THE ANGEL OF EDEN FALLS

A SWEET, MARRIAGE OF CONVENIENCE ROMANCE

TINA NEWCOMB

The Angel of Eden Falls

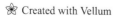 Created with Vellum

DEDICATION

To Chris, Marnie, Carly, Sara,
Kristen, Andrew, Richard , Stefan

Without whom this book would have been completed three
years earlier.

JK (not really)

CONTENTS

CHAPTER 1

Mac Johnson trudged up the porch steps of the renovated Victorian house. Welcome, Owen Danielson, Attorney at Law was emblazoned on a plaque next to the door. Tempted to knock the cheerful sign off the wall, he sucked in a deep breath, hoping the extra oxygen would calm his raging heart. If only he'd skipped his trip to the mailbox yesterday. The manila envelope he carried felt like a hundred pound weight. He wanted to rip the contents to shreds or set the thing on fire, but neither option would solve his problem.

When he entered the large foyer, Owen's receptionist turned from her computer screen with a smile. "Hi, Mac. Owen is taking a call, so it will be just a few minutes."

"Thanks, Jolie."

"Can I get you something to drink while you wait?"

She made the offer as if today was like any other, but then she didn't know the envelope's contents were eating away the lining of his stomach. "No. Thanks."

Mac glanced around. He'd never been in Owen's offices before, hadn't needed the advice of an attorney in years.

"How's Beck?"

He gripped the blasted envelope at the mention of his son. "He's good."

"I bet he's looking forward to the Harvest Festival."

Mac smiled. Probably his first of the day. "Yeah, he is."

"Have a seat. Owen should be out any minute."

When Jolie turned to her computer, Mac stuck the envelope under his arm and walked across the room to a magazine rack mounted on the wall. After flipping through the pages of *Field and Stream*, which failed to grab his attention, he put it back and yanked out one on fitness. "How's Jeff?"

Jolie looked up. "He's good."

"Still in Montana?"

"Yes."

He shoved the magazine back in the holder and walked to a window, staring at nothing. "How's JessAnn?"

"She's fine."

"She lives in California, right?"

"Yes, and Jeremy is working in Spokane," Jolie said, finishing off her "J" siblings. "Mom and Dad are good, too," she added before he could ask.

He sat on the edge of a chair and glanced at his watch for the third time. He'd arrived early, praying he could get in sooner. Now Owen was five minutes late.

Jolie glanced over her shoulder with raised brows.

"What?"

She nodded at his bouncing knee, which made the wood floor under his foot squeak.

"Oh. Sorry." He wiped a palm down his pant leg. "Nervous."

Jolie swiveled her chair to face him. "Owen is very good at what he does. I'm sure he'll be able to help you, and if he can't, he'll find someone who can."

A door down the hall opened and Mac leapt to his feet,

sending the offending envelope skittering across the floor. Owen scooped it up. "Hey, Mac."

"Thank you for seeing me so soon," Mac said, shaking Owen's outstretched hand.

Owen smiled. "The way Jolie put it, I didn't have much of a choice."

"Sorry, but this can't wait," Mac said, nodding to the envelope Owen held.

"Well, come on back and let's see what's so important."

Owen led him into a spacious office with deep green walls, the bottom half covered with rich wood paneling. Built-in bookshelves lined both sides of a beautiful wooden mantelpiece. A small conference table near the bay window overlooked a garden where pots of fall flowers surrounded a fountain. Owen's massive mahogany desk faced the soothing view.

The comfortable room and setting beyond settled the queasiness that had seized Mac's stomach ever since he opened the envelope sixteen hours earlier.

Owen gestured to one of the wingback chairs in front of his desk before circling to take his own chair. "How's Beck?"

"Good." Mac sank into the soft leather and pointed at the envelope Owen still held. "That will explain my impatience to get in as soon as I could."

Owen opened the envelope, tugged the contents free, and spread the papers out on his desk. Mac watched his eyes move back and forth while he read and then reread each sheet. Mac tried to decipher his expression, but Owen's features remained neutral. When he finally looked up, Mac released the breath he'd been holding.

"Were you and"—Owen glanced at the letter he'd placed on top of the pile—"Mrs. Lynwood married when Beck was born?"

"No. We were married, but divorced before his birth."

Owen rested his forearms on the desk and laced his fingers together. "Start at the beginning."

Mac looked down at his own fingers, twisted in tension. "Our marriage was a mistake. We were college kids, dumb and drunk in Las Vegas with a group just as dumb and drunk. Dares were thrown out and, before I knew what was happening, Cheryl and I were in one of those sleazy chapels saying, 'I do'.

"We were together a week before she moved out, saying she'd have divorce papers delivered." Guilt and embarrassment of a long ago mistake tightened his chest muscles. "I don't know if she dropped out of school or what, but I never saw her on campus after that. She did send divorce papers. We shared no property, so it was uncontested. I showed the papers to an attorney, signed them, and the divorce was final. I didn't hear anything from her for a year and a half.

"Then one morning, before dawn, there was a knock on my apartment door. When I answered, I found Beck in a baby carrier with a 'He's yours' note attached with a safety pin."

Owen's eyebrows rose, wrinkling his forehead. "She left him on your doorstep?"

Mac nodded. "A bag of formula, a few diapers, and a birth certificate that had me listed as the father and Cheryl as the mother were in a paper sack next to him."

Owen reached for a legal pad and jotted a few notes. "How long were you married?"

"She sent the divorce papers about a month after she left, so a month and a week."

"Which means there was a fifty-fifty chance she knew she was pregnant when she filed for divorce."

"I don't know much about those things, but my guess is yes."

"You didn't talk to her that morning?"

"No."

"Did she stick around long enough to make sure it was you who opened the door of the apartment?"

"No. I'm not even sure she's the one who dropped Beck off."

Owen looked up and Mac saw the surprise on his features.

"I ran down the stairs and out the front door of the apartment building, but didn't see anyone."

"After Beck was dropped off, did she have any contact with him? Or you?"

"None."

Owen's pen stopped scratching over the surface of the legal pad a second time. "None? She never sent birthday cards or Christmas gifts?"

"No."

"Did you ever receive money for Beck's support?"

"Zero contact."

Owen nodded slowly and resumed writing. "What does Beck know about his mother?"

"Not much. He asks about her occasionally, and I try to be up-front without hurting him." Mac rubbed the base of his skull where a tension headache was starting to throb.

"What do you tell a kid whose mother leaves him on a doorstep when he's only six months old? I've never bad-mouthed her, but I've never made excuses either. I'm not going to lie to my son or get his hopes up. Cheryl never told me why she did what she did. She never even told me she was pregnant." He met Owen's steady gaze. "Yes to your next question. Beck is mine."

Owen ran an index finger under his bottom lip. "Do you have the paperwork to prove it?"

"Yes."

While Owen made more notes, Mac held his own questions at bay. His what-ifs and should-I-haves were lined up like little soldiers, marching through his mind. *I should have made sure there were custody papers drawn up. What if Cheryl has a case because I didn't? I should have checked with an attorney before moving to Washington. What if Cheryl takes my son away because I left California without permission?*

"How old was Beck when you moved back to Eden Falls?"

"Almost five."

"Why did you move back?"

"When it was time for kindergarten, Mom and Dad offered to help, and the police department here was hiring, so I moved. Before that I'd hired a nanny. I thought being near family was the right choice. It never occurred to me to check with an attorney before I took Beck out of California."

Owen steepled his fingers and rested his chin on top. "Why haven't you remarried, Mac?"

Mac knew the surprise had to show on his face. Of all the questions he'd imagined Owen might ask, that wasn't one of them. "Does it matter?" He noted the defensiveness in his tone. *Of course it matters. I'm a single dad. Judges usually rule for moms.* "Between work and Beck, my days were full. *Are full.* When would I have time to date, and where would I meet a woman? There isn't an overabundance of single women in this small town."

Owen held up a hand in surrender. "I was just curious, Mac. I wasn't passing judgment."

"Would it help my case if I were married?"

Owen turned his hand over, palm up as if weighing his answer. "It wouldn't hurt, but that's not why I asked. You don't still have feelings for—"

Mac snorted. "No. Cheryl and I barely knew each other. Our marriage was a stupid, immature action on both our parts. Our relationship…" He shook his head. "There was no relationship. Our time together was purely physical. Over before it started."

"Why do you think Cheryl wants custody after all these years?"

Mac sat back in his chair as the pressure in his head pounded along with his heartbeat. "I have no idea."

Owen nodded and looked down at his notes. "I understand you not wanting to get Beck's hopes up. I feel the same with clients, because anything can happen. If this goes before a judge, you never know how he or she will rule. However, you have several things going for you. Cheryl abandoned Beck, she's never tried to contact him, and she's never contributed to his support."

Mac narrowed his eyes. "I hear an another unspoken however hovering in the air."

Owen took off his glasses and polished the lenses with a cloth he pulled from a desk drawer.

He's stalling.

"However, we don't know why." Owen replaced his glasses. "There may be extenuating circumstances that a judge would find justifiable. This letter says she's remarried and has two stepchildren she cares for, which shows responsibility. Do you know anything about her family? How she was raised, if she has siblings?"

Mac shook his head.

"Why did Cheryl leave?"

Mac shrugged, too ashamed to admit his relief when she packed her bags. Grateful she was the one to leave rather than forcing him to make the decision. "Other than going to the same school, we had absolutely nothing in common. I hated the music she played. She hated mine. She was vegan. I wasn't. I could go on and on, but really, what does it matter?"

Owen tapped the eraser end of a pencil on his desk.

"I'm not letting Beck go, Owen. She abandoned him on

my doorstep nine and a half years ago. Beck was a defense-less baby and she left him with a note pinned to his chest. She hasn't called once to ask how he is, if he's healthy, or happy. She's never taken him to the dentist or a ball game, never attended a parent-teacher conference, or one of his school performances."

"How would you feel about this letter if she had?"

Another surprise question, one that made him pause. "I'm not sure. My guess is I'd still be in California and we'd be sharing custody, so there wouldn't be a letter."

Mac dropped his head back and stared at the ceiling. "I want to do what's best for Beck and I don't believe uprooting him, completely changing his lifestyle, is the answer. He doesn't know Cheryl at all and he shouldn't be forced to *live* with her because she's suddenly changed her mind." Mac met Owen's gaze. "He's happy here, Owen. He's doing well in school, plays on several sports teams, and has great friends. He's close to my parents, sees them everyday. They've played as big a part in his life as I have. The situation would be different if I was an unsupportive parent or unable to care for him, but that's not the case."

"Would you be willing to discuss visitation?"

"Do I have a choice?" Mac pressed his fingertips together, desperate to regain the control slipping away. "Yes. If Beck wants to meet his mom, I would be willing to discuss visita-tion, but it has to be here, in Eden Falls. I'm not going to ship him off to California."

"If you wish to retain my services, I'll send a letter to Mrs. Lynwood's attorney expressing your concerns, and your willingness to negotiate." Owen pushed up from his chair. "That willingness will go a long way with a judge, if this goes that far."

Mac assumed their meeting was over, though he felt far from the relief he'd hoped for. He stood. "I appreciate anything you can do for me, Owen. Beck is my life, has been since he was six months old. I can't just send him off with someone he doesn't know."

Owen came around the desk. "I'm sorry you're going through this, Mac. I can't imagine how I'd feel if it were my boys. We all have things in our past that seem to rear their ugly heads at one time or another." Owen opened his office door and started down the hall. Mac had little choice but to follow.

"We didn't discuss fees."

"This meeting is a free consultation. Jolie will go over my fees with you, but let's hold off until I hear back from Mrs. Lynwood's attorney. Jolie, will you make copies of these papers for Mac's file?"

Mac held his hand out and Owen shook it. "Thank you, Owen. And thank you for fitting me in so quickly, Jolie. I appreciate it."

"You're welcome." Jolie turned to the copy machine.

"As soon as I hear anything, I'll be in touch," Owen said. "Until then, try not to worry."

Mac hoped to leave Owen's office with his promise that nothing would come of the contents of that brown envelope. He wanted to feel secure in the knowledge that Beck was going nowhere, except bowling on his tenth birthday. What he got was, "Try not to worry".

A shadow fell over him when he stepped outside as clouds obscured the sun. He pocketed the sunglasses he'd just pulled out. The gloom settling over Eden Falls matched his mood.

Mac hoped bad weather held off until after the town's Harvest Festival. Rain would dampen the celebration and his nine-year-old son's excitement.

He climbed behind the wheel of his truck and headed for Town Hall where the police station was located. From there he'd change into his uniform and spend the night keeping Eden Falls, Washington safe.

~

*N*oelle Treloar rubbed her eyes and yawned. Today had been good. Summer tourist season was over, but business was still bustling. She closed her laptop and stood up to stretch. If the café continued to have weeks like this, she'd be able to pay off the loan for the kitchen's new appliances by the end of the year, three months ahead of schedule, which called for a celebration.

The wall clock taunted her, its hands standing straight up at attention. The café closed three hours earlier, and she'd been crunching numbers ever since—something she missed from her previous life. Numbers had been her business.

She stretched, hands high overhead, then bent at the waist until they lay flat on the floor. She held the position for thirty seconds before slowly straightening. Time to go home.

First a victory dance, because she couldn't help herself. The idea of owning a café, even after eighteen months of actually running it, still seemed surreal. She owed it all to a distant uncle she'd never met and a letter she wrote for a fourth-grade genealogy project. After the uncle answered her questions about the Treloar family tree, their spotty correspondence continued for several years.

When her letters started coming back with Return to Sender stamped on the front, she wondered what had happened to this wandering uncle. Then she received a certified delivery from Attorney Owen Danielson. The one-page letter informed her that Jeremiah Royal Treloar had died and left her a restaurant in Eden Falls. After an internet search, she learned Eden Falls was a small town in the middle of Washington state. She contacted Owen, who hired someone to board up the place. She paid the back taxes and promptly forgot about the restaurant and Eden Falls for five years.

A few stolen clients and a backhanded business deal two years ago had her booking a flight to Seattle to escape the cutthroat company she worked for and her overly-aggressive parents, who were pushing her toward insanity. What better place to hide out for a month than an estranged uncle's stomping grounds?

She opened the door to her office and wandered around the polished-to-perfection kitchen, the accomplishment of her fabulous staff. What would she do without each and every one of them? She didn't want to find out.

Pushing through the swinging doors into the front of the café, she spun one of the red vinyl stools. The linoleum floor shone from a recent mopping. She straightened a few glasses and made sure the bin that held rolled silverware was full. She fished a quarter from the front pocket of her jeans, slipped it into the slot of her prized possession, a nineteen-sixties jukebox, and selected C-5, her go-to song when she was alone.

Kelly Clarkson's "Stronger" poured from the speakers while she threw herself into a victory dance of freedom. Gone were her days of anxiety and scrambling for the next big deal. Gone were her mother's harping words and her father's disappointed looks. She was free from stress and frustration. Free to live her life the way she wanted to live it. Suffer the consequences of her mistakes without her family breathing disapproval down her neck.

She grabbed spray cleaner, a roll of paper towels, and polished the glass on the jukebox she'd purchased on a whim. As the song wound down, she rechecked the lock on the front door. The hardware store, and then the big tree in the square, the one the town decorated for Christmas every year, were both burned to the ground recently. She knew the police chief suspected someone, but there wasn't enough evidence to convict. She wasn't going to take a chance with her baby.

After one more look around, she flipped off the lights and walked through the kitchen for her coat.

Outside, Indian summer still prevailed. It was almost balmy for the middle of October, although rain was on the way. She just hoped it held off until after Eden Falls' Harvest Festival, or a lot of people would be disappointed.

She made sure the door was shut tight, then turned as a patrol car swung into the parking lot. Handsome Mac Johnson leaned his head out the open window.

"I saw lights go out in the front of the café and thought I'd drive around to make sure everything was okay."

One of the many reasons she loved this little town. Residents—not just the police—watched out for each other. On top of the fires, there had been a loony stalker on the loose a few months earlier. He was apprehended and all was quiet again, but the events had shaken Eden Falls' residents' usual sense of security.

"Everything's good. Thanks for checking. Will you and Beck be in tomorrow night?"

"Same time as always."

Father and son were Friday night regulars unless Mac was on duty. "Albert made a to-die-for pumpkin cheesecake."

His white-toothed grin appeared in the glow of the dashboard lights. "I remember his cheesecake from last year. Choosing between that and your apple pie will be a hard decision. How about you save us one of each."

"Anything for my two favorite customers."

She waved as he backed out. The town was in good hands, patrolled by Eden Falls' finest. Everything was just as it should be.

CHAPTER 2

M ac pulled his patrol car to the curb and turned off the siren, but left the lights flashing. As he climbed from behind the wheel, he blew out an exasperated breath. Why did this always happen right before quitting time?

The tiny woman driver, a look of determination etched into her tense profile, would somehow make her speeding ticket his fault. He rapped on the driver's side glass. "Roll the window down, Rita."

As soon as the window lowered, Rita Reynolds squawked.

Luckily, he'd known the odd woman and her bird-like habits since he was a toddler, or the sound would have startled him. She peered up, the thick lenses of her glasses magnifying her brown eyes, and flapped her hands. Another fowl tendency.

"Do you know why I pulled you over?"

"You haven't reached your quota for the month, so you thought you'd pick on a defenseless old lady?"

He dropped his chin to his chest and met her gaze over

the top of his sunglasses. She held a black belt of some sort and owned the tongue of a viper. "Defenseless?"

"Don't you start with me, Macoy. *Squawk!*"

Rita was the only person in town, other than his mom, who used his full first name. He continued to stare at her.

She pointed a bony finger at his chest. "I have something on you that I've kept secret for years."

"I doubt that." Rita hadn't kept anything secret for an hour. She was known to be the town's biggest gossip, spreading tales whether they were true or not.

"I'll tell JT it was you who started that fire in Frank Powell's field when you were a kid. He'll throw you in jail."

He pushed his sunglasses into place so she couldn't see his eyes. What would she say if she knew JT Garrett, Eden Falls' Chief of Police, was with him that day? His dad and JT's made them work at Frank's place for two summers to pay for the damage. "Never proven."

"It may have never been proven, but I know you did it." She scowled, trying to look menacing, difficult for a five-foot-nothing, ninety-pound-when-wet woman to pull off. She stuck her head out the window and sniffed. "Wait! Is that alcohol I smell on your breath?"

"Nice try, but I haven't touched the stuff since college. Do you know why I pulled you over?"

She sat up a little straighter, a glimmer of hope in her eye. "If I guess right, will you let me go?"

He bit back a chuckle. "Another nice try, but it doesn't work that way."

She slumped against the seat. "Then I don't want to play your guessing game."

"You were speeding."

"Not by much."

"Forty-three in a thirty." He opened his posse box. "What's the rush?"

"The movie theatre charges an arm and a leg after five." She looked at her watch. "And you're going to make me miss the four-forty-five showing, along with the previews."

He pulled a pen from his shirt pocket. "License, registration, and insurance card."

"*Squawk!* Can't you look that information up at the station?"

"The longer you stall, the more previews you miss."

His words prompted immediate action. Rita dumped her purse upside down on the passenger seat. "Lotion, toothpicks, glass case, pantyhose…"

Mac shook his head and glanced around while she rummaged. Today was probably the last warm day Eden Falls would enjoy this year. Temperatures were supposed to dip tonight. The leaves of the maple tree he was standing under were just beginning to change color. In another week, burning reds and burgundies would be displayed in all their brilliant fall glory.

Rita's hand came out the window. "Here you go, Mr. Gunslinger."

Mac took the license and insurance cards and began filling in the blanks of Rita's ticket.

"JT would be a gentleman and let me off with a warning."

"I'm not JT."

"You're right about that. What is the complete opposite called? Oh, yeah, a bully!" She exhaled loudly. "Can't you just bring the ticket to me at the post office tomorrow?"

"You don't work on Saturdays." He held out her license and insurance cards. "I still need your registration."

"Oh, for Pete's sake!" She pulled the glove box open and fumbled through the contents.

He wasn't usually so inflexible, but thirteen miles over the speed limit through their sleepy town was ticket-worthy. He caught the registration as it sailed out the window. "You need to slow down, Rita. An hour earlier, you would have been speeding through a school zone, and the fine would be double."

"If I was an hour earlier, I wouldn't be missing previews. *Squawk!* I'm going to tell your mother about this. The very idea that you make me sit here with my window open in the cold is police brutality."

"It's seventy-two degrees, Rita, and preventable if you'd obeyed the speed limit."

Rita snatched the registration and ticket away from him, started the car, and drove away. She'd have him painted as a drunk by morning.

He climbed behind the wheel of the patrol car and stared at the brown envelope sitting on the passenger seat—the cause of his surly mood. He'd brought it with him in an effort to keep the contents from his son. Not that Beck would understand any of what the letter said, but he wasn't ready to answer his curious son's inevitable questions when he spotted the envelope.

At the station, Mac climbed out of the patrol car just as Layne Yancy exited the back door.

"I was coming to see if you were here yet." Layne caught the car keys Mac tossed.

"Sorry, I should have radioed. Rita Reynolds decided speeding through town was acceptable when rushing to see movie previews."

Layne laughed. "Glad you were the one to catch her. She still blames me for egging her house that Halloween she gave out toothbrushes instead of candy."

Another of my childhood sins.

"When I was home with chickenpox," Layne added.

Mac remembered writing Layne's name in toothpaste on Rita's front porch steps. "It's crazy that she blamed you."

Layne cut a look his way. "Yeah, crazy."

Mac walked inside, headed for the break room and his locker. He placed the envelope on the top shelf under his police cap. After changing into street clothes, he added his uniform to the bag of laundry at the bottom of his locker, and slung it over his shoulder.

He stopped in JT's office to drop off Ms. Kennedy's grocery list. JT would do her shopping, and she'd repay the kindness with enough baked goods to keep the station on a sugar high for an entire afternoon.

On his way out of the station, he waved to Layne's wife, who was manning dispatch for the night.

"Wait!" Gianna held out a piece of paper. "Patsy Douglas called to remind you of the pie-throwing contest you volunteered for tomorrow."

"Pie in the face. Kind of hard to forget, Gianna."

"You're ornery."

"Sorry. Long couple of days."

She flexed her arm. "I might have to spend my break practicing my aim."

"I've seen you throw. I'm not worried you'll get better overnight."

"Hey!" she yelled as he pushed through the back door.

He dumped his bag of laundry into the bed of his truck and walked around to the front of the building. Town Square was a beehive of activity as people erected tents for Saturday's festivities. Quiet Eden Falls wouldn't be so quiet tomorrow.

Beck bounded out of The Fly Shop. They stared at each other a long moment, then both took off running. Beck beat him to the door of Noelle's Café by half a step.

"Ha! I won."

"Lucky duck."

Beck grinned. "It's not luck, it's skill."

His son's smile brightened his mood. He pulled Beck's

baseball cap down over his eyes. "You're still a lucky duck to have me as your dad."

Beck straightened his hat. "Quack quack."

Mac laughed and caught Beck in a hug that was returned with gusto.

"Are we still going to the festival tomorrow?"

Mac glanced up at the sky. "We always do, unless it gets rained out. Are you going to bob for apples this year?"

"I always do unless it gets rained out." Merriment danced in Beck's brown eyes.

Mac wrapped a hand around his son's neck. "Wise guy."

Once inside, Mac scanned the room. Working in Los Angeles for five years had instilled habits he couldn't shake. The pace was fast and furious compared to slow, uneventful Eden Falls. Not that he minded slow and uneventful. He loved being back in his hometown and the life he and his son had built. Their house was easy walking distance from school and town. His parents were close by to help when he worked nights and weekends. Life was good…until he collected the mail two days earlier.

Beck stopped in his tracks and looked around. "Cool. Noelle decorated for Halloween. Look at the bats over the jukebox."

"That is pretty cool. They look like they're following each other out of a cave." Mac pointed in the opposite direction. "I like the witch that smashed into the kitchen door."

Beck laughed.

Because Beck liked the swivel stools, they wove their way through the crowd, until they reached their usual spot at the counter. "What're you having tonight, buddy?"

"Mmm," Beck hummed as he contemplated a menu they both knew by heart. "I want that special grilled cheese Noelle makes and fries. Can I go to Evan's birthday party next Friday?"

"I don't see why not. How old is he going to be?"

"Daaad," Beck said with an exaggerated eye-roll. "He's going to be ten just like I am *in five weeks*."

Noelle set two shakes in front of them, her gaze on Beck. "Wait. Didn't you just have a birthday last year?"

"Everybody has a birthday every year." Beck unwrapped his straw.

Noelle propped her forearms on the countertop and faked a grimace. "Don't remind me."

Mac nodded to their shakes. "Thanks."

She winked and glanced at Beck. "What are you doing for your birthday?"

"We're going bowling!"

"I've never been bowling."

"You've never been bowling?" Beck asked with wide-eyed disbelief.

Noelle shook her head, a wisp of brown hair settling on her cheek.

Mac pushed his straw into the chocolaty goodness. "How is that even possible?"

She lifted a shoulder in a half shrug. "Is it fun?"

"It's a blast!"

"Well, there you go. My parents don't believe in fun."

"You didn't ever go with friends?" Beck raised his straw from the shake and ran it through his lips, then stuck out his tongue to try to catch the pooled chocolate before it dripped on his shirt.

As if on cue, Noelle reached under the counter, shook out a napkin, and set it near Beck's elbow. "Studying got in the way of bowling and movies and friends."

Her remarks intrigued Mac. "You weren't allowed to have friends?"

She produced a second napkin for him. "Yes, at school, as long as they didn't interfere with homework."

Her comment wasn't said in a way that solicited pity. He asked for information and she gave an answer. "Were you a geek?"

She scrunched her nose in the cutest way. "Define geek."

"Studying because you found it more enjoyable than going out with friends."

"Nope, not a geek." She glanced at Beck. "So, how do you have a party at a bowling alley? Do you take a cake with you?"

"Yeah, plus they have a snack bar that serves pizza and hotdogs and really good cheese-fries. The only yucky part is they make you wear funny shoes that thousands of other people wear before you."

"Gross." She wrinkled her nose again. "So you should definitely wear socks."

Beck laughed. "Yeah. Hey, you should go with us! It's going to be *a lot* of fun." He pushed his straw back down into the shake, sucked until his cheeks concaved, then squeezed his eyes closed. "Brain freeze."

Noelle smiled as she reached under the counter and retrieved two sets of silverware wrapped in napkins. "I'll have to check my schedule."

For some odd reason, his normally bashful son opened up for Noelle every week. Mac half listened while Beck continued to fill her in on important nine-year-old stuff, his mind wandering back to the envelope in his locker. It was like a time-bomb ticking away precious minutes of his life. He had to set time aside to discuss the situation with his wise parents.

He'd played his discussion with Owen over and over in his mind. How much of a difference would it make if he was married? He just couldn't stop thinking about that question. In the ten years since Cheryl left, he hadn't found anyone he wanted to spend forever with, not that he had much time to date. Beck was front and center in his life, and always would be.

"I wish we could go camping for my birthday, but it's always too cold."

"I sure wouldn't want to sleep outside in the cold." Noelle straightened and reached for the order pad in the pocket of her apron.

"We don't sleep outside. We have a trailer. It's like a house on wheels and even has a bathroom with a shower."

"A bathroom can be a valuable resource in the wilderness." Noelle pulled a pencil from behind her ear. "I've never been camping, either."

Beck smirked. "That's because girls don't go. They're too scared of bugs and snakes. Right, Dad?"

Mac raised an eyebrow. "I'm not going there with the woman who'll be serving our dinner."

"Wise decision. Do you men know what you want?"

After ordering, Beck went into a play-by-play description of his day at school. Mac loved hearing every detail, down to what he had for lunch. He listened even more carefully when Beck mentioned the girl who sat behind him. "She always asks *dumb* questions like, 'How come you like Jason? He's so mean,' and says things like, 'You're so strong, Beck,' just cuz I can climb the rope in gym." Beck shrugged. "It's no big deal. Everyone can climb it except a few of the girls. Can I have a quarter for the jukebox?"

Mac pulled a quarter from his pocket and handed it to his son. "No crazy, head-banging stuff."

"Oh, to be young again," Noelle said when she set their dinners on the counter.

She wore a whimsical smile on her pretty face. When she wasn't paying attention, her East Coast accent was more pronounced. "Where are you from, Noelle?"

"Bwoa-ston."

He chuckled at her comical pronunciation. "What brought you to Eden Falls?"

She waved a dismissive hand. "Long, boring story. Ask me on a night when you don't have a patty melt on rye and fries getting cold."

He squirted ketchup onto the extra plate Noelle set between them. She knew Beck didn't like his fries touching the ketchup before they were dipped. He glanced over his shoulder. "Beck, come and eat."

Beck talked all through dinner, helping to keep his mind off Cheryl. When they finished, Noelle collected their plates. "What's it going to be gentlemen? Pumpkin cheesecake or apple pie?"

"Cheesecake!"

Mac held up two fingers. "For both of us."

"Coffee?" She placed a cup and saucer in front of Mac. He wasn't sure why she asked. They always ended their meal with a slice of something sweet, him with coffee, Beck with a glass of milk, which she set on the counter next.

"I like your Halloween decorations."

"Thanks, Beck. Do you and your dad decorate for the holiday?"

"We have a scarecrow sitting on a bale of hay on our porch. His head is a jack-o-lantern. We carved a scary face this year, huh, Dad?"

"Sure did. Beck dressed him in overalls and an old flannel shirt."

"And my dad's work boots!" Beck fiddled with the clean fork Noelle put on a napkin in front of him until she stilled his hand with a touch.

Noelle set a slice of cheesecake in front of each of them. "He sounds spooky. I may have to do a drive-by and see."

"We'll be home tomorrow night. You could come over."

Mac glanced up, curious to see Noelle's reaction to

Beck's impromptu invitation, surprised that he hoped she'd accept.

She smiled and pushed Beck's glass of milk away from his active elbow. "Wish I could, but I switched shifts with Gertie. I promise I'll drive by to see your decorations before Halloween."

After Beck gobbled down the last of his cheesecake, he held out his hand. "Can I have another quarter?"

Before Mac could react, Noelle pulled two quarters from her apron pocket. "I'll buy this one if you'll play B-17 for me."

Beck bounced off in the direction of the jukebox. "Is B-17 a favorite?" Mac asked.

"B-17 and C-5 are the reason I bought the thing."

Joan Jett's "I Love Rock 'n' Roll" filled the café, and Mac laughed. "Appropriate."

When Noelle started moving to the beat, Mac wondered why she was single. She was attractive, smart, and playful. She was great with Beck. Why hadn't he ever thought to ask her out?

She propped her hip against the counter and flashed her beautiful smile. He caught a slight whiff of perfume. "You have a great kid there."

"Yeah, I do." They watched Beck flip through the cards in the jukebox. "Do you remember much about that age?"

"Sure. Don't you?"

She had the bluest eyes he'd ever seen, the color of two mountain pools in late afternoon shadows. "Bits and pieces. I remember getting into trouble a lot. I always seemed to be doing something I shouldn't."

"Like?"

"Rita Reynolds reminded me earlier today of the time I set the field behind Frank Powell's house on fire."

"On purpose?"

He chuckled and sent another glance Beck's way to be certain he wasn't within hearing distance. "No. JT and I were lighting up a stolen cigar. We both got to coughing so hard we set the lit cigar down, and, poof, the dry field went up in flames."

"You and the chief of police set sweet old Frank's field on fire. You're lucky you didn't burn down his house."

"A neighbor saw the smoke and called the fire department. That was just one of the many times I caused trouble."

She picked up their plates and set them in the bin behind her. "I wouldn't have taken you for a bad boy."

"I wasn't bad. I just had a keen ability for finding trouble."

"And now you're a respectable law enforcement officer."

"Didn't you ever get into trouble?"

"Absolutely not." She put a hand to her chest. "I was a good girl."

"How good?" He straightened so she could wipe the counter. Then she freshened his coffee and placed the packets of sugar at his fingertips before he could reach for them.

"I went to a strict, all-girls Catholic school. Step out of line and you got a ruler to the knuckles."

"Harsh." He dumped two packets of sugar into his cup and then added a dollop of Beck's milk. "I've heard about schools like that, but thought they were urban legends."

She held up her fisted hand and pointed to a white crescent scar on her middle knuckle. "Sister Jane was the worst. I got this for asking a question about boys." She rubbed the knuckle. "I was never sure if I was reprimanded for asking the question without raising my hand or because of the question I asked."

"What'd you ask?"

A twinkle of mischief made her eyes bluer. "Why God gave boys a penis."

Mac choked on his sip of coffee.

"What?" She shrugged. "I thought it was a valid question, and who would know the answer better than a nun?"

He was afraid to ask, but had to know. "What was the answer?"

She held up her hand. "A rap on the knuckles and a note sent home. My parents weren't amused." She batted her eyelashes innocently. "I'm thirty-three years old and I still don't know the answer."

Mac choked again. "Didn't nuns teach the birds and the bees in that school?"

Beck slid onto the stool next to his dad. "We learned about bees last year. There are three different bees in the hive. The Queen, the worker, and the drone." He held up three fingers as if to prove his point. "Did you know bees are the only bug that makes food people eat?"

"That is fascinating, Beck. I just learned something new." Noelle winked at Mac. "How about you, Dad?"

She leaned over the counter, hugged Beck, and something unfamiliar stirred in Mac's chest.

CHAPTER 3

Noelle walked into her apartment and headed straight to the shower to wash the fried-food smell off her skin and hair. A cup of herbal tea always followed, which she took to her bedroom, grateful Gertie had asked to trade shifts the next morning. Gertie and her husband, Albert, were participating in the Harvest Festival's square dance competition tomorrow night. Noelle was sorry she'd miss it. She couldn't imagine little Gertie and three-hundred-pound Albert do-si-do'ing around each other. She'd have to ask someone to record the event for her.

Gertrude Rollins was her assistant manager extraordinaire, a gray-haired spitfire who made the café hum like a tightly strung bow. Instead of a traditional interview, Gertie insisted Noelle come to her home where her husband, a retired Navy chef, served homemade lunch. Noelle hired both Gertie and Albert on the spot.

Joseph, her dishwasher and assistant to Albert, was a transient she found sleeping in her abandoned restaurant. He'd turned out to be a blessing hidden under long hair and filthy clothes. Albert ran the kitchen with quiet efficiency, Gertie ruled the front of the café with a steel hand and a kind heart, and Joseph handled everything between.

She settled back against the headboard, not quite ready for sleep. The book on her nightstand was tempting, but her mind was too busy flitting around to settle on the story.

The events that caused her to move to town were never far from her mind. Mac asking the question tonight brought it all forward and reminded her to appreciate her good fortune. She believed she'd been led to this little town for a reason, but the reason still wasn't clear. It couldn't simply be to offer home-cooked goodness to residents of Eden Falls and tourists who visited the little town.

Those thoughts were too deep to encourage sleep, so she changed course.

Beck's face popped into her mind. She had to admit she was just the tiniest bit jealous of Mac and Beck's relationship, the happy smiles they shared with each other. She could probably count on two hands the times she and her mom and dad had laughed together.

Enough! She'd never get to sleep with those thoughts either.

Tomorrow she'd stop at the festival's farmer's market and pick up some fresh squash. The Saunders would be there with apples harvested from their orchards, and the Sawyers would be selling organic vegetables from their gardens. Albert was genius at coming up with new ways to incorporate local produce into the menu.

Then, if she had time before her shift at the café, she'd wander through the craft booths.

She heard the front door open and close softly, her cousin Mike coming home from his bartending job at Rowdy's Bar and Grill.

After being left at the altar by his fiancée, he'd decided to get away from Boston. Noelle had an extra bedroom, so she invited him to stay with her for a while. That was five months earlier. She knew he wouldn't be going back. As big as Boston was, it wasn't big enough for Mike, his ex-fiancée, and his ex-best friend—especially after the two exes announced their engagement. Luckily, Rowdy was hiring, and Mike had worked as a bartender in college. She could have used him in the café, but he made twice as much in tips at Rowdy's. Quiet and clean, Mike had turned out to be the perfect roommate, and it was nice having family she liked close.

"Come in," she said at the soft knock.

Mike opened the door. "Hey."

"Hey yourself."

"I saw your light. Can't sleep?"

"Actually, I just got home. It was a busy day."

He leaned against the doorjamb. "Rowdy's was busy, too. Must be something in the air."

"Tourists coming for the Harvest Festival. Last year Eden Falls was packed all weekend."

"So, it's a big deal, huh? I've seen the signs posted around."

Noelle lifted her cup and saucer from the nightstand. "The festival draws a lot of people. Craft booths, baking and canning contests, games, prizes, music all day. Do you have to work?"

"Not until four. How about you?"

"I go in at two."

Noelle sipped her tea while studying her cousin. He was as blond as she was dark, but they had the same blue eyes, which came from her mother's side of the family. Cool, calm, and collected on the outside, she knew he was jittery with pent-up energy. Rowdy's was always busy and relieved some of that, but Rowdy's was also short-term, a make-do job until

Mike found a new path. Noelle just hoped whatever he found wouldn't take him too far from Eden Falls.

"Your mom left a message on the answering machine. She wants you to call."

He exhaled enough to make his shoulders sag. "Yeah, I know. She wants me to come home for Thanksgiving, so she and Dad can talk some sense into me. They're worried about their baby in the wilds of Washington State, living with his crazy cousin who left her Wall Street job to open a café. I think they're afraid you'll rub off on me."

Noelle smiled. "Have I?"

Mike returned her smile. "You and Eden Falls."

"Is that a bad thing?"

"Not to me. I can see why you stayed. I like it here." He shoved his hands into the front pockets of his jeans. "I don't want to ask Rowdy for time off anyway. I'm the new guy, low man on the totem."

"Is that the truth, or do you not want to go back to Boston?"

He looked down at the floor. "Both. If I go anywhere with friends, I'm sure to run into my ex and…" He shook his head.

Noelle could relate. Boston—actually, Massachusetts—wasn't big enough for her and her parents. After college, she escaped to New York to get farther away.

She set her tea on the nightstand. "I know you only planned to stay for a couple of months, but you're welcome here as long as you want, Mike."

He ruffled his hair until it stood on end. "I appreciate the offer, but I hate imposing. I've been here since June."

"You help with rent, utilities, and you buy half the groceries. That's called a roommate."

He grinned. Her handsome cousin had been devastated, but not destroyed. After months of sulking and sitting in the apartment alone, he was finally accepting invitations for poker nights with the boys, and the smile she remembered so fondly was showing up more often.

"The Forest Service is hiring. I saw a post on their internet site."

The notion surprised her. "I thought your degree was environmental science."

"And forestry. They need a river conservation associate."

"Are you qualified?"

"It requires a bachelor's degree. I have my master's."

"Wow, I say go for it, if you're interested. What will Rowdy do without you?" *What will I do?*

"The job is local. I could possibly stay on at Rowdy's on weekends." He shrugged. "If I even get the job."

"I'd love it if you could stay close, but working those hours, you won't have much time for a social life."

"I've found having a social life is highly overrated."

She winced at her thoughtless comment. "I'm sorry. Sometimes I don't think before I speak.

"Don't be sorry. You're right about the hours, but I like being busy. Leaves me less time to think." He backed into the hall. "I'll see you in the morning."

"'Night, Mike."

❧

*M*ac parked behind Town Hall, glad his designated parking space was still available in spite of the Festival. Beck was out of the truck and gone before Mac even opened his door. He wouldn't see his son for hours except in passing, or when Beck ran out of money.

He walked around the building and looked toward Town Square. Vendor tents, lined up in neat little rows, filled the space, and people crowded the displays. Today would be good for Eden Falls' businesses. He crossed the street to

The Fly Shop, which was full of men whose wives and girl-friends were probably shopping the craft booths. His dad was behind the counter helping a customer, so Mac wandered over to a display of reels.

Growing up, he'd spent as many hours here as he had at home. He'd worked alongside his dad selling fishing supplies and licenses for the rivers and lakes around the area ever since he was tall enough to reach the cash register. Mac considered himself a novice fisherman compared to his expert father. People came from around the country to take lessons from Rance Johnson.

His dad stopped at his side. "Hey, son, you headed to the festival?"

Mac nodded. "On my way over. You have classes today?"

"Fly-tying at two."

"Your mom bought a box of Saunders' apples this morning. I'm sure you'll be gettin' some of 'em," his dad said, smoothing a hand over his bald head with its fringe of white around the edges.

Mac pulled a rod from a nearby rack. The weight felt good in his hand. "Best apples in the state."

"Your mom entered her mixed berry jam and peach preserves this year."

"She'll come home with at least one blue ribbon."

"Always does." His dad took the rod from Mac and handed him another that felt even better. "You have something on your mind?"

Mac had never, even as a kid, been able to put one over on his dad. From bad grades to stretching cellophane over the toilet seats in the teachers' lounge, his dad knew as soon as Mac walked through the door. "Yeah. I want to talk to you and Mom about something that's come up."

"Tomorrow after church?"

Mac shook his head. "I don't want to talk when Beck is around. Can we meet for lunch on Monday?"

"Sure. I'll get Warren to cover the shop. How about Renaldo's at twelve-thirty?"

Mac didn't have to work until five. "Sounds good."

"You going to tell your mom, or am I?"

"I'll walk over to the library now." Mac slid the fishing rod back into the vacant bracket and pointed to a man with a puzzled look on his face. "You have a customer."

His dad studied him a moment looking for a clue, then clamped him on the shoulder. "I'll see you and Beck tomorrow."

Mac watched his dad greet the stranger as if they were life-long friends before he left the shop. Patsy didn't have him scheduled for a pie-in-the-face for thirty minutes, so he crossed behind Town Hall to bypass the crowded square and sidewalks. He took the library steps two at a time and pushed open the heavy wooden doors to another familiar place. His mom had been Eden Falls' first librarian at the age of eighteen. She met her husband in the western fiction section, and had been rushed to the hospital in the middle of children's story time to deliver Mac.

Seeing his mom behind the checkout counter calmed the frazzled nerves that had buzzed through his system since opening that envelope. Her reassuring smile was like a warm hug to his unsettled inner being.

"Hey, honey. Where's your other half?"

"He ran to meet up with buddies as soon as I parked the truck." He rested his palms on the scarred wood counter. "Dad said you entered a few of the festival's contests. Congratulations."

Her lips quirked into a half smile. "I haven't won yet."

"You will."

She swatted at him playfully. "The last few years haven't

even been a competition. I don't think this new generation has any idea how to can or bottle anything."

"Maybe you should offer some classes."

She gazed at him thoughtfully. "Actually, that's not a bad idea."

"You could use the library's basement kitchen."

She nodded before sliding a stack of books in front of her. "Rita came by earlier this morning. She told me you stopped her for no reason."

"She was doing thirteen over the speed limit."

"She also hinted you might have a drinking problem."

Mac could tell by the smile playing at the corners of his mom's mouth she didn't believe the town gossip. He lifted a shoulder. "Yesterday was slow."

She shook her head. "Have you walked through the square yet?"

"Patsy roped me into taking pies in the face to raise money for the Humane Society. I have to take my spot"—he glanced at his watch—"in about twenty minutes."

"Patsy can be persuasive."

"She promised me a few free donuts."

"Is that all?" His mom laughed. "She promised Colton a dozen."

"I'll have to hit her up for more. Why didn't she just sell the donuts she's giving away and donate that money to the Human Society."

"Don't you dare ask for more. The money she's raising is for a good cause. Do it for the puppies, not the pastries."

He tapped the counter with his fingertips. "I came by to see if you're free for lunch on Monday."

Her face brightened. "I am. What's the occasion?"

"I want to talk to you and Dad about something. Dad said he could get Warren to mind the shop."

The brightness was replaced with concern. "Everything okay?"

"I hope so. Monday, twelve-thirty, at Renaldo's. And don't say anything to Beck."

Lily nodded.

Mac thumbed over his shoulder. "Time to get coconut cream in the face."

"Have fun." Her worried expression didn't match her cheery tone.

~

*N*oelle loved the feel of small town celebrations. She wished she could bottle the excitement and sell it as a happy elixir on dreary days. The slightly cooler temperature and the scents of popcorn, cotton candy, and fall floating through the air made for the perfect Harvest Festival. Children bobbing for apples or getting their faces painted made her smile. She stopped to watch a caricature artist draw a young couple, enlarging the female's engagement ring to gargantuan proportions.

A group of teens dressed in black hovered near the corner of Main and Orchard Avenue. Two stood out. A tall male with skin so white it almost looked translucent and a short boy with bright orange hair. She didn't recognize any of them, but watched them scatter like leaves in a breeze when Eden Falls' chief of police started in their direction.

Noelle dropped off her bounty of vegetables in the café's kitchen, then joined her cousin for more fun. They watched a cluster of boys, Beck Johnson among them, trying to win prizes by throwing darts at a board filled with balloons. They moved over to enjoy the faces of children participating in the cupcake walk.

Families were out enjoying time together. Couples

strolled hand in hand, moms pushed strollers, dads had toddlers riding on their shoulders. She never thought about having a family while working on Wall Street, where the pace was fast and the competition brutal. A husband and children hadn't entered her thoughts until she moved here. Now she found herself wondering what it might feel like to meander through the booths hand in hand with a man or pull a wagon with a couple of wide-eyed children who resembled her…or him.

She shook her head when Mac and Beck popped into her mind, raising unexpected melancholy. She certainly didn't want Mike to notice a change in mood. It was too beautiful a day for sadness or regret.

They split up when Mike decided to watch an arm-wrestling match and she wanted to walk through the crafts section. A hand-carved pocketknife, a perfect Christmas gift for Mike, caught her eye. While she purchased the knife, a group of boys watching a group of giggling girls held her attention. The sight took her back to high school and those long-gone days of uncertainty.

"It's always the same—the girls ignoring the boys."

Noelle smiled at JT who'd appeared next to her. "I don't think they're ignoring, just playing hard to get."

He frowned. "That's even worse. Learning to play games so early in life."

"Somebody woke up on the cynical side of the bed this morning."

He snorted. "I guess I did. Sorry." He held out his hand. "What did you buy?"

She handed him the pocketknife. "A stocking stuffer for Mike."

JT examined the workmanship. "Has Mike decided to stay in Eden Falls?"

I hope so. "I don't think he knows for sure yet."

Laughter and cheering turned them toward a tent in front of Patsy's Pastries.

"Pie throwing booth," JT said.

"Really? I want to see."

They reached the booth just as Colton McCreed emerged covered with lemon and meringue.

His wife—the mayor of Eden Falls, and JT's sister—ran her finger down Colton's cheek and popped it into her mouth. "Mmm, you taste good."

Patsy Douglas laughed. "You two lovebirds take your tasting behind closed doors. There are children and jealous adults present."

"Closed doors." Colton pulled Alex against him. "My thoughts exactly."

Alex shrieked and tried to escape when Colton nuzzled her neck, smearing lemon meringue into her hair.

Patsy waved her forward. "Let's see how good a throwing arm you have, Noelle. It only took Alex two tries to clobber her husband. Five dollars a pie. The Humane Society needs you."

"The Humane Society would make a mint off me. I haven't thrown more than bread dough on a counter in years."

JT steered her forward with a hand on her back. "I'll fund this one, Patsy. It's for a good cause, and I wouldn't feel right throwing a pie at one of my officers."

Shouts of encouragement rose behind her as Mac Johnson stuck his head through a hole in a board painted to look like a clown without a face. A look of relief crossed his handsome face when he saw her standing at the front of the line.

"Attaboy!" Patsy accepted the ten-dollar bill JT handed to her.

Noelle tried to back away. "I really can't throw, JT. You'll be wasting your money."

JT patted her shoulders. "I have faith in you."

"Imagine Mac is a person you'd love to double up your fist and clobber." Patsy held out a pie in a foil pan.

"I heard Mac say, just last night, that the food at the café tastes like it comes out of a box," Colton said from behind her.

"Fighting words," she mumbled.

"Colton lies, Noelle. You know Beck and I love the café food."

"I heard him spreading rumors about ants. On the tables." JT lifted her hand and set the pie on her palm.

"She doesn't need help from any of you yahoos," Mac said. "Noelle, you know it isn't true."

Suddenly, Beck and two of his friends were beside her. "Dad, I need more money."

"Got you covered, Beck." Colton pulled a ten from his wallet. "Stay and watch. Your dad is about to get hit by berries and cream."

"Cool. I want to see your dad get hit," one of Beck's friends said.

"You've got two tries, Noelle," JT said. "Pretend he's a rat in the café's kitchen."

Noelle wrinkled her nose. She had to do this. Too many people were crowded around not to try. "Sorry," she mouthed at Mac as she took aim, threw, and missed by three feet.

Mac laughed.

Colton leaned in. "That was a good try, sweetheart, but it isn't going to kill the rat."

"Neither is a berry and cream pie," she retorted.

"Try again." JT handed her a second pie. "The rat just crawled onto the kitchen counter."

"Try again. Try again. Try again," Beck and his friends started chanting.

"Aim a little further to the right this time." Colton pointed at Mac's face. "The rat just got into a bag of sugar."

Noelle took aim and fired. The pie landed even further away than the first try. Mac laughed harder.

"Give us another pie." Colton snatched the ten away from Beck and handed it to Patsy.

"Dad, I need more money!"

This time Noelle took aim at the still-laughing Mac. She launched the pie and hit him square in the face.

The crowd went wild.

CHAPTER 4

Monday afternoon, Mac walked into Renaldo's Italian Kitchen in a cloud of discouragement hanging as heavy as the dark clouds overhead.

His mom and dad knew the story of his Vegas marriage. His mom read him the riot act when she learned what he'd done. His dad just shook his head and said, "Getting drunk is the same as ingesting a stupid pill, but learning from our mistakes is part of life."

His parents came through the door hand in hand and Mac felt a familiar twinge of shame. Before lunch was over, he'd disappoint them once again with the same stupid decision he made long ago.

His mom always asked for a table by the front window, but Mac steered her to a booth in the back corner. Watching people on the sidewalk would be a distraction. He needed his parents' full and undivided attention for thirty minutes. He didn't want ears overhearing and the information somehow getting back to Beck before he had a chance to talk to him.

His mother scooted onto the bench. "I know something is going on with you, Mac. Tell us."

"Let's order first." Mac picked up his menu as their waiter delivered water and a basket of bread to the table. Renaldo's menu hadn't changed much since the day he opened the restaurant, so browsing didn't take a lot of time. They each had their favorites. Once their drinks were delivered and they placed their order, Mac tugged the letter out of his pocket and pushed it across the table for his parents to read. They both took a moment to skim the contents, then raised their heads simultaneously.

"What is this?" his mom asked.

"It's pretty clear what it is." His dad glanced at the letter again and shook his head.

"I don't understand."

The quiver in his mom's voice hurt Mac's heart. Besides him, she'd been Beck's main caretaker since they moved to Eden Falls. He'd never thought about it before, but suddenly realized that, as an only child, he was their sole provider of grandchildren. Beck might be his parents' only grandchild and Cheryl wanted to take him away.

"Beck's mom wants him back." Despite having seen an attorney, Mac saying the words aloud made the situation more real, beyond daunting.

"Did you tell her she can't have him?"

"It doesn't work that way, Mom."

"It does to me. She abandoned him—left him on your doorstep in Los Angeles with a note attached. You didn't even know you had a child." She took a shaky breath. "This can't happen. She can't just decide to take Beck from every-thing he knows. She gave up her rights," she added, leaning forward and lowering her voice when his dad patted her hand.

His dad wrapped his arm around his wife's shoulder. "Have you talked to Owen Danielson?"

"Last week. I wanted his opinion before I said anything to you."

"What did he say?" Lily asked.

"Cheryl has abandonment and no-contact-since going against her. However," he said, using Owen's word, "she is remarried and has two stepchildren she cares for."

"That doesn't make her a good mother," his dad said.

"No, but it does mean she's grounded. 'Responsible,' Owen said." He made quotation marks with his fingers.

"So are you." His dad's fist bounced off the table, shaking their silverware and glasses. "You've been taking care of Beck since he was a baby with no help from her."

Conversation stopped as the waitress set salads in front of them.

"I spent the weekend researching California laws and Washington laws," Mac said after the waitress left. "Beck living here since he was five years old is a plus. Eden Falls is really all he remembers. He has friends and family here. It would disrupt his life to move him."

Questions crowded his mind again. "The thing that worries me, I took Beck from California without permission. I should have consulted an attorney first. I also didn't check with an attorney about drawing up custody papers. We were divorced before I knew Beck existed, so custody wasn't mentioned. And since she abandoned him, it never occurred to me that she might want him back. I should have closed and locked that door before leaving California."

Silence fell again when the waitress picked up the salad bowls none of them had touched and delivered their lunch plates. Mac looked down at his chicken parmesan with no appetite. His dad picked up his fork, seemingly lost in his own thoughts. Other than the worry line between his mother's eyebrows deepening, she was still.

His dad leaned his forearm on the table and looked at her. "We'll handle the situation the way we always have, one day at a time. Mac is a good father. He accepted responsibility when Cheryl ran from it. He took his son in before he even had proof Beck was his and has been raising him alone ever since. I don't believe a judge will rule against that.

"Beck is smart and happy. We need to have faith this will turn out right in the end. If the case goes to court, this whole town will vouch for Mac. He's provided a good home and loves Beck enough for two parents. Beck does well in school. His teachers will testify about the type of father Mac has been, so will Beck's coaches. I'm sure Preacher Brenner will come if we ask. Beck is an exceptional boy, and that right there says a lot."

Guilt surfaced as it always did when his father defended him. Mac made a lot of mistakes in college and getting married in Vegas was at the top of his list of dumb.

His mom blotted under her eyes with a napkin. "But sometimes the bad guy wins. If that happens, Cheryl will take our grandson to California. We might never see him again."

Mac reached across the table and took his mom's hand. "That's not going to happen, Mom. Even if Beck has to go to California, Owen will do his best to make sure it's only for the occasional holiday or summer break." He wished he carried as much conviction as his words. He met both his parents' gazes head on. "We have to believe this will turn out right." *I have to believe this will turn out right.*

"But what if—"

"There is no what if here, Lily. Owen will fix this. We have the law on our side. Mac has been a good father. We have to be optimistic—for Beck's sake, if nothing else."

Lily squeezed Mac's hand. "Do you need money? This may get expensive."

"No. I've got money." He'd work two jobs before asking for help to fix the mess he'd created.

His mom straightened her back and gave him a watery smile. "Okay, then, we'll all think positive thoughts. We'll be optimistic that everything will work out. You've raised that boy alone and done a wonderful job of it. Like your dad said, everyone around here will vouch for that."

"I didn't raise him alone." Mac's gaze bounced from one parent to the other. "I couldn't have done it without you two. You were there for me when we moved back to Eden Falls. You helped us get settled in, you watch Beck while I work. You both have had as much influence over Beck's life as I have. He loves you, and it would break his heart to leave here."

"Then, we'll just have to make sure that doesn't happen," his mom said with resolve, while drying her tears again.

Yes, I'll have to make sure that doesn't happen.

～

*T*uesday, long after the lunch crowd had emptied the cafe, Mac still sat at the booth where he had lunch with JT, Alex, and Colton. They'd enjoyed a lively conversation punctuated with lots of laughter. Now Mac sat alone with a single piece of paper on the table in front of him while he sipped a soft drink.

Noelle wiped down the counter, checked condiments, and made sure there was enough silverware rolled for the dinner crowd. She started a fresh pot of coffee and slid a couple of pies Albert baked into the display case. Finally, she walked over and slid into the opposite side of Mac's booth where he was attempting to build a Giza pyramid with sugar packets.

"Still mad at me?"

He glanced up and blinked his brown eyes, as if he'd forgotten where he was. Then his mouth quirked up in a crooked smile. "I was never mad, but I am still blowing whipped cream from my right nostril."

"You shouldn't have laughed."

"Lesson learned." He went back to stacking sugar, but his mind was a million miles away.

"Tell Beck I drove by and saw his scarecrow."

"Yeah?" He raised his brows, but kept his attention on the tilting pyramid. "I'll tell him."

"Day off?"

He turned his wrist and glanced at his watch. "No. I work tonight."

Noelle leaned forward, her forearms resting on the table. "Want to talk about whatever's bothering you?"

His lips flattened into a thin line as he shook his head. Then he looked up and stared at her a moment. "Yes. Actually, I do. Have you got a minute?"

She motioned to the almost empty café. "I think Lisa can handle things."

He unfolded the piece of paper he'd been reading earlier and slid it across the table. She straightened the edges with her fingertips. The address on the top listed a Los Angeles attorney. She read it, and then reread it, before glancing up at him. "Does this mean—?"

"My ex-wife is trying to take my son—the son she hasn't seen since he was six months old—away from me."

Noelle had never asked about Beck's mother. She heard tales and rumors as they floated through the café, but didn't pay much attention to gossip. There was always another side to every story. "This says she lives in California."

Mac nodded.

"Do you want to tell me what happened?"

"Long story."

She waved a hand around indicating the empty café. "I've got time."

Mac leaned back against the red vinyl of the booth and told her about a drunken Las Vegas wedding to someone he barely knew, how she'd walked out after a week of marriage.

Her expression must have registered surprise, because he raised an eyebrow. "Are you appalled by my stupidity?"

"Not appalled, just…surprised."

"Why? Because you thought I was a sensible, responsible person?" He stacked another sugar packet. "I told you I got into trouble a lot."

"I'm sorry she left."

He scoffed. "Don't be sorry. The wedding was the result of a ridiculous dare that I was stupid enough to take. There was no love or sense of loss on either of our parts when she walked away."

She was surprised again by his emotionless comment. "Even after you discovered she was pregnant?"

"I didn't know she was pregnant until she left a six-month-old baby on my doorstep."

Noelle closed her mouth when she realized it was hanging open. "She never told you?"

"Nope."

"Are you sure Beck is yours?" She immediately regretted asking. Beck looked too much like Mac, shared too many mannerisms to doubt.

"Yes, he's mine."

Noelle refolded the letter and slid it back to him. "She just dropped him off and hasn't seen him since?"

He tapped a pack of sugar on the table. "Never heard from her again."

"No support?"

"None."

"Wow."

He raised his gaze to hers. "Yeah, wow."

They were both quiet for a long moment, her with her own thoughts, him stacking sugar packets. The clink of glasses as Joseph unloaded the dishwasher carried into the front of the café.

She took a breath and blew it out, not sure if her words would help, but hoped to ease the worry around Mac's eyes. "I doubt a judge would take Beck away from you. Your ex didn't tell you she was pregnant, hasn't seen Beck since he was six months old, has never gotten in touch to check on him, and has done nothing to help with support. You've raised him by yourself and you've done a fabulous job." She attempted a reassuring smile. "You're a great father. Beck adores you."

Mac shook his head. "I won't go from seeing my son every day to visits on holidays. If Cheryl takes him to California, I won't even get to see him on weekends. She would turn his whole world upside down to satisfy her own selfish desires."

The café grew dark and then light as the sun played hide and seek with passing clouds. She breathed in the scent of Albert's cornbread coming from the kitchen. It would be served alongside the beef stew for tonight's special. "What does Beck say about all of this?"

"I haven't told him yet." Mac rubbed fingers along his jaw and Noelle heard the scrape of whisker against skin.

"Does he ask about his mom?"

He glanced out the window. "Occasionally. I tell him she had blond hair and blue eyes. She liked to listen to music and had a nice smile. We barely knew each other before the dare, only lived together for a week after. What else can I tell him?"

"She was the one who left and filed for divorce?"

"Yes, but I sure didn't do anything to stop her." He looked at her. "The whole thing happened a long time ago."

"Have you talked to an attorney?"

"I saw Owen last week. He's going to send a letter to Cheryl's attorney, let her know I'm willing to talk about visitation. He said being willing to work with her would go a long way with a judge."

"I'm sure that's hard, but he's probably right."

He gathered the packets of sugar and put them back in the container. "He intimated my case would be stronger if I was married."

Noelle shrugged. "I suppose that would be a better scenario." When he raised injured eyes, she added, "But there are a lot of single fathers out there, Mac. Judges don't just side with mothers anymore—especially when the mother abandons her child on a doorstep. I'm sure Owen will do everything he can to help you."

"But will it be enough?"

Not being a parent, Noelle had no idea what Mac was going through, but the pain in his voice and the worry in his eyes had words escaping her mouth before her mind caught up. "I'll marry you."

He snorted. "Yeah, that would make the situation all better." Then he stared at her, all amusement gone. A medley of expressions crossed his face before he shook his head. "No. That's crazy."

"That's me." She tipped her head and crossed her eyes. "Crazy."

"No one in their right mind would believe a marriage between us." He chuckled.

"I just hate to see you so worried."

Mac scraped his fingers along his jaw again. "Can you imagine the reaction I'd get if I up and married you? People would think I'd lost my mind."

Noelle raised a brow.

"We don't know each other any better than I knew Cheryl. I mean, that is really a crazy idea." His earlier "lesson learned" was forgotten as he began to laugh.

Her blurting out a proposal might be crazy, and she might

be crazy for thinking it could help, but it wasn't *that* crazy. "You'd better stop while you're ahead."

"Come on, Noelle, the notion is too insane to even contemplate. Marriage between us would never work." Another snort. "No one would believe it was for real. We haven't even been on a date. We know nothing about each other."

She cocked her jaw to the side as he continued snorting and snickering, as if she'd told the funniest joke he'd ever heard. "Actually, I know a lot about you."

"Yeah"—he leaned forward planting elbows on the table —"like what?"

"Besides being a good father, I know you enjoy fishing and camping. And bowling, apparently. You like coffee with a teaspoon of sugar and a splash of milk."

"That's common knowledge. Things everyone knows about me."

"You love cheese on your burger, but no ketchup or raw onion. You hate broccoli and turn up your nose at eggplant, but would never say so aloud, because it might influence Beck to never try them." *You're handsome and kind.* "Your favorite song on the jukebox is D-12, though you never remember the letter or number and always have to search."

His laugh faded.

"You are loyal to friends, love your parents, and haven't been on a date with *any* woman since I've known you." *You have a great smile and beautiful brown eyes.* "You love sweets. Anything chocolate is your favorite."

The smile slid from his face.

"Your favorite color is probably blue, maybe green, because those are the colors you wear most often." *You have an enviable relationship with your son, one I wish I had with my parents.*

A crease appeared between his brows.

"And you pull that face"—she pointed at the bridge of his nose—"when you get freaked out or embarrassed by a question."

He sat back, reached for his glass of diluted soft drink, but didn't lift it. "It's stalkerishly weird that you know all that."

"I'm a people-watcher. I can tell you the same kinds of things about most of my customers."

"All I know about you is that you own a café, you ask nuns inappropriate questions, and you have pretty eyes."

She fluttered her eyelashes. "Thank you. My favorite color is purple, my favorite food is pizza, and if you add black olives, I'm in heaven. I love to cook, I haven't been on a date since I moved to town, have never been in love"—*and never slept with a man because, well, you obviously remember the part about nuns and being a good girl*—"and my middle name is Mistletoe."

The line between his brows reappeared. "Your parents named you Noelle Mistletoe?"

She smiled. "I just said that to see if you were paying attention. Want me to continue?"

"Please do."

"I have three brothers, a master's in finance, I used to make a high six-figure salary on Wall Street, and I had an imaginary dog, the only pet my mom would allow. His name was Mr. Poopaloop." She took a deep breath. "And I want to be a mermaid when I grow up."

He stared wide-eyed. "You gave up a six-figure job on Wall Street to buy a restaurant?"

"I didn't buy it, I inherited it." She crossed her eyes, again. "Crazy, remember?"

She slid from the booth and pointed at his glass. "Would you like a refill?"

He shook his head, eyes still wide.

She knew his gaze followed her when she swung through the kitchen door.

~

$\mathcal{M}$ac watched Noelle disappear into the kitchen while her information dump ran through his head. She said she was crazy, and he believed it. You'd have to be out of your mind to offer to marry a complete stranger or leave a six-figure job to run a café in Eden Falls.

And the fake dog and mermaid thing? Was she serious—about any of it?

She knew a lot about him, which made sense. He and Beck ate here every Friday, and sometimes more often than that. She always asked questions and they answered. What did it say about him that last Friday was the first time he'd ever learned anything about her?

He left money on the table and walked the few blocks to Riverside Park. He found an unoccupied bench and sat.

Crazy as it was, her offer wouldn't leave him alone. He couldn't marry Noelle, of course, but if he found a woman, fell in love quickly, and proposed…would that satisfy a judge enough to keep Beck in Eden Falls? He thought of the single women he knew. There were several. Women he knew and liked, but none he would want to marry. He probably didn't have time to go online to some dating site before Cheryl's attorney took action. His thoughts circled back to Noelle. He liked her. More important, Beck liked her. She obviously liked them or she wouldn't be offering a possible solution to his very big problem.

Of course, they'd divorce as soon as the judge ruled in his favor.

Was a marriage of convenience considered falsifying evidence?

Could he and Noelle make a marriage believable enough?

It's possible.

He shook his head. He was as nuts as Noelle to be thinking along these lines. Another loveless marriage would crush his mom and dad.

Or would they understand he did it for Beck?

Truth be told, he'd be doing it as much for himself as Beck. He couldn't lose his son.

He tried to recall details he knew or had overheard about Noelle. She seemed like a happy person. Her employees liked her. Eden Falls liked her. She'd gotten a roaring round of applause when she nailed him in the face with a pie. He knew her cousin lived with her because of some trouble back home. He'd never seen her drunk—which probably had something to do with being schooled by nuns.

She was compassionate, cared about others. She had a pretty smile and a nice sense of humor. When she laughed, her eyes seemed to grow bluer.

Maybe that was the crazy coming out.

Once word got out Cheryl was suing him for custody, a sudden marriage would look suspicious. Everyone in town would know they hadn't married for love.

He couldn't believe he was even considering Noelle's offer. He'd already been married to a woman he didn't know or love, and here he was thinking about repeating the same scenario. He was as crazy as she was. A marriage between them couldn't work.

But what if it did?

They probably wouldn't see much of each other. She worked long hours at the café and his shift rotated. If she was willing to move into his house and stay with Beck when he worked, his mom and dad could have some time off. They'd probably appreciate the break.

What would Noelle expect from the union? She'd never

said, but surely she'd want something for her time. He didn't have a lot of money, but he'd give her everything he owned if it meant Beck would stay with him.

He glanced at his watch. He'd been sitting in the same spot agonizing for more than an hour. Noelle was crazy to offer and he was even crazier to consider. An impromptu wedding wouldn't work.

The breeze rattling the leaves seemed to whisper, *But what if it does?*

~

*N*oelle climbed out of bed, grabbed a sweater, and made her way down the dark hallway to the front door. She expected Mike, wearing a contrite expression for forgetting his key, but it was Mac's profile she saw when she peered through the peephole. He was in his uniform, bottom lip between his teeth.

She opened the door a crack and he turned to face her. "I think you have the wrong house. I didn't call the police."

He glanced down at his boots. "Sorry to wake you."

"That's okay." She flipped on the small porch light of her apartment and opened the door wider. "Is everything okay?"

He looked past her into her dark apartment. "Were you serious when you offered to marry me?"

"Uh…" *Was I?* Thoughts of Mac and Beck at the café counter on Friday nights, Mac's worried expression earlier today, Beck doubled over with laughter when she clobbered his dad with a pie, all ran through her mind. "Yes."

"You paused."

"I did. Marriage is a big step." *Huge. Gigantic. A my-parents-will-disown-me step.* "But I was serious."

He frowned, looking very much like his son when something was bothering him.

"Then I'd like to set up an appointment to discuss it."

She laughed and batted her eyelashes in as a flirtatious gesture as she could manage given the hour and the circumstances. "An appointment? Why, Mac Johnson, is that your attempt at asking me on a date?"

His frown turned to a scowl. "Look, I'm new at arranged marriages. Can you cut me some slack?"

Under the glow of the porch light, he emitted a shiny aura, as if he was made of glass so thin, the touch of a finger would shatter him. "Sorry. Sure, we can make an appointment."

A muscle in his jaw flexed, but the scowl fell away. "Could we talk Friday night? Beck will be at a birthday party."

Friday would work because she and Gertie had traded shifts again this week. "Friday will be fine." He nodded and turned away as the tips of his ears turned red. Too cute. "Do you want to come here to talk or should I meet you somewhere?"

"I'll pick you up at seven. We can go to dinner." His gaze raked over her, from her ratty sweater to her sheep-covered sleep pants, and ended on her bare toes. "Somewhere nice."

She'd never seen Mac so tense. Or serious. Even earlier today, with all that had been on his mind, he was more relaxed than at this moment. "Okay."

He pointed at her head. "I've never seen your hair down."

Expecting Mike, she hadn't looked in the mirror before answering the knock. She ran fingers through her hair, pulling it away from her face. "It gets in my way at work when it's down."

"I like it." He glanced around, as if afraid someone might overhear. "It looks nice."

"Thanks."

"Mermaid, huh?" he asked, possibly an attempt to lighten the atmosphere that crackled around them.

"Anything is possible." She rubbed her chin. "If I could get this beard to fill in, I'd apply for mall Santa, though that would be seasonal."

His expression remained staid.

Okay, so he isn't in a kidding mood. Still, she had to try for a smile or he'd have a long, ornery night ahead of him. "I considered unicorn wrangler, but have you ever tried to control a herd of unicorn? Impossible."

His lips twitched the tiniest bit. "I'll see you Friday." He turned and walked away.

Okey-dokey. She shut the door and leaned against it. *What have I gotten myself into?*

She'd always been a people-watcher and had observed Mac and Beck together many times. She would hate to see anything or anyone come between them. Mac also treated his parents with deep love and respect. They were a close family. *Something I'd love to be included in.*

She'd make a good wife. Unlike most, she enjoyed domestic duties, but didn't have many living with Mike, who cleaned up after himself for the most part. This would give her an opportunity to cook somewhere besides the café.

She didn't know much about being a mom. She certainly knew what *not* to do. She could watch Beck when Mac worked nights, or get him off to school on the mornings she was home. They could bake cookies together and she could help him with homework.

I sound like I'm trying to talk myself into a job I've already committed to.

If their stilted conversation just now was an indication of things to come, sitting through a nice dinner might be long and uncomfortable. She'd become an expert with uncomfortable lunches and dinners while working on Wall Street. If two hours with Mac was worse than some of those, they would be in big trouble.

The prospect of going out wearing something nicer than jeans and a tee gave her a thrill of anticipation and angst at the same time. She'd dressed in boxy tailored suits and sensible shoes in New York to try and blend in with the male-dominated field of finance. To some she'd been a threat, hadn't been taken seriously by others. She hadn't dressed for a date in a long time. Though, he hadn't actually asked her out. This would be a business dinner, at which she excelled.

She pushed away from the door and started down the hall. Out of desperation, Mac was considering her offer. She sent up a silent plea, for all their sakes, that she hadn't made a terrible mistake.

CHAPTER 5

Mac trudged through the open door of The Fly Shop the next afternoon. He could hear his dad's voice coming from somewhere in the back of the store. Moving to the window, he stared across the street at the café, fighting the urge to go in and tell Noelle he couldn't go through with their dinner. He'd temporarily lost his mind to even consider her offer. He spent a long night questioning her sanity—and his—over this crazy idea. What woman proposed marriage to a man she barely knew? True, he and Beck had been going into Noelle's Café since she'd opened her doors two years ago, but seeing someone in passing wasn't the same as knowing them.

"Hey, son, what brings you in today?" his dad asked, suddenly at his side.

Mac rubbed a hand down the side of his face. "Just wandering, and generally out of sorts since I received that letter."

"Don't blame you a bit there." His dad straightened some fishing magazines. "Have you talked to Owen again?"

"No. I'll wait until he contacts me. I'm sure he doesn't know anything new yet."

His dad leaned against the counter and ran a hand over his bald crown. "Your mom has been tossing and turning at night since seeing that letter."

"I probably shouldn't have told her until I knew more. I didn't mean to worry either of you." What had he been thinking to tell them before he had more news?

"You did the right thing by telling us. No need to carry that weight by yourself."

Mac spotted Noelle pulling a sweater on as she left the café. She waved to someone she passed as she crossed the square, coming this way.

Why would she come to The Fly Shop? She wouldn't mention her proposal to his dad, would she? He wasn't sure he wanted his parents to know he was actually contemplating a marriage of convenience in order to keep Beck with him. His heart thumped hard as she drew near, but she passed without a sideways glance and turned into Pretty Posies. He released the breath he was holding, startled by his hot cheeks and tight chest.

"You okay, son?"

"Yes." Mac glanced at his dad and noticed the concern on his face. "Yeah, I'm fine. I just stopped by to say hi." He thumbed over his shoulder. "I'd better go."

His dad patted his back. "Don't worry too much, Mac. Things will work out."

"I could say the same to you, but you'd still worry."

"You're right," his dad replied on a chuckle. "It's not fair, what she's doing, after all you've given up to raise your son."

"I've never felt like I was giving anything up. Quitting my job with LAPD has never been a regret. Beck's happy here and I love my job. I don't worry about him as much as I would if we were still in Los Angeles." He shook his head.

"I've never felt like I missed anything by having Beck. I can't imagine what my life would have been like these past ten years if I didn't have him, and I don't want to find out what the next ten would be like without him."

"You won't find out. Worst case scenario, you follow them, get your job back with the police department. As parents, we do what we have to do."

His dad was right. If Cheryl won this custody case and took Beck to California, he would follow.

A thought crossed his mind. If he and Noelle were considering this insane plan, he might as well set some groundwork. "I do have some news that will make Mom happy."

His dad's face brightened. "That's what we need, some good news."

"I have a date Friday night."

Rance raised his gray eyebrows. "With someone we know?"

"Noelle Treloar."

~

*N*oelle loved stepping into Pretty Posies where funky armoires held pots of autumn flowers. Bats, spider webs, and plants hung from the ceiling. Pumpkins shared shelf space with unique pieces of art from local artists. The whole place smelled divine—comfort food for the senses.

Alex came from the back room. "Hi, Noelle."

"Hey. I love your Halloween decorations."

Alex leaned against the counter. "Thanks. Charlie is jealous of the witch that smashed into your kitchen door."

Noelle smiled. She loved Alex's seven-year-old son, Charlie. His happy smile never failed to delight her, and he had inherited that smile from his mother. "Yeah, he got a kick out of Hazel."

Alex smiled. "He said he helped name her."

"He did. He came in with JT the other day and said she needed a name. We all agreed she should be Hazel." Noelle bent to smell a rose. "I need a birthday gift for my mom."

"Are you looking for something specific?"

Noelle waved her hand around. "I'll take one of everything."

"I'll wrap it all up and have it sent over to the café. Then retire." Alex straightened a pot of flowers sitting near her elbow. "Not sure how well that would work—my author husband and I together all day in that small house of ours. One of us might not come out alive."

"I heard through the ever-reliable Eden Falls gossip line that you're building a new home."

"We are, but it won't be ready until next summer." She scrunched her nose. "Have you ever built a home with a man?"

Noelle shook her head.

"Take my advice. Don't. Especially a man who's used to getting everything he wants."

Alex and her husband, *New York Times* bestselling author Colton McCreed, were the epitome of a darling couple. Two people from different backgrounds, who were the complete opposites, could not be more perfect for each other. Colton's mom was an actress, and his father, a screenwriter. Growing up spoiled and privileged, he'd come to town a sworn bachelor, but it hadn't taken Alex and Charlie long to work their way under his callused edges.

Noelle met Alex soon after coming to town. Not only did she own the only flower shop in Eden Falls, but she was also the mayor and sister of the police chief. The petite blonde, who was possibly the sweetest person Noelle had ever met, welcomed her before she even started the renovations on her café.

"Last time I was in I noticed some—aww, there they are." Noelle moved to a shelf that held an array of wooden candlesticks. She pulled two from the shelf. "I think my impossible-to-please mom might like these."

"They're unique, aren't they?"

Noelle set the pair on the counter near the cash register. "Do you happen to have a box?"

"No. I do have bubble wrap, but you'll have to get a box from the post office. My dad keeps odd sizes in the back room. I can call and see if he has something that will work."

"Thanks, Alex."

When Noelle left the flower shop ten minutes later, she spotted Mac standing in front of Patsy's Pastries looking straight at her. She turned in that direction and stopped next to him. "Hello."

"Hi." He glanced at the bag she held.

"I bought something for my mom's birthday. Alex always has the perfect gifts." She pulled a candlestick from the bag. "She said Leo Sawyer carved these."

"He was always a good artist in school. Do you know Leo's history?"

Noelle lifted a shoulder. "I've heard rumors."

"Leo developed a dot-com something or other, moved to Silicon Valley, then sold the company for millions a couple of years ago."

～

*N*oelle grinned, her blue eyes brightening the gloomy day. "Maybe I offered to marry the wrong man."

She had an uncanny ability to make him laugh. Her sense

of humor wasn't in your face, but rather, small snippets thrown in at the right moment. He liked the wink she flashed to let him know she was teasing. In the long run, and the short, Leo Sawyer would be a much better catch.

He took the bag and held it open when she struggled to put the candlestick inside. "Are you headed to the café?"

"No, the post office. Denny Garrett has a box and I need to get these in the mail today."

"I'll walk with you."

She shook her head. "You don't have to do that."

He also liked her smile. "I want to and"—he inhaled—"if we're seriously as insane as I think we are, we should be seen together. People won't be quite so shocked if we…you know…get married."

She leaned close. For a second, he thought she was going to kiss him, which might be kind of nice…if anyone was watching, of course. "You make it sound as if we're planning something dirty. It's just marriage."

Just marriage? "How can you sound so flippant?"

"Because it's not real."

"Marriage?"

"No, silly. Us. Our marriage won't be real, just a means to an end."

Mac pulled out his cell and entered her comment in his search engine. "Means to an end—doing something undesirable to reach a goal." He glanced at her. "I can't think of a more unromantic way to describe what we're contemplating."

A mischievous smile tipped up the corners of her mouth. "I didn't know you wanted to be romanced."

"That's not what I meant, but now you mention it, don't you think…we should probably act a little romantic towards each other if we're to be believed?"

"I thought you were still straddling a fence over marriage."

"I am, but it wouldn't hurt to lay the groundwork…just in case."

"Then we're headed in the right direction." Her blue eyes twinkled as she wrapped both hands around the crook of his arm and set their pace toward the post office. "The biggest town gossip, a.k.a. Rita Reynolds, will see us together, and word will spread like a wildfire in an August drought. Of course, she'll add that I'm pregnant. Why else would we get married so quickly?"

Great.

"Little will she know this marriage will be in name only."

Oh—he hadn't thought that far ahead, but of course it would be in name only. A little enthusiasm leaked from his farce wedding balloon.

She looked at him and grinned as if reading exactly where his mind had gone. "To be believable, you should probably put a smile on that handsome face."

Did she really think he was handsome? He couldn't tell if she was serious or not, but he wasn't going to ask, because she might take it back. Marriage to her would certainly be interesting, and he didn't mind walking down the street with a woman hanging on his arm or boosting his ego with compliments. Even if they were empty.

Maude Stapleton, who owned Pages Bookstore, walked outside her shop to adjust a wreath on the front door. She turned toward them with a frown. "You two look awfully cozy. When did this happen?"

"When did what happen?" Noelle asked.

Maude moved a pointed finger between them. "The two of you. Are you—?"

"Together? We are." Noelle flashed him a flirtatious smile. "Aren't we, boogabear?"

"Sure are…snookums." Mac chuckled at the look on Maude's face. She was a woman who never ran out of words or snarky comments, and they left her tongue-tied, her mouth opening and closing like a beached trout.

"Have a nice day," Noelle said over her shoulder as they passed. "You couldn't come up with anything better than snookums?" she said when they were out of earshot.

"Oh yeah, boogabear is so much better."

She shrugged. "Okay, so we both need to work on our pet names for each other."

"How about we call each other Mac and Noelle?"

"Booorrring."

"At least we left Maude speechless." Mac pulled the elbow Noelle clung to closer to his body.

"Which is an epic feat," Noelle added.

It felt nice to share a laugh together.

"It won't last long. She's almost as big a gossip as Rita."

Mac had dated here and there, but kept things light since moving back to Eden Falls. He didn't have the time or energy for dating games. He was a what-you-see-is-what-you-get kind of guy. He was also very careful about who he introduced into Beck's life. He didn't want his son to become attached to a woman only to have her walk away like his mother had. Which was exactly what Noelle would do when their marriage was no longer necessary.

But if he retained custody, they would still see her every Friday at the café, so she wouldn't be out of their lives.

As soon as they walked into the post office, he knew being seen with Noelle was the right thing if they were going to pull off this charade. Rita was behind the counter and squawked loudly. "Macoy and Noelle, Macoy and Noelle," she repeated like a talking mynah. "Before you get too attached, Noelle, you should know Macoy Johnson is a bully. He gives tickets out to innocent senior citizens."

"Really?" Noelle asked wide-eyed. "And I was just starting to like the guy."

"You were speeding, Rita."

Rita leaned over the counter and pointed her finger at him. "He also has a drinking problem. *Squawk!*"

Denny Garrett came out of his office. "Hey, Mac. Come on back, Noelle. We'll get those candlesticks wrapped up for you."

Noelle turned to Mac while Rita flapped her hands as if she was about to take flight. "Thanks for walking me."

Mac glanced from her to Rita. "I'll see you Friday night." He turned to leave, but Noelle caught him by the front of his jacket. "No goodbye kiss?"

Seriously? In front of Rita?

Noelle tugged him close and kissed him. It was fast and so surprising he just stood there like a dummy. When she stepped away, she winked in that sexy way of hers. Rita squawked so loud he jumped, and Denny chuckled.

"See you Friday, boogabear," Noelle said, low and seductive.

Mac walked back to the police station aware of the silly grin that wiggled at the corners of his mouth. Maude was bound to tell every woman who walked into the bookstore. Denny wasn't a gossip, but he'd tell his wife, Alice, who would tell their daughter, Alex, who would tell her brother, JT, who would tell everyone at the station, who would tease Mac relentlessly. Rita would alert everyone else.

Their secret was out. One brief fifteen minute walk and he and Noelle Treloar were a couple.

◈

They sat around the table in the break room, JT at the head. To his right was Eli Atkins, newbie to their small police force. He came to them from a little town northeast of Eden Falls. They'd been shorthanded for two months and it would be good to be fully staffed again.

Mac took a muffin from the box with Patsy's Pastries embossed on the top and set it on a napkin. He held the box for Phoebe Adams, whose hand floated over the box twice.

"They're all blueberry."

"I know. I'm looking for the smallest one."

"Cut one in half if you don't want a whole one."

"But then I'll just eat the other half before this meeting's over. If I pick a small one, I'll eat two small halves instead of two large ones." He made the selection for her and passed the box down the table.

"While we're waiting for Gianna to make some copies, I'll start this meeting with introductions. Please welcome Eli. He graduated from the University of Arizona last spring." He glanced at Eli. "We're glad you've decided to join us. Next to you is Layne Yancy, an Eden Falls native, who's been with the department for six years. He and Gianna, our office assistant slash dispatcher, are married. Macoy Johnson goes by Mac. He moved back to town five years ago. Before that he was with the LAPD. Phoebe Adams, also a native, has been with the force for eight years. Drew Zahn joined the force a year ago."

"Welcome, Eli," Phoebe said. While Gianna walked around the table setting a piece of paper in front of each of them, Phoebe leaned toward Mac. "He's cute."

Mac lifted an eyebrow. "And too young for you, cougar."

She slapped his arm. "Be nice."

JT held up the paper Gianna had passed out. "Our suspects were back in town for the Harvest Festival. I want to go over their information again. The tall one is Anthony Harris, known as Thorn by his groupies or followers. The kid with the orange hair is Aaron Meeks, aka Blaze. The fire marshal found his cell phone under the burned tree on the square." JT glanced at Eli. "You have the report of that fire and the one at the hardware store in front of you. When Aaron Meeks was questioned, he said he lost his phone at the concert on the Fourth of July. We can't prove otherwise, even though the phone was used after the fourth."

"What about phone records?" Phoebe asked.

"We have them, but they don't prove he had the phone in his possession."

JT pushed back from the table and walked to the window. "Blaze is small enough to have fit through the break in the chain-link fence at the lumberyard."

"Being small and losing a phone isn't enough—"

"Evidence," JT said, interrupting Drew. "I know."

"Do they have a motive?" Phoebe asked.

Layne snorted. "Kids don't need motive."

"I mean, if Thorn has groupies or a gang of followers, is lighting fires some sort of initiation for admission into the gang?"

JT turned back to face them and blew a breath out, his frustration visible. "Good question."

"Phoebe may be onto something. Initiation or lighting fires may be a way for Blaze"—Mac used quotation marks as he said the name—"to prove he's tough enough for this gang. He's small for his age, so he dyes his hair, changes his name, and lights fires so he will be accepted."

Everyone around the table nodded.

"Good angle," Layne said.

"In my opinion, if it is Blaze, and if he's lighting fires for that reason, he'll continue to do so until he's caught. He's gotten away with two and will begin to feel invincible. Losing his phone was a mistake. He'll make another." JT walked over and planted his palms on the table. "If you happen to see one of these two in town, call me day or night. As you can see, they're easy to spot."

"Why are you zeroing in on these kids? Are there no other suspects?" Eli asked.

"None." JT shook his head. "And I'm zeroing in because my gut tells me to. It's a hunch I can't shake. The way these two look at me, it's like they're taunting me. As soon as they spotted me at the Festival, they scattered, but Thorn—it's almost as if he wants to make sure I see him."

"Do you know what they drive?" Drew asked.

"Thorn drives an old Ford Bronco. Mac, do you remember the other makes and models from the Fourth?"

"One kid was driving an older Subaru, dark green or blue. One of the girls with them was in a burgundy Jeep Cherokee, also older."

"I know we don't have any evidence, but I'm going with my gut on this." JT straightened with hands on his utility belt. "That doesn't mean to ignore the possibility it could be someone else. I don't want us to get sloppy, because I suspect these kids. But I want to keep an eye out for them and call me if you see either one of them around town."

"You got it, Chief," Phoebe said.

JT glanced at Mac as a self-satisfied grin settled over his face. "I don't have anything else except the news that Mac and Noelle Treloar were caught kissing in the post office."

"What?" Phoebe turned to Mac with wide eyes. "When was this?"

"Wednesday afternoon," JT said, walking around behind Mac and shaking him by the shoulders.

Layne whacked Mac on the back while Phoebe pointed a finger at his nose. "You can't deny it, because your ears are turning red."

Mac held up his hands in surrender. "I'm not denying anything."

Drew leaned forward. "You and Noelle?"

Mac didn't want to commit to anything, so he stood. "Eli, you ready to roll? I'll show you around town."

～

"Okay." Gertie cornered Noelle in her office Friday after the lunch rush. "I just stopped at the post office and Rita started questioning me about you and Mac Johnson. She said you kissed him shamelessly in front of her two days ago."

Noelle smiled, surprised the information had taken so long to get back to Gertie. "She's right. I didn't feel much shame at that moment, or since."

"I didn't know you and Mac were dating. It seems no one else knew you were dating either," Gertie said cutting an eye at Noelle. "Want to tell me what's going on?"

"Nothing's going on. Mac and I are dating."

"You haven't been on a date since you moved to town.

Go wipe a counter, Gertie.

"It's about time, in my opinion."

"Then you should be happy."

"I am happy, and Mac is a nice man. I just wonder how this has been going on under my nose. What does Beck think about you and his dad?"

"I'm not sure Mac has told him yet. He's very careful where Beck is concerned."

Gertie nodded. "As he should be. He's a good father."

Noelle had been answering the same questions all day. She didn't imagine they'd stop coming until everyone was used to seeing her and Mac together. The mention of Beck concerned her, though. She hadn't thought of Beck when she kissed Mac. Not smart. If she was to become a stepmom, Beck had to be front and center in her thoughts.

"Gertie, would you mind if I leave a little early? I have an errand."

At Gertie's nod, Noelle grabbed her coat and ran out the back door. She crossed the square and entered Pretty Posies. Alex and her assistant looked up when the bell over the door jangled happily.

"Hi, Noelle," Tatum said. She wore a Morticia Adams dress, and not because it was almost Halloween. The scuttlebutt around town was that Tatum ran out of gas passing through town a few years earlier. She'd walked into Pretty Posies looking for a job to fill her tank. Alex hired her, and Tatum never left.

She dressed like a punk-rocker with ever-changing hair color. Today it was jet black and pulled back just enough to show the jeweled spiders hanging from her ears.

Alex set a book on a shelf to her left. "Twice in one week. I feel special."

"I need your help."

Alex's expression turned from happy to concerned. "Of course, anything."

"I have a date tonight and I have no idea what to wear or what to do with my hair."

Tatum squealed and clapped her hands like a child in a toy store. "Please, let me do your makeup. Please, please, please."

Noelle must have looked appalled as she stared at Tatum's black eye shadow and lipstick, because Alex took her hand and led her around the counter. "Believe it or not, Tatum is an expert with makeup."

"I am. I really am. I have everything I need here."

In the backroom, Alex pulled a stool out from under a large worktable for Noelle to sit on. Tatum hefted a huge bag from a locker.

This was a mistake. Noelle, not much of a makeup

person, sat as still as possible while Tatum worked on her face and Alex, using a curling iron—*do they always carry all this stuff around?*—worked on her hair.

Alex leaned around Noelle's shoulder. "I assume the rumors I've been hearing are true and this date is with Mac."

"It has to be with Mac." Tatum lifted a brush from Noelle's cheek. "It's all over town you two were kissing in the post office." She glanced at Alex as she stepped back. "What do you think?"

Alex studied Noelle with a smile. "That looks great."

"You don't wear much makeup, do you?" Tatum asked as she swirled a large brush over the top of what she'd already applied.

"Just a touch of mascara."

"Your cheeks look luminescent," Alex said

"Is that good?"

"Beautiful." Tatum pulled more pots and brushes from her bag. "Now for your eyes. Should we go for hot and sexy or smoky and sultry?"

Alex grinned. "Hot and sexy."

"How about normal?"

"Too bland." Tatum loaded a brush with eye shadow. "You have stellar eyebrows."

"Is that good?"

⁓

"**W**hy are you dressed up, Dad?" Beck asked when he bounced into the bedroom.

Mac glanced down at the trousers and sport coat. "I'm not dressed up."

"Yeah, you are. You're wearing a tie."

Too much. Mac loosened the knot of his tie, pulled it over his head, and straightened his collar again.

"Where are you going?"

Mac ran a hand down the front of his jacket. "I'm going on a date."

Beck snickered. "With a girl?"

"Well…yeah." He turned sideways and sucked in his stomach. "I'm taking Noelle to dinner."

"Noelle?" Beck flopped onto Mac's bed. "That's kind of weird."

Mac sat on the edge of the bed and pulled Beck into a headlock. "Why do you think it's weird?"

Beck shrugged as he scratched at the side of his nose. "I don't know. I guess because we know her already. Aren't you supposed to date people you don't know?"

"No. There really isn't a rule book." *Though that would be nice.* "You just kind of make it up as you go along."

"I don't want to date."

You'll change your mind before I'm ready. "You like Noelle, don't you?"

"Yeah, she's cool."

Mac ruffled his son's dark hair. "I forgot to tell you, she drove by to see our Halloween decorations."

A smile spread across Beck's face. "Did she like them?"

"She said she did." Mac stood and studied his reflection a moment. "Do I look okay?"

Beck tipped his hand back and forth. "You kinda look like you're going to church."

Mac jerked a thumb over his shoulder. "Get your stuff, wise guy, or you'll be late for Evan's birthday party."

CHAPTER 6

M ac stood at Noelle's door, his stomach jumping like he was back in middle school, standing before the principal. He'd considered flowers, but decided against them.

This whole idea was ridiculous. He should get back in his truck, call Noelle, and tell her thank you, but he couldn't go through with it. Which was just as ridiculous. He'd already asked her out, and they'd go. He owed her that much. They'd have a nice dinner and, afterward, he'd tell her he appreciated her offer, but a wedding wouldn't guarantee he could keep Beck. Where would that leave them? He'd been reckless to even consider her offer.

He knocked and wished he'd stopped for flowers after all.

Noelle opened the door and took his breath away…just a little.

She looked different, softer somehow. She was wearing a slim skirt with a flowered sweater and stuff on her eyes. And lips. Pink stuff that looked nice. He'd never seen her in anything but jeans and a T-shirt or sweater. Or pajama pants and a ratty sweater that needed replacing. And she was wearing her hair down, curled softly around her face. It looked pretty and temptingly touchable. As his eyes moved down her body, she pulled on the short hem of her skirt.

"I borrowed it from Tatum. I'm taller than she is."

"Goth chick Tatum has normal clothes?"

She laughed. "That's what I said when she pulled it out."

Her over-the-knee boots covered too much of her legs. *Marriage in name only, buddy.* "You look nice."

"Thank you. So do you."

His attention was on her legs rather than what he'd worn. He looked down. Right, his tweed sport coat. When he glanced up, her mischievous smile was back.

"Come in while I get my coat."

He stepped inside her apartment and looked around. She kept a neat home. Important in his book. Cheryl had lived like a pig. He took the coat she picked up from a chair and held it while she slipped her arms in.

"Thank you."

"You're welcome."

She turned to him. "Are you nervous?"

He shoved his hands in his pants pockets. "For some reason, yes."

"Don't be. We're just going to dinner to talk. That's all. No promises or commitments have to be made. If you'd rather call it off, I'm okay with that. Or we can go as friends and I'll pay my way."

He wished he could go back, all the way back to the moment he decided to open up about his talk with Owen. If he could go back that far, she wouldn't have approached him with this ridiculous idea. "No. I asked you to dinner. I'll pay."

"Okay, if you're not going to take an easy out, let's go." She picked up her purse and shut the door. "Was Beck excited about the birthday party?"

"Yes." He stopped short of touching her back as they walked to his truck.

"Was it a sleepover?"

"Yes."

"I guess he's at the age where no girls are allowed."

"Yes." His son was at the age where girls still had cooties.

"Are you still nervous?"

"No. Yes."

Her mouth angled to the side, drawing his gaze to the color. He'd have to make a concerted effort to keep his eyes off her mouth tonight.

"I need to restructure my questions, so I can get more than a yes or no answer."

Her smile told him she was teasing again. "No," he said with a half laugh.

"Seriously, Mac, we don't have to go to dinner. I won't be offended and trash your name all over town for standing me up."

"What will you say?"

She waved a hand down her body as if it was behind door number one. "Obviously you're gay."

He glanced at her mouth again. "I'm not gay and I didn't stand you up." He opened the passenger door.

She held her hand to her mouth as if talking into a walkie-talkie. "Houston, I think we have a problem."

She was pretty in her purple coat back-dropped by a red maple. "What's wrong?"

"To get into your truck, I'll have to hike my skirt up to the Netherlands. Then you'd have to arrest me for indecent exposure. Your maybe, pretend, fiancée in jail would not look good to a judge, because I won't be a model prisoner."

Without a thought, he scooped her up and settled her in the passenger seat. "Problem solved."

She flashed a smile. "Okey-dokey."

He closed the door, ran around to the driver's side, and slid behind the wheel. Her perfume floated through the cab, soft and flowery. He'd never had a woman in this year-old truck. "I thought we should go somewhere private to talk. No prying eyes or ears."

"Probably a good idea."

"Do you like Chinese?"

"Love it."

"Have you ever eaten at Formosa Gardens in South Fork?"

"No, but I've heard it's good."

Their twenty-five-minute ride was on the quiet side. Mac wasn't shy and hardly ever short on things to talk about but, for the life of him, he couldn't think of anything to say that wouldn't sound forced. Being more nervous than he'd ever been on a date didn't help. He blamed it on the knowledge this date could possibly end in matrimony.

Why was he thinking along those lines? Before he knocked on her door, he'd decided against the idea.

Once parked, Noelle slid from the seat and hit the ground safely before he could get around to open her door. They were shown to a table and he held her chair. While they perused the menu in silence, Mac racked his brain for a topic of conversation.

"What's good?"

"I've never been disappointed with anything on the menu."

After they placed their order, she spread a napkin over her lap. "So, I guess we should do a background check. Would you like me to start?"

He had no idea what she was talking about.

"The long or the short version?"

"We have all night," he said, and then hoped she didn't take that the way it sounded.

She leaned both forearms on the table, as if settling in. "I was born and raised in Boston. My mom, dad, and three brothers are goal-setting, overachievers—neurosurgeon, cardiothoracic surgeon, pediatric surgeon, orthopedic surgeon, ophthalmic surgeon, and then there's me—the black sheep…"

Ahh, background check—backstory. Little slow on the uptake there, Mac.

"At my father's insistence, I entered medical school. We didn't fit well, so I dropped out without my parents' knowledge and went the financial route. My parents were furious, but settled on irritated annoyance when I received my master's degree and landed a job in New York City."

A waiter appeared with their salads. Noelle flashed a beauty pageant smile. "Thank you. This looks delicious."

The kid was instantly smitten. "If you need anything—"

"We'll let you know," Mac said.

"My estranged uncle dashed even those hopes and dreams for my parents when he died and left me a rundown, rodent-infested restaurant," she said after the waiter reluctantly wandered away.

"Marrying me will really add to the family disappointment."

She waved a dismissive hand. "You'll get over it. I did."

A marriage in name only, in-laws who will despise me, and three, probably very protective, brothers…this gets more enticing by the minute. "So, old Jeremiah was your uncle?"

Noelle nodded as she picked up her chopsticks and expertly popped a carrot slice into her mouth.

"That restaurant was boarded up for so long, I'd forgotten it used to be Jeremiah's Place when I was a teenager."

"Jeremiah was eighteen years older than my dad. He ran away from home after high school and eventually ended up here in Washington. He was the reprobate no one ever talked about. Mmm, this dressing is divine."

He forked some lettuce into his mouth.

"Don't you use chopsticks?"

"Can't. I've tried."

She got up from her chair, walked around behind him, and pulled his chopsticks out of a silk sleeve. Reaching around him, she showed him how she held them in her own fingers. Her hair tickling the side of his face was extremely distracting. "Now you try."

"I have tried. I'm hopeless."

She wrapped her much smaller hand around his and placed the chopsticks between his fingers. "Nothing's hopeless."

Her breath fluttered across his cheek. He attempted a piece of lettuce, almost making it to his mouth. Before he could try again, he felt the tip of her finger just above his ear.

"Did you know you have the cutest little mole right here by your temple?"

He turned his head until their lips were almost touching. "You're distracting me."

The twinkle was back. "Sorry. Try again, but keep your ring finger tucked under the bottom chopstick."

His gaze wandered to her mouth. She smiled and moved back to her chair.

He waited until she spread her napkin and picked up her chopsticks. By then his erratic heartbeat had settled to normal again. "So, back to Uncle Jeremiah."

"When I was in the fourth grade, we had a genealogy assignment. My dad produced a Spokane address for his estranged brother, said he would know more about past family history, so I wrote, and Jeremiah wrote back."

She continued her story as if they hadn't just shared a moment and Mac fought to keep his gaze off her lips. Had she felt the air sizzle around them? If so, how could she act so nonchalant?

"We corresponded back and forth sporadically over the

years, and then the letters stopped. I got a few Return to Senders, so I assumed Uncle Jeremiah had moved on, which he obviously had. You're doing really great, by the way," she said, nodding toward his lettuce-to-mouth attempts. "You'll get better with practice."

"I'll also starve."

"Just use your fork, silly."

He attempted a withering look.

She winked.

"Back to your story."

"Right. Then I received a letter from Owen Danielson informing me of my uncle's passing and that he'd left me a restaurant."

"So, just like that, you left your life in New York and moved to Eden Falls."

Noelle laughed. "Not exactly. There were back taxes to be paid, and vagrants had broken in, so the town wanted something done. Owen hired a handyman to board up the place securely for me. I caught up the taxes and forgot about it.

"Then one stressful day, I decided a much-needed vaca-tion was in order. I booked a flight to Seattle, rented a car, and ended up in Eden Falls. My plan was to find a realtor and put the restaurant up for sale, but something about the building spoke to me. I fell in love with Eden Falls on sight and could see the potential in the boarded-up restaurant. I sat across the square at East Winds eating Chinese, staring at my uncle's place. Before paying the bill, I opened my fortune cookie and it said, "Big changes are in the air". What bigger change could there be than renovating the restaurant rather than selling? And here I am."

Noelle was smart, came from a smart family. Did those kinds of things matter in a custody hearing? Would a judge ask about her background?

Mac set the chopsticks down and picked up his fork. "That's a crazy story."

She crossed her eyes and he chuckled.

"Tell me how your cousin came to be here."

Noelle wiped her mouth with her napkin then arranged it over her lap. "He moved in after a bad breakup. Us under-achievers have to stick together." She laughed at her own joke, which made him smile. "Actually, Mike was engaged to be married, and his fiancée left him at the altar—*and* ran off with his best friend. Now that the exes are engaged, Mike decided the East Coast wasn't big enough for the three of them. I had a spare bedroom and he needed a place to crash for a while. Rowdy was hiring at the time, and Mike bartended in college, so Rowdy offered him a job. He only planned to stay for the summer, but he likes it here."

She pushed her salad bowl back and pointed a chopstick at him. "Your turn."

"What would you like to know?"

"Let's start with Beck. I know he plays baseball in the spring. Does he play any other sport?"

Mac set his salad bowl inside Noelle's. "He likes football and soccer, but baseball is his first love."

The waiter served their dinners, picked up their salad bowls, then waited like a puppy wanting a pat on the head.

"This looks delicious." Noelle smiled up at him.

The waiter—no more than twenty, twenty-one at the most—gave her a goofy grin. "I'll be back in a minute to make sure everything's okay."

After the kid walked off, Mac said, "Should I be offended that he's flirting with my date?"

"Don't be silly. He's just doing his job." She leaned over her dish, closed her eyes, and breathed in deeply. "This smells divine."

Noelle's enthusiasm over her food was fun to watch. She

was always serving. He'd never seen her eat before. She picked up a tiny bite of kung pao chicken and put it on her tongue. "It's as delicious as it smells." She picked up another bite and held it out to him. "You have to try this."

He leaned forward and allowed her to feed him a bite. He tried to savor the flavors, but was too mesmerized by watching Noelle's tongue swipe across her bottom lip. She had a beautiful mouth. And her expressive eyes... One minute they were wide with surprise, the next they were dancing with merriment. Would the blue deepen in the throes of—"

"Good, huh?"

Her question brought him back to Formosa Gardens. "Delicious."

"What else does Beck like to do?"

"He likes to do the same thing most boys in Eden Falls enjoy. Summers are spent fishing, swimming, hiking, playing ball."

She took another bite and chewed daintily. "Does he help your dad at The Fly Shop?"

Mac nodded. "And my mom at the library at least one afternoon a week for a few dollars. He likes to read. He's doing well in school, has good friends."

"What does he like to read?"

The waiter had taken his fork away with his salad bowl, so Mac attempted a clump of rice with his chopstick, only to have it disintegrate at a touch. Noelle laughed and passed him her fork.

Mac took a bite of his beef with mushrooms and snow peas. It was as delicious as Noelle's dinner. "I think I need another chopstick tutorial." *But not with you standing behind me, or we may be here all night.* She smiled. She really had a pretty smile.

"Back to Beck and reading." She ran the chopsticks through her lips.

Mac tried to pull his focus away from Noelle's mouth. "He reads just about anything my mom brings home. We both do. She drops a tote bag of books by the house about once every two weeks."

"You have great parents."

He nodded. "I do. They're the best."

"Did you tell them where you were going tonight?"

Mac smiled. "I told my dad, who told my mom, who told everyone at the library. By the way, I endured all kinds of flack after that kiss in the post office."

"If you thought that was a kiss, you haven't been kissed in a very long time." She raised an eyebrow in the most provocative way.

They ate in what became comfortable silence, but curiosity about her posted questions on his internal message board and Mac finally had to ask. "Do you like to read, Noelle?"

"I love to read, a little bit of everything, but mostly fiction."

He picked up his water glass. "What else do you like to do?"

She looked thoughtful, then expelled a half laugh. "I enjoy a lot of things, but never seem to have the time."

"Like?" he prompted.

"I like to hike and bike. I enjoy wandering through antique shops, love the hunt for a great bargain. I'm thankful, every day, for the café. love the people I work with." She smiled. "Do you like being a police officer?"

"I can't imagine doing anything else." He swirled the liquid in his glass. "It's one of those boyhood dreams, but mine actually came true."

"Do you miss policing in a big city?"

He shook his head. "No, I'm happy in Eden Falls. It's a safe place for Beck. Or I thought so before…"

"The letter," she said, finishing his sentence, addressing the elephant in the room.

"A marriage certificate won't guarantee I'll keep Beck."

"You're right, there is no guarantee." Noelle set her chopsticks down and leaned her forearms on the table. "I only offered marriage as a friend, Mac. I won't be offended if you decline. The decision is completely up to you."

He stabbed a slice of beef. "I didn't love Cheryl when we got married. Now I'm thinking of repeating that mistake a second time." Embarrassment hit him hard in the chest. He raised his gaze to meet hers. "I'm sorry. That came out wrong."

She reached across the table for his hand. Her fingers felt cool against his skin. "Will you stop being so serious. I'm not in love with you, either."

"I just keep thinking how disappointed my parents will be if I marry you." He closed his eyes. "Sorry. That came out wrong, too."

"It's a good thing I'm not easily offended."

"Still, I owe you better."

"You don't owe me anything, Mac." She squeezed his wrist before retracting her hand. "Maybe you should talk to your parents about this. See what they think."

That was an idea he hadn't considered. Talking to them would be wise. "What about your parents? Do you plan to discuss it with them?"

～

"Heavens, no." It wouldn't make any difference. She could marry a millionaire with the highest IQ known to man and it still wouldn't be enough.

"What about your brothers? Are you close to any of them?"

"Not really. The youngest is five years older than me. They are all very busy with their careers."

Mac moved the food around on his plate with his fork. "I don't know if I can do this."

"Then don't." She sat back, sorry she'd caused him more frustration by making the offer. For him it wasn't a solution, but more stress. "Let's enjoy the rest of our dinner, split the bill, and forget I mentioned marriage."

A frown creased his brow. "I'm not splitting the bill."

"Okay, I'll let you pay." She pointed at his plate. "Eat your dinner."

He stabbed a mushroom. "You sound like a mom."

True, I just sounded like my mom, except she would have criticized the way I held my fork or the way I chewed my food. "It's probably better we do forget about this whole thing, because I don't know the first thing about being a parent. My only reference is my own mom, and growing up with her was tough. Even the best was never good enough."

"You're great with Beck."

She looked down at her plate. "I never imagined becoming a wife and mother, though I guess I always assumed I would one day." She met his gaze. "I was raised by parents that believed career comes first. Nothing is more important. Not even family."

"Kind of depressing, don't you think? Life is full of so much more than work. I can't imagine my life without Beck." He chuckled. "Even with all this mess, it's hard for me to think badly of Cheryl when she gave me such a fantastic son."

"You're a good father."

He lifted a shoulder. "I believe you'd be a good mother."

The waiter appeared to clear their plates away. "Are we going to have dessert tonight?"

She pointed at Mac. "He's paying, so of course we're having dessert."

As Mac glanced over the dessert menu, Noelle took the time to study his facial features up close. His strong jaw, prominent brow line, the shape of his nose. His features were sharp, but his sexy mouth, kind eyes, and nice smile smoothed everything out. She imagined watching his eyes open first thing in the morning and a lazy grin appearing. She blinked at the thought. *Never going to happen. Marriage in name only, if there is a marriage.* Still, he was about six-two to her five-seven. They might have made a decent-looking couple, under different circumstances.

After the elephant had been discussed, the evening flowed more smoothly. Their conversation lightened. They talked like they did at the café or when they met by chance on the street. He lifted her into his truck after dinner and they tried to outdo each other with stupid knock-knock jokes all the way home. She slid from his truck quickly when they reached her apartment with, "You don't have to walk me up."

He got out anyway and took her hand. "Does your offer still stand, Noelle?"

Did it? His indecisiveness was making her dizzy. And a little leery. This was a big—*huge*—decision, but he was bouncing back and forth faster than a ping pong ball. She thought of father and son at her counter on a Friday night and nodded. "Yes. It does."

He glanced at the door of her apartment. "Would you be okay moving into my place? With all that will be going on, I don't want to uproot Beck. I can help financially if you have to break your lease."

"Whoa," she said, holding up a hand. *Uninterested at*

dinner, now he was moving full steam ahead. "First, do you have an extra bedroom?"

"Yes. I'll take it and you can have the master."

Nope, but that can be discussed at a later date. "As far as my apartment goes, Mike might enjoy having the place to himself."

"Right. I forgot about your cousin. Still, if he's used to your half of the rent—"

"Remember the six figure job on Wall Street? I'm not doing this for money, Mac."

"I was just—"

He stopped when she held up a hand, again. "I know you were offering because you're a good guy, but I don't want any talk that I'm marrying you for money."

"Okay." He shoved his hands into his back pockets. "When is your next day off?"

"I take Tuesdays and Sundays off."

"I checked on the Washington State laws. We both have to be present to apply for a marriage license. Then there's a three-day waiting period."

"Okaaay." She was surprised by his research, a little alarmed at how quickly he wanted to move forward, and still not convinced he was ready to take the plunge. "Sounds like we can't do anything until Tuesday, so let's both take the weekend to make sure."

He glanced up at the streetlight. "If we decide to go through with this and it works"—he shook his head—"even if it doesn't, I'm not sure how I would ever be able to repay you."

"I'm not doing this for repayment, monetary or otherwise. I'm doing this to help a friend."

She could tell he was desperately struggling for words, so she got on tiptoe and kissed his cheek, then turned toward her apartment. "Thank you for dinner. It was a treat to eat somewhere bedsides home or the café," she said over her shoulder.

"You're welcome."

"Good night, Mac."

She knew he watched while she let herself inside and closed the door. This time next week, she might be a wife and mother. Instead of the expected jumpy skin pinpricks of *What have I done?*, she felt oddly calm. As calm as she'd felt when she decided to resign from her Wall Street job and renovate a restaurant.

Mike would be shocked, as would the residents of Eden Falls. Her parents would write her off, if they hadn't already. That was reason enough to rejoice.

"My life, my decision," she said to the empty apartment.

CHAPTER 7

Monday morning Mac got the call he was dreading and waiting for at the same time. Jolie said Owen wanted to see him. He texted Phoebe Adams, who said she could come in for her shift an hour early. He called Jolie back and scheduled a four o'clock appointment.

The day dragged after that. He delivered the groceries JT picked up for Ms. Kennedy. She fed him enough homemade fudge to make him sick. He helped George Ames fix a downed fence, then made an appearance in Beck's class for career day. By three-thirty, he was so hyped up with worry, he felt he'd finished off an urn of coffee by himself.

The minute Phoebe came into the station, he left, walking the two blocks to Owen's office. Luckily, Jolie waved him down the hall as soon as he entered the Victorian, or he might have broken Owen's door down.

"Have a seat, Mac," Owen said, after they shook hands.

Mac sat on the edge of a chair and rubbed sweaty palms down his thighs.

Owen took his chair and rested his forearms on the desk,

lacing his fingers together. "I know you're anxious, so I'll dispense with small talk."

"Good. Thanks."

"I received a response to the letter I sent Mrs. Lynwood's attorney yesterday. She has asked to meet Beck the first Saturday in November."

"Yeah well, my mom has asked me to eat cabbage since I could sit at a table. Doesn't mean she gets what she wants."

A slight smile tugged at Owen's mouth. "I know how…" He stopped and shook his head. "It's not fair for me to say I know how you feel, because I don't. I can say, if you agree, it will go a long way with a judge."

Mac slumped in his chair as despair shrouded him. "So ultimately I don't have a choice. Does Beck? Does he have rights as far as the law is concerned? What if he doesn't want to see her?"

"He does have rights, but it would be best if you both agree to this first meeting. Talk to him, Mac. Tell him his mom wants to see him. You and I will be with him the whole time. I'll tell Mrs. Lynwood's attorney it's the only way we'll agree to the meeting."

"The first Saturday of November. That's in two weeks." Mac ran the fingers of both hands through his hair. "Where are we supposed to meet?"

"We can meet here in my office, if you'd like, or I can book the conference room at The Dew Drop Inn. I think her attorney will accompany her. I'm not sure if she'll bring her husband and his children. I'll advise against it. I think Beck will have enough to digest with just his mother there."

Mac nodded in agreement. "I'd rather meet here, if you don't mind. It'll be more private."

"Not a problem." Owen made a note on a legal pad sitting at his elbow. "Have Beck bring something along to show his mom. School work, an art project, something to make the hour less stressful for him."

Mac nodded again. He didn't like feeling out of control, and this situation was about nine-point-eight out of ten on his feeling-helpless meter. "Why is she doing this, Owen? She wanted nothing to do with Beck after he was born."

"People can change, Mac. You said yourself, you were both young and stupid. Perhaps, now she's remarried, she regrets her earlier decisions."

"But she's never reached out to Beck in all these years."

"Maybe it wasn't possible until now."

Mac stood and stalked to the window. "You can't tell me sending a birthday or Christmas card wasn't possible." He turned to Owen. "She's never cared enough to call and ask about him. She knows nothing about her own child and has never taken the time to find out. Then, out of the blue, she wants to take him away from everything he knows? It doesn't make sense."

Mac's heart felt as if it would leap out of his chest. Unfamiliar emotions were stampeding through his system, and Owen wanted to tell him it might not have been possible for Cheryl to pick up a phone in this day and age? He rubbed the back of his neck where tension was building to the point of meltdown.

"You said it might help my case if I'd gotten remarried. Do you really believe that?"

"There are no guarantees, Mac." Owen pulled the legal pad closer and jotted a few notes. "Marriage gives a sense of stability, but even you know how false that sense can be. Every case is different. Every set of circumstances has an exception."

Mac didn't feel any better when he left Owen's office than he had the last time he walked out. Only one thing had changed. Cheryl was coming to meet Beck.

His mom was moving around her kitchen fixing dinner when he entered the back door. She turned from the sink and sent a silent plea for information.

"Where's Beck?"

"He just ran to the bathroom." She nodded toward the table. "He's been doing his homework."

Mac stepped to the kitchen door and glanced down the hall to make sure his son wasn't within hearing distance. "Cheryl wants to meet Beck the first Saturday in November. Both Owen and I will be there, too."

She yanked a tissue from a box near the phone and blotted the tears that filled her eyes. Mac wrapped an arm around her shoulders. "It's going to be okay, Mom. We'll work this out. I know this is asking a lot, but there's something I have to do. Would it be possible for Beck to stay here tonight?"

"Yes." She looked like she was about to ask a question, but Beck ran into the kitchen saving him from the lie he'd prepared.

Beck snickered. "Did Dad tell you he went out on a date?"

His mom pasted on a smile. "No, but Grandpa told me." She glanced at Mac. "Did you have a nice time?"

"I did." He was surprised by his answer. Until that moment, he hadn't really thought of his and Noelle's date as more than a business meeting. Suddenly, he hoped she'd had a nice time, too.

"Dad, can we get a puppy? Christian's dog had seven puppies and he has to find homes for all of them. He said we could have one."

Mac and Beck had been discussing a dog for about a year. Maybe it was time to do more than discuss. "We'll talk about it after dinner, son."

"You always say that, and then we never do."

The doubt in his son's eyes had Mac pulling him into a tight hug. "This time we will, I promise."

∽

*A*t least this time when she peered through the peephole on the front door she wasn't in her pajamas. For some reason, she'd known it would be Mac when she heard the soft knock. She twisted the deadbolt and opened the door. "Hi, there."

"Hey."

She opened the door wide enough for him to enter. "Bad day?"

He stepped inside. "Not great."

"Is it too late for a cup of coffee?"

"Not today."

She felt the frustration vibrating through Mac as she closed the door and helped him shed his coat. She draped it over the back of the sofa. "Come into the kitchen."

He followed her and sat down heavily in the chair she indicated, while she pulled a carton of milk from the fridge and set it and the sugar bowl on the table.

He stretched out his legs. "Thanks, Noelle."

A minute later, she set a steaming cup of coffee in front of him and sat in a chair across the table.

He spooned sugar into the brown liquid and added a dollop of milk. "You don't drink coffee this late?"

"Another tidbit about me, I don't drink coffee at all."

He gazed at her thoughtfully, as if filing the information away for later.

"Want to talk about it?"

"Cheryl wants to meet Beck the first Saturday in November. Would you consider marrying me before then?"

Two weeks. "You've decided this is what you want to do?"

"Yes."

She studied him a moment. The worry around his eyes and the fear etched in the rigid line of his mouth concerned her. "Have you talked to your parents?"

He shook his head.

"I think you should."

"Asking them puts them in a position to answer. What are they going to say? If they agree and it doesn't work, they feel guilty. If they disagree and it works, they feel guilty. I can't put any more pressure on them."

"Okay. Talk to Owen."

"This is between you and me." He reached for her hand, rubbed his thumb across her knuckles. "Just tell me you're sure about this, Noelle. Really, really sure."

She squeezed his hand. "I wouldn't have offered if I wasn't."

"Can you go with me to get a license tomorrow?"

She nodded.

"Since there's a three-day waiting period, we could have a small ceremony Saturday."

"Okay."

"Will that give your parents enough time to get here?"

Six months wouldn't be enough time for them to rearrange their schedules. "I don't need my parents' permission, Mac."

"Don't you want them here?"

"I'll ask Mike to come with me."

What showed in his expression looked an awful lot like pity. She stood, tugging her hand from his. "Not everyone has a perfect relationship with their family like you do."

She got a cup from the cupboard, filled it with hot water

from a tea kettle, and pulled a teabag from a basket on the counter. "Do you want a refill?"

"No thanks." He cleared his throat. "I'd like my parents to be there. They obviously missed my first wedding."

She sat down, again, and dunked her teabag into the water. "Of course."

"Are you okay with Josh Brenner performing the ceremony?"

"That's fine."

He twisted his coffee cup in a one-eighty on the table. "You sure you don't mind?"

"I'm sure—Oh, you're asking because I don't go to church."

"Mind if I ask why?" He glanced up to meet her gaze.

Ack! She hated talking religion or politics. Or her parents. "My parents didn't take us."

"But you went to a school run by nuns?"

"Ironic, I know. You'd have to understand my parents." *Which is impossible.*

He turned sideways and hooked an elbow over the finial of his chair. "Do you believe in God?"

A valid question for a father with an impressionable son. "Yes."

"If you'd rather have someone besides Josh—"

She held up a hand. "Josh is fine, if he agrees."

He leaned forward, put his elbows on his knees and lowered his head to his hands. "This is a mess, Noelle. Here I am, rushing you through this without asking what you would like." He stared at her a long moment. "Women want sparkling rings, white gowns, lots of flowers."

If her parents were involved, they'd want the huge wedding for their only daughter so they could invite all their important friends. There would be wedding planners, hundreds of invitations, and thousands spent on flowers, a dress, and multi-tier cake. The venue would be elegant. There would be dancing and cases and cases of champagne. She would be in hell for months. "You're in luck. I've never given much thought to a wedding, or dreamed of white gowns. A ring from a gumball machine would be fine with me."

Mac stood, pulled her to her feet, and gathered her in his arms. His hand on the back of her head felt warm from his coffee cup. She breathed in the cotton scent of his shirt, felt the muscles on his back bunch under her hands. When was the last time she'd been held by a man? So long ago, she couldn't remember. The warmth from the contact felt heavenly.

When she turned her head to say something, his lips met hers in a kiss that startled her. He tipped his head to deepen the kiss and she let herself fall… Just as suddenly as it began, he released her. If the kitchen table hadn't been behind her for support, she would have toppled over.

He stepped back, wide-eyed. "I'm sorry. I shouldn't have done that."

She was sorry he was sorry, because that kiss was pretty spectacular. She put a hand to her chest to calm her pounding heart. "Good practice if we're going to make this believable."

He grabbed his coat, but stopped at the door. "Do you like dogs?"

"Sure, I guess. I've always wanted one. Why?"

"I promised Beck he could have one in six weeks."

She smiled. Even though she didn't know much about dogs, a pet occupying Beck's thoughts might be good right now. "Good to know."

∾

*T*heir drive to the county courthouse in Harrisville was tense, but Noelle didn't mind the quiet. She'd been trying to come up with a way to tell her cousin he'd soon have the place to himself. Not that she thought Mike would mind.

She'd also gone over several scenarios to tell her parents. Every time she talked to them, they asked if she was dating. Her first six months in Washington, she answered no to the question, but her no became yes to get them off her back. Of course that hadn't worked. They just changed their questions from why not to who is he, and what does he do. But since it had been yes for a while now, maybe a whirlwind wedding wouldn't be a huge surprise.

"What are you thinking?"

Noelle glanced at Mac. She would soon be married to this man she really didn't know. If her parents knew the truth, they'd flip out. "Just odds and ends kinds of things."

He chuckled. "What are odds and ends kinds of things?"

She liked the crinkle at the corner of his eyes and the rumble of his laugh, even though she knew it was mostly nerves. "Nothing in particular. My mind is kind of bouncing all over the place."

He looked her way. "Mine too. I need to talk to Beck, but I'm not sure how to broach the subject. I need to tell my mom and dad, but decided to get the license first. I was also thinking, even after we get a license, we don't have to go through with a wedding. Believe it or not, the piece of paper we leave with comes with an expiration date."

Poor guy was still wavering on the edge of her insanity. But he knew how she felt, so she didn't respond.

When they arrived at the county building, Mac came around to get her door. "You don't have to do that, Mac."

"Do what?"

"Open my door."

"It's habit. Besides, my mom would box my ears if I didn't open doors for women."

She laughed at his choice of words, but she could totally picture Lily bopping him on the head.

They went inside and sat at a desk to fill in the blanks of the online form. She learned his date of birth and that Macoy was actually his middle name. He was Rance Macoy Johnson the fourth after dad, grand- and great-grand. Mac's ex broke the chain by naming their son Beck. She knew he lived on Evergreen Way, but had never been inside his house. *Probably should check out how this man lives before offering marriage.* She didn't tolerate filth well.

He smiled at her middle name, Belle, and seemed surprised to see she had a Christmas birthday. "Hence the first name," she teased.

"You also told me your middle name was Mistletoe."

"Yes, but this is an official document. I promise, my birthday is Christmas day."

Once the forms were filled out, they took a number and sat in plastic orange chairs with about twenty other people there for various reasons. His knee started to bounce. After a minute, she touched it with a fingertip and it stopped. "Nervous habit."

She smiled. "Because you're nervous?"

"No. Yes." He turned to her. "Why aren't you?"

She shrugged, oddly calm. "Because I don't have as much at stake as you do, I guess."

"You don't know anything about me. I could collect airline barf bags, or have dead bodies buried in my backyard, or sleep in a coffin."

"Do you?"

"What?"

"Collect airline barf bags?"

His incredulously comical expression tickled her. "You're not worried about dead bodies in my backyard?"

"I'm not worried about anything, Mac. I won't be sleeping with you, so if a coffin is your thing"—she shrugged —"have at it. I'm sure dead bodies in your backyard would have circulated around town by now, and a barf bag collection might be kinda cool to see."

She took his hand in one of hers and rubbed his arm with the other. "It's not too late to say no. Like you said earlier, even if we get a license, we don't have to go through with the wedding. You have up to the moment of 'I do' to change your mind."

Mac's shoulders relaxed slightly. "Do you think we should get a prenup?"

"If you'd like, but I promise—and will put it in writing— whatever you have going into this marriage, you will keep afterward. I'm not in this to gain from the situation, Mac." *Time to reveal a little more backstory.* "Remember the Wall Street job? I have money and can help with court costs and attorney's fees."

He threaded their fingers together. "I would never take money from you, Noelle, but thank you."

She smiled.

After a moment, his knee started to bounce again. "Do you think we should send out announcements?"

"Tell Rita Reynolds and we won't have to."

His laugh didn't hold much humor.

When their number was called, they took seats at a desk. A cute little gray-haired lady straightened the papers in front of her. "You two make a darling couple."

"Oh, we're not—"

"Thank you," Noelle said, squeezing Mac's knee. "People tell us that all the time. Don't they, snookie bear?"

He kissed the tip of her nose. "Yeah, all the time…pookie."

Mac's mood lightened by the time they walked back to his truck. They ate lunch at a little diner and spent more time getting to know each other. When he stopped at the curb in front of her apartment, she climbed out before he opened his door. "I can get out and I promise not to tell your mother that I opened my own door."

"Thanks for today, Noelle."

She winked. "See you soon, honeybun."

~

*M*ac picked Beck up after school and they drove to Christian's house to pick out the puppy they'd take home when it was old enough to be separated from its mother. Soon they'd have two new additions to their family. Beck was ecstatic about the dog. Mac hoped he'd be as excited about Noelle.

They went to South Fork for hamburgers at a favorite restaurant by the river. Rain clouds were rolling in, but it was warm enough to sit outside at a picnic table.

"Did you have a good day at school today?"

"You already asked me that, Dad."

I did? "Sorry. How'd you do on that science project?"

"Daaad."

Over-fried brain cells. He couldn't remember what Beck's answers had been, but they had to be positive or he would have reacted. "Are we still going bowling for your birthday?"

Beck nodded around a mouthful of hamburger.

"Have you thought of a name for the puppy?"

Beck lifted a shoulder. "I kinda like Ernie."

"Ernie?" Mac chuckled. "Where did Ernie come from?"

"Remember how I always liked Ernie and Grover from *Sesame Street*?"

Mac nodded. He had fond memories of Beck's *Sesame Street* days.

"Well, I don't think the puppy looks like a Grover."

"I like Ernie."

"I wish we could bring him home now."

"Christian's mom explained why the puppy needs his mom. All babies need their…" Mac's words faded away. Beck had done just fine without a mother, hadn't he? "Beck, I need to talk to you about something."

"What?"

Mac wished it was something fatherly, like chew with your mouth closed or don't wipe your fingers on your jeans. Instead, the subject would change both their lives. "Your mother wants to meet you."

Beck stopped chewing. What thoughts were speeding through his son's mind? *Losing you would be like clouds perpetually covering my sun. My world would become dark and gloomy.*

"Why?"

Mac pulled in a ragged breath. "Because you are the best thing in the whole wide world."

"I know," Beck said, with a heart-melting grin.

"Seriously, son, she's coming to Eden Falls to meet you."

Beck put a fry in his mouth and looked away.

Mac set his own burger down and wiped his hands on a napkin. "Want to talk about it?"

"Do I have to meet her?"

So unfair. He wanted to say, no, you absolutely don't have to. He wanted to rage at the injustice, but raging would do no good. "It would be best if you did."

"Will you be there?" Beck asked, careful his gaze didn't meet Mac's.

"Yes."

Beck pursed his lips and then pressed them together. "Do I have to talk to her?"

The kid melted his heart. Mac reached across the table and ran a hand over his son's hair. "I think she'll do most of the talking, but it would be nice if you would answer some of her questions."

"What kind of questions?"

Mac pushed his half-eaten burger to the side and put his elbows on the table. "She'll probably ask how you like school and if you have a lot of friends. She might ask what sports you play, if you like your teacher, those kinds of questions."

Beck finally looked at him. "Why does she want to know that stuff?"

"She'll be curious. She hasn't seen you since you were a baby."

"How come she never came before now?"

"I'm not sure, Beck, but I think we need to give her a chance. I promise I won't leave your side."

They finished their dinner with only the sound of the river nearby. Once the trash was thrown away, Mac wrapped an arm around Beck's neck and they walked down to the water. "There's one more thing I need to talk to you about. It's kind of important."

"Okay."

Mac turned Beck by his shoulders so their eyes met. "What would you think about me getting married?"

Beck scrunched his nose. "To who?"

"Noelle."

Beck's lips quirked to the side in a familiar smile. "Will she live with us?"

"Yes."

"I guess that would be okay," he said, like it was a question he answered every day. "Does she like dogs?"

"She said she's always wanted one. We might be able to talk her into cooking for us once in a while. She loves to cook."

"No duh, Dad. She has a café."

Mac took a step, but Beck kept him from walking further with a hand on his stomach. "Grandma said you aren't married because you don't love anyone. Do you love Noelle?"

Mac hung his head. *How to answer?* "Sometimes life…is a little more complicated than that."

"But if you're getting married, you have to love her."

If only it were that simple. He pulled Beck into a hug and shamefully crossed two fingers, out of sight. "Yes, I love her." *As a selfless friend.*

∿

*M*ac pushed through the door of Noelle's Café. She flashed a smile from behind the counter when he slid onto a stool at the far end.

"Coffee?"

"Orange juice, please."

She set a glass of orange juice in front of him. "How are you feeling this morning?"

He blew out a breath. "Actually, I'm good. I just talked to Josh Brenner. He has plans this Saturday, but can perform our ceremony next Saturday, which will work better for me. How about for you?"

"If we wait until next Saturday, I may be able to get the whole day off," she replied with exaggerated wide eyes.

He took her hand. "And the café isn't open on Sundays, so we'll have the weekend to move your things in. We can…acclimate."

She leaned toward him and her perfume made him want

to pull her closer. Instead, he inhaled to keep the scent with him longer. "Are you forgetting this is a marriage in name only, honey bunny?" she whispered close to his ear.

He turned his head slightly so his mouth was bare inches from hers. "Believability, cherry blossom."

"Aww, good idea, sugar lips." Her gaze dropped to his mouth.

He was tempted to kiss her, and she licked her lips as if reading his mind. "Go ahead. You know you want to. This would be the perfect time to flaunt that believability, because we have an audience."

He was still embarrassed by his impromptu kiss at her apartment. The current that shot through his system when their lips touched still crackled just under the surface. He racked up his lapse of sanity to overwhelming gratitude.

As for the moment and in honor of believability, he closed the minute distance between them and connected with her in a short, sweet version of their last meeting of lips. When he drew away, she was grinning.

"With a few more of those, we'll have this town believing we are the new golden couple. Move over Alex and Colton."

He smiled as he pushed up from the stool. "I have to go over to the station and talk to JT."

"Okay, sweetie pie," she said when he stood. She batted her eyelashes. "I miss you already."

"See you later, snickerdoodle."

He jogged across the square, trying to erase the stupid grin on his face. Noelle had a way of lightening his burden.

Inside the station, he turned to JT's office, glad the chief was behind his desk. He closed the door. "Morning."

JT looked up from whatever he was working on. "Hey. What's up?"

"I have a favor to ask." Mac fell into one of two chairs in front of JT's desk. "I need the last Saturday and Sunday of the month off. Layne and Drew already agreed to cover my shifts and I'll make sure the changes are on the schedule."

JT lifted a takeout cup of coffee from Patsy's Pastries. "A little vacation?"

"My wedding."

"What?" JT choked out after spewing coffee on his desktop calendar.

Mac would have to get used to the reaction. Actually, it was the same way friends and family had reacted after his first wedding. "Noelle Treloar and I are getting married."

JT grabbed the napkin sitting under his cup and held it to his mouth until he finished coughing. "Did I miss something? You just started dating her, didn't you?"

Mac made a snap decision. JT would be the one person who'd know the truth. They'd been friends since they were kids. He trusted JT as much as he trusted his parents. "I got a letter from my ex-wife's attorney. She's remarried and wants custody of Beck. She wants to take him to live with her in California."

"What does that have to do with Noelle?"

"Owen intimated that it might be helpful if I was married. Noelle offered—"

"Wait." JT held up a hand. "I understand why you think this might be a great solution, but there has to be another way."

"Noelle and I have talked. She's willing to help. We'll be married in name only. She'll be free to move on after all this is over."

JT's eyebrows came together like thunderclouds over a mountain peak. "Noelle's okay with this?"

"I told you, she offered."

"Have you talked to your parents? Do they think this is a good idea? Because I don't."

"I'm going to tell them after we finish here."

JT shook his head. "You have to come up with something else, Mac. This is a mistake."

"Like what?" Mac stood and planted his palms on JT's desk. "I'm desperate, JT. I am not going to sit back and watch my ex take Beck away."

"But marriage…" JT mumbled, still shaking his head. "What if it doesn't work? What if you two get married and your ex—"

"We know it's a possibility, but I'm going to do whatever I have to do to keep Beck with me." He straightened and turned toward the glass door. Phoebe, Gianna, and JT's assistant scattered. *Great.*

JT stood and started pacing behind his desk. "You're making a mistake you might not be able to undo." He turned to Mac. "Nothing against Noelle—I mean, I like her, but you need to think long and hard before you go through with this."

"Do you think I haven't?"

JT looked him in the eye. "You didn't the first time you got married."

Mac sank into his chair. "Not fair."

"Maybe not, but it's a valid point, and you know it."

Mac blew out a breath, his resolve wagging a finger in his face. "Look, JT, I don't need a lecture. I just need next weekend off. I've worked the schedule out. If you have a problem with what I'm doing, pretend I'm going fishing. Noelle and I will have a small get-together on Sunday to announce—"

"Announce what? Your mockery of matrimony?"

Mac stood and turned toward the door but paused before twisting the knob. He looked at JT. "Beck's mother abandoned him ten years ago. She'll be here the first Saturday of November to introduce herself to the son she left on my doorstep. I'm not going to let her waltz in and take him away. This is the only way I can think to stop her."

JT came around the desk. "I'm sorry, Mac. I would probably do the same thing if it were happening to me. I have no right to judge, I just hate to see you and Noelle make a mistake that might ruin your friendship. Or worse."

"Me too, but Cheryl has me backed against a wall. I don't expect your support, but you can keep your opinions to yourself."

CHAPTER 8

Next came Mac's parents. He crossed the street from the police station to Patsy's Pastries. His mom and dad always enjoyed a cup of coffee and a pastry before work on Wednesday mornings. Usually the sweet-smelling scents of sugar, vanilla, and cinnamon enticed him to the counter, but today his mind was centered on one thing.

His parents sat in the front corner of the shop at a table for two. He waved to Carolyn behind the counter. "Can I get a cup of coffee?"

"Sure." She filled a takeout cup. He pulled out his wallet, but she waved him away. "There's cream and sugar at the end of the counter."

Mac doctored his coffee, then grabbed an empty chair and set it at his parents' table. "Morning."

"Morning, hon," his mom said.

"Glad you could join us," his dad added.

He decided to get right to the point, glad for the vacant table next to them. "Did Mom tell you Cheryl wants to meet Beck the first Saturday in November?"

His dad nodded. "Have you talked to Beck?"

"Last night. He asked a few questions, wasn't real eager, but said he'd meet her as long as I'm there." Mac paused a beat as his chest tightened. "I have more news. Noelle Treloar and I are getting married."

"What?" both parents said simultaneously.

"I know it's quick, but we've been talking—"

"Didn't you two just go out on your first date?" his mom asked.

"Yes, but when you reach our age, you know what you're looking for."

"Your age." His dad laughed. "You're closer to thirty than forty and already been married for what? A week? How can you know what you want?"

"I might not be as old and wise as you, but I do know what it's like to be raising a son alone. Noelle is great with Beck and he likes her."

His mom set her hand on his arm. "Honey, dating is our way of trying someone out to see how they fit. Marriage after one date is crazy. You and Noelle don't know enough about each other."

Picking up his coffee cup, his dad stared into the black liquid as if looking for some words of wisdom. "Have you talked to Owen about this?"

"It's none of Owen's business."

His dad met Mac's gaze. "No, but as your attorney, he will have an opinion as to how it might affect your case."

Mac decided not to elaborate that Owen hinted marriage could help. "How can it hurt?"

"You're rushing *because* of the case," his dad said

"We might be rushing things a little, but we've decided this is what we want. Preacher Brenner agreed to perform the ceremony a week from Saturday. I'd like you both to be there."

"What's the hurry, Macoy?"

Mac smiled at his mom. "Why not? I'm not sure what this meeting with Cheryl will do to our lives. Noelle and I can get settled before any disruption Cheryl might cause."

His mom pressed her lips together as she looked at his dad. "I like Noelle."

"I do, too. But…I'm not sure marriage between her and Mac is the answer." His dad glanced at Mac. "I'm afraid a rash decision could work against you."

His dad already suspected.

His mom reached for his dad's hand before turning to Mac. "Noelle is a very nice woman, and if you think this is the right decision, we'll support you."

Next it was back to the café to tell Noelle the deed was done. Every table in the café was taken, as was every seat at the counter, and a line had formed at the door. When he rounded the group, Gertie held up a hand, eyeing him suspiciously. "You're going to have to wait."

"I'm just here to see Noelle."

"She's busy."

Okaaay. Seems Gertie has taken a sudden dislike. "I'll only take a second of her time."

Gertie's lips flattened to a rigid line. "She's in the kitchen helping Albert."

"Thanks." Mac wormed his way through the tables and pushed into the kitchen. Noelle was pulling biscuits from the oven, and his stomach growled at the smell. Had he eaten this morning? She looked up at the sound of the door.

"Can I talk to you?"

"Ah, now isn't a good time. We're really—"

"Busy. I know, I see the crowd, but it will only take a second."

She set the pan of biscuits on the top of the stove and walked to her office.

He followed her in, shut the door, and fought a sudden urge to pull her into his arms. *Gratitude. I'm grateful she's agreed to help me.* "I hope you don't mind that I told JT the truth. He won't tell anyone, but I felt like I owed him."

"I don't mind."

"I just thought you should know. I also told my parents about the wedding."

For this piece of news she sat. "How'd they take it?"

He inhaled. "They weren't thrilled." She frowned, so he added, "But both reassured me they like you. I think my dad suspects what we're doing."

"Your parents are smart. Before this is over, I'm sure a lot of people will suspect."

He rubbed the back of his neck where tension was suddenly building to monstrous proportions. "I'll let you get back to work."

She stood and smiled, setting his heart beating in erratic patterns. "I appreciate you letting me know. Have you eaten today?"

He chuckled. "I honestly don't remember."

"Sit," she said, pointing to the chair behind her desk, and left the office.

He did as he was told.

A moment later she was back with a steaming plate of biscuits with sausage gravy and a tall glass of orange juice. "Eat."

~

Thursday dawned cold and rainy, but the weather didn't stop Noelle's customers from lining up. The café was busy with locals ordering hot breakfasts and lots of coffee. She moved easily around the tables, delivering food and topping off cups. She loved this part of the business. She enjoyed chatting about the change in weather and upcoming Halloween.

As the crowd thinned, she noticed JT at the end of the counter. Lisa, who'd been working the counter since they opened, was on break, so Noelle went over to see if his coffee cup needed filling.

"Morning, Chief Garrett."

"Noelle," he said with a nod. "You've had quite a crowd this morning."

She leaned a hip against the counter, glad for a moment of quiet. "We've been busy all week, but stormy days are always my best. You'd think people would stay indoors instead of going out for breakfast—not that I'm complaining."

JT's smile was off. Not quite as friendly as normal. "Are you okay this morning?"

"Do you have a minute to talk?"

"Not until Lisa comes back from her break."

"I'll wait."

She pointed at his cup. "Can I get you something besides coffee?"

"Nope, I'm good."

Noelle hesitated for a moment before moving down the counter to deliver an orange juice refill. By the time Lisa came back, JT had moved to a booth in the back corner.

"Lisa, I'm going to take a quick break. Holler if you need help."

"Sure thing."

Noelle poured herself a cup of hot water, grabbed a herbal teabag from a basket under the counter, and scooted into the booth opposite JT. "What's up?"

He hooked his finger through the handle of his coffee cup but didn't lift it. "Mac asked me for a couple of days off next weekend."

Oh.

"To get married."

"He mentioned that he told you."

JT tipped his head down, but kept his eyes on her. "I think you're both making a mistake."

"Did you tell him that?"

"Yes. Now, I'm telling you. I understand you're only trying to help, but you need to rescind your offer. He's in the wrong state of mind to make a decision of this magnitude. He's desperate, willing to do anything to keep Beck."

"That's why I made the offer. I'm not holding a gun to his head, JT." She heard the defensiveness in her tone, but didn't care. "I've reminded him repeatedly, he can say no at any time. There is no contract. I don't have a hidden agenda."

"Then why are you doing it? He's marrying you for the wrong reasons."

"I'm helping a friend."

"I didn't know you two were such good friends."

"He and Beck come in every Friday night, and sometimes a night or two during the week. I know them both well enough to know if Beck moved to California, it would kill Mac. And vice versa."

JT sat back against the red vinyl of his seat. "He doesn't love you, Noelle."

Ouch. Even though she knew, said that bluntly, the comment still stung.

"What do you stand to gain from this? Is he paying you?"

Noelle was tempted to throw her cup of tea into the police chief's face. "I'm not doing this for gain, JT. I offered to help Mac. It won't hurt my feelings if he changes his mind and it won't change the friendship we share." She stood, finished with the conversation. "I'm not rescinding my offer."

She disappeared into the kitchen, but didn't stop there. She went straight out the back door, where she leaned against the brick wall under the protection of the overhanging roofline. Still, the rain splattering off the roof, wet her hair and face.

Even though she'd held her ground, JT planted doubt in her mind. She'd been asking herself what in the world she was doing from the start. Then she'd think of Mac and Beck together at the counter and felt she was doing the right thing. She wouldn't rescind her offer. She'd made it and she'd stand by it.

She touched her lips. Her heart did a little dance every time she thought of the kiss she and Mac shared in her apartment. It hadn't lasted thirty seconds, but she could still imagine the pressure of his lips on hers, and the way he smelled, and how warm she felt with his arms wrapped around her. She just might emerge from this with a broken heart. The thought didn't scare her. Except by family, she'd never had her heart broken before. Wasn't it something everyone should experience at least once in their lives?

∼

*L*ater, Noelle sat at her desk with a pile of papers in front of her when Mac walked in, bringing the scent of rain with him.

"Hello. What brings you in on this rainy afternoon? Wait! I know. JT sent you over to make sure my business wasn't a front for cross-breeding leprechauns and trolls."

His look of confusion was cute. "What?"

She waved a dismissive hand.

"Have you got a minute?"

"Of course." She indicated a chair. "Would you like something to drink?"

"No, I'm good." He glanced toward the kitchen where

Albert was moving around. "Do you mind if I close the door?"

"Not at all."

After the door was shut, he took a moment to look around her small office. He pointed to her collection of lighthouse pictures. "I noticed those this morning. Do you like lighthouses?"

"They fascinate me."

She could see the indecision weighing his shoulders down. He knew nothing about her, yet he was thinking of trusting her with his son. And there was nothing she could do to calm his fears.

He sat and lowered his elbows to his knees, fingers laced together. "Are we crazy?"

She lifted a shoulder. "Possibly. JT sure thinks we are."

"He talked to you?" Mac straightened. "Ah, the leprechaun-troll comment."

"He thinks I'm trying to gain something from my offer."

Mac shook his head. "He shouldn't have said anything."

"He's your friend, he's concerned. He says you're in the wrong state of mind to make a decision of this magnitude."

"Maybe he's right." Confusion twisted his features. "I don't know what to do."

"I do." Noelle came around her desk and took both his hands in hers. His fingers were long and strong, and cool from the outdoors. "I won't marry you if you're this unsure."

Confusion clashed with worry. She hated creating more grief, but this was a big decision for him, one he'd have to make on his own. They seemed to be compatible. They wouldn't be sharing a life as much as sharing a space. She was going in with her eyes wide open. He needed to do the same.

"JT raised questions. I don't want to hurt you, Noelle."

"How would you hurt me?"

"You'll be a divorcee because of me."

His concern touched her. She stared at him a long moment. "I knew that when I offered, Mac."

*G*ertie stomped into her office shortly after Mac left. "Okay, what's going on? And don't say 'nothing,' because I'm hearing all kinds of rumors."

"Mac and I are getting married the last Saturday of the month."

"You and Mac Johnson just went on your first date and you're getting married? Are you crazy?"

Noelle smiled inside and out. "Apparently."

"Why?"

Noelle made a snap decision. She had to talk to someone, and Gertie had become a surrogate mother of sorts. She knew Gertie would keep her secret. "Have a seat."

She filled Gertie in on Mac's ex-wife, the letter, and Owen's suggestion that marriage might help. "I'll close the café, because I'd like you and Albert to be there."

"Of course we'll be there, but there has to be another way. You can't seriously—"

"I'm as serious as when I decided to renovate this place. I've made more friends in Eden Falls than I've had my whole life. You all mean so much to me. If I can do this one small thing to help Mac, I'm going to do it, and nothing you say will change my mind."

∼

*S*weeping in front of the café the next morning was a simple pleasure for Noelle. Since moving here from the big city, she'd begun to notice these little gifts of quiet or reflection. Clouds building over the mountains, a breeze chasing leaves down the sidewalk, the smell of autumn in the air were all things she'd been too busy to notice before her life slowed to a trickle instead of the raging river of New York City.

She'd been on the fast track since graduating *cum laude*, the only woman in her department of men fighting and clawing their way to the top. She was at the office before dawn and left long after dark most days. There'd been no time to date or have much of a personal life. Her weekends were spent working to avoid her family. She was still busy, working long hours, but it was on her time, doing what she enjoyed.

"Hi, Noelle."

She looked up and smiled as Alex approached. "Hey, Alex."

Alex nodded toward the café. "I have a lunch meeting, but thought I'd come by a little early and apologize for my brother."

"Apologize?"

"He said you and Mac are getting married. I'm not sure what's going on, but he told me he came down kind of hard on you."

"I didn't take offense. He and Mac have been friends for a long time."

Alex hugged her. "Congratulations. When is the wedding?"

"Next Saturday."

"What can I do to help?"

Noelle leaned on the broom handle. "Nothing, but thanks for the offer. We're just having a small ceremony."

"Have you picked out a wedding dress?"

A wedding dress? She hadn't even thought about what she'd wear.

Alex must have read her mind by her surprised expression. "When is your next day off?"

"I have Tuesday off, but I don't need a fancy dress, Alex. When I say the ceremony is going to be small, I mean just Mac's family, and my cousin Mike," *who I still have to tell*, "Gertie and Albert."

"You can't get married for the first time in one of your business suits. I'll pick you up at ten Tuesday morning for a little girl time."

"Alex—"

"No arguments. See you Tuesday."

Noelle watched Alex walk through the door of her café and decided she was right. Maybe not a full-blown wedding dress, but something nice was in order.

"Yoo-hoo, Noelle."

She mentally groaned when she heard Lily Johnson's voice. She plastered on a smile, hoping it looked genuine. She didn't want to do this without Mac. "Good morning, Lily."

"Goodness, it's turned chilly. It won't be long before it snows." Lily pulled her jacket tighter around her slight body. "I was hoping you had a minute for a chat."

Noelle looked skyward, having a hard time meeting Lily's gaze. *Can't believe I'm going to do this.* "I do. Would you like a cup of tea or some hot cocoa?"

"Oh, hot cocoa would hit the spot."

Noelle led Mac's mother inside, then through the kitchen door to her office where they could talk in private. "Have a seat. I'll be right back."

She came back minutes later with two hot chocolates and a plate holding a slice of Albert's pumpkin bread. Feeling a little sick to her stomach, she set the plate and hot chocolates on her desk. "I think I know—"

Lily held up a hand. "Please, have a seat. That sounds

silly, me telling you to sit in your own office, but…please, Noelle."

Noelle slid into the chair behind her desk and waited.

Lily took a sip of cocoa and hummed in pleasure. "That is good." She set the cup and saucer on the desk and folded her hands in her lap. "I'm here because of the upcoming wedding. I want to say thank you."

Noelle's mouth fell open in surprise. She snapped it shut.

Lily laughed. "You thought I'd be mad, and I might be if I wasn't so selfish. Oh, not at you, dear. I'd be mad at Mac for planning another wedding without my help. At least this time he told me." She broke a small piece from the pumpkin bread and popped it into her mouth. "I love Albert's bread. Anyway, I want to thank you for what you're doing for Mac and Beck. I should say you shouldn't, but I can't, because I don't trust the legal system enough to make the right decision about a single father. Macoy is a fabulous dad, but a judge won't know that. Knowing you'll be in the picture may allow me to sleep at night—at least for a few hours."

Noelle wasn't sure how to respond, so she didn't.

"Do you love my son?"

Noelle turned away, which wasn't fair, so she looked her future mother-in-law in the eye. "I respect him. He and Beck come here often, and I've seen the fabulous dad in action. Beck is a sweet and kind boy because of Mac, you, and Rance. It would break Mac's heart to lose him."

"What if Mac wins the case? What will happen between the two of you?"

"We'll remain friends. I have no motive other than to help Mac and Beck." She felt her cheeks heat with the admission she was about to make, and she almost decided not to, but felt it was important for Lily to know. "This marriage will be in name only, Lily. We'll keep it as simple as possible for Beck's sake."

Lily wrapped the pumpkin bread in the napkin Noelle had provided and stood. "Mac might not have found love, but he found a good woman. I admire what you're doing for my son and grandson, and look forward to adding a chair to our Sunday dinner table."

Lily walked around the desk. When Noelle stood, she hugged her tight. "You are an angel."

❧

*M*ac pulled the patrol car to the curb when Alex waved him down. He lowered the window, but she opened the door and slid into the passenger seat.

"I'm taking Noelle wedding dress shopping Tuesday."

"How did you find out?"

"How do you think?" She flapped a hand. "Oh, don't worry. JT won't tell anyone else. He was worried and needed an ear, so I listened. Then I went over and apologized to Noelle. He was a little hard on her, but she understood."

Her words were coming so fast, all he had time to do was nod.

"You're getting a good one there, Mac. Noelle is a keeper. She's one of the sweetest women I know. And a good cook to boot. You and Beck will be well fed."

When she stopped to take a breath, he was finally able to ask, "What do you mean JT was hard on her?"

She fluttered a hand. "I'll take care of JT. Anyway, we're throwing Noelle a shower at Rowdy's Tuesday night. I know you work, but stop by if you get a minute. Oh, and you should probably buy a new suit." She climbed from the car and shut the door before he could respond.

❧

"*N*oelle, open up."

Noelle came awake at the shout from the hall and jumped out of bed. Her ratty sweater held up in front of her, she pulled her bedroom door open to Mike's dark silhouette. "What happened? Are you okay?"

He pushed into her room. "Seems I missed something, because I just heard you're engaged."

A sense of relief with a touch of apprehension settled over her pounding heart. "You scared me to death."

"Sorry."

She looked up at him through squinted eyes when he flipped the overhead light on. "You don't look sorry."

"I'm not. Imagine my surprise when I was asked about your wedding. Want to explain to me what's going on?"

Noelle climbed into bed and plumped and extra pillow against the headboard. "You might as well have a seat."

"I'm afraid if I sit, I'll fall asleep." He yawned on cue.

"You do look tired." She patted her bed in invitation. "Didn't you sleep well last night?"

He blinked the tired from his eyes, kicked off his shoes, and sat down, leaning against the headboard shoulder to shoulder with her. "I had an early morning interview for that forestry job and didn't get much sleep before my shift." He pinned her with a look. "And this isn't about me. You and Mac Johnson were the talk of the bar tonight. Did you forget to tell me some important news?"

"I didn't forget, I just haven't had time. Everything has been moving so fast."

"When did it happen at all? I didn't even know you two were dating."

"We went out once," she mumbled while rubbing a finger over her lips to obscure her answer.

"Once? And you're getting married?"

She took a deep breath. Mike should probably know the truth, so she told him about her offer of marriage.

"You can't be serious about this. You don't even know the guy. What if he's a serial killer?"

"I do know him, and he isn't a serial killer. He's a cop."

"So was Russell Walsh!"

He had her there. Russ, a member of Eden Falls police force for two years, had been breaking into Carolyn West's house and stalking her for a couple of months before he was caught. "There haven't been any murders around here, so he's not a serial killer. And I know he doesn't collect airline barf bags."

Mike's face fell along with his jaw.

"I did ask some questions."

"Oh, well, as long as he doesn't have any bizarre collections, everything's good."

"He and Beck have been coming into the café at least once a week since I opened the doors. He's a great dad, with a great son, and they don't deserve what his ex-wife is attempting."

"That's not reason enough to get married. What would you say if someone told you I was marrying…oh, I don't know, Tatum?"

Noelle sat up straighter. "You have a thing for Tatum? She's darling."

He looked at her as if she'd grown another nose. "How can you tell under all that"—he circled a finger in front of his face—"Goth stuff she wears."

"She has a great personality and she's probably gorgeous under all that Goth stuff. Why didn't you tell—?"

"How did you just change the subject, again? We were talking about—"

"I didn't change the subject." She lifted an eyebrow. "You're the one who mentioned Tatum."

He glared.

"Okay. Tell me what is so wrong with helping a friend?"

"This isn't making dinner for someone who's sick or helping change a flat tire, Noelle. This is a lifetime commitment." Mike's glare softened under sleepy eyes. "This game you're playing is a dangerous one. I don't want to see you hurt."

"I'm not playing a game and it won't be a lifetime commitment. Mac and I are well aware of what we're doing. Besides, how can I get hurt if my heart isn't involved? I'm simply helping a friend."

Mike tipped his head back and stared at the ceiling. "When is this mock wedding?"

"Next Saturday."

"Have you told your mom and dad?"

"Not yet." She bumped her shoulder against his. "Will you walk me down the aisle?"

His glare was back. "Do I have to dress up?"

She laughed. "Yes, but it's going to be a very small ceremony, just a few friends."

He gave her a strange look. "Small?"

She nodded

He stifled a yawn. "What about living arrangements?"

"I'll move into his house and you'll have this place all to yourself. I'll help with rent, though, since I'm dumping this in your lap."

"I can pay my own rent, Noelle."

"Don't get your nose bent out of joint. I'm only offering because I didn't give you any notice. How did the interview go?"

"I got the job. I start in February."

"Congratulations." Noelle gave him a sideways hug. "That's great news. Will you have to leave Eden Falls?"

"Nope, I can stay right here."

"Love that!"

"I've got to get to sleep." Mike scooted off the bed and walked to the door, but turned before leaving her room. "I wish you'd rethink this, Noelle. I know you want to help, but there are some problems you can't solve."

She lifted a shoulder. "I can try."

CHAPTER 9

Noelle had many friends in Eden Falls, but no on she was close with. So it was a special treat to be shopping with Alex. They went to a bridal boutique in Harrisville. After the fifth try, she emerged from the dressing room in what Alex exclaimed was the perfect wedding dress. She'd specified simple and modest. From the scalloped neckline and sleeves to the flattering mermaid silhouette, it was classic elegance. And the price was right.

"Ohh," Alex breathed on a sigh. "You look lovely."

Twisting her hair behind her head, she held it in place. "I should call Dahlia's Salon today. Maybe Misty could do something with this mop Saturday morning."

Alex pulled her phone out. "I'll call right now."

Noelle stared at her reflection, mesmerized by the pristine white of the gown, feeling elegant for the first time in years. Maybe ever. She wasn't one of those girls who'd dreamed of a big, beautiful wedding day surrounded by bridesmaids, layered with flowers and tulle. She had no visions of wedding cakes and piles of presents and photographers freezing the moments for eternity. Yet here she stood, feeling the excitement of her upcoming wedding.

Alex appeared in the mirror behind her. "Are you okay?"

"I just never dreamed I'd be doing this." She smoothed a hand over the elegant fabric. "Trying on wedding dresses."

"You never dreamed of weddings as a little girl?"

Noelle shook her head. "I've never imagined myself married."

Alex came around her. "You never dreamed of finding the perfect man and walking down the aisle on your father's arm?"

"No. I always thought I'd fill my days with work, scrambling to get to the top, climbing higher to please my parents."

"Well, your parents are going to think you're the most beautiful bride."

"They won't be here."

Alex's eyebrows shot up. "Your parents can't make it?"

"I'm not inviting them. They wouldn't approve of me marrying a police officer."

"Because…?"

"He's not successful enough, not rich enough, doesn't come from a family with a high-profile name. I could go on and on."

"Is that going to cause problems between you and your family?"

"There are already irreparable problems." *Problems caused when I wouldn't conform, when I left medical school, when I quit my Wall Street job... I'm sure their expectations are about zero now.*

There were no expectations with Mac. She would stay with him as long as was necessary to protect him and his son, and then they'd get a very quiet, uncontested divorce. There would be no property to split, no assets to divide. They would simply move on with their lives in separate directions. She hoped they could remain friends. Eden Falls was too small for enemies. She also hoped she could maintain a friendly relationship with Beck.

This whole thing should be non-emotional, so why was she feeling teary-eyed?

A dress, shoes, and jeweled hair clip later. Alex pulled into the parking lot behind Rowdy's Bar and Grill. "Now, dinner."

"No, Alex. I've already kept you from home all day."

Alex opened her door. "We both have to eat."

Noelle climbed from the car and followed Alex. Inside, she came to a stop. A corner of the wood paneled room was decorated with streamers and balloons. Noelle stood open mouthed while her eyes finally did fill with tears. Sisters Stella and Phoebe Adams, Amy Saunders and her daughter, Jillian, Misty Garrett, Lily Johnson, Gertie, and a half dozen other ladies clapped and cheered. Never before had anyone done something like this for her.

"We couldn't let you get married without the traditional embarrassing bridal shower." Alex put an arm around her waist. "Don't cry. This is a happy day."

"But…" she stopped short of spouting, *It's not real. Our marriage is for appearances' sake only.*

Her gaze landed on Lily, who smiled and gave her a firm nod.

As the festivities went on around her, Noelle felt like she was swimming through a fog. Food and drinks were served, followed by toasts. And presents—naughty nighties that would never be worn and monogrammed pillowcases that wouldn't share the same bed. Lily gave her an apron with Mrs. Johnson embroidered on the front. She unwrapped a personalized cutting board from Gertie.

The evening overwhelmed her with guilt. Mike stared at

her from behind the bar with raised brows, making her feel even worse.

She wanted to tell everyone the wedding wasn't on the up-and-up. She was sure, for Mac's sake, they would keep the real reason a secret, but Lily's reassuring hand on her arm kept her quiet. She knew she'd grow to love her mother-in-law very much over the next few months.

≈

*M*ac entered Rowdy's and Alex waved him over to a corner decorated with girly balloons and tangles of streamers. Noelle sat on a stool, a veil of toilet paper crowning her head. She tried to smile, but it wobbled slightly when she held up a coffee mug with Mrs. Johnson printed on the side.

Surprised by the emotion that swamped him, Mac took a deep breath. He ignored the jokes and innuendos thrown at him as he moved to her side and put a protective arm around her. "Wow."

She nodded. "Yeah, wow. Totally unexpected." She glanced at Alex. "But very sweet."

He touched the toilet paper veil. "This is attractive."

"That's nothing. You should see her dress," Alex said. "Talk about wow."

He glanced down at her with raised brows. "Yeah?"

"Kiss, kiss, kiss," Stella chanted and soon all the women joined in.

He had no choice, and hoped his apology was conveyed in the half-smile he sent Noelle. He lowered his head. Noelle put her hand to his cheek. Her fingers were warm and reassuring. When their lips touched, she pulled him closer.

He turned his head slightly and she ran her fingers over his ear, sending a pleasant zing of energy down his neck. He opened his mouth and wet her lips with the tip of his tongue. Her lips parted. They enjoyed their first quick tango of tongues in front of a group of clapping, cheering women. When he pulled back, he spied the same wonder he was feeling reflected back at him. She pressed her lips together and he smiled.

He gave her another swift kiss. "I'll see you later."

She nodded.

He glanced at his mother who was grinning from ear to ear.

"You ladies have a wonderful time, and thank you for doing this. It was nice. Noelle and I appreciate it very much."

Stella held a black scrap of lacy cloth in front of Noelle. "You can thank me and Phoebe on your wedding night."

"I'll look forward to seeing that on, and then taking it off."

Noelle's scarlet blush made him laugh.

❧

The weather turned cold and rainy. Noelle wondered how it would affect the trick-or-treaters in a few days. In her New York world, Halloween had been just another day, but in Eden Falls, the residents went all out. People had costume parties, and the shop owners around the square dressed up and handed out candy. Noelle found it great fun. She loved to see all the kids, big and little, in their variety of costumes.

Funny, but she spent more time choosing her costume than she had her wedding dress. The thought bothered her. She and Mac were getting married for other reasons, but she would take her vows seriously, even if they were short-term. They mattered. She would make them matter.

She walked into the café from the kitchen and smiled.

Beck was sitting in his usual Friday night place, wearing a curious expression, but there was no Mac. "Hi, Beck."

"Hi."

"Where's your dad?"

Beck lifted a shoulder in a half shrug. "He's probably on his way."

"Want the usual chocolate shake while you wait?"

"Yes, please."

After Noelle set a shake in front of Beck, she stayed close, suspecting he'd come in early to talk. She didn't have to wait long.

"Are you going to move in with us when you and my dad get married, or are we going to move in with you?"

She rested her crossed arms on the counter between them. "My place is too small for all of us, so it would work out better if I move in to your house. Are you okay with that?"

Beck performed another shoulder lift as he unwrapped a straw. "I guess. Our house is kinda big. My dad's bedroom is really big and has a bathroom."

Please, don't go there. "I promise not to take up too much space."

He worked the straw up and down through the thick chocolate shake. "Did you know my mom is coming to meet me?"

"Your dad told me." When he didn't elaborate, she asked, "Do you want to talk about it?"

"No."

She decided to bring up a lighter subject. "Your dad told me you're getting a dog."

He smiled, his troubled eyes brightening. "I was going to name him Ernie, but now I like Quincy."

She'd wanted a pet so badly when she was young, but her plea was always answered with a resounding No! "I like Quincy. What kind of a dog is he?"

"Mmm, I can't remember the name."

"Is he big?"

"No, he's too little to take away from his mom." Beck pulled the straw from the shake and swiped it through his lips.

A brand-new puppy ought to make life interesting. Note to self: keep shoes put away. She set a napkin at his elbow. "What are you going to be for Halloween?"

That question produced a second smile. "Count Dracula," he said in his best Transylvania accent.

"Spooky," she replied in her best shaky voice. "I'm going to be Little Red Riding Hood."

"That's kind of cool. My dad's going to be a werewolf. A scary one."

"A really scary one," Mac said sliding onto the stool next to Beck.

Noelle's heart did an unexpected salsa. She straightened. "Another milkshake coming up."

❧

"*H*ow's it going?" Mac asked his son when Noelle walked to the far end of the counter.

Beck looked up at him, his brown eyes so trusting. "I got a hundred on my math test."

Mac wrapped his hand around his son's neck and squeezed. "That's fantastic. I'm proud of you."

Beck leaned forward so he could see around Mac. "I like Noelle."

Mac glanced in her direction. His milkshake was blending and she was laughing with a customer close by. "I like her, too. She's a very…thoughtful person."

"What does that mean?"

Mac looked back at his son. "I mean she thinks of others. She likes to help people."

"Is my mom thoughtful?"

Mac took a moment to answer. "Your mother had other nice qualities."

"How nice is leaving you when you're only a baby and never coming back?" Beck mumbled just loud enough for Mac to hear.

"Beck," Mac reprimanded. He'd been careful to never bad-mouth Cheryl all these years. He wouldn't start now. He tried to pick his words carefully, using some stolen from Owen. "She might have had a good reason why she couldn't stay."

"Yeah, but she could have called or something."

"What's it going to be tonight, gentlemen?" Noelle asked as she set Mac's milkshake in front of him, saving him from having to defend his ex-wife. "You going to have your usual, or are you going to shake things up a bit?"

Beck tipped his head. "Shouldn't you guys kiss or something?"

"Right." Mac stood and leaned over the counter, holding a hand over Beck's eyes.

Noelle bent toward him and their lips touched in too brief a second. Hints of her perfume mingled with French fries.

Beck groaned. "Are you going to do that a lot?"

Noelle giggled against Mac's lips before she stepped back and tugged an order pad from her apron pocket. "Are you ready to order, young man?"

"I'm going to have a burger."

The black lacy thing Stella held in front of Noelle three nights earlier ran through Mac's mind. "I think I'll shake things up a bit and try the Goblin Special."

Noelle winked at Beck. "Your dad is brave. There's no telling what Albert put in the Goblin Special today."

After Noelle walked away, Mac swiveled toward his son. "Want to talk about what's bothering you?"

"How do you know there is something?"

Mac swiped a finger between Beck's eyebrows. "You get a little line right here when you have something on your mind. Is it Noelle, or your mother's visit?"

Beck became very engrossed in trying to stir his shake with his straw.

"Tell me what you're thinking."

"I don't want to see her."

Mac ran a hand over Beck's back. "It's just for an hour and I'll be right there with you."

"But after she meets me, then what?"

This was the part that scared Mac. "Your mom is remarried, Beck. She lives in California and would like you to go live there."

"No. I'm not going." Beck shrugged Mac's hand away. Then just as quickly, he leaned sideways and clung to Mac's shirt. "Don't make me go, Dad. I don't want to go there without you. I promise I'll never do anything bad, ever again."

His son's plea ripped his heart from his chest—an agony he'd go through to keep Beck safe. But the choice could be taken from him, right along with his son, by a judge who didn't know them at all. Mac had to believe the court would take Beck's feelings into consideration.

In the end, there was only one thing Mac could say. "Where you go, I go."

"What do you mean?"

"I mean I will always be close by, Beck." *No matter what happens, no matter what the judge decides, I'll always be as close as possible.* "If you move to California, I move to California."

The flip side of the coin was Beck meeting Cheryl and

becoming dazzled by her promises. How would he handle the situation if it was Beck's decision to move to California? Anger toward his ex-wife resurfaced, an emotion he'd tucked away years ago. Anger was wasted energy. Cheryl didn't care what his feelings were, so it was time that could be better spent, but now it was rearing its ugly head and breathing fire into the pit of his stomach.

Noelle came through the kitchen door with their dinners and their talk ground to a halt. Mac could only hope marriage was the answer that would keep Beck with him.

~

*P*lain. That was the word anyone would use to describe her. She wasn't beautiful, didn't have any outstanding features. She had okay eyes and nice lips. Her hair was thick, a pretty shade of brown, with no evidence of gray yet. She was on her feet all day, which kept her in shape. She loved food, but worked off the calories by running between tables and the kitchen.

Plain, except today. Today she looked almost pretty. Misty had done a wonderful job of sweeping her hair up and using the fancy clip she bought to hold it all in place. For a second time, Tatum preformed miracles with her makeup.

Noelle's gaze dropped from her reflection in the mirror to her wedding dress. Not necessarily memorable, but elegantly simple. She felt very feminine and hoped Mac liked it.

The door squeaked open and Alex stuck her head in. "Oh, Noelle, you look beautiful."

Noelle turned back to the mirror and smiled. "Thank you."

Alex stepped inside and held out a bouquet. "Mac asked me to bring you this."

"It's gorgeous, Alex." Noelle held the flowers to her nose

and inhaled the sweet mingling with tangy scents, then looked at Alex expectantly. She knew Alex used the language of flowers when building her bouquets, and wondered if she'd applied them here.

"The orange callas are beauty, sunflowers for adoration, and yellow roses, friendship. Magenta zinnias are lasting affection and the wheat is for prosperity. I threw in the orange roses for fascination, because who doesn't like a little of that in their lives?"

"Did Mac have anything to do with this bouquet?"

"He asked for something as special as you are." Alex put an arm around Noelle's waist. "I think what you are doing is amazing. The church is full of people who've come to celebrate with you."

"What?"

Alex smiled. "Everyone is waiting for the bride."

Noelle turned, gripping the counter behind her. "What do you mean the church is full?"

"I mean several of us put together a very fast wedding celebration. There's a party at The Dew Drop Inn afterward."

"Who did this?"

"Mostly Lily. She missed Mac's first wedding and didn't want to miss his second one." She leaned close, as if sharing a secret. "She already loves you."

"How many people are out there?"

Alex took her arm. "Enough to show their support. Are you ready?"

No! This was supposed to be a quiet affair with just a few people to witness the vows. "Do I have a choice?"

"Yes, you do. I'm sure Mac won't hold it against you if you change your mind." Alex tucked a wisp of hair that had escaped under a bobby pin. "I think you and Mac make a perfect couple. I also think you'll be happy together. Beck needs someone around besides his grandparents. Don't get me wrong, Lily and Rance are the best, but a boy could use a womanly influence other than his grandma. Who knows, maybe things will work for longer than you both imagine?"

No, that's not how it's supposed to be.

Alex tipped her head toward the door. "Mac is waiting and, if I may say so, he has never looked more handsome."

Mike, who was leaning against the wall outside the women's restroom, stared wide-eyed when she stepped through the door. "Wow."

"Do you really think so? From a guy's viewpoint?"

"You look beautiful, Noelle." He held out his arm. "Just so you know, if your dad shows up at my door with a bat, I'm sending him Mac's way."

Alex laughed. Noelle tried to, but her stomach felt as if it had risen to clog her throat.

"Do you have something old?"

Noelle shook her head in confusion.

"Something old, new, borrowed, and blue?"

"My dress and shoes are new."

Alex unlatched a pearl necklace and draped it around Noelle's neck. "This was my grandmother's, so old is taken care of." She unhooked pearl earrings. "These are mine, so they're your borrowed."

"Aren't you supposed to wear a blue thingy around your thigh?" Mike asked, waggling eyebrows.

Noelle thumped her forehead with her palm. "I can't believe I forgot my garter."

"Hold on." Alex disappeared down the short hall and through the chapel doors. A minute later she was back with a blue ribbon. "Compliments of Sophia Garrett. Her hair will be in her eyes during the wedding ceremony, but you'll have your blue. Hold up your dress."

Down on one knee, Alex tied the blue ribbon around

Noelle's thigh. When she stood, she gave Noelle a quick hug. "All set."

Alex went back to the door of the chapel and waved a hand. An organ playing Pachelbel's *Canon in D* floated through the open door.

~

*M*ac couldn't recall much about his first wedding. Vegas was no place to get married, especially when both parties were too drunk to remember. There should be a law.

This time around he wanted to remember. Even if it was short-term, he wanted to remember the way his heart was beating, the smile on his mom's face, the beauty of the music, and Beck, as best man, looking handsome in his suit and tie.

He wanted to remember Noelle's expression, the blue of her eyes as she walked down the aisle on her cousin's arm, her pretty smile. He wanted to remember how beautiful she looked in her white dress, the vibrant color of the flowers she held, her nervous smile.

He wasn't prepared for the assault of emotions that threatened to overwhelm. Or the tender feeling that swamped him when tears filled Noelle's eyes at the sight of all their well-wishers. He wasn't prepared for the moment the sun popped through the clouds, shining through the stained glass at the front of the church just long enough to light the top of Noelle's head in a halo of glow, reminding him what an angel she was for her selfless act on behalf of him and his son.

Noelle glanced at her cousin as if seeking support. Mike smiled at her and patted the hand that held his arm hostage.

When she reached the front of the chapel, Mac took her free hand in his. Her fingers were cold. He rubbed his thumb across her knuckles and then squeezed lightly, trying to convey everything was going to be okay. *Please, let this be right. Please, don't let the result of this decision harm Noelle or Beck in any way. Please, let us be happy together.* "You look beautiful," he said near her ear.

She smiled and held onto his hand like it was a lifeline. They recited their vows and said their "I do's". His complete attention was on her as she gazed back at him.

"Do you have a ring?"

He released her hand long enough to turn to Beck, who pulled a ring from his pocket. He was so proud of his son at that moment. He put a hand on the side of Beck's face and smiled. Beck grinned back.

He took her hand, again, and slid the simple silver band with a single row of diamonds along both edges onto Noelle's finger. Too big.

When she lifted her eyes, he noticed tears. She mouthed quietly. "Thank you."

Preacher Brenner glanced at her. She reached into a tiny bag she had attached to her wrist and, to Mac's surprise she pulled out a silver band. She slipped the ring down to his first knuckle. Too small. They shared a private just-between-the-two-of-us smile.

"You may kiss the bride."

Mac had been anticipating this moment. They had a room full of people watching, so he gathered her close before touching his lips to hers. He memorized the moment. The way her dress rustled, the look in her eye, the rosy pink of her lips, the way she felt against him, her perfume as it enveloped them. He would commit this moment to memory. He wouldn't let what she was doing for him and Beck be forgotten. Ever.

When he leaned away, she reached up and wiped his lip. "I'm not sure rose is your color."

"It looks really nice on you."

Suddenly, organ music rang through the chapel. They turned to face their friends. He tucked her hand into the crook of his arm and they made their way out of the church as Mr. and Mrs. Macoy Johnson.

⁂

*B*esides the high school gymnasium, which no amount of tulle could transform—even then the smell shouted high school gym—The Dew Drop Inn was the only spot for wedding receptions in Eden Falls. The banquet room overlooked the river. With a backdrop of mountains, it was a magical sight when the sun dipped behind the peaks, suffusing the world in a golden hue.

As bride, Noelle felt she was financially responsible for this party and embarrassed that Rance and Lily had funded it. She knew it wasn't what should be running through her mind at a time like this, but couldn't quite relax because of it. She would find a way to pay them back.

"It was a nice ceremony. The party's even better. Have you tasted these jalapeno poppers?" Mike asked from beside her.

She touched her stomach. "I'm not sure I can eat anything." She eyed him suspiciously. "Did you know about this reception?"

She watched his Adam's apple bob as he swallowed the popper. "Yes."

"Why didn't you tell me?"

"If you remember, I started to the night you told me the wedding was going to be small. I was afraid I'd ruined a surprise."

She blew out a breath. "It was a huge surprise. I didn't expect to have all those people watching us recite vows."

"Does it make you feel dirty to be lying about this false

wedding?" He glanced at the table of presents. "If you don't need those bed pillows, I'll take them off your hands. They look pretty plush."

"You're not getting the pillows. I'll return everything. And give people their money back when this is all over."

"When are you breaking the news to your mom and pop?"

"Soon." Noelle turned to her cousin. "Thanks for taking over father of the bride duties. I really appreciate it."

"Not a problem, but I'm telling your folks you black-mailed me into it."

She smiled. "No need. The blame is all mine. I'll take it with head held high, like the black-sheep Treloar that I am."

Mac approached and held out his hand. "Time for the bride and groom to dance."

When Noelle noticed a band setting up in the corner of the room, she'd hoped for this moment. She liked to dance, but usually pranced around alone after the café doors were locked and the blinds closed.

The music was slow and country, just the way she liked it. Mac pulled her into his arms and expertly moved them around the dance floor. She was surprised he danced so well. They fit together nicely, which wasn't a surprise given the few times they'd kissed.

"I'll never be able to thank you enough for what you did today, Noelle."

"Please stop saying that. If it helps you keep Beck, that's all the thanks I need."

He turned her a few times before she said, "Mac, did you know about this reception?"

"Total surprise to me."

"I want to pay your parents back, especially since this wedding isn't real."

"I hate to tell you, snookums, but this marriage is real. A piece of paper and the rings on our fingers say so."

He was right. She was dancing at her wedding reception with her husband. "You know what I mean."

He smiled and her heart did a silly little pitter-patter. "You married me. I'll pay them back for the party."

"It's the bride's responsibility."

"It's my responsibility." He lifted her hand to his lips and kissed the ring he'd placed on her finger. "We'll have our rings sized sometime this week."

"I know the only jewelry you wear is a watch. I bought the ring to show you I was serious, but you don't have to wear it."

"It's an honor to wear this ring, Noelle. It means a lot to me that you bought one."

She glanced at her ring finger still in his hand. "I feel the same. This ring is so beautiful, but I wish you hadn't spent so much."

"I saw it and thought of you."

"Why?"

"Simple, beautiful, sparkly."

She stared up at him a moment. How nice that he thought of her that way. "Sparkly?"

"You have a sparkly personality. Simple because you seem very low-maintenance and beautiful because you are."

Her heart pattered a little harder. Did he really think she was beautiful or was he just blind from gratitude?

When the song ended, Rance asked her for a turn around the floor, a moment she'd been dreading. She and Rance hadn't talked since he found out about his son getting married. He didn't wait to say what was on his mind.

"You make my son happy."

She glanced around until she spotted Mac. He was watching them with a smile. "Do I?"

"Why are you surprised? Don't you think you can make a man happy?"

Not the way you mean.

"I know this wedding was planned because of Mac's ex-wife threatening to take Beck away. Like Lily, I appreciate your sacrifice."

Noelle wrinkled her nose. "That's a strong word. I don't feel I'm sacrificing anything."

"Whatever you want to call it, Lily and I appreciate what you're doing for Mac and Beck. I'm not sure it's the answer, but it can't hurt, right? Anyway, Mac has smiled more since you two agreed to marry than he has in years."

"I hope us marrying doesn't give him false hope."

"No, honey. You gave us all the spark of hope we needed."

After their dance ended, Noelle glanced around for Mac and found him in a corner with Owen Danielson. She didn't want to interrupt whatever they were discussing, so she went in search of Beck. He was sitting at a table looking as bored as he should at an adult event.

"Hi, handsome."

His smile was a replica of his dad's.

"Will you dance with me?"

She was surprised he stood so willingly. He laughed with pure joy as she taught him the two-step. Their second dance involved lots of twirling and giggling. When the music stopped, she asked, "Do you have any questions for me?"

She could imagine the wheels of his mind turning as he shifted his weight from foot to foot. "Will you come with me when I have to meet my mom?"

She put a hand to her chest, so touched that he'd want her there. "I will, if it's okay with your dad."

"I want you to go."

When she nodded, the relief in his expression twisted her heart.

"It's time for the tossing of the bouquet," Alex announced into the microphone.

Before Noelle knew what was happening, Mac swooped her into his arms and stood her on the chair in the middle of the room. The warmth of his hands on her waist seeped through her dress, sending a delightful tingle up her back. Her husband. This man holding her steady, his handsome face smiling up at her, was her husband. The thought was oddly comforting and terrifying at the same time.

Alex walked out onto the floor and handed Noelle her bridal bouquet, then nodded when the single ladies were in place. Noelle tossed the bouquet over her head, straight into Stella Adams's hands. She was at the function with her boyfriend, who looked like he'd swallowed a bug when she showed him her prize.

Mac lifted Noelle off the chair and she sat to the cheers of the men in the crowd. "Please tell me you have a garter. I didn't think to get one."

"Neither did I. Luckily, Alex confiscated a blue ribbon from little Sophia Garrett and tied it in place before the ceremony."

He knelt in front of her "How high up is it?"

She smiled. "Just above my left knee."

He rolled her dress up once, twice, thrice—higher than necessary, but he got the applause he was after.

"With your teeth, Mac!" was yelled in chorus.

CHAPTER 10

Noelle had pre-packed an overnight bag to take to Mac's after the wedding. She would move her clothes and some personal belongings into his house, but leave her furniture for Mike to use.

Rance and Lily took Beck home with them after the reception. For this plan to work, everyone had to believe their marriage was the real deal.

Mac carried her bag into the master bedroom. She looked around at the beige walls with white trim. The king-size bed was covered with a basic forest green comforter. A chair of the same color sat in one corner. A dresser was backed against the opposite wall. Blinds covered the windows and a picture of a river scene hung over the bed. The room was nondescript, almost devoid of color, and kinda boring.

"This is your room, Mac."

"It was. Now, it's yours."

"No. I'll take the guest room."

He took her hand and led her to the bed where they sat side by side. "We keep surprising ourselves with scenarios we haven't discussed."

"Like me sleeping in the guest room."

He smiled. "Okay, I won't argue, because I like my bed, but to make this believable for Beck…"

Right. We have to make this believable, even for Beck. Noelle nodded. "Who watches him on your night shifts?"

"He stays at my parents' house."

"He can stay with me now, except when I have an early morning shift and you're still at work. Maybe I can change the schedule around slightly so I can be with him more mornings."

"How are we going to hide sleeping in separate rooms?"

"I'll make sure I'm up before he is. That way he won't see me coming out of the guest room. I'll keep my clothes in your closet—if you don't mind making room."

He stood, walked to the closet, and pulled one door open. "Already done." She must have shown surprise, because he added, "I'd planned for you to stay in this room, remember?"

She could see the master had a bathroom attached. "Is there room in there for my girly things?"

He smiled. "Yes. The left half of the vanity is cleaned out, as is the left side of the dresser."

"Thank you." She stood. "I hope my stuff won't inconvenience you. I won't bring much over."

"Bring as much as you want, Noelle. I want you to feel at home." Mac took her fingers in his—something he did that she liked. "What about on the nights we're all home?"

Noelle nodded toward the chair. "If we go to bed at the same time, I'll stay there and read until Beck falls asleep, or sit in the family room. He won't know we aren't sharing a bed." *Not ideal, but workable.* "Unless he has a habit of walking in here."

Mac shook his head.

"I forgot to tell you, Beck asked me to be at the meeting

with his mom next Saturday. I told him I would if it was okay with you."

Mac released her fingers and shrugged out of his suit coat. "I think it's a great idea. Cheryl will get to see how comfortable he is around you."

"I saw you talking to Owen at the reception. Did he have anymore news?"

"No, he was reading me the riot act for getting married." He loosened the knot of his tie. "I told him he was the one who suggested marriage would be a plus. He said that didn't mean I should go out and get married."

"He doesn't think this will hurt your chances, does he?"

"He didn't really say." The buttons of his shirt came open under his fingers. "He's concerned they'll think we got married to make my situation look more stable."

"Which we did."

Mac smiled as he unbuttoned his cuffs. "Yes, but they don't know that. You are now Mrs. Macoy Johnson. How does it feel?"

He's undressing. Time to get out of here. "I feel the same as I did yesterday. Maybe I'd feel different if we were, you know, in love or something."

"Yeah, I know." Noelle watched him fiddle with the ring that stopped at his second knuckle. "First chance we get, let's get these rings sized, or exchanged for ones that fit."

Noelle nodded.

"You looked really beautiful today."

Pleasure settled over her. "Thank you." She touched the suit jacket he'd laid on the bed. "You looked handsome."

Noelle picked up her bag. "I'll use the hall bathroom tonight."

He followed her to the door. "Thanks for—"

Noelle held up a hand. "No more. Let's just hope it helps. Good night, Mac."

"'Night, Noelle."

$\sim$

*N*oelle learned her way around Mac's kitchen the next morning. She'd bring a few gadgets from her apartment. Mike wasn't a big cook and would never miss them. She started the coffee pot for Mac and was just dishing a vegetable omelet onto a plate when he walked into the kitchen.

"Morning." He rubbed a hand over his hair, still tousled from sleep. "How'd you sleep?"

"Surprisingly well."

"I've never slept on that mattress. I hope it was comfortable."

"It was wonderful."

"I have to say, I've never woken up to such enticing smells since I lived at home with my parents."

"You're just in time for breakfast. Would you like some toast?"

"I don't want to eat your omelet."

"I chopped enough vegetables for two. I hope you don't mind. I went through your refrigerator."

"It's yours now, too."

She didn't feel a piece of paper gave her the right to his property and she would replace the things she used. She set the omelet on the table and pulled silverware from a drawer. "Eat while it's hot." She poured him a cup of coffee, popped two pieces of bread in the toaster, and set butter and milk on the table.

"You don't have to wait on me, Noelle."

She batted her eyelashes. "I'm trying to impress my husband with my cooking skills."

"I've been impressed with your skills since you opened the café."

Noelle went back to the stove and broke two eggs into a bowl.

"Mmm, this is as good as it smells," Mac said from behind her.

When her omelet was done, Noelle pulled out the chair opposite Mac, then stopped. "Where does Beck normally sit?"

"Here, next to me, so that chair is fine."

She spread a napkin over her lap. "I don't want to step on his toes or make him feel threatened in any way, so please tell me when I overstep my bounds."

"Beck is pretty laid-back. I haven't had to set a lot of rules or boundaries around here yet."

"You're lucky."

"Very."

They finished breakfast and cleaned the kitchen together, which felt surreal to Noelle, to the point she laughed.

"What?"

She leaned back against the counter. "I just never imagined myself here." She waved a hand around. "Cleaning a kitchen with a husband."

⟳

"*I* kind of like it," Mac said. And he did. He'd liked waking to the smell of coffee and breakfast. He liked knowing Noelle had slept just down the hall from him —though he'd tossed and turned for over an hour, wondering if she was wearing that black lacy thingamajig Stella taunted him with at the shower.

He liked knowing she'd be with them when they met with Cheryl next Saturday.

She smiled at his answer. "Me, too."

"Would you like to spend the day together?"

"I guess we should be seen out and about together."

Mac backed up against the opposite counter. "What do you normally do on your days off?"

"Clean house, do laundry."

He laughed. "Me, too, but not today. Let's do something fun. It looks nice outside. Let's drive to Seattle. We can do a little touristy sightseeing and have a nice dinner on the bay."

Her blue eyes lit at his suggestion.

They spent the ride talking about their childhoods. He'd fished, explored the woods, and built forts with friends. He told her about the stunts that had gotten him into trouble, and the ones that had never been discovered.

"You were a bad kid."

He glanced her way. She'd worn a blue sweater that made the color of her eyes stand out. "Not really bad, just…experimental."

She laughed. "Is that what you tell Beck when he hears these tales?"

"As far as I know, he hasn't heard any of them. And I'd rather he didn't," he added with a sidelong look.

She pretended to lock her lips with a key.

"My childhood was the complete opposite. My parents had very high expectations. I had a few friends at school, but they weren't allowed at the house. *Horsing around cuts into study time*," she said in a deep, fatherly tone. "I only got invited to a few birthday parties, because I usually couldn't go. I didn't go to football games and boyfriends were discouraged, so I was never asked to prom."

From the wistfulness in her voice, he imagined she'd lived a very lonely childhood. He would have expected her to be a stodgy, subdued adult from all the restrictions. Or completely wild, sowing some of the oats she hadn't been allowed to during adolescence. Instead she was friendly, personable, and fun to be around. People liked Noelle. And she liked people.

She probably pushed herself now because of the expectations she grew up with, though she might not realize it.

In Seattle, they shared a bowl of clam chowder at Pike Place Market, went to the top of the Space Needle, and walked through Chihuly Garden and Glass. They finished with dinner at a restaurant overlooking Elliott Bay.

Mac decided on the way home, while Noelle dozed in the passenger seat, today was hands-down the best day he'd ever spent with a woman.

～

*N*oelle gave a quick swipe of red lipstick, then studied her reflection in the mirror. Little Red Riding Hood was an easy costume, requiring little effort in the makeup department. She left the café bathroom and smiled as Albert the cowboy, a costume consisting of a suede vest and a ten-gallon hat, sauntered past. Gertie swung into the kitchen wearing her flirty square dancing dress and shoes that had been tapping over the café floors since her one o'clock shift started.

"I let Lisa go early. It's pretty dead out there and she had a party."

Gertie being a softy was unheard of. Noelle lifted her eyebrow in question.

She shrugged. "It's Halloween."

Noelle grabbed Red Riding Hood's basket of goodies and walked into the front of the café. Main Street was overrun with ghouls, goblins, and popular movie characters this evening. She positioned herself by the door, but didn't wait long. Her first trick-or-treater, Sophia Garrett, came in her father's arms. She was dressed as a princess, and fit the part, with her jet-black hair and eyes of blue. Beam was dressed as one of the seven dwarfs. By the dunce hat he wore, Noelle guessed he was supposed to be Dopey, though he was anything but, and Mama Misty wore the wicked queen costume. Like her daughter, she fit the part, though her wickedness had been subdued by a patient husband and sweet daughter.

Noelle touched the tip of Sophia's nose. "Aren't you too little for candy?" She glanced at Beam. "What is she now, seven months?"

"Eight and a half."

Sophia blew a raspberry.

Noelle laughed. "I have some fruit and veggie pouches is the fridge."

"She's fine, but I'll take one of those Tootsie Rolls," Beam said, gazing into her basket.

Misty held out a plastic pumpkin. "As you can see I have two kids on my hands. How's married life?"

Noelle opened her eyes wide for emphasis. "Still getting used to it all."

Actually, the transition had been smoother than she could have imagined. This morning, she and Mac had moved around each other like they'd been married for years. Beck was coming home tomorrow night. She hoped it would be a smooth transition for him, too. She was determined to make as few changes as possible, so he'd feel comfortable.

"No honeymoon?"

"Eventually, down the road, when things aren't so hectic. We didn't want to be gone for Halloween. Beck loves the holiday."

Her second trick-or-treater was Alex's son, Charlie. He and his tow-headed friend Tyson pushed through the door as Batman and Captain America.

"Trick or Treat!"

"I don't know any tricks and I don't want you playing any on me, so I guess I'll have to give you treats."

"My dad knows how to pull a quarter out of his ear," Tyson said.

"It's really cool!" Charlie added.

Noelle dumped a handful of candy into each boy's pumpkin. "I'll have to get him to show me the next time he comes in."

The theme of the night for little boys was superheroes. Most girls dressed as princesses. The slightly older crowd got a little more creative. She saw a Maleficent, Pocahontas, Beetlejuice, and Minnie Mouse. Wreck-It-Ralph had to be explained to her, as did Baymax. She asked Beck about the last two when he showed up in his Count Dracula costume.

As the sun set, Noelle let another waitress and the dishwasher go so they could attend parties. She closed early, and once the doors were locked, she pushed through the cleanup in the front of the café while Albert and Gertie tackled the back. Luckily for her, Halloween fell on a Monday and she had tomorrow off. As the three of them left by the back door, a werewolf stood waiting. Unexpectedly, the sight of Mac quickened Noelle's heartbeat.

"Great costume," Gertie said. She eyed Mac and then Noelle. "You two match in some kind of twisted fairy tale way."

"I don't think there was a werewolf in Little Red Riding Hood," Albert said.

Gertie humphed. "No, but in this fairy tale there might be."

After Gertie and Albert climbed into their car, Mac turned to her. "Gertie used to like me."

"She still does. Like JT, she's protective. She's worried one of us will come out of this hurt."

"And by one of us, she thinks you."

Noelle shrugged. "She's become like a substitute mother since I moved here." *And much sweeter than my real one.* "She makes sure I eat my veggies and get plenty of sleep." She didn't add that she'd confided in Gertie.

"I guess our wedding has been the talk of the town."

"We'll only be talked about until the next scandal."

He tipped his head. "You think of our marriage as a scandal?"

"No, but I've already been asked my due date by Maude and Rita. Both tonight."

Mac shook his head with a laugh. Then, in a move that surprised her, he put his arm around her. "Are you too tired to walk down to Rowdy's? There's a Halloween party going on. It will be a nice place to be seen together."

His hand felt good on her waist, though she'd never say so aloud. "Where is Beck?"

"Mom took him home. She was the one who suggested Rowdy's."

"Sounds fun." She'd never attended a Halloween party.

Rowdy's Bar and Grill was packed with people dressed for the occasion. Noelle took time to appreciate the costumes. Real thought had gone into a few.

Walking through the crowd was fun and strange at the same time. Mac kept his arm around her or her hand in his while they mingled as a couple. She'd never been a couple before. Ever. It was a little intoxicating, a feeling she wanted to keep close.

She caught Mike's eye a few times. He was working hard behind the bar, but seemed to enjoy the crowd.

"Are you having fun?" Mac asked close to her ear.

"I am. Thanks for bringing me." She took his arm to turn him towards the back of the bar. "Look at the guy dressed like a bowl of spaghetti. That's hilarious."

Mac burst out laughing, but it wasn't at the bowl of spaghetti. It was at the Robin Hood coming their way. "How did you get Colton into that costume, Alex?"

"Believe me, it wasn't easy."

Colton scowled. "She made all kinds of sexual promises that she'd better keep."

Mac bowed. "You look beautiful, Maid Marian."

"Thank you," Alex replied, swishing her skirt back and forth.

"And you look delectable, Little Red Riding Hood," Colton said.

Noelle curtsied. "Thank you. I love your green tights."

"Yeah, it was all done with promises that will come after the party." He lifted the red gingham cloth over her basket. "Aren't there supposed to be some eatable pleasures in there?"

"Long gone," Mac said with a laugh.

Colton wrapped an arm around Alex. "I didn't expect to see you two. No honeymoon?"

Noelle glanced at Alex, surprised she hadn't told Colton the truth. Alex's wink was undetected by everyone but Noelle.

Mac pulled her into his side. "We could only get away for a night. Noelle had to be back at the café and I didn't have enough vacation time. We'll go somewhere nice soon."

Noelle knew her attempted smile was weak at best. The list of people who knew their marriage wasn't the true-love, eternally-besotted sort was growing.

"Rita Reynolds' costume is appropriate."

Glad for the change of subject, Noelle turned to look. The postal worker was dressed as a bat. She held her arms out to display her webbed wings.

"She definitely has the senses of a bat. Her hearing is impeccable, especially if it's gossip," Alex said.

"Don't bats squeak instead of squawk?" Colton asked, and they all laughed.

"Attention, you spooky ghouls."

Rowdy stood on the bar, a microphone in hand. "The votes have been counted. We have winners of the costume contest to announce."

As Rowdy called the winners forward, Noelle applauded along with the other partygoers. She was sorry to see the night winding down. Life in Eden Falls was so different from the life she'd lived before moving to Washington.

She glanced at Mike again and wondered if he missed Boston and his big, noisy, so-different-from-hers family. She'd loved spending time with his family on holidays. Their moms, who were sisters, were as different as night and day. He probably missed the gaiety typical of his big family gatherings. Then again, Mike might appreciate the quiet of Eden Falls.

"Aaannnnd the winners of the best couple costume— Noelle and Mac Johnson!"

Noelle turned to Mac, who looked as surprised as she felt. Colton gave them both a nudge forward. "Go claim your prize."

Mac led her forward to a round of applause and chants that Mac should take a bite out of Little Red. Rowdy handed Mac a small trophy, which he held up. The chanting continued, so he bent her over his arm. The shock of his teeth on the tender flesh of her neck almost had her struggling to stand, but he kept her still as his tongue laved the spot just under her ear to thunderous applause.

"Sorry," he whispered close to her ear before pressing a soft kiss to her lips.

She felt dizzy when he raised her to standing position. Lucky for her, he kept his arm around her waist, tucking her humming body against his. He'd gone for believable, and, if she hadn't known the truth, it would have been enough for her. She glanced at Mike, whose expression she couldn't read —probably just as well.

Mac raised the trophy over their heads to more cheering, then leaned close. "Are you ready to go?"

Her silly heart was thundering like a teenager on a date with her first crush. She did her best to nod.

"You okay for a minute? I'll get our coats."

She performed another bobble-head nod and leaned against the bar as he walked away.

Mike moved over to her. "That looked like more than a marriage in name only."

"Shhh." Noelle glanced around. "It was for show."

"Riiight. Have you told your parents you're married yet?"

"Don't you have better things to do than harass Red Riding Hood?" she fired back.

~

*M*ac found Noelle rummaging through the fridge the next morning. She stepped to the counter, wrote something down, then went back to rummaging. Bent over, her black exercise pants showed curves that were covered by a huge sweatshirt when she straightened. He tugged his gaze from her rear the second time she bent over.

"Morning."

She stood and glanced his way with a smile. "Hey, I was just making a grocery list. What would you like for dinner?"

He leaned a shoulder against the doorjamb. "Beck and I are pretty easy to please."

"How about pot roast tonight?"

"I work."

"Right, but I have the day off, so I thought I'd start it early. You can take some for your dinner break." She wrinkled her nose. "I assume the station has a microwave and you get a break."

"That sounds great. I usually just pack a sandwich." She'd spoil him with this kind of cooking. His mom sent him to work with leftovers occasionally, but pot roast would be a treat. "You know, on the nights I work, you can stay in the master bedroom."

"Okay, if you're sure you don't mind." She went back to rummaging, and he went back to watching.

"Do you like—" She turned her head in time to catch him.

"Yes." He pushed away from the door and headed for the coffee pot with a grin.

She straightened and cocked a hip. "Do you like most vegetables?"

She was already spoiling him. She had a cup, spoon, and the sugar bowl next to the coffee pot. "Yes. So does Beck. I can't think of anything he really doesn't like."

She pulled the milk from the fridge and set in near his elbow, then turned to the pantry. On tiptoes, stretching just enough that the sweatshirt played peek-a-boo with her behind, she moved boxes of dry cereal around on the top shelf. He sat at the table, trying to keep his eyes on the once-a-week Eden Falls Chronicle she'd set at his place.

"Would you like French toast this morning?"

"Where did that come from?" he asked, looking at the fresh loaf of bread in her hand.

"The grocery store."

"You've already been to the grocery store this morning, and you're making another list?"

"I used the eggs for breakfast yesterday morning, so I ran to get more. I thought you might like French toast."

"I would. Thank you, but you don't have to cook for me, Noelle. I don't expect breakfast in the mornings or home-cooked meals every night. Beck and I have been on our own for a long time."

She lifted a shoulder. "You have to eat and I love to cook."

He enjoyed every bite of French toast.

After Noelle left for the grocery store, Mac went into the yard to rake leaves and clean up the front porch scarecrow. When he came in to shower for work a few hours later, she'd added two comfy-looking pillows to the sofa and centered a framed picture of him and Beck from the wedding on the mantle. He studied the additions and decided they made his and Beck's very male house a little more like a home.

～

*O*ver the next week, Mac and Noelle worked out a "Beck schedule." On the nights he worked, Noelle picked Beck up from his parents' house or Beck walked to the café from The Fly Shop or the library. If Mac had to work early, she got Beck off to school. On the mornings they both had to work early or Mac wasn't off yet, his mom or his dad came to the house and took Beck to school. And Beck seemed happy as a clam with the arrangement.

On the dreaded Saturday morning, he and Noelle made a quick trip to Harrisville to pick up wedding rings that fit, after dropping Beck off at basketball practice. Mac wanted them both to be wearing rings when they met with Cheryl and her attorney that afternoon.

They stopped for lunch at a small Italian restaurant before heading back to pick up Beck. Over salads, he reminded her about the dog he'd promised Beck.

"Beck mentioned it a couple of times this week. He said he was going to name him Quincy."

"Quincy? I thought he'd decided on Ern..." His words

faded away when his ex-wife entered the restaurant, followed by a man who looked much older than her. Cheryl was carrying on an animated conversation, using wild hand gestures. He'd forgotten that about her.

When she spotted him, she held up her index finger and walked toward their table, leaving the man staring after her.

He stood.

"Mac."

Before he could react, she threw her arms around his neck.

"It's good to see you."

"Is it?" He pushed her back a step.

She flashed a smile as beguiling as he remembered. "You seem so much…taller. And your hair looks darker."

He turned when she reached out to touch his hair. Vaguely aware of Noelle standing up from her seat, he reached for her and she stepped into place as if they'd orchestrated the movement. "Cheryl, this is my wife, Noelle." His words sounded stiff and defensive to his ears.

Cheryl's wide-eyed surprise was like a *cha-ching* in his favor. "I didn't know you'd remarried."

"Hello." Noelle extended her hand, but it was ignored as the man who was with Cheryl approached.

Cheryl took his arm. "Simon, this is Mac Johnson *and his wife*"—she glanced at Noelle—"I'm sorry, I didn't catch your name."

"Noelle. Johnson." Mac studied the man in front of him. The way Cheryl was hanging on, Mac assumed Simon was her husband. His overcoat probably cost more than Mac made in a month and the diamonds hanging from Cheryl's ears could pay his mortgage. For months. Not good. If this custody thing got ugly, they'd have the money to fight long and hard.

Mac could get a loan, take out a second on the house.

Would money make a difference? Beck didn't get everything he wanted, but he didn't go without, either.

The man held out his hand. "Simon Lynwood."

Mac and Simon shook hands, then they stood for a long uncomfortable moment before the waitress appeared with their lunch.

"See you in a little while." Cheryl waved her fingers as Simon led her away.

Mac held Noelle's chair as she sat down and replaced her napkin on her lap. He sank into his own chair.

"Wow."

Mac glanced over, still thinking about what he could sell to finance a court battle. Noelle's lips were pressed together, her eyes wide. "What?"

"Your ex-wife is gorgeous."

Mac turned to look at Cheryl. She picked up her menu and chanced a glance his way. He picked up his water glass. *Yes, she is.*

"She makes me look like a turnip."

He had just taken a sip and almost snorted water through his nostrils. The image of Noelle coming down the aisle on their wedding day flashed through his mind. He reached for her hand. "Please, don't be intimidated by her looks. You are one of the most beautiful women I know, Noelle. Both inside and out."

CHAPTER 11

Mac parked behind Town Hall, and Beck came running from the library to greet them. Noelle ran a hand over Beck's hair. "How was practice?"

"It was fun."

Mac and Beck's conversation centered around basketball while they walked to Owen's office, but Noelle's thoughts lingered on Cheryl. At the restaurant, she'd removed her coat to reveal a clingy red dress that showed off curves Noelle would only dream of having. Her long blond waves put Noelle's brown locks to shame. The diamonds dangling from her earlobes were something Noelle might have been wearing if she still rubbed elbows with the elite crowd of Wall Street.

She'd left it all behind and hadn't looked back...until now. Could money win a custody suit? Would a judge look at Cheryl's money as an advantage for Beck's welfare? She had money, too, a significant savings account, and a 401K that she'd never mentioned to Mac. In New York, she'd lived below her means, putting as much aside as possible. She'd only used a small amount to open the café, but would be happy to provide bank statements if it would help Mac.

She looked down at her jeans, sweater, and knee-high boots—appropriate attire for Eden Falls—and felt dowdy, a feeling her mother hammered into her since childhood.

What would Beck think of his mother when he saw her? Would he see similar features staring back at him? Would he recognize he'd inherited his mother's nose and her mouth? Would she make him offers that would be hard to refuse?

Cheryl couldn't have her son's best interests at heart or she wouldn't be so determined to take him away from everything familiar. Was she aware of the anxiety she was heaping on father and son? Did that matter to her? Or was she only thinking of herself?

Mac opened the door of Owen's office and they walked into the reception area. Since it was a Saturday, Jolie was off, but Owen came out to greet them. He was a short man, slightly balding, with frameless glasses perched on the tip of his nose. The memory of his and Mac's conversation in a dark corner at their wedding made her nervous, but her apprehension faded when he greeted her with a smile.

"I didn't get a chance to tell you congratulations last weekend. I wish you and Mac many years of happiness."

"Thank you, Owen."

"Are you three settled in? Everything okay?"

He doesn't want any irreconcilable differences showing up while Cheryl is here.

"Everything is great," Mac said, and seemed to mean it, which eased Noelle's anxiety. After seeing Cheryl, her self-worth was wavering. She'd always fallen short of her parents' expectations—she was never pretty enough, or smart enough —and she didn't want to do the same with Mac and Beck. She hadn't gone into this marriage to prove anything. Or had she? Maybe her reason for helping Mac wasn't as selfless as she believed. Maybe she'd recited vows to prove she was good at something her own mother failed at—at least in her eyes.

Mac wove their fingers together, bringing her back to the moment. The look in his eye asked if she was okay. She flashed a smile.

"How are you, Beck?" Owen asked.

"Fine." But the quaver in his voice told them otherwise.

"I hope you're not too nervous about today. We'll be with you the whole time."

Beck nodded and glanced at Noelle.

She put her hand on his shoulder. "Are you sure you want me to be there?"

Beck nodded, then glanced at Owen. "Noelle can come, too?"

"Yes. She's your stepmom now, so it's perfectly fine if she's there."

Owen led them through the renovated Victorian home. They entered a room with a fireplace on one wall and two long sofas facing each other in the middle of the room, separated by a coffee table. "I thought this would be a more comfortable setting than the conference room. Can I get you anything to drink before the others arrive?"

"Maybe some water," Mac said.

Beck maneuvered himself between her and Mac before they sat on one sofa.

"I don't want to meet her," Beck said to his dad after Owen left the room. The panic in his voice broke Noelle's heart.

"I know, son, but this will be over before you know it. How about a movie tonight? We can go to the theatre or grab a DVD on the way home."

Noelle winked at Mac. "If we go home, I could make my caramel corn, which is the best you'll ever eat."

Beck's smile trembled around the edges, but he nodded bravely.

Owen returned with three bottles of water that he placed on the coffee table. "I just saw a car pull into the parking lot. I'll go out and meet them, give you a few more minutes together."

They heard the street door open and, to Noelle's surprise, Beck snuggled into her side rather than his father's. She glanced at Mac as she placed an arm around Beck's quivering shoulder. Voices floated down the hall toward them, but she couldn't make out the words. As they came closer, she and Mac stood, with Beck secured between them. Cheryl and Simon entered, trailed by another man. All three exuded an air of superiority and tension. Owen followed them into the room and closed the door.

Cheryl headed straight for Beck with open arms, but Mac stepped between them. When Beck backed into Noelle, she wrapped her arm across his chest, securing his trembling body against hers.

"He doesn't know you, Cheryl."

She glanced at the man Noelle assumed was the other attorney. "He's turned my son against me. I told you he'd do that. I want to talk to Beck alone."

Owen held up a hand. "Your attorney and I agreed we'd all be together for this first meeting, Mrs. Lynwood."

"I didn't agree to that," Cheryl said.

"We can reschedule for another day, if you'd rather change the terms of our agreement," Owen said, his expression neutral.

Cheryl shook her head.

Owen introduced the Lynwoods and their attorney, Brian Fischer.

"We ran into Simon and Cheryl at lunch," Mac said, shaking hands with both men.

"Let's all have a seat." Owen waved the other party to the sofa opposite Mac, Beck, and Noelle. He set a chair next to Noelle and balanced a legal pad on his knee. "Before we get started, I have—"

"I want to see Beck alone."

"That's not going to happened, Cheryl. I go where Beck goes," Mac said.

Mr. Fischer glanced from Cheryl to Owen. "I don't see any harm in allowing—"

"We agreed that Mac would be with his son for this first meeting," Owen said, to the attorney. "Mac and Noelle are here at Beck's request. You'll respect his wishes, or we'll forgo this meeting all together."

"I'm his mother. I should be allowed—"

Owen stood and Mr. Fischer turned to his client. "Let's play the game by their rules today," he said in a stage whisper.

Owen pinned the attorney with a look. "This isn't a game."

While the debate continued, Beck burrowed into Noelle's side. She kept a tight arm around him. Mac crossed his arm over them protectively, his hand resting on Noelle's thigh.

Cheryl's husband looked irritated by what was going on between his wife and her attorney. "Cheryl, enough," he finally said. "You're here to see the boy, not argue."

Cheryl turned to glare at Mac. "When did you get married?"

Mac raised his brows. "Do you really want to spend your hour asking me questions?"

Several emotions crossed Cheryl's face before she pulled a sheet of paper from her handbag, smoothed it over her lap, and turned an exaggerated smile on Beck. "How do you like school?"

Noelle glanced at Mac in astonishment. This woman who

hadn't seen her son in years, who wanted him to live with her, had to read prepared questions from a piece of paper?

Mac blinked slowly. She knew he was trying to hide his disgust. "Beck," he said, "why don't you tell Cher—your mom about school? You could start with your favorite subject."

Beck kept his eyes on Mac rather than look at Cheryl. "I like science."

"My favorite subject was…" She flapped a hand. "Actually, I didn't like school much."

"Tell her about your teacher," Mac prompted.

Cheryl's eyes lit. "Yes, do you like her?"

Beck nodded.

"What do you like about her?" Without waiting for an answer, Cheryl launched into a story about a teacher she had who ate prunes during class. "The whole room smelled like prunes." She laughed while everyone, including her husband, stared at her. Unfazed, she glanced at the sheet of paper again. "Do you play sports?"

Beck nodded.

"Which is your favorite, Beck," Owen prompted.

"Baseball."

Cheryl told another story about playing tennis in high school. Each time she asked a question, she followed with a story about herself. This went on for an uncomfortable thirty minutes before she ran out of questions. She didn't seem the least annoyed that most of Beck's answers were only one word.

At some point, Mac had lifted his arm to the back of the sofa and began to rub a thumb over the side of Noelle's neck, oblivious to the delicious sensations he was sending down her spine.

Brian Fischer scratched away on a legal pad the whole

time. Noelle wondered what he could be writing. There was nothing noteworthy to record, other than Beck's one-word answers. He finally lifted his pen. "Perhaps Beck would like to ask a question."

All eyes turned to Beck, who looked down at the thumbnail he'd been picking at for fifteen of the thirty minutes.

"Is there something you'd like to ask your mom?" Mac asked.

Beck shook his head without looking up.

"I can tell you some things about me, Beck. I"—she glanced at her husband, who hadn't spoken since his reprimand—"we live in a really big house very close to the beach. Simon has two sons that come to our house two weekends a month. They swim in the pool and play tennis. You would love it there. We have a golf cart the boys drive around the grounds."

"My dad has a four-wheeler. We drive it when we go camping."

"On weekends, we go to parties," Cheryl continued as if Beck hadn't told her something very important about his life. "Sometimes the hostess has a chocolate fountain for the kids."

Noelle bit her lip as she imagined the look on Mac's face. Tragically, Cheryl was so self-absorbed, most of the hour had been spent talking about herself.

Owen cleared his throat. "Do you have another question for your mom?"

Beck nibbled his lower lip a moment, then leveled Cheryl with a look of hope. "Do you know how to make caramel corn?"

Cheryl frowned and glanced at Simon, as if he could make it happen. He stared at her, also waiting for an answer. "I'm sure our cook knows how to make it."

"Can you make chocolate shakes?"

"I don't eat ice cream."

He didn't ask if you ate ice cream, Noelle wanted to shout.

"Do you like to camp?"

The look on Cheryl's face almost sent Noelle into a fit of giggles.

"Too many bugs."

"Do you like dogs?"

Cheryl smiled. "We have three dogs, pugs with curly tails. You would love them."

"How old are the boys that come to your house?"

Cheryl glanced at her husband.

She doesn't know the age of her stepsons.

Simon tapped his fingertips together. "Simon senior is seventeen and Jeffery is fifteen."

Beck took a moment to digest this information while worrying his bottom lip.

Boys that age won't be interested in the same things Beck likes. She made them sound much younger. Noelle glanced at Owen, wishing she could read his thoughts.

Owen leaned forward. "Do you have any more questions, Beck?"

Beck shook his head.

Cheryl lifted her husband's arm and glanced at his watch. "I'd like to take Beck to dinner tonight. It will give us a chance to get to know each other better."

Beck almost crawled into his father's lap. "I don't want to go with her, Dad."

"You're not taking him anywhere, Cheryl."

"You don't make the rules, Mac," Cheryl said.

Owen stood and faced Cheryl's attorney. "We'll take this slowly, as agreed, or the next time we meet will be in a courtroom."

Simon stood. "The boy doesn't want to go, Cheryl. He doesn't know you."

"But he will. If we take him to dinner, he'll—"

Mac shook his head. "Not going to happen, Cheryl."

"Enough." Owen glanced at Noelle. "Will you take Beck into the reception area?"

Beck grasped her hand and they left the room, closing the door behind them.

"She can't make me go with her, can she, Noelle?"

She hated that Beck's hand trembled in hers. "Mr. Danielson is going to do everything he can to prevent it, Beck. Let's walk to the café. Maybe Albert has some pumpkin pie."

"With whipped cream?"

"Tons of whipped cream." She pulled her cell phone from her pocket with her free hand and texted Mac where he could find them.

~

$\mathcal{M}$ac was so relieved when he walked out of Owen office, he didn't know whether to laugh or cry. He'd left Cheryl and Simon arguing about trying to force Beck to dinner. Owen signaled him to the reception area when their attorney stepped into the middle of the fight.

"You saw how Beck feels, Owen. You can't let her take him without me being there."

Owen nodded in what Mac hoped was agreement, but he didn't want to stick around long enough to ask, or he'd have to see Cheryl again. He wanted out.

He headed in the direction of the café, but first a stop at Pretty Posies. He owed Noelle big time for today. She'd been a rock, their lighthouse, while a storm named Cheryl surged and crashed around them. Beck had leaned into her during most of Cheryl's thoughtless questions, which she'd probably found on the internet—Fifty Questions to Ask the Kid You Haven't Seen in Nine Years.

"Hi, Mac," Alex said from behind the counter when he entered the flower shop. "How are you?"

"Could be better. I need a huge thank you bouquet."

"For Noelle?"

"Yes."

"Okay." Alex held up a rose. "Deep pink represents gratitude. I could add a few flowers to make a pretty autumn bouquet."

"Perfect."

"Budget?"

"Uh…whatever, just don't break the bank." He met her gaze. "Make it really nice."

Alex pulled several orange roses from a bucket. "Of course. Do you want to wait, or would you like it delivered?"

"Will you deliver it to the café?"

"Sure. Do you want to pick out a card?"

"I'll thank her in person." He already had a hand on the doorknob, anxious to be with Noelle and his son. "Thanks, Alex. I'll come by Monday to settle up."

"See you then," Alex called out before the door closed behind him.

When he entered the front of the café, Gertie pointed toward the kitchen. Both Noelle and Beck were on stools at the worktable while Albert spooned whipped cream on top of two slices of pie.

"You got any more of that, Albert? I sure could use a piece."

Noelle stood and pulled another slice of pie toward Mac. "Got you covered. Hit him with some whipped cream, Albert," she said while she indicated the stool she'd just vacated. When he started to decline, she nodded toward the stool. "Sit and eat some pie with Beck."

Beck looked up, Mac's brown eyes reflected back at him. "Did she go back to California?"

Mac released a breath while he stroked a hand down the back of Beck's hair and gave his neck a squeeze. "Not yet, buddy. We're going to meet her again next Saturday."

"Nooo."

"I wish there was something I could do, but my hands are tied for now."

The first bite of pie stuck in his throat as he watched his son's long face. Noelle lightened the mood by telling Albert a knock-knock joke. Always serious Albert tried to play along, but his hesitancy was funnier than the joke. After three, they had Beck laughing. One more reason to be grateful Noelle was in their life. She'd saved him today.

"Knock-knock."

Mac could almost hear Albert's silent groan. "Who's there?"

"Noah."

"Noah, who?"

"Noah good place we can get something to eat?"

Albert turned a stink eye at her. "Now you're hitting below the belt."

She threw her arms around the big man's neck and kissed his cheek. "You know I'm kidding, Albert. No one cooks better than you."

Beck pointed at the rose colored lipstick imprint Noelle left on Albert's cheek and broke into giggles. Noelle put a finger to her lips so Beck wouldn't give away their secret. Mac enjoyed the glow of appreciation in Noelle's eyes when Gertie appeared with the flowers.

Noelle looked at Mac over Beck's head. "Who could these be from?"

"Your boyfriend!" Beck said.

"Shh." She held a finger to her lips. "Don't tell your dad."

He broke into another round of giggles that warmed Mac's soul. Noelle was just what the doctor would have ordered for Beck's panic of an hour earlier.

Gertie marched up to Albert with hands planted on her slim hips. "Who's been kissing you, old man?"

Beck almost fell off his stool laughing.

*O*nce they got home and dinner was out of the way, they snuggled on the sofa, Beck in the middle, with a bowl of the best caramel corn Mac had ever eaten. It was still warm and gooey from the oven. *The Goonies*, Beck's choice, played on the television that bathed them in the only light in the house. He glanced over Beck's head when he felt Noelle's eyes on him.

"Thank you for the flowers," she whispered.

His gaze stayed on her mouth longer than necessary. "Thank you for today," he whispered back.

She winked, and he would have kissed her if it weren't for his sweet son sitting between them.

When she turned back to the movie, one she said she'd never seen, he watched her. Why, in the couple of years since she'd moved to town, hadn't he ever thought to ask her out? He'd watched her interact with Beck at the café. She was kind and thoughtful even before she made the ultimate offer of marriage.

She glanced his way and smiled. "What?"

Mac shook his head and turned his attention to the television screen. But a minute later he was irresistibly drawn to stare at her again. She was laughing with Beck and the merriment looked good on her.

As the final credits rolled ninety minutes later, Beck turned to Noelle. "Why don't you go to church?"

She lifted a shoulder. "I wasn't raised a religious person."

"Does that mean you don't believe in God?"

Noelle looked at him over Beck's head. Should he give her an easy out and tell Beck it was time for bed?

"I do believe in God, but my parents were too busy to take me to church. They're both doctors. They spend a lot of time at hospitals and in their offices."

"You could come to church with us tomorrow."

Mac realized he'd been holding his breath, waiting for Beck to ask.

She ruffled Beck's hair. "Yes, I guess I could. What time should I be ready?"

"Dad will wake you up." Beck smiled at him in delight. "Won't you, Dad?"

"I'd be happy to."

~

*N*oelle lay watching the moonlight play across the comforter, reflecting on her life as a married woman. Mac made her heart do the tango more than once over the past week and she was working hard to keep this whole "marriage in name only" thing in perspective. She couldn't let emotions or weak moments take them to a place they might not be able to return from.

She held up her hand. The tiny diamonds around both edges of her ring sparkled in the dim light. Like a wedding, she'd never spent much time thinking or fantasizing about rings, but if she had to pick from a boatload, this would be the one. Funny that Mac seemed to know her taste so intimately.

After the odd lunch with Mac's ex-wife sitting across the room, and the even odder meeting at Owen's office with the same woman, she, Mac, and Beck had spent a cozy evening watching a cute movie and licking caramel from their fingers.

Her thoughts circled back to Cheryl. She'd felt so inferior to the woman during lunch, but after the meeting in Owen's office, those insecurities evaporated. Cheryl was beautiful, granted, but inside she was mostly fluff, with little substance. Strange that a man like Simon would be attracted to her. He couldn't have chosen her as mother material for his two sons, since they were with them so seldom.

If Beck had to go with her, would she and her husband be capable of taking care of him? Would they spend any time with him? Cheryl didn't seem the type to be interested in anything a boy would want to do. After asking an initial question of Beck, she hadn't taken the time to delve deeper into his answers. Instead she seemed more intent on talking about herself.

Noelle rolled onto her back. It was time for sleep. She'd promised Beck she would attend church in the morning.

Getting married to a police officer, watching *The Goonies*, and going to church…what would her parents say about her lifestyle change? The thought made her smile.

∼

*B*eck scooted into the pew next to Lily and Rance, followed by Noelle and Mac. Sitting through an hour-long sermon would be a first for her. She hoped the ceiling didn't collapse or lightning bolts wouldn't shoot from the sky and hurt these good people simply because she was here.

Preacher Joshua Brenner came into the café at least once a week. He always left a nice tip and a note on the back of the ticket inviting her to join his congregation. When he stood at the podium and acknowledged her with a smile, she expected the sermon to be directed at sinners like her who never went to church. Instead, Josh talked about patience and tolerance, which turned her thoughts to Cheryl. The person in the restaurant had seemed so poised and put together. In Owen's office, that same person was completely out of her element. Which person had Mac married? Which person would they be fighting? If her questions were any indication, they'd be dealing with the out-of-her-element one.

After the service, she was greeted by people she knew and some she didn't. Beck took her hand and led her to Josh's side.

"Good morning, Beck."

"A few weeks ago, you said we should try to bring our friends with us, so I brought my stepmom."

"I see that." Josh took her hand in his. "Welcome, Noelle. I hope you enjoyed yourself."

She *had* enjoyed herself and Josh's sermon. She liked sitting next to Beck and the feel of Mac's arm along the top of the bench, barely touching her back. "I did. You're a very good speaker."

He smiled. "Kind of comes with the job."

At the door, Mac held her coat while she slipped her arms in. The action made her feel old and special at the same time. Warmth spread through her when he gave her shoulders a squeeze. She liked that, too.

~

*N*oelle sitting at his parents' table felt right. Even though he'd married a cook, she happily agreed to their traditional Sunday dinner at his mom and dad's. He knew she appreciated that his parents had extended the invitation to her cousin, too. She flashed a smile when she noticed him watching her and an unexpected emotion zinged through him. An emotion he'd never felt before, one that felt good and scary at the same time. One he might like to investigate.

After church, Noelle spent time helping Beck with his English homework. Now she was exchanging recipes with his mom. She'd moved into their small world effortlessly. And his family accepted her as if she'd been with them for years. Even her cousin Mike seemed comfortable at their table.

When his mom, Noelle, and Beck disappeared into the kitchen, his dad stood. "Before dessert, I want to show you something I've been working on in the garage. You're welcome to come too, Mike."

They entered the garage through the mudroom. Along with other updates to the house, his dad had added a work-shop to the back of the garage. Over the years, he'd become as skillful working with wood as he was at fishing.

His dad removed a tarp and revealed a chest with a lift top.

"That's a nice piece, Dad," Mac said moving his hand along the smooth-sanded wood.

"Really beautiful," Mike added.

"I'm giving it to Noelle for a Christmas present. What do you think?"

Mike glanced at Mac, making him wonder if Noelle had told her cousin about their marriage of convenience. If so, maybe he was wondering if Noelle would still be with them for Christmas. The few times he'd seen the cousins together, they seemed close.

Mike traced the shape of a hand-carved rose with his fingertips. "I think she'll love it."

"Mike's right. She'll love it," Mac said, understanding why his father wanted to bestow such a beautiful gift. "Thanks, Dad."

"How did the meeting with Cheryl go yesterday?" his dad asked.

"It went better than I expected, but not as well as I hoped. Cheryl had a list of prepared questions she asked, more or less interviewing her son. Beck was a trooper and answered them all, even asked a few of his own."

"I'm glad Noelle could be there. That shows Cheryl a united front."

"Beck asked her to be there. She was a rock through it all."

"Noelle likes Beck," Mike said.

Mac moved around the chest, taking in the details. "Beck likes her back."

"Do you?" his dad asked.

Mac glanced at his dad. *Are you kidding me? You're going to ask me that, with her cousin standing next to me?* "I always have."

"She likes you back," Mike repeated, easing the uncomfortable moment. "But I do have my reservations about this whole thing," he added.

So, Noelle did tell him.

His dad patted Mike's shoulder. "I'm sure you do. Lily and I did at first, but if it works…"

Mac looked up at the canoe his dad stored in the rafters during the winter months. "I remember the grand opening of Noelle's Café. The town was so curious about where this woman came from and what the café would be like. Anyone who remembered old Jeremiah Treloar didn't have much confidence the place would be clean enough to eat at. But everything was different. New floors, booths, kitchen. Noelle stood at the door, handing out sliders and small paper cups of chocolate shakes. She bent down and offered a cup to Beck. He's been a fan of hers ever since."

His dad chuckled. "Noelle is nothing like her Uncle Jeremiah. That old codger was a menace, flying around this town in his old truck. The rust was the only thing holding that old beater together." He glanced at Mike. "Sorry, I shouldn't talk like that about your family."

"I'm related to Noelle on her mom's side. I never knew the man."

Beck ran into the garage. "Grams just dished up dessert!"

CHAPTER 12

Noelle jumped up when the alarm sounded. She quickly made the bed and straightened the room before heading to the master bedroom. This scenario—her going into the master bath to shower while Mac was asleep—had only come up once since their wedding. She could probably shower in the hall bathroom, but she and Mac had agreed, for appearance's sake, this was the smarter solution.

She opened the door as quietly as possible and crept inside. There was enough light to see Mac was facing away from the door, and seemed to be sleeping soundly. She showered quickly and donned the clothes she'd picked out the night before. Her hair had enough natural curl that all she had to do was towel dry. She'd pull it into a ponytail before leaving for work. After applying a little makeup and straightening the bathroom, she turned out the light and opened the door.

"You don't have to be quiet. I'm awake."

His rough, sleepy voice sent a nice shiver through her. *Marriage in name only. Marriage in name only. Marriage in...* "Sorry to wake you."

He rolled toward her. "You didn't. Thinking about Cheryl kept me awake most of the night."

Ouch. His words hurt, but of course they also made complete sense. Cheryl was a movie star, compared to her… It was too early to think of a comparison.

He threw the covers aside and she turned away. *Marriage in name only.* "Albert and Gertie are opening, so I have time to make breakfast."

"How about I make breakfast this morning?"

She caught a glimpse of his muscled back before he disappeared into the closet. "Do you cook?"

He leaned his head out as he pulled a T-shirt over his broad chest. "How do you think Beck and I survived before you?"

"Lily."

"My ego is bruised." He ducked into the bathroom. The water in the sink came on. A moment later, he was next to her, toothpaste outlining his mouth. "For your information, I make a mean buffalo chicken omelet," he said around his toothbrush.

Noelle lifted the hamper lid and dropped her sleep pants and tee inside. "That sounds delicious."

"I'll meet you in the kitchen."

~

*M*ac stopped brushing long enough to watch Noelle leave the room, her perfume trailing after her. He lied when he said thoughts of Cheryl kept him awake. A dream of him and Noelle together—in his bed— woke him up an hour before she came in to shower. He kept telling himself dreaming of Noelle was normal. They spent the better part of the weekend together. He and Beck survived their first meeting with Cheryl because of her. They'd leaned on her. Saturday night, they watched a movie together, snuggled up just like a real family. She attended church with them, joined them at his parents' weekly Sunday dinner, so to dream of her was only natural.

Mac finished his teeth and ran a brush through his hair. He'd shower after he got Beck off to school. He leaned his palms on the vanity and stared at his reflection. The dream had been so real, the feel of Noelle's skin under his fingers… *Stop!*

"What are you doing?"

He jumped slightly at the sound of Beck's voice right behind him. "Wondering how you got to be so goofy-looking when I'm so handsome."

Beck laughed. "It's the opposite, Dad. I'm the handsome one. Just ask Noelle."

She'd probably agree with you. "I don't need my ego bruised twice in such a short time."

"What's an ego?"

"On the negative side, ego means conceit or self-importance, but there is also a positive side, which means self-esteem or self-image."

"Did you mean the negative one or the positive one?"

Mac hugged his son with a chuckle. "Probably the negative. How did you sleep?"

Beck rocked his hand side to side as he'd seen Mac do when asked the same question by his parents. "Noelle said you're making breakfast."

"It'll be ready by the time you get out of the shower." He hiked Beck over his shoulder and deposited him in the hall bathroom. "See you in fifteen, clean and combed and dressed."

Beck saluted. "Aye, aye, captain."

Passing the family room, Mac noticed Noelle straightening the throw on the back of the sofa and picking up one of

Beck's school books. He took a step back. "I'm glad you're here."

She glanced his way with a puzzled look on her face.

He walked into the room until they were standing toe to toe. "I'm glad you're here. I'm glad I met you, and that you're my friend. You've made a difference—a positive impact—on our lives, and I'm glad you're here…with us."

A smile lit her face. "I'm glad we're friends, too. I hope when this is over we remain so."

"Absolutely."

Thirty minutes later, Noelle pushed back from the table and groaned. "That was delicious, and I'm impressed." She glanced at Beck. "Your dad's a good cook."

"And he thinks he's handsome."

Noelle glanced at Mac with raised brows.

He lifted a shoulder. "The kid had to get his looks from somewhere."

She laughed as she stood. "Beck, run and brush your teeth while I clean the kitchen. I'll take you to school so your handsome father doesn't have to go out in the cold."

"I'll take care of the kitchen," Mac said, wondering if she really thought he was handsome.

"I won't argue." Noelle carried her plate to the sink, then went to the back door and wound a scarf around her neck.

Mac began clearing the table while she slipped her coat on and buttoned it to her chin. Beck ran into the kitchen and grabbed his coat and backpack. Mac joined them at the back door and pulled his son into a hug. "Have a great day. I'll pick you up after school."

"Okay."

Noelle snugged a navy knit hat with a bright pink flower on her head. "Zip your coat, Beck. It's really cold out this morning."

"Dad, aren't you going to kiss Noelle goodbye?"

Noelle looked amused. They'd been able to avoid a parting ritual so far.

"Gramps always kisses Grams if she goes to work before him."

"I was in such a rush I forgot." Noelle wrapped her arms around his neck and delivered a sweet kick-his-heart-rate-into-high-gear kiss. "Goodbye, sweetheart. Have a nice day. I'll miss you."

Little minx. "You, too, snookums."

Beck broke into a fit of giggles at his endearment.

She winked.

Yep. He was glad she was here.

~

The next four days passed quickly and uneventfully. Beck called Mac out two additional times for not kissing Noelle goodbye. Both were chaste quickies that still sent Noelle's heart into wild flutters. Mac always smiled afterward, but didn't show any signs of feeling the same flutters.

Other than those moments, their routine became settled and familiar. If Mac was home and she at work, he would make dinner and help Beck with homework. If he worked the late shift, she'd pick Beck up from Lily and Rance, and they'd make dinner together, then tackle homework. Beck was usually asleep before she went to bed, but if he wasn't, she sat in the chair in Mac's room reading. If Mac was due home, she'd sneak down the hall to the guest room for the night...kind of a crazy setup, and completely backwards from the direction most people would be sneaking. When Mac worked all night, she'd sleep in his bed, with his musky scent enveloping her in secure comfort.

In the two short weeks since their wedding, Noelle felt

herself growing closer to the two men whose lives she'd invaded. Beck sidled up to her often, as if wanting to be reassured she wasn't going anywhere. Beck worrying his lip happened when he was struggling with something. She would put an arm around his shoulder or run her hand over his head to let him know she was there for him.

Mac's mannerisms also became familiar. After dinner, he'd settle into his recliner with a book, his reading glasses perched on his nose, a crease between his brows. She loved the way he looked just before leaving for work, all clean and starched and handsome in his uniform. She loved the curl of his hair when he was fresh out of the shower. Beck's hair had the same wave, his eyes the same color of caramel around the pupils.

She grew increasingly nervous as Beck's birthday party approached, afraid she'd make a fool of herself in front of a gaggle of boys. She wished she'd thought to ask Mac ahead of time for bowling pointers. Too late now.

The morning of, she woke early and prepared a special breakfast for her stepson. Since she'd never experienced a birthday party of her own and only been allowed to attend very few, she didn't know what else to do for him. She'd wrapped an artist notebook, paints, and colored pencils, because Beck liked to draw after he finished his homework. Upon opening, he seemed thrilled with her small present.

She arrived at the bowling alley early, strung crepe paper, and hung balloons over the two picnic tables reserved for their party. She didn't go with a theme since Beck didn't seem to be into superheroes, but colorful tablecloths with bright plates and cups made even the bowling alley tables look festive.

Beck and Mac showed up first, then Lily and Rance. Beck thanked her several times for the decorations. When the kids arrived and the bowling began, Noelle pulled out her cell phone and snapped pictures until Mac took her hand.

"You can't put this off forever."

"I can try."

He ran a finger between her brows, relieving a bit of the bowling tension, while building on another. "You get a little crinkle here when you're nervous or worried about something."

The thought that he'd been observing her telltale signs sent a warm tingle all the way down to her belly.

"There's nothing to be nervous about. If these kids can do it, you can, too."

Luckily the lane they were using was the last one, and against the wall so there wouldn't be many observing. The kids were too wrapped up in their games to pay any attention.

Mac helped her select a ball and she walked up to the line just as she'd seen the kids do. Mac surprised her by coming up behind her. He put one arm around her waist and his other hand under the ball. "As you take three steps forward, you swing the ball behind you. Try to set it down gently, but with enough momentum to make it to the pins. Aim for the middle arrows running down the lane."

She nodded. Normally she liked it when he got this close, liked his breath brushing her cheek and the weight of his hand on her waist. Her thoughts turned to what Lily and Rance must be thinking, which heated her face. He stepped back and she followed his directions, slid too far into the lane, and released the ball with a *thud*. It rolled forward, almost halfway down the aisle before curving into the gutter that ran alongside.

Lily clapped. "Great try, Noelle. You'll be a natural before you know it."

"Not bad for your first attempt," Mac said

She pointed at the side of the lane. "Why is that there?"

"What? The gutter?"

"If it wasn't there, my ball would have hit at least one pin."

Mac laughed and picked up her ball when it came out of a chute by their little scoring table. "You get another turn," he said and handed the ball to her. He came up behind her, again, and tucked her close. "Try to relax."

"I can't with you standing so close."

"Really?" His breath tickled her temple. "We might have to come bowling more often. We can work on your form."

"Go sit down, and no laughing."

"I don't know. I kind of like this position."

Though she probably shouldn't in front of his parents, two could play this game. She nudged the front of his jeans with her bottom.

He straightened immediately and took a step back. "O—kay. I think she's got it."

Lily laughed.

"Atta girl," Rance said.

Noelle didn't stand a chance at winning, but caught Mac watching *her form* more than once, so felt she'd scored pretty high.

$\sim$

*M*ac opened the door of Owen's law offices for Noelle and Beck, proud when Beck allowed Noelle to enter first. "Good job, son."

Beck leaned close. "Grams has been teaching me some eti…"

"Etiquette."

Beck's face brightened. "Yeah. That's a fancy word for good manners. She says you know all about them and I should watch you. Noelle will like that, huh?"

Note to self: Provide a good example. "Yes. Noelle will like that."

Owen showed them into the same room they'd used for their first meeting. Beck positioned himself between them on the sofa.

Cheryl strolled in like a fashion model and acting as if it was just an ordinary day. Her attorney followed her in, but her husband was absent.

Beck played with the bottom button on his shirt while his mom bombarded him with new questions. Most were answered with a yes or no. She didn't take the time to probe further. It was as if she had a quota of questions to fulfill and she just kept them coming, one after the other. Beck only looked up or answered with more than one word when he or Noelle coaxed him to do so.

"Beck, do you have any questions for your mom?" Owen said after forty-five minutes.

Beck glanced at Mac with an expression he couldn't decipher. "Do you have a question?"

"I want to know why she left us."

Cheryl leaned forward. "I didn't hear him. What did he say?"

Mac ran his hand over the top of Beck's head, memorizing the feel of his hair, the shape of his skull. "You have to speak up."

Beck looked at his mom through a curtain of lowered lashes. "Why did you leave me and Dad?"

Blazing blue eyes turned on Mac. "You told him to ask that!"

Mac moved his hand from Beck's head to his shoulder when he flinched at her shout. "I don't coach him before we come here, Cheryl. He's curious. You would be, too."

Cheryl's attorney stood. "Cheryl, I have a plane to catch."

Relief flooded Cheryl's face. She didn't have a prepared answer. Her job here was done until the next visit.

She left in a flurry, without saying goodbye to Beck. After the door closed, Beck glanced at Noelle. "She didn't tell me happy birthday."

Noelle lifted a teary gaze to meet Mac's and then hugged Beck. "Her attorney was in a hurry to catch his plane, honey, that's why she forgot."

Beck shook his head. "No, she forgot because she doesn't care."

Owen hadn't touched the legal pad balanced on his knee this time, opting to watch Cheryl. He stood. "I'm so glad you mentioned your birthday, Beck. I keep a drawer full of things for special occasions and a birthday is a very special occasion. Come to my office so you can pick something out.

Once Owen and Beck left the room, Mac shoved to his feet and stalked to the window, just as Mr. Fischer and Cheryl pulled out of the parking lot. He turned to Noelle, who swiped tears from under her eyes. Beck was paying for a stupid mistake he'd made years ago. Ironically, if not for that drunken weekend, he wouldn't have his son, which he wouldn't trade for anything.

*M*ac sat in his patrol car on the outskirts of town, watching for his wife and son to pass on their way to an arcade in Harrisville. Noelle was spoiling Beck, but if he wasn't working, he'd be doing the same. Cheryl forgetting their son's birthday was unforgiveable. He'd parked in the open so they'd be sure to see him. They did, honking and waving as they drove past.

He hated spending time apart from Beck tonight after what had happened. In truth, it wasn't just Beck he wanted to be with. Noelle was winding a silken threat around his heart.

He spent a lot of time looking across the square at the café when she was working, watching her move around the kitchen at home. Following her trail of perfume from room to room was becoming one of his favorite pastimes, along with seeing a pair of deep blue eyes watching him from across the dinner table.

Beck turned to her for help. He liked that his son had someone to go to besides him or his parents. Noelle touched Beck often, stoking his back or patting his shoulder. Beck responded well to those touches of affection, making Mac a little jealous that he never received any physical attention.

A blue, older model Ford Bronco passed and Mac's attention clicked into high gear. Pulling onto the highway, he followed at a distance, not really caring if he was spotted. He couldn't tell how many passengers were in the SUV, but did recognize the driver as the older kid JT had asked his staff to keep an eye out for.

Mac followed the car into Eden Falls. He stowed the police cruiser behind the station when the kids parked in front of Noelle's Café and piled out. Three boys and two girls went inside. He drew his cell phone from his pocket and scrolled to JT's number, glad he was on shift tonight.

"Hey, Mac," JT said after the second ring.

"Where are you?"

"I'm at the Sawyers' farm. It looks like someone tried to set an old shed on fire. The wood was too wet from the last rainstorm to burn, but Mr. Sawyer noticed the scorch marks and called me. What's up?"

"I may be following the perpetrators as we speak. Blaze, Thorn, and three other kids just went inside Noelle's Café."

"Go inside and let them know we're watching. I'll be there in fifteen."

Mac disconnected the call and walked across the square. Through the window, he saw the kids had taken a table in the back corner. Gertie was standing over them like a hawk watching a rabbit's burrow. When he entered, the kid with the orange hair was flicking a lighter and then extinguishing the flame. On, off, on, off.

"Pocket the lighter, kid, or you're all going right back outside," Gertie said.

"There's no law that says I can't—"

"Knock it off, Blaze," one of the girls said when she spotted Mac at the door.

"Put the lighter away," the vampire-looking kid who went by Thorn said. He glanced at Gertie. "I'll have a burger and fries."

Mac sat at the end of the counter while Gertie took their orders. The kids were dressed in black, with multiple piercings, and enough makeup to join a circus. *Please, don't let Beck go through a Goth phase.* All the kids but Thorn glanced his way occasionally. Gertie brought him a cup of coffee and a slice of pumpkin bread slathered in butter, just the way he liked it. Mac finished both before JT walked in.

"Any trouble?"

"Nah, just kids being kids. Gertie handled them and Albert's aware they're here. He's looked out a couple of times. The orange-haired kid was flashing a lighter when I first walked in. Thorn told him to stow it."

"There's nothing out at the Sawyer place—no footprints, no candy wrappers—the site's clean. I can't find a shred of evidence that points to them, but my gut tells me at least one of these kids is guilty."

Too bad. Mac knew a gut feeling wasn't enough to go on in an arson investigation.

∾

*N*oelle got up the next morning and got ready for church before Mac came home. She'd take Beck so Mac could sleep after his night at work. The building hadn't fallen in on her and Josh's sermon touched a spot in her heart last Sunday. After their meeting with Cheryl, she hoped he could touch that spot again.

She threw a breakfast casserole she'd put together the night before in the oven. Then she went to wake her stepson. He was in the shower when Mac came through the garage door. His eyes grazed over her in a heart-jumping way.

"You look nice."

"You look tired."

He chuckled and ran a hand down the side of his face. "I am. Where are you going?"

"I'll take Beck to church so you can sleep. There's a casserole in the oven. Would you like to eat before you go to bed?"

He walked over and tucked a strand of hair behind her ear, a simple yet extremely intimate gesture. "Actually, I want to take a shower and go to church with you."

"Are you sure?" She hoped she didn't sound as breathless as she felt.

He nodded. "I'll only be a few minutes."

Noelle set the table and popped two English muffins in the toaster.

Beck came into the kitchen smelling clean and looking handsome in his shirt and clip-on tie. "Did Dad come home?"

"He's in the shower."

"Is he coming with us?"

"He says he is." She handed him a container of orange juice. "Will you set this on the table and get the butter, please?"

Mac came into the kitchen, looking just as handsome as

his son and more so than a man who'd been up all night should. The shower seemed to have opened his eyes a little wider.

"Hi, buddy. You look spiffy."

"So do you. Doesn't he, Noelle?"

Noelle was at the stove dishing the casserole. She glanced over her shoulder. "You both look amazing. Beck, can you get the jam from the fridge?"

She brought two plates to the table, and placed one in front of each of her men, then went back for her own. She put the toasted English muffins on a plate and set it in the middle of the table.

"Want orange juice?" Mac asked, pouring some for Beck.

She held out her glass. "Yes, please. Thanks for your help this morning, Beck."

"You're welcome."

Content, she smiled at her little make-believe family and the world she was becoming too fond of. Going back to being by herself would be hard when this was over.

*N*oelle scooted into the pew next to Lily forty minutes later, and Beck followed her in. She was glad he was between her and Mac. She'd felt his eyes on her several times during breakfast, but kept her own down or on Beck.

Throughout the sermon, the weight of Mac's arm was warm against her back and his hand circled her shoulder. His fingers ran up and down her arm, sending goose bumps popping up all over her skin. She was glad for her sweater, or he would have felt the effect his touch had on her. She glanced his way. He had the audacity to wink, turning her flirty tables around on her.

*Marriage in name only…Marriage in name only…*ran

through her mind like a news ticker running across the bottom of a television screen.

We have to keep things light, uncomplicated, but the silly shiver of anticipation that moved through her told a different story.

She turned her attention to Josh. His sermon was on choices and their consequences. Noelle thought of Cheryl once again. Was she tired of paying the consequences for the choices she made so long ago? Did she believe she had Beck's best interests at heart by upsetting his way of life?

Noelle could understand wanting her child if Mac was an irresponsible father, but he was the best, and everyone in town would vouch for that. If this case went to court, what would Cheryl use as her defense? She'd left her son on a doorstep, hadn't tried to get in touch with him since that day. She'd even forgotten his birthday. If she truly cared, how could she have overlooked such an important date in her son's life?

She felt sorry for Cheryl. She'd spent all these years missing Beck's firsts, his first birthday and his last, his first skinned knee, first day of school, first lost tooth, first baseball game. The list went on and on. Noelle wanted to ask her, why now? Why, all of a sudden, did she want Beck with her?

*W*hile Mac was sleeping and Beck went to lunch at a friend's house, Noelle picked up her cell phone and closed the guest bedroom door. Her intention was to leave a pleasant, upbeat—non-defensive—message on her parents' home phone. Chicken? Yes. This time of day, they were usually at the hospital doing rounds, or in their offices going over charts. Her mother's businesslike "Hello" had her sinking onto the edge of the bed.

"Hi, Mom."

"Noelle?"

I'm your only daughter. "Of course it's Noelle."

"We were beginning to worry. We haven't heard from you in a couple of weeks."

Six weeks, Mom. It's been six weeks, and phones work both ways. "I've been crazy busy."

"With what, dear?"

Running a restaurant, getting married, taking care of a ten-year-old. Not that any of those things would be of interest to you. Her mom saved lives every day, was cool as a cucumber under pressure, and little emotion ever showed. "Life."

Her mom's laugh was like fingernails on a chalkboard. What she did in her life was insignificant to her parents. "Crazy busy with life" to her was equivalent to catching butterflies on a summer afternoon to them.

Well, here you go, Mom and Dad. "I don't have much time to talk, but I wanted to let you and Dad know I got married two weeks ago."

"You what?"

Ahhh. Now I have your attention. "I married a wonderful man. He's a police officer here in Eden Falls. He comes from a really nice family and has a ten-year-old son." *How's that for insignificant?* "I'll text you my new address. I'm having dinner at his parents' house, so I have to run, but I'll call again soon. Tell Dad hi."

She disconnected the call, her heart pounding like a snare drum on a high school parade route.

Wimp.

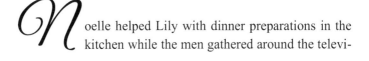 oelle helped Lily with dinner preparations in the kitchen while the men gathered around the televi-

sion to watch a football game. Beck's cheers floated into the kitchen.

Lily smiled. "I love hearing that happy voice." She turned to Noelle, who was slicing carrots for a salad. "You make my boys happy and that makes me happy."

She wished her parents could hear Lily's statement. *I can make someone happy. I don't need a medical degree to make a difference.* She'd felt liberated since telling her mom she was married. A little rebellious. A lot euphoric. "I'm not sure about happy, but I hope I've eased their anxiety a little."

"You have."

"I also hope this situation doesn't confuse Beck. I'm afraid things are going to get a whole lot more complicated for him before this mess with his mom is over."

"I think you give them both some peace of mind. I appreciate that." Lily clapped her hands. "Enough gloom and doom. Let's talk about Thanksgiving. It's only a week and a half away. I'm not sure how you celebrate the holiday, but I would like to include you in planning. Mac has to work that morning, so normally I would serve dinner after he gets off."

"It's been so long since I actually celebrated with a sit-down dinner."

"Really? What do you do on Thanksgiving?"

"I've spent the last two years at the Eden Falls Shelter, cooking and serving meals. Before that, I usually worked on Thanksgiving and grabbed takeout on my way home."

"You ate takeout on Thanksgiving?"

Noelle laughed when Lily sank against the counter, as if she might faint at the idea.

"It wasn't that bad. The supermarket around the corner from my apartment in New York had a deli that served turkey with all the trimmings."

"Your family doesn't celebrate Thanksgiving?"

"When I was young, we usually went out to a restaurant after my parents finished their hospital rounds."

Lily shook her head as if the idea was completely beyond comprehension.

"I like helping at the shelter."

"Doesn't Amy Saunders head that up?"

Noelle added the carrots to the salad and went to the sink to wash a bunch of radishes. "She does."

"Is there a crowd of people who help?"

Noelle lifted a shoulder. "More like a handful."

"We can work around your time at the shelter."

"I had planned to take Beck with me, since Mac works."

"That sounds wonderful. It would be good for Beck to be exposed to helping others. What can I do?"

"I'm not in charge of volunteers. I usually contact Amy. She lets me know what needs doing."

"I'll call her tomorrow. How late do you usually work at the shelter?"

"We finish cleaning up around three."

"And Mac gets off at four, so that will work. We'll plan our family dinner for five."

Family dinner. The idea of sitting at a table with Lily, Rance, Mac, and Beck for Thanksgiving sounded wonderful, like the dinners they had at her aunt and uncle's. She could picture it in her mind so clearly. "Can I invite Mike?"

"Of course. Tell him he's welcome to bring a date. The more the merrier, as Rance would say."

"What can I bring that I can make ahead?"

"We have the traditional turkey, stuffing, mashed potatoes, and gravy. Vegetables can be anything. Of course, Beck likes the green bean casserole. I make a couple of pies."

"I can make the pies this year. What does everyone like?"

"Surely you know by now, these men aren't picky about

their desserts. They like the traditional pumpkin pie, but they'd be happy with anything."

"I'll bake them early and bring them over on Wednesday. I'll make the green bean casserole ahead, too. All we'll have to do is stick it in the oven."

Lily pushed away from the counter. "What time do you have to be at the shelter?"

"I cook several turkeys and a few side dishes at the café and take them over just before noon, when the doors open."

"We'll take Beck for you that morning. I'll have Rance drop him off at the café at eleven, so the two of them can help you get everything to the shelter."

"That would be great."

Beck walked into the kitchen. "Why are Gramps and I going to the shelter?"

"I hope you'll help me serve Thanksgiving meals to people who haven't got a place to eat dinner."

"What do I have to do?"

"Just stand behind the counter and scoop food onto plates." Beck came over to her and leaned against her hip. She smoothed an errant strand of hair from his forehead. "You'll be fabulous at it."

"Cool."

CHAPTER 13

Noelle hustled, a tray overhead, out of the kitchen. It was the usual Monday morning rush and the café was bustling.

"Here you go, gentlemen." She set plates in front of Beam, Rowdy, and JT Garrett. "What else can I get you?"

Beam held up his empty orange juice glass. "I'll take a refill when you get a minute."

"And some hot sauce," Rowdy added.

She glanced at JT, who'd been standoffish since the wedding. "I'm good. Thanks, Noelle."

"I'll be right back."

"Noelle, can I get my coffee topped off?"

"Sure thing, Frank." She stuck a bottle of hot sauce in her pocket, filled another glass with orange juice, and grabbed a coffee pot on her way around the counter.

"Noelle, we're low on potatoes," Gertie called from the kitchen.

"Send Joseph to the grocery store," she hollered back. *Mental note: Order more potatoes.* "How are you this morning, Rita?"

Squawk!

Frank, who was sitting next to Rita at the counter, jumped, spilling the coffee Noelle had just poured into his cup.

"Dagnabbit, Rita."

Noelle grabbed napkins for Frank, refilled his coffee, set the glass of orange juice in front of Beam, and handed Rowdy the hot sauce from her pocket, all in a smooth motion she hadn't realized she was capable of two years earlier. This was her life, and she loved it.

"Have you decided, Rita?" she asked pulling an order pad from her apron pocket.

"I'll have the special with French toast instead of pancakes."

"That's not the special. That's number thirteen on the menu and two dollars more."

Squawk!

Frank sloshed more coffee. "Would you stop that squawking!"

Noelle grabbed a bar rag and wiped the counter before filling Frank's cup again.

After the morning rush, Noelle settled behind her desk to get the potato order in, along with everything else they were low on. She added extra bags of regular and sweet potatoes to be sent to the shelter. People wouldn't go hungry while she was in town.

"Noelle," Marianne said at her open office door. "There's a woman out here asking to see you."

"I'll be right out. Have you had your break yet?"

"Just got back. I'm going to start wrapping silverware for lunch."

Noelle nodded as she pushed back from her desk. She poured some hot water into a cup and grabbed a herbal tea bag from the basket on the kitchen counter. When she entered the café, she was shocked to see Cheryl sitting at a booth by the front window.

Marianne tipped her head in that direction when Noelle came around the counter. Cheryl had a cup of coffee sitting in front of her, so Noelle slid into the opposite side of the booth.

"Good morning."

"Noelle, right?"

She'd made her way to Noelle's Café, asked to see her, but couldn't remember her name? *Nice try, Cheryl.* "Yes. What can I do for you, Cheryl?"

Cheryl motioned in a circle with a pink manicured nail. "This is your place?"

Noelle wondered if she was as insincere on the inside as her smile. "Yes."

"You have money?"

"I inherited the café from an uncle." Noelle took a sip from her teacup.

"I didn't know Mac had remarried." Cheryl tucked a lock of blond hair behind her ear, exposing her gargantuan diamond earrings.

Yes, I know you have money.

"How long have you two been together?"

No need to elaborate. "A while."

Cheryl pointed to Noelle's ring. "I noticed that in the attorney's office. It's cute." She twisted her own huge diamond wedding and engagement rings.

Noelle sat back against the red vinyl bench. "Why don't we skip the small talk, since neither one of us is really interested? What can I do for you?"

Cheryl took a deep breath and exhaled. "I want you to talk to Mac about letting me have Beck. I'd be willing to settle for joint custody."

Noelle studied the woman across the table from her. Even dressed in jeans and a heavy sweater she was gorgeous, but she had lonely eyes. Noelle wondered what her background was. How had she grown up? Did she have family, or was it just her, Simon, and the two boys they saw every other weekend?

"Why do you want Beck? Why now?"

"It's really none of your business, but…now that I'm remarried and have stepsons, I think Beck should be with me."

Noelle wasn't buying her reason, but wasn't sure why.

"Simon and I can give him things Mac can't. He will go to the finest boarding school, take sailing lessons, and learn to ride horses—"

"Boarding school? You want custody, only to send him away?"

"He'd get the best education. Both of Simon's sons go to the same school. Beck's choices here are limited. With us, he will have the world at his disposal."

Noelle laughed and received an indignant glare from Cheryl. "Sorry. I'm trying to understand why you think taking Beck from his father, the man who's taken care of him since he was six months old, would be to Beck's advantage."

Cheryl leaned forward. "Are you listening to me? I could give Beck things Mac could never afford."

"Money isn't the most important thing in life, Cheryl. Beck is happy here. He loves his father and enjoys spending time with his grandparents. He has lots of friends. He's on a basketball team. He plays baseball in the spring." Noelle also leaned forward and crossed her arms on the table. "I'm not saying a mother shouldn't see her son, but why would you want to take him away from everything familiar, everything he loves, only to send him off to an unfamiliar boarding school? Maybe you should consider what Beck wants."

"How can a child know what he wants?"

"Would you have liked to be taken from everything familiar

at Beck's age?" When Cheryl didn't answer, she added, "Don't you think a judge will take Beck's feelings into consideration?"

Cheryl released a huff. "Simon will take care of the judge."

That statement sent shivers up Noelle's spine. "What do you mean?"

"Once Beck gets to California, he'll love it…the warm weather, the big house, the pool and tennis courts."

Noelle wasn't getting through to her. Cheryl believed money would make Beck happy. Maybe it was what made her happy—though she didn't look it.

"Will you talk to Mac?"

Noelle wondered if seeing Mac and Beck together in a setting other than an attorney's office would change Cheryl's mind. "Do you have a number where I can reach you?"

Cheryl opened her handbag, wrote her name and number on a piece of paper, and slid it across the table. "I'm leaving for California today, but I'll be back the Saturday after Thanksgiving. We usually spend the holiday in Italy, but we're staying here this year."

Cheryl stood and walked out of the café. Noelle noticed Mac across the street and Cheryl headed in that direction. The thought of telling Mac about boarding school flitted through her mind, but she decided against it. There was no reason to worry him further, but telling Owen was a must.

~

*M*ac was walking the square when he spotted Cheryl leaving the café. What was she doing in there? She saw him and crossed the street in his direction.

"Good morning, Mac." She glanced around. "Where's Beck?"

"In school," he said with as much disdain as possible. *A mother should know that.*

"Oh, sure, I forgot it was Monday."

Right. "Having breakfast?" he asked nodding toward the café.

"Heavens, no. That place smells of year-old grease."

"When did you become such a snob, Cheryl?"

"I'm not a snob." She pulled her coat together at the neck and shivered. "It's cold out. Why don't we go talk in that cute pastry shop?"

"I'm on duty."

She smiled. "You look handsome in a uniform."

"If you weren't eating breakfast, what were you doing in Noelle's café?"

"I wanted to talk to your wife. I was hoping she'd be less stubborn than you."

"About what?"

She rolled her eyes. "Beck, of course. I want her to talk some sense into you. By the way, did you settle on her because the choices"—she surveyed their surrounding—"around this tiny town are so thin?"

He bit his tongue. Noelle was three times the woman Cheryl would ever be, but he wouldn't get into a back-and-forth war with an audience. He'd caught sight of Patsy at the window of her pastry shop. "There's no sense to talk into me. I don't want Beck moving to California and I'll fight you with every resource at my disposal."

"Well, I want him with me, and I'll fight you. And I can call on far more resources, which is the whole point. Besides, mothers usually win custody suits."

Not moms who abandon their children. Again, he held his tongue. Town Square wasn't the place to air their dirty laundry.

"Anyway, I hope you'll come to your senses. I don't want to drag Beck into court, but I'll do it if forced."

That was the sentence that pushed him over the edge. "You would, too, wouldn't you, Cheryl? You'd make your son's life miserable to get what *you* want, even if he doesn't want to go. You would drag him into court to satisfy your own selfishness. Notice I didn't say needs. You've gone nine years without showing any interest in Beck—no cards, no letters, no calls. Then, all of a sudden, you want to barge into his life and turn it upside down. Just because you gave birth, doesn't make you a mom."

"We'll see who wins this court battle, if that's what you want to make it into, Mac."

"This isn't about winning. It's about our son and what's best for him. Dragging him off to California, a place he doesn't know, isn't fair to him."

"You should have thought about that before *you* took him from California."

"You should have thought, *period*, before you abandoned him on my doorstep. You didn't even wait long enough to make sure I answered the door. What kind of mother does that?"

Someone touched his arm. "Mac, this isn't the place."

He sucked in a deep breath, his body quivering with rage, as he glanced down at Noelle.

"We'll see you the Saturday after Thanksgiving, Cheryl," Noelle said, pulling on his arm.

Once they were out of earshot, he tried to release the tension in his jaw. "I swore I wouldn't get into it with her on the street, but she pushed every wrong button available."

"She tried to push mine, too." Noelle squeezed his arm. "You okay?"

"I am. Thanks for coming to the rescue." He covered her hand with his own. "I feel like I'm always indebted to you."

"You're not, so stop. Everything will work out, Mac."

"I wish I had your optimism."

Noelle smiled. The sight lightened his spirits. He liked that she could change his mood so easily. In fact, the more he was around her, the more fond of her he became, which might end up being a problem.

*M*ac came home to laughter from the kitchen and smells that set his stomach growling. His son's happiness warmed his heart. He'd been worried how Beck would react to the jagged edges Cheryl introduced into his life, but Noelle had a way of smoothing those edges with gentleness and stability. And maybe even some love.

He took his time removing his coat and boots, enjoying their animated conversation before emerging from the mudroom. Beck was perched on a stool peeling carrots while Noelle tossed a salad.

"Hi, Dad."

"Hey, buddy. What's going on?"

"Noelle put me to work."

Mac laughed and hugged his son. "Good for her and you. It's about time you started earning your keep."

"Beck helped me put the whole dinner together."

On his way to the oven to take a peek at what was cooking, Beck grabbed the back of his uniform shirt.

"Dad, you forgot to kiss Noelle. Again."

Noelle put a hand on her cocked hip. "Yeah, Dad, you forgot to kiss me."

Mac turned and looked down into her pretty blue eyes, which were dancing with mischief. "Sorry, sweetheart. My hunger got the best of me. Whatever's cooking smells delicious."

She placed both hands on his face and brought him closer for a kiss before he had the chance. "Your cheeks are cold."

"Your hands are warm."

Her lips were soft, pliant...and sweet. She ran the tip of her tongue over the seam of his lips and he pulled back to narrow his eyes at her. "Where is it?"

She smiled. "It's too close to dinner. You'll have to wait."

"Where is what?" Beck asked.

"You guys had chocolate before dinner."

Beck snorted. "How did you know?"

Noelle pressed her lips together and raised a brow.

"Lucky guess." He turned to the oven and flipped the light on. "It smells great. Mmm...meatloaf. We love meatloaf, don't we, Beck?"

"I already told Noelle that. Guess what she let me put in it?"

Mac leaned a hip against the counter and folded his arms. The table was already set with new place mats and cloth napkins. They made the kitchen look homier somehow. So did the new dishtowel hanging from the fridge handle. He liked the subtle, feminine changes Noelle periodically added to his and Beck's masculine world.

"Dad, guess."

Mac smiled at his son. "I have no idea. Onions."

"Everybody puts in onions." Beck glanced at Noelle. "Don't they?"

"Pretty much."

"How about broccoli?"

Beck rolled his eyes. "He's never going to guess. Can I tell him?"

Noelle nodded as she took the half-peeled carrot from Beck and finished the job.

"Barbecue sauce."

Mac opened his eyes wide for Beck's benefit. "What? I've never heard of that."

"I know, but it smells good, doesn't it?"

"It smells great. I'm going to change clothes and wash my hands. How about if you get the milk out of the fridge, Beck?"

Beck hopped off the stool. "Okay."

Never before had it been this easy to get his son into the kitchen. He walked down the hall to change, the aroma of dinner following him. After closing the bedroom door, he slipped his gun from his utility belt and locked it in the lockbox in the top of his closet. He changed quickly, not wanting to be left out of what was going on in the kitchen.

"Dad, will you pour the milk?" Beck asked when he returned to the kitchen.

Mac almost laughed at his son's request. "Sure."

Noelle opened the oven and bent over to pull the meatloaf out. Mac's gaze followed the line of her back over her—he diverted his eyes in case Beck was watching. "What can I do to help?"

"Can you get a bowl for the green beans? Beck, will you put the salad on the table and pick the salad dressing you like? Mac, what would you like on your salad?"

"I'll take creamy Italian."

Noelle bumped Beck with her hip. "That sounds good. I'll have the same."

The three of them danced around each other while dinner was set on the table. Mac thought, once again, he could get used to this.

Their dinner talk started out complimenting Noelle on meatloaf with barbecue sauce. Next, Noelle turned the conversation to the A Beck got on his History test. Mac congratulated him. Beck changed the topic to the puppy they were going to pick up on Friday. Quincy was still the name of choice. Noelle had promised they'd go shopping to pick out a bed, some toys, and puppy food tomorrow after school.

"Can you go with us, Dad?"

"As a matter of fact, I can. How about we go out to dinner after our Quincy shopping spree?"

"Yay!"

"That means you have to come straight home after school and do your homework," Noelle said.

Mac couldn't believe Noelle had doubted herself as mother material. She was doing a great job and Beck adored her.

Beck added butter to his baked potato. "Did you have a dog when you were my age, Noelle?"

"No. I wasn't allowed to have any pets."

"Not even a goldfish?" Mac asked.

"Nope. Too messy. We were allowed to do homework and then read books."

Since Beck had brought up the subject of her past, Mac decided to dig a little deeper. "I know I've asked before, but there had to be something you were allowed to do besides study."

"No, that's pretty much all my brothers and I did. Studied, or read. Sometimes, when my parents had a minute and were in a good mood, we played board games. Not fun games, but ones that challenged our minds."

He had a sudden need to know more. "How often did you go over to friends' houses?"

"Maybe once a month." Noelle shrugged. "It's hard to make friends when you aren't allowed to socialize."

"Were your mom and dad mean?"

Noelle smiled at Beck. "Not mean, just strict and…regimented is the best word I can think of to describe them. We were on a tight schedule because of the hours my parents worked and we were expected to stick to the schedule. I learned to cook because it was my duty as a member of the family. Lucky for me I liked my duty. One of my brothers had to do the laundry and he didn't like his job at all." She laughed. "Now he's a grown-up, he sends all his laundry out."

Beck wrinkled his nose. "Even his underpants?"

Noelle laughed. "Even his underpants."

Mac sat back in his chair and studied the woman across the table. She didn't have a regimented schedule anymore. She didn't seem to mind their spur-of-the-moment life. How did someone grow out of that kind of childhood? Had she done a one-eighty and tried to be completely different? "What made you change?"

"What do you mean?"

"Why aren't you living that strict sort of life anymore?"

"I guess I was for a while. In New York I was up by four, in the gym by four-thirty, showered and in the office by seven. I rarely left before dark. If I didn't have a business dinner, I'd grab a bite to eat and work at home until ten. Fall into bed—wash, rinse, repeat."

Amazing. And lonely. "I see why you love Eden Falls so much."

The twinkle in her eye was back. "You think?"

∿

*N*oelle pulled the chocolate pie she and Beck sampled earlier from the fridge while Mac cleared the table and Beck ran to take his shower. She set it on the counter and turned to get the whipped cream just as Mac reached around her to put leftovers in the fridge. Their foreheads collided.

"Ouch!"

"Whoa!"

They rubbed their heads, laughing.

"I was going—" Mac said. "I needed—" she said at the same time.

They both laughed again.

He moved her hand. "Let me see."

She leaned away. "It's okay."

He ran the pad of his thumb over her forehead. "It's red."

"It's nothing. I'm fi…" Her words trailed away when his lips touched the tender spot once. Twice. She could smell his cologne, faint after his long day. His Adam's apple bobbed and she imagined pressing her lips against it.

He slipped his fingers down the side of her face and lifted her chin until their eyes met. She saw the raw desire there, and wondered if her eyes revealed the same. The moment seemed suspended. His pupils contracted slightly before he lowered his mouth to hers.

And she was lost. Tumbling in a tangle of emotions far more intense than the teasing kiss she'd given him earlier, or the quick pecks they shared at Beck's insistence. Overpowering and primal, yet soft and alluring, the kiss pushed her forward with the force of an incoming tide, then receded back soft as the tickle of a feather, only to come rolling in again.

His arms encircled her, pulling her flush against him, and she went willingly, longing to be closer. His fingers tangled in her hair as he turned her head so their mouths could meet more fully. Their tongues moved in a sensuous dance that caused her knees to shake. Sensations, emotions rushed together in a matter of seconds making her light-headed, yet craving more. She leaned into him. He turned them so he was standing with his back to the counter and she was tight against him.

I love Mac. I love Beck. This is why I'm in Eden Falls. This is where I belong. I've found my purpose.

Those thoughts struck her so forcefully, she jerked back and stared at him.

He appeared as dazed as she felt, his eyes wide. Before she drew her next breath, they were intertwined again—limbs, tongues, scents all moving together as one.

"Is it time for—ewww, get a room."

Noelle broke away and gulped for air.

Mac turned toward the sink with a chuckle. "Where on earth did you learn that, son?"

Beck grinned. "I heard Gramps say it once."

Please, don't ask under what circumstances. Noelle didn't want to hear about Rance's disapproval of some teenagers making out in a parked car or on a Town Square bench. Thankfully, Mac only glanced her way. Self-conscious, Noelle ran fingers through her hair hoping it wasn't sticking out. *Oh, we shouldn't have done that.*

She glanced at Beck. "I'll dish up the dessert," she said, her voice too bright. "Beck, will you get the whipped cream?"

After grabbing three plates from the cupboard, she cut the pie. Mac added dollops of whipped cream. They sat at the table and enjoyed the sweet treat in comfortable silence, she and Mac stealing glances every chance they got.

*A*fter dessert, she sent both men to the family room to watch television for an hour while she emptied the fridge for a good scrubbing. She needed space and time to clear her muddled brain. *Sharing that kiss was incredibly dumb. And letting Beck catch us was even dumber.*

She emptied the vegetable drawers, washed and dried them while her thoughts scattered like ashes in a breeze. She was becoming too attached to Mac and Beck. If she didn't retain her perspective on the situation, they would have her whole heart before she knew it.

As she was reloading contents, Beck came in for a good

night hug. Mac leaned against the doorjamb, his eyes on her. "Interesting choice of songs."

"What?"

"You were singing 'Crazy Love' just now."

"I was?" *Poco, D-13 on the jukebox.* She glanced at Mac's grin and felt her cheeks heat. *Oh, great. Perfect song for Mac to hear me singing aloud after we kissed.*

Beck grinned. "Yeah, me and Dad were laughing."

Mac held up a hand. "Not at your singing, just that you were singing. You have a nice voice."

"Are you going to pick me up after school?"

She bent down and gave Beck's cheek a smooch. *Thank you for changing the subject, cutie pie.* "I'll be there. Sweet dreams."

Mac pushed away from the wall and walked Beck down the hall to his bedroom. Noelle scrambled into the master bathroom to wash her face. When she finished, she found Mac standing near his bed. His eyes moved down her sweat-shirt and poodle-patterned pajama pants. And back up.

She grabbed her book from the nightstand. "I'm going to read for a little while."

"You can read in here."

"I don't want to keep you up."

His smile was slow and didn't quite make it to his eyes. "I'm not tired."

"I think reading in the family room is a better idea." As she passed, his index finger caught hers. They looked back at each other over their shoulders, linked only by a touch. It was a movie moment, one you'd see on the Hallmark Channel. *THUD.* "Ouch!"

Or a comedy, right before the heroine runs into the doorjamb.

"Oh," he said with concern. "Are you okay?"

"Fine." She rubbed the new spot on the side of her head.

"Here, let me see."

That might lead to another make-out session. Yes, please, her heart cried. "No. I'm fine." She fled, but felt his gaze follow her down the hall.

She settled onto the sofa, still rubbing her head, and opened her book, but after reading the same paragraph three times, she gave up. Her mind wouldn't settle after the kiss she and Mac shared, and being caught by Beck made it worse. If he became attached as she was, it would hurt him when she and Mac separated. She needed to build boundaries and stick to them.

There will be no more kissing.

～

*M*ac tried to read, but put the book down after two pages. He flipped the television on and then turned it off. He tossed and turned, and finally fell asleep only to awaken with dreams of Cheryl waving to him as she drove away with Beck. His heart pounding, he climbed out of bed for a glass of juice. When he opened his bedroom door, he noticed a light still shining in the family room.

Curled on one end of the sofa, with a throw pulled up to her chin, Noelle was sound asleep. Mac sat on the coffee table and watched the slow rise and fall of her shoulder, the slight twitch of her eyelid. She was beautiful, his saving angel, and deserved better than she was getting.

Tonight was only the second time he'd felt such an intense impact from a kiss or spent so much time thinking about it afterward. The first time was Halloween night. Now he wanted to do it again. And again.

She sighed, and he leaned closer, resting his elbows on his knees, and continued to watch in a stalker-ish sort of way while his thoughts bounced to love—a word people threw around too easily, in his opinion. Yet what other word was strong enough to describe what he felt for Noelle? Friendship seemed trite. The emotion filling his chest, his mind, his bones, was much more than friendship. He and Noelle had formed a bond, with Beck as their nucleus, and he knew they'd always share it, no matter the outcome of this custody battle with Cheryl.

And what if Cheryl did win and took his son to California? What would happen between him and Noelle? She wouldn't come to L.A. with him. She had a café to run. Would they be limited to a twice-yearly visit, when he brought Beck to see his parents? He wouldn't want to go that long without seeing her or hearing her voice. Funny how he already knew that.

What if this *was* love? He'd never been in love before, which sounded extremely shallow, given the fact he'd been married and had a son. Yet the feelings running through him seemed an awful lot like what he'd heard described as love.

He lifted a strand of her hair and ran it through his finger and thumb.

He wasn't opposed to falling in love. In fact, the idea sounded rather nice to him at the moment. He liked coming home to Noelle, could easily imagine a life with her, imagine the three of them together. Or four. Possibly, a dark-haired little girl who resembled her momma.

Crazy that a kiss could conjure such images.

Noelle scrubbed at her nose with the back of her hand and snuggled deeper under the throw.

Mac pushed up from the coffee table and turned off the lamp. With the room in darkness, he went over to the gas fireplace and flipped the switch. Once the fan kicked on, she'd be warm enough. The light from the fire flickered over her beautiful face.

Good night, Noelle.

CHAPTER 14

Mac stalked into Get Fit ready to work off some tension. He'd let his three times a week visits to the gym dwindle away after his wedding and it was time to get back to working out. He checked in with Jillian Saunders, who was behind the front desk, then headed for the locker room. Peeling off his coat and street clothes, he donned his workout gear.

He hit the treadmill for a warm-up and was joined by JT a few minutes later.

"Howdy."

Mac chuckled at JT's standard greeting.

"Haven't seen you here in a while."

Two miles down, Mac bumped up the speed. "Yeah, I've been busy."

"How's married life?"

Frustrating. "Good."

"Yeah?"

Mac nodded and bumped the speed up another notch. He didn't want to talk about married life or Noelle. He'd gotten very little sleep last night, thanks to thinking about her.

JT laughed. "Here to work off a little sexual frustration, since this marriage is in name only? Or did she redecorate your den without asking?"

"Shut up." He slowed the treadmill to a stop and moved over to the free weights, because the treadmill was doing nothing to relieve anything, and JT only made it worse. He'd had another dream of Noelle. She was in her wedding dress, and they were dancing at their wedding, but there had been lots of kissing involved. Suddenly they were in his bed and there was nothing but that black thingamajig Stella had taunted him with at Noelle's shower.

JT approached wearing a contrite expression. "Sorry, Mac. I know you're under a lot of pressure from the ex. I saw you two having a conversation on the sidewalk in front of Patsy's. It didn't look like it was going well."

"Nothing with Cheryl goes well." He picked up two weights and moved to a bench for some inner-biceps curls. "She went into the café to persuade Nicole to talk to me."

"What did Noelle say?"

Mac stopped lifting. "She didn't say. I'm sure she told Cheryl she was being ridiculous."

"And how is Noelle fitting in as Mrs. Johnson?"

"We get along great and Beck loves her." He didn't tell JT how much he liked coming home to dinner in the oven, the sound of his son's laughter, or the smell of Noelle's perfume.

～

*W*ith all the doggie necessities purchased, they drove to a little diner Mac had discovered with buddies in high school. Beck was beyond excited about the puppy and counting the days until Quincy came to live with them.

Noelle seemed just as excited.

Mac couldn't imagine growing up in the environment she described. He hoped when Beck looked back he'd remember his childhood fondly. Mac's younger days had been filled with discovery, lasting memories, and friendships he still enjoyed.

He ran around the truck and opened Noelle's door. She eyed Rosie's Countryside Diner while Beck climbed out of the back.

"If it hasn't changed hands, I promise the food is great," Mac said, pulling the diner's door open. The place looked exactly the same as the last time he'd been here. It even smelled the same. He just hoped the food was as good.

"Mac Johnson, is that you?" came the squeal of a female voice.

He turned in time to catch a woman who launched herself into his arms, knocking him back a couple of steps. His head was pulled down and lips began kissing his entire face. He finally got his hands under her armpits and peeled her off.

"It's me," she said pointing to the ample chest he *did* remember. "Mary Jo Bond. Don't tell me you don't recognize me. It hasn't been that long."

Oh, boy. Mary Jo had been a high school setup. They dated for about three weeks before she started writing Mary Jo Johnson on everything in sight. He was seventeen and far from ready for a serious girlfriend. The breakup hadn't gone well.

He glanced at Noelle, who wore an amused grin. Beck's eyebrows were raised almost to his hairline. Mac turned back to Mary Jo. "Sure. I remember you."

She ran a finger down his chest before he could step out of reach. "You look really great. I always knew you'd be tall, dark, and handsome."

He took that step back and sent a plea for help to Noelle. Her smile grew.

"I'm married." He grabbed Noelle's arm and pulled her in front of him.

Mary Jo's face fell. "You're married?" The words came out more a whine than a question.

"Yep. Married. This is my wife, Noelle." He tugged Beck close. "And my son—our son, Beck."

Beck gave a half wave.

"It's nice to meet you, Mary Jo." Noelle dropped an arm around Beck's shoulder. "Come on, Beck. Let's get that vacant table by the window and give your dad a few minutes to catch up with his friend."

Little minx. She could see he didn't want to be left alone with Mary Jo. She led Beck away while Mary Jo prattled on about the time a group of them drove to the lake for a moonlight skinny-dipping party. When he spotted a waitress approaching Beck and Noelle, Mac held up a hand to stop Mary Jo's blow-by-blow rehash of that night. "I better get to my family. It was great seeing you."

Mary Jo leaned forward for a kiss, but he ducked, and pointed to his ring finger. "I have a very jealous wife."

A moment later, he slipped into a chair next to Noelle. "Thanks for abandoning me."

"We wanted to give you time to reminisce. I promise I'm not the jealous type."

Beck pointed at his cheek and laughed. "You look like Albert."

Noelle dipped the tip of her napkin in her glass of water and handed it to him. "That shade of fuchsia looks good with your complexion."

Mac sent her a glare while he scrubbed at his cheek.

"How do you know that lady, Dad?"

Noelle bit back a smile as she pointed to Mac's chin.

"You think this is funny."

"Pretty amusing."

"Dad?"

Mac blew out a breath. "I dated her in high school. Layne set us up because he was dating her friend."

"The swim party at the lake sounded fun."

Beck's eyebrows puckered in a frown. "What is skinny-dipping?"

Mac rolled his eyes at Noelle. "Thanks for bringing that up."

"You still have pink lips everywhere," Beck said.

Mac pushed back from the table. "I recommend the raspberry shakes. Will you order one for me while I wash my face?"

"Dad? What is skinny dipping?"

Noelle grinned, merriment dancing in her eyes.

$\approx$

The café was busy despite snow blowing sideways just outside the door. After the lunch rush, Noelle pulled her cell phone from her pocket just as Mike pushed inside.

"Spooky timing." Noelle held up her phone. "I was just about to call you."

Mike unwound his scarf and stomped snow from his boots. "About?"

"Thanksgiving. The Johnsons invited you to join us for dinner, if you're not going home for the holiday."

One side of his mouth scrunched in a frown as he hung his coat on a hook by the door. "I'm not going home, but I also don't want to horn in on Johnson's family dinners all the time."

"What are you talking about? Thanksgiving is for family." She gave him a tight hug. "And you're family. Lily said you can bring someone."

"What time?"

She took his arm and led him toward a booth. "Five-ish. I know for a fact Rowdy's is closed, so you can't use work as an excuse."

"How do you know I don't have a date?"

"Because you're not ready to date or I would have seen you around town with someone by now. Please come. I'd really like you to be there."

"I'll be there," Mike said as he slid onto the vinyl bench.

"How about some lunch?"

"Perfect timing. I'm starved."

"Burger and fries?"

Mike nodded. "Sounds great."

"Marianne, can you get Mike a drink?"

Noelle went into the kitchen and came back a few minutes later with his lunch and a nice salad for herself.

"Are you doing okay with rent?" she asked as she set a plate in front of him.

"I'm a big boy, Noelle. I can handle rent."

"I didn't mean it like that, Mike. We were splitting everything when I was living there. I kind of left you high and dry."

"I make plenty at Rowdy's. Saved a bunch on the cancelled honeymoon."

"Sorry."

He shrugged in a what-you-going-to-do gesture and squirted ketchup onto the side of his plate. "Rent here is cheap compared to what I used to pay."

Noelle laughed. "It is, isn't it? When I first moved here, I felt guilty for paying so little. I got used to it in a hurry, though. My wages as a café owner are quite different from my Wall Street job."

"Thanks to your investment advice, I built up a healthy savings account before I left Boston."

She huffed a breath on her nails and polished them on her shoulder. "I will admit, I was quite the entrepreneur in New York. But the café is doing great. I paid for my new appliances without dipping into any of my savings."

Noelle enjoyed thirty minutes with her cousin. She missed their late-night talks. He didn't have any more news about the river conservation job other than it started in February and he was looking forward to it.

"Rowdy is going to miss you. He told me he hasn't had such reliable help since he opened the bar and grill."

Mike waved her comment away. "He'll find someone." He took a bite of his burger and glanced out the window. "I got a call from Lora yesterday."

The pain of losing his fiancée was still evident in his voice. "What did she want?"

"She and Eddie were fighting. She thinks she might have made a mistake."

Noelle set her fork down and crossed her arms on the table. "What do you think?"

Mike pushed his almost empty plate back. "That I still love her."

Noelle reached across the table and touched his flannel-clad arm. "Did you tell her?"

"No." Mike lifted his gaze to hers. "I'll admit, her admission boosted my ego a little, but I'm not sure I'd want her back. They say love is blind, and it is. Now that I think back, there were things she did that bugged the crap out of me."

"What are you going to do?"

"About her?" Mike released a huff of air. "Nothing. She's Eddie's problem now. I like it here and I'm looking forward to my new job."

Noelle was happy to see his smile return. She hadn't seen his genuine smile since he arrived.

"Lora would be miserable in the wilds of Washington." He stood and pulled his wallet from his back pocket.

Noelle slid from the booth and held up her hand. "Lunch is on me."

"Thanks."

She took his arm as they walked to the door. "I'm sorry about Lora."

"It was bound to happen." He shrugged into his coat. "I was getting too cocky about my new job and my great surroundings. Her call humbled me."

"That's it. Put a positive spin on it." Noelle wrapped his scarf around his neck.

"Thanks again for lunch."

"Sure." She patted his cheek. "I've missed your face. Thanks for stopping by. And thanks for agreeing to Thanksgiving dinner."

"What can I bring?"

"How about that great dip you used to make when we were kids, the one with shrimp? I haven't had that in years. That, a box of crackers, and a big appetite."

"I can do that." He reached for the doorknob and then turned. "Did you tell your parents?"

"I told my mom. Haven't heard from them since."

Soon after Mike left, Beck and Lily came in, bringing a swirl of snow with them. Beck unzipped his coat. "Hi! Me and Grams came for hot chocolate."

Noelle swiped the snow from Beck's shoulders, then helped Lily out of her coat. "Then you've come to the right place."

Beck held up a shiny coin. "I have money for the jukebox."

She pulled a quarter from her apron pocket. "Play E-2 for me."

He grinned and bounded away.

"How about some tea?"

"That sounds lovely." Lily rubbed her hands together. "It's really cold out there."

She led Lily to the booth farthest from the door and went behind the counter for mugs of hot water, tea bags, and hot chocolate for Beck.

"What brings you in today?" Noelle asked once they settled at the table.

Lily nodded toward her grandson. "Beck wanted to see you. He's been asking questions about his mother today." She sighed while watching him bounce to the beat coming from the jukebox. "I think knowing you're near gives him a sense of security."

"I can't guarantee him security." Noelle dipped a tea bag into the hot water of her mug as her chest tightened. Foolishly, she hadn't taken Beck's feelings into consideration when she proposed marriage. She hadn't counted on him becoming as attached to her as she was to him.

"You've given him love and the experience of a family environment. He's never had that."

"A false family environment. When this custody issue is over, Mac and I—" She stopped when Beck slid into the booth beside her. He took a sip of hot chocolate and grinned at his grandma. "I caught Noelle and Dad kissing in the kitchen."

Heat moved up Noelle's neck. Fabulous. She was telling Lily one thing, and Beck was telling her another.

Beck snickered behind his hand. "I told them to get a room."

Lily's laugh skittered through the café. "That sounds like something you picked up from Gramps."

"I did."

The song Noelle asked Beck to play started and he turned to her. "Why do you like this song?"

"Because the music and the words make me happy."

As Beck licked the chocolate from his mouth, Noelle could almost see the wheels turning in his head. "D-3 makes me happy."

Trying to recall what D-3 was, she handed him a napkin.

He took another sip and scooted from the booth. "I'm going to see if Dad's at the station, Grams."

"Okay, honey. I'll be there in a minute."

"Zip your coat," both Noelle and Lily called as he raced for the door. They shared a laugh.

~

*M*ac caught Beck by the shoulders as he ran into the station. "Whoa, where you going in such a hurry?"

"I came to see if you were here."

"You have a hot chocolate mustache."

Beck swiped at his mouth with the back of his hand. "I had some at the café. Grams and Noelle are talking. Did she tell you I get to help serve food at the shelter?"

"Whoa, again," Mac said with a laugh. "Did who tell me you get to help serve food and when?"

"Noelle. She said I could help her serve food at the shelter on Thanksgiving."

"What about our dinner at Grandma and Grandpa's house?"

"We're eating there after you get off work. Noelle is cooking a bunch of things for the shelter and me and Gramps are going to help her carry it over."

Mac turned when the door opened and his mom trudged in. With her scarf wrapped around her face, her eyes were all that were visible. "Hello, son," came out muffled.

"Hey. Beck was just filling me in on all kinds of goings-on."

"Like the kiss you and Noelle shared in the kitchen?" his mom asked with a raised brow.

Mac frowned down at Beck.

"What? You didn't say it was a secret. Besides, aren't you supposed to kiss when you're married? Jason's mom and dad kiss all the time."

Lily covered her grandson's eyes with gloved fingers. "Don't you hurt Noelle," she mouthed.

Mac looked at the ceiling with a shake of his head. "What's this about Beck serving food at the shelter?"

"Noelle helps at the shelter on Thanksgiving and she said Beck could help. I think it's a wonderful idea."

"Yes, as long as someone is there to help him."

"Noelle will be there and I'm going to send your dad over to lend a hand. We'll eat after you get off work. Same time as always."

Mac's glanced toward the café as he tugged a wool bomber hat over his ears. "I'll walk you to your car, since I have to take a turn around the square."

They went out together and he gave his son a hug before he opened the passenger door. "Be careful driving home. We've had reports the roads are icing over in places."

"We'll be careful."

He bent down so he could see his mom. "I'll pick Beck up after work."

"No need. Noelle said she'd pick him up when she gets off."

It felt strange that someone was taking over the duties he'd performed alone for so long. "Buckle up," he said to Beck. "I'll see you in a few hours."

He watched them drive away before turning toward the café. The lights in the windows were bright and inviting, as were all the shops around the square. He wanted to see Noelle, but did an about face.

Across the square, he pushed through the door of Pretty Posies. The bell over his head announced his arrival. Alex was behind the counter with her right-hand helper, Tatum. "Hey, ladies."

Alex flashed a smile, which was as contagious as a yawn. "Hi, Mac. In need of another bouquet?"

"Yeah. Can you deliver something festive to my mom before Thanksgiving?"

"A centerpiece for the table?"

He nodded and glanced around the shop.

"Anything else?"

"Yeah." He heard the uncertainty in his voice and wondered if Alex noticed. Her knowing smile told him she did.

She walked around the counter to a huge armoire and picked up a candlestick. "Noelle bought a pair of these for her mom's birthday. Maybe she'd like a pair for the house?"

Mac glanced over his shoulder, relieved to see Tatum disappear into the back room. "I'd like something a little more…"

"Personal?" Alex prompted. She motioned him to a table and selected a necklace of pink and green beads strung on silky-looking threads. "How about a rose quartz, peridot, and pearl necklace?"

He could picture the necklace against Noelle's skin. He took the delicate strands from Alex.

"She was wearing a pink sweater the other day when I was in the café. This would look nice with it."

"I'll take it."

Alex smiled. "Good choice. Would you like it wrapped?"

"You do that?"

"Of course." Alex took the necklace. "I take it things are working out well for you and Noelle."

"Things are…" He blew out a breath. "Complicated."

"Want to talk about it? I'm a great listener, better than JT. He says he's a good listener, but he interrupts with questions, and then wants to fix everything."

Yes, JT was a fixer, but so was he.

"So"—Alex placed the necklace in a small box—"Noelle has fit into the Johnson household better than you ever expected. Or anticipated. She's great with Beck, gets along with your parents, and everyone knows she's a wonderful cook. She's smart, so I bet she's helping Beck with home-work, which relieves some of your daddy duties, and who doesn't love coming home to dinner in the oven? I bet your heart goes pittypat just thinking of her."

She wrapped the box in a piece of colorful paper and taped the ends. "And that wasn't meant to happen. Noelle was just supposed to throw a monkey wrench into the ex's plan to take Beck away, but here she is making you experi-ence all kinds of unexpected emotions. You're wondering why you didn't think to date her before. She's pretty. She's successful. She's sweet, kind, thoughtful. And sexy, but you have to keep your hands to yourself, because this is a marriage of convenience. You never thought you'd fall in love, but you did. Fall in love." She topped the box with a ribbon and held it out. "How close am I?"

Just listening to her talk about Noelle made him short of breath. Alex was completely right. He was in love.

Alex grinned.

He turned toward the door, but before going out, he said, "You might as well set up an account for me," and left without looking back.

◞◟

*T*hanksgiving dawned cold and snowing. Noelle left the house hours before dawn to get the café ovens on and the turkeys roasting. The stuffing would be prepared separately so that wasn't an issue. Cleaning the huge birds was. She wrestled them into the utility-sized sinks, got them washed, patted dry, and seasoned. Once they were tucked into roasting pans and in the ovens, she scrubbed out the sink, made a cup of hot chocolate, and went into her office to start the schedule for the month of December.

She sank into her chair, her hands wrapped around the warmth of the mug and sipped. The last week, filled with restless energy and sleepless nights, was catching up with her. Even though the café was closed, today would be a long one.

Beck's excitement about helping at the shelter made her smile. He'd become even more tenderhearted once he spent the afternoon serving meals to the less fortunate.

A knock on the back door startled her. She wasn't expecting Rance and Beck for hours and Gertie and Albert were spending the day in Tacoma with family.

She stepped to the peephole and her insides did the stupid little dance they'd been doing whenever Mac was close. She unlocked the heavy door and pushed it open.

Mac's shoulders and cap were covered with snow, which he brushed off before stepping inside and closing the door. "Brrr, it's cold out there this morning."

"Do you have time for breakfast? Bacon, eggs, hash browns?"

His smile heated her more than her hot chocolate. He pulled his police radio from his pocket and set it on the work-table. "I do have time."

"Want a cup of hot chocolate or coffee while you wait?

"Hot chocolate sounds great."

One thing she'd known about Mac before they got

married, he liked meat and potatoes, but he also loved sweets. "With marshmallows or whipped cream?"

He looked at her like the question was absurd. "Both."

She laughed. "If I put cold whipped cream on your marshmallows, they won't melt into your hot chocolate."

"I guess I'll just have to go with the marshmallows this morning." He shed his gloves and coat. "It already smells good in here. How many turkeys are in the ovens?"

"Four big birds. Patsy has another two in her ovens over at the pastry shop and Amy Saunders will bring two more."

"That's a lot of turkey."

"Eden Falls serves Thanksgiving to all the homeless in the area. Harrisville takes over for Christmas and South Fork supplies Easter dinner. School buses will transport everyone here."

Mac nodded while pulling out a stool. Noelle went to the fridge for a jug of milk. She poured some into a pan and heated a burner on the stove. Then she got a mug and went into the large pantry for a bag of marshmallows.

"Do you know how beautiful you are?"

The look on his face told her he was as surprised by his comment as she was. "Mac…"

"What?"

She poured hot milk over the cocoa mix and set the mug and spoon in front of him. As she turned away he caught her hand. "Noelle, you are beautiful. I'm not saying that because I feel it's my duty as your husband or to be kind. I say it because I see your beauty. You are beautiful on the outside, and on the inside. You are kind and thoughtful and…I could go on and on about your positive characteristics."

"Stop." She pulled free, opened the fridge, and pulled out bacon and eggs.

"Hasn't a boyfriend ever—"

"I never had a boyfriend." At the look on his face, she

almost laughed, even though tears were close to the surface for some reason. Mac just couldn't wrap his mind around the fact that she hadn't dated or had much fun growing up. It was as if he wanted to discover some secret life that she'd never lived. "I've told you before, my focus was always on school and grades." She added several slices of bacon to a skillet.

"Not in college?"

She pulled two potatoes from a bag and a peeler from a drawer. "No time."

"What about when you moved to New York?"

"Life there was about the next advance, the next big deal, the next promotion. There was always a next something that was higher priority than a date."

Mac stood, picked up a pair of tongs Noelle had left near the stove, and flipped the bacon. "So you've never been in a serious relationship?"

"Nope." She was careful to keep her back to him while she peeled the potatoes. She knew exactly where his mind was traveling. She was thirty-three years old and had never slept with a man, never had sex. And he'd be right.

She pulled the grater from a shelf under the counter and grated the potatoes into a hot skillet. She grabbed a plate, layered it with paper towels, and set it next to his elbow. He took the bacon from the skillet and placed it on the paper towels to drain while she flipped the hash browns.

"Never?"

She turned. "What part of my pathetic previous life don't you get, Mac? I didn't date much because I wasn't allowed. By the time I went away to college, I was too focused on what I had to do to get my parents off my back. I never dated a guy more than once or twice, because after a while, a guy just stops asking. This…" She waved a hand around in frustration. "A man in my life is all new to me."

"I'm sorry. It's just that…knowing you, the kind of person you are, makes it hard to believe."

She turned back to the stove. "Believe it, because it's true."

A few minutes later they were seated at the worktable eating breakfast side by side.

"Thanks for this."

"Of course. A wife can't let her husband go to work with an empty stomach." She was embarrassed by her earlier outburst, but she wouldn't apologize for who she was and hoped he'd finally accepted the truth. "I'm glad you stopped by."

"Me, too." He reached over and linked their fingers, pulling her around to face him. He swallowed and she thought he would try to kiss her. She would let him. Instead he laughed, which surprised her.

"What's funny?"

He shook his head and looked at their joined hands. "You are going to think I'm crazy." He met her gaze. "I think I'm crazy—this whole thing was crazy from the beginning, so I'm not sure why this is happening. " He shook his head again and looked away.

"I don't understand. What are you talking about?"

He pressed his lips together, looked at the ceiling, and released a breath. "Crazy. This is crazy," he mumbled before looking into her eyes. "I think—No, that's not fair. If I'm going to say this, I have to be truthful with you. I don't think…I know. I'm falling in love with you. I'm in love with you. I love you."

Noelle's mouth dropped open as his words tumbled around in her mind, looking for a place to take hold.

"I don't expect you to say anything or return the senti-ment. I know it isn't what you signed up for, but…I don't know." He shook his head as if trying to clear cobwebs away. "I thought you should know."

A smile twitched at the corners of her mouth while she tried to wrap her mind around the idea that a man might actually love her. Was it possible? She glanced around, expecting to see the disapproving glares of her parents.

He cleared his throat. "I lied. I do expect you to say something. I mean…I don't expect you to return my feelings. I know this was supposed to be a temporary marriage. But… would it be so crazy if it worked? I think it is working. I like what you, me, and Beck are building. It feels comfortable and…right. I know Beck thinks the world of you. I don't know what we would have done without you at these meetings with Cheryl. I mean…we would have survived, but you being with us…as a family… I'm rambling. Please, say something. Anything. Tell me to get out and I'll go."

She suspected tears would upset him, but she couldn't stop them.

"Oh, geez, I made you cry. Please don't cry."

"You didn't…well, you did, but only because I feel… happy. I've been so happy with you and Beck. Your mom said the same thing about you on Sunday night—said you seem happy—and it made me happy—you know, to think I might be making you happy."

She couldn't open her heart enough to tell him she loved him back—loved them both.

Not because she was afraid of being hurt. Between her parents and her job in New York, she'd developed pretty tough skin. But what if the judge ruled for Cheryl and Mac had to move to California to be near Beck? She'd invested a lot of energy and heart in her café. She couldn't just leave. Yet, she knew—deep down in the pit of her stomach—she'd leave if he asked. The thought scared and excited her at the same time. She would leave Eden Falls if Mac invited her to come to California with them.

On the flip side, what if the judge ruled for Mac? Would his feelings change when he didn't need her anymore? It wasn't that she didn't trust Mac, but when circumstances changed…

And what of Beck? She wouldn't risk hurting the little boy she loved as deeply as her own when he was already going through so much.

Their marriage seemed to be working so well. She loved the life she'd fallen into. But how could it possibly last when it had been build on pretense? Sure, she'd added a few touches of femininity to their bachelor home here and there, but nothing that couldn't be bagged up in ten minutes and hauled to the trash after she was gone.

Mac placed the hand he still held flat on his chest. He skimmed his other hand around the back of her neck to cup her head before tugging her into the sweetest kiss she'd ever experienced.

She loved kissing him.

CHAPTER 15

Mac left Noelle's café after a nice breakfast and many more kisses. He left with the realization that he wanted more from her, more than a live-in stepmother for Beck and a pretend wife. He wanted her as a real wife in the full sense of the word. As he slid behind the wheel of his police cruiser and pulled onto the almost deserted streets of Eden Falls, his thoughts went back to their conversation.

There had been no declaration of love on her part, and, to tell the truth, he hadn't expected one. His intention, when knocking on the café's back door, hadn't been to blurt out his feelings, but for some reason he felt compelled to tell her.

He wasn't sorry, he just wished he'd waited for a more… romantic moment.

He wondered if she'd told her parents she was married and what they thought of their underachieving daughter marrying a cop. She said she was happy, that he and Beck made her happy, and he believed, from her tears, that she meant it.

He could still smell her perfume on his clothes and the scent of roasting turkeys still lingered around him. Twin aphrodisiacs—which made him think of another part of their conversation. She said she'd never been in a serious relationship or had a boyfriend. Did that mean she was still a virgin? How was that possible in this day and age? Though not on the same level, she'd admitted to never bowling or having a pet before, either.

His windshield wipers slapped at the fat flakes as Mac circled the square, headed toward Ms. Kennedy's place. Her son picked her up yesterday to spend the holidays in Bellingham, but JT asked him to go by and check that her doors were locked.

Mac drove carefully down her long drive, which had been plowed by one of her good neighbors. The people who lived this far out of town had to fend for themselves. Ms. Kennedy had been on her own since her husband passed, but remained adamant she wouldn't become a burden on family. So Eden Falls rallied. People took turns checking on her, shoveling walks, mowing lawns, and buying groceries. He knew JT's mom came out regularly to get Ms. Kennedy to doctor's appointments and into Dahlia's Salon. Ms. Kennedy repaid everyone with plates of award-winning baked goods.

Both the front and back doors were locked tight, as were all the windows. He grabbed a shovel near the rear stoop and cleared the front steps and walks—might as well keep it manageable.

After kicking the snow from his boots, he climbed back into the cruiser and headed to the Polanski house to count the old man's chickens. Mr. Polanski was known for his sightings of Sasquatch and was sure the mountain beast nabbed a chicken regularly. Mac suspected kids playing jokes, but was never fast enough to catch any suspects.

He headed back to town around lunchtime. A comfy sofa, a warm fire, and Noelle tucked against him flitted through his mind—definitely an appealing after-dinner prospect.

He entered Eden Falls Shelter parking lot, surprised by the number of people bustling about. He parked next to his dad's car and went in through the back door. Noelle was mashing potatoes in a huge pot. He walked up behind her and took the masher from her hand. "Let me do that for you."

She smiled in pure appreciation. "Perfect timing. My arm feels like it's about to fall off."

"Doesn't that deserve something?"

She stood on tiptoes and pecked him on the lips.

"That's it?"

She raised her eyebrows. "We don't have time for anything else."

This was the Noelle he was used to before marriage. She'd always been playful and fun at the café. Her more subdued side hadn't surfaced until after they tied the knot. He liked the playful one. "We'll have time later."

"We'll have to negotiate."

"Negotiate?"

She flicked her finger toward the pot of potatoes. "Mash. We need those."

She disappeared through a door. A moment later Beck dashed through the same door. "Hey, Dad!"

"Hey, buddy. Whatcha doing?"

"I've been helping Noelle. There are a ton of people out there. I ask them if they want a roll or cornbread and put the one they pick on their plate."

"How come you're back here, then?"

"Noelle said we should eat something when you're done with the potatoes. Gramps is taking over for me."

His dad, who usually spent the morning watching parades and the afternoon yelling at football players on the television, was serving food at a shelter. Noelle had turned their traditional Thanksgiving topsy-turvy without even trying. Once he finished the potatoes, he and Beck went to the back of the line to wait their turn.

"Grams told me not to eat too much. She wants us hungry when you get off work."

Mac put his hand on the back of Beck's neck and steered him toward the counter. Alice Garrett served the turkey slices her husband Denny was carving. Scooping stuffing were Amy Saunders and her daughter, Jillian. Alex was on potato duty and Colton ladled gravy. Rance asked if they wanted a roll or cornbread and Noelle added cooked carrots to their plates. There were plenty of behind-the-scenes hands bustling about, refilling whatever ran low.

Mac decided this was how he and Beck would spend the Thanksgivings he didn't work from now on. They would give back to the community by helping at the shelter when the need arose.

After lunch, he walked around the square. It was so quiet he could almost hear the snowflakes landing on awnings and light posts. He took the patrol car out for a final circle around the town. The streets were mostly empty, just a few cars carrying people here and there to enjoy dinner and family. At four he parked behind the station and turned the keys over to Phoebe, who said she'd enjoyed the day with her parents and four sisters.

He was looking forward to getting home to his own family.

His parents' house was warm with familiar sights and sounds. His dad snored away in front of the television while the scent of roasting turkey filled the air. His son lay on the sofa reading a book. His mom was at the sink and his wife waited with a hot cup of cocoa. Life couldn't get much better.

As they were loading the kitchen table with all the goodies, the doorbell rang.

Noelle glanced at the clock over the sink. "I can't believe

Mike's so late. He promised to bring an appetizer." She smiled at Rance. "He must have been sleeping in front of a football game, too."

"I wasn't sleeping." Rance grinned. "Just resting my eyes."

"And snoring," Beck added with a laugh.

"I'll get the door," Mac said.

He pulled the front door open and there stood Noelle's cousin with an older couple scowling behind him. "Mike, glad you could make it. Noelle was getting worried."

"Mac, these are Noelle's parents, Benjamin and Eleanor Treloar."

Noelle's mother stepped forward. "I assume you're my daughter's husband."

"I am. It's nice to meet you. Please, come in. We were just sitting down to dinner. Have you eaten?"

"We're not here to eat. Could you please get our daughter?"

Mac decided it would be best not to put his arm around Noelle when she came to his side. "Mom? Dad? What are you doing here?"

Lily and Rance moved forward. "How lovely you came to Eden Falls for Thanksgiving. I'm Lily, and this is my husband, Rance. Please, come in and join us for dinner."

Mr. Treloar waved Lily's invitation away. "That's a kind invitation, but we can't stay. Noelle, get your coat."

Noelle turned to Mac. "I'm going to go with them and talk. I'll meet you at the house later."

Mac fought the urge to take her arm and keep her with him. Who did her parents' think they were, to show up and take her away like she was a misbehaving child? Did they know anything about her and how amazing she was? He stood at the door and watched his wife drive off with his in-laws who were, obviously, not happy about their daughter's marriage.

"Where is Noelle going, Dad?"

Mac put his hand on Beck's shoulder. "She's going to talk to her mom and dad. She'll be okay."

"Is she coming back? It's Thanksgiving."

I hope so. "If she doesn't, we'll see her at home."

Mike was apologetic through dinner, trying to explain his aunt and uncle's behavior. "I'm really sorry I brought them here, but they insisted on seeing Noelle immediately. They are incredibly successful, and have always had extremely high expectations for their kids. Noelle falls short of those expectations, no matter what she does."

"But she's successful and loves what she does. How can they find fault with that?" Lily asked. "They should have witnessed how hard she worked today. She donated not only her time, but turkeys and potatoes. She was up way before dawn cooking for others."

"Anything less than medical school equals failure in their eyes. Noelle never was interested in medicine, but they pushed and pushed. She says she left her New York job because of the pressure and some backhanded deals, but really she was escaping her family." Mike added gravy to his mashed potatoes. "Wall Street was a walk in the park compared to her mom and dad."

"How sad, to have such a beautiful daughter and not appreciate her for who she is." Lily sat back and wiped her mouth.

Yes, very sad. They had no idea of their daughter's self-less acts.

.   .   .

*B*eck ran into the dark house before Mac could get out of his truck. He gathered the leftovers his mom sent home for Noelle, because she was worried her daughter-in-law hadn't eaten since lunch.

Beck met him at the door. "She's not here."

"Her car is here." Which meant the Treloars had returned her to his parents' house to collect it, but she hadn't come in.

"She isn't in the living room or the bedroom."

Mac put the leftovers in the fridge. "Get ready for bed, son. It's late." When Beck started down the hall, Mac added, "Don't forget to brush your teeth after all that pumpkin pie."

Once alone, he checked the counter for a note, but found none. There wasn't a message on the landline. He pulled his cell from his pocket for at least the tenth time since Noelle left with her parents. No message. Where was she?

He turned off the lights and started down the hall, but stopped when he reached the guest room. Noelle lay on top of the comforter, facing away from the door. Beck had zoomed right past without looking since he thought Noelle slept in the master bedroom. Mac continued to Beck's room where he pulled the graphic novel out of his son's hands. "Not tonight. You had a long day and tomorrow will be longer. Lights out."

"I'm too excited to sleep."

"You're going to need all your energy for that new puppy, so try."

Beck rolled onto his side. "Are you worried about Noelle, Dad?"

Mac held up his thumb and index finger, a small measure of space between them. "But I believe she'll be okay."

"How do you know?"

"Because she has us."

Beck grinned. "Yeah, she has us."

Mac kissed his sons forehead. "Go to sleep."

"Sweet dreams, Dad." Beck mimicked Noelle's usual good night as he rolled to his other side.

"Sweet dreams, son." Mac pulled Beck's door shut and debated whether to go to Noelle or to his own room. Noelle won. He stopped in the doorway for a moment and watched her shoulders to see if they were moving in sleep.

"You can come in."

The invitation was whispered so quietly he almost missed it.

He closed the door so Beck wouldn't hear. "Are you okay?"

"Yes."

By her nasally answer, she'd been crying. He felt for the bed in the dark and sat on the edge. "Do you want to talk?"

"I want to apologize for running out on dinner, but my parents would have turned a beautiful holiday into an ugly scene. I'll apologize to your parents tomorrow."

"That's not necessary, Noelle. They understand."

"Still, I want them to know…" She took a shuddering breath. "I want them to know I'm nothing like my parents. I feel like I've been apologizing for them my whole life." Her small laugh sounded strangled with pain. "Funny, they probably say the same about me."

"They were noticeably disappointed in your choice of a husband."

"Don't take offense."

His eyes had adjusted to the dark enough that he saw her glance over her shoulder.

"They would be disappointed in anyone I chose," she mused. "They had their hearts set on a Congressman or the CEO of a Fortune 500. They thought my move here was a silly phase. They believed I'd come to my senses after a few months and return to my job—though I'm sure they really hoped I'd go back to medical school." She turned away.

She wasn't really talking to him, just voicing her thoughts aloud.

"They can't accept the fact that I'm not going back. When you're doing something that isn't right for you, it upsets the balance of life, and I can't go back to that unbalance."

Lying down behind her, he pulled her against his chest and smiled when she snuggled closer. He hated that her parents made her feel less than she was. Why couldn't they accept her as the exceptional person he and Beck knew? Would it soften their hearts to know what she was doing for him, or would the knowledge anger them more? He couldn't imagine living without his parents' support. Yet, that was her life.

"Anyway, they left, eternally disappointed in me. I'm okay with that." She took another shaky breath and turned to face him.

He pushed her hair from her face. "Mom sent a plate home for you. I'll warm it up if you're hungry."

"I'm not." She tipped her face up and kissed the side of his mouth. "Sorry to dump on you. Not very nice of me to do on Thanksgiving."

"I forgive you." He gently combed his fingers through her soft hair. "For what it's worth, I'm glad you didn't become a doctor. I'm glad you ended up in Eden Falls with a café. So is Beck."

"Me, too."

She surprised him with another kiss, one that sent his heart into overdrive.

"About this morning."

"I'm sorry I made you uncomfortable. I just thought—"

She put her index finger against his lips. "You didn't make me feel uncomfortable. Your declaration just surprised me. I thought I was the only one falling in love."

He wanted her to say it again, but decided he'd rather kiss

her. She met him in the middle, two sets of lips crushing together in their eagerness, two hearts beating against each other.

He was the one who pulled back this time. "We should stop. This might lead—"

"Good," she said quietly.

~

*N*oelle parked her car in front of the café since the lot in back hadn't been plowed yet. She paused to watch the huge snowflakes glisten as they floated down under the streetlights. The early morning world was quiet, as if life was at a standstill except for the white falling from the sky.

She'd awakened in a fog of bliss, memories of her and Mac's lovemaking still swirling sweetly through her mind and body. She'd extricated herself from Mac's arms as gently as possible and snuck into the bathroom. Naked, she stared at herself in the mirror. *You are in love, deep and true, for the first time in your life.* Her smile alone would alert anyone to her feelings.

She turned on the shower, remembering Mac's gentle hands followed by his kisses. In his arms, she'd experienced an uninhibited love, a complete uniting of souls. She'd given her whole self to another for the first time in her life. After a night of discovery, how did a person get up and shower for work, as if it was just another ordinary day?

As snowflakes tickled her face, she came back to the present, though the past was such a glorious place to be. Before Mac and Beck came through the door last night, she'd felt very alone. Now she had a purpose. She wasn't just a stand-in. She truly was a wife and a stepmother.

She wondered if her parents were up yet and on their way to the Seattle airport. Last night they'd yelled, bribed, and her mother had even resorted to tears. Through it all, she kept thinking, *It doesn't matter what I do, you will never be satisfied. Maybe if I'd been born a boy...* They seemed happy enough with her brothers.

She was sure her mother got little sleep, she was so angry over her daughter's choices. Her father said she was making mistakes she'd always regret, and unless she gave up her silly little restaurant and marriage to a policeman, he was done. They hadn't given her a chance to explain why she married Mac. They hadn't even given her a chance to introduce Mac and Beck or the Johnsons.

She shivered. None of it mattered anymore. They would be back in Boston soon and she was in Eden Falls to stay.

She headed around the café to the back door and noticed footprints in the snow—two sets, leading to the dumpster, which had been pushed up against the back wall. Another set of prints led to the back door. She smelled the smoke before she noticed the dumpster smoldering. Careful not to step on any of the prints, she hurried over to the dumpster, yanked her glove off, and held her hand out without touching the metal. It was hot.

She pulled her cell phone from her purse and punched in three numbers.

"Nine-one-one. What's your emergency?"

"Gianna, this is Noelle. Can you send someone over to the café?"

"You okay?"

"Yep, but it looks like someone tried to set the back wall on fire."

"Hold on a minute."

Noelle tried to see if the building had been damaged, but there wasn't enough light. She looked skyward and uttered a silent prayer of thanks for the snow, which was still falling wet and steady.

"Noelle? JT is on the way."

"Tell him not to pull into the back parking lot."

She'd barely disconnected the call when a patrol car pulled up to the curb. JT stepped one foot out and grabbed the car radio. "Gianna, wake the fire station. Tell them to bring a truck over to spray a little water on a dumpster fire."

The radio crackled. "You got it."

JT hung up the radio and shut the door. "You okay?"

Noelle nodded. "I've been careful not to disturb any footprints. Two sets go to where the dumpster belongs, the other, to the back door."

Watching his step, JT started taking pictures with a camera he pulled from a pocket.

"Is it okay if I go inside to start the ovens? I can use the front door."

JT walked her around the building and waited until she'd relocked the door. After turning on the ovens, she went out to start coffee. Albert let himself in the front door, a look of concern on his face. "JT said you're okay."

"I am, and so is the café, thanks to all this lovely snow."

He blew out a breath. "I can honestly say I've never been grateful for snow until this morning."

She got up on tiptoes and kissed his cold cheek. "I want to send coffee out for JT and the firefighters, along with some muffins. Can you whip up a batch?"

JT walked in an hour later. "The state fire marshal is on his way from Seattle. He'll have some questions for you."

"I can't tell him much. I saw what you saw." She set a cup of coffee in front of him.

"Thanks." He pulled off his gloves and wrapped his hands around the hot mug. "Why did you park out front this morning?"

"John Kelly plows my lot and I could see he hadn't been by yet. We park out front until he gets the lot cleared."

JT glanced out the front windows, and Noelle noticed a tick in his jaw.

"What is it, JT?"

"I was on patrol last night and those kids floated in under my radar," he said without looking at her.

"You can't be everywhere all the time. Once word gets out, maybe someone will come forward with information."

He turned to look at her. "I've been meaning to talk to you."

"About?"

"How hard I was on you before your wedding."

She waved a dismissive hand. "You were worried about a friend."

"So were you." He lifted his mug and took another sip. "Has Mac heard any more from Owen?"

"No. Beck has to meet with his mom again tomorrow."

"Look, I am sorry. I just didn't feel like marriage was the solution. I'm still not convinced, but Mac seems happy. Really happy."

Noelle tried to bite back the smile on her face, but it was impossible, so she pulled the order pad from her apron pocket. "How about some breakfast on the house?"

~

*M*ac glanced at the screen of the cell phone when it vibrated on the kitchen table before connecting the call. "Hey, JT. After working the night shift, I thought you'd be in bed long before now."

"I'm just leaving the café. Someone tried to burn the place down last night."

"What?" Mac leapt to his feet. "Is Noelle okay?"

Beck ran into the kitchen. "What, Dad?"

"She's fine. Our arsonists pushed the dumpster close to

the back wall and used an accelerant to start it on fire. Luckily, the snow was wet enough to keep it from getting out of hand. The fire scorched the back wall and the soffit a little, but there's no other damage."

Mac sank back into his chair as relief washed over him. Beck sidled up close. "She's okay, son."

"What happened?"

Mac held up a finger to quiet Beck. "Any evidence?"

"None. Phoebe didn't see anything, either. Thanksgiving night and everyone was home with family. Noelle said when word gets out, someone might realize they did see something and come forward."

"Right. Thanks for calling, JT."

Mac disconnected the call and stood, again.

"What happened?" Beck chewed his bottom lip the same way he did when he was around his mother. "Why were you asking about Noelle?"

"Someone started a fire in the parking lot of the café, but the heavy snow put it out."

"Did she come home last night?"

Mac could see the worry around his son's eyes. "She did, and she's okay."

"Can we go see her before we pick up Quincy?"

Mac wrapped his son in a headlock. "Yep."

In town, Mac found a spot in front of The Roasted Bean because the café's parking lot was taped off. From the sidewalk, he could see JT was right. The snow had most likely saved the building.

While Beck rushed inside, Mac paused to survey the square. Shoppers were out hunting Black Friday deals. A town worker was on top of a cherry-picker, brushing snow off the huge pine planted to replace the tree Alex and JT's grandfather planted many years earlier. That tree was set on fire and burned to the ground by their arsonist in August. The old pine had served as Eden Falls Christmas tree since before Mac was born.

Just past the tree stood a group of teenagers dressed in black—spiked hair and long trench coats. Mac recognized them as the kids causing trouble at the Fourth of July Concert on the Square, the same kids JT suspected in their two—now almost three—fires. He glanced toward Town Hall. JT stood on the stairs, hands on his waist, watching. Rance walked out of The Fly Shop and took up the same stance. Alex appeared in the door of Pretty Posies, and Maude Stapleton stepped out of Pages Bookstore. Had JT called the shop owners or had they spotted the Goth group and come out to show a united front? He looked back at the kids. Were they expecting to see another building burned to the ground like the hardware store?

Noelle, wrapped in her coat, came up to his side. "Beck said you were here. What are you doing?"

"Nothing." He wrapped an arm around her, pulling her close. "JT called. Are you okay?"

"Just a little anxious about what could have happened."

He lifted her chin and kissed her sweet mouth. "How are you feeling this morning?"

Her blush was adorable. "I'm okay"

"No regrets?"

"None." Her eyebrows drew together. "How about you?"

"My only regret is that I have to work tonight."

They gazed into each other's eyes for a long moment before she shivered. He turned her toward the café. When he glanced over his shoulder toward the square, the teens were gone.

CHAPTER 16

Noelle spent the rest of the morning anxious and grateful. The fire could have destroyed everything she'd built over the past two years. Her parents would have been delighted in a we-told-you kind of way.

How did one protect against an arsonist? She couldn't be here twenty-four hours a day. None of the business owners could. After the lunch rush she sat at her computer to research security cameras.

"Knock, knock."

She glanced up and smiled at her cousin. "Hey, come in." She indicated the chair in front of her desk. "Want some lunch?"

He sat. "No, I only have a minute. Rowdy told me about the fire. I wanted to check on you."

"Only minor damage." She turned her laptop screen toward him. "Thought a security camera might be a smart idea."

He smiled. "Rowdy is researching the same thing for the bar and grill."

She slouched back in her chair. "I would have thought he'd already have one."

"He said there's never been a need." Mike pulled off his beanie and ruffled his hair. "About last night. Your parents showed up just as I was—"

Noelle held up her hand. "Not your fault."

"I didn't know what—"

"I know how they are, Mike." She leaned her forearms on her desk. "They're gone—probably never coming back—furious at their failure daughter and disappointed, once again, that I won't bend to their way of thinking. Dad said it was the Uncle Jeremiah in me." She shrugged. "Maybe it is. Unfortunately for them, it's the part of me I like best."

After Mike left, Noelle went out front to help with the second wave of shoppers piling in for a late lunch. At four, the door opened and Cheryl walked in. She spotted Noelle at the counter and slid onto a stool.

Noelle pulled her order pad from her apron pocket. "I'm surprised to see you here."

"A girl's got to eat."

Noelle leaned a hip against the counter. "Are you staying in Eden Falls?"

"Not that it's any of your business, but yes." She waved her hand around. "This is exactly why I didn't want to stay married to Mac. I'd be working as a waitress in a place like this."

The verbal slap across the face made Noelle smile. If Cheryl felt the need to sling mud, Noelle would rather it be at her than Mac or Beck.

Cheryl slumped. "Sorry. That wasn't nice."

Noelle was surprised at the admission.

"I'm just nervous about seeing Beck again. I wish Simon was here, but he couldn't get away." Cheryl slipped her coat off and laid it on the empty stool next to her. "He doesn't agree with what I'm doing."

"No?" The information and the fact that Cheryl shared it surprised Noelle a second time. She was a fountain of information. Noelle remembered she'd meant to talk to Owen about the boarding school Cheryl mentioned on her last visit to the café.

Cheryl shook her head. "He thinks I should leave Beck where he is."

Nice to know.

Cheryl folded her hands on the counter in front of her. "He doesn't understand the unfulfilled need I feel inside."

Get a hamster.

"Simon's boys are too old to be mothered. They don't really like me anyway. The house is full of tension when they're home."

And you want to place Beck in that environment? All good info, Cheryl. Thanks for sharing. "Do you work?"

"I'm a housewife." She held up a hand. "I know what you're thinking. I have a rich husband, we have housekeepers and such, but there's still a lot to do."

Noelle was trying to find a soft spot for Cheryl, but the woman made it impossible. "I'm not passing judgment."

Cheryl picked up a menu. "You and Mac look happy together."

Noelle smiled while scenes from last night flitted through her mind. "We are."

"And Beck seems to really like you."

"I love Beck. Mac has done a fabulous job of raising him."

"I agree. He has done a fabulous job, but I think I can do a good job, too."

"You forgot his birthday."

Cheryl frowned before a panicked expression settled over her facial features. "When?"

When? Cheryl couldn't remember the day she gave birth to her only child? *Nope. Still no soft spot.* "Two weeks ago today."

Cheryl lowered her head to her hands. "Did he notice?"

"Of course he noticed! He was terribly hurt."

Cheryl set her jaw in what Noelle interpreted as determination, an expression she'd seen in Owen's office during both visits with her son. It was the expression of someone out to prove something. It stirred curiosity.

"Well, if he comes to live in California, I won't forget."

"What if he doesn't want to go to California?"

"Look, I know I've made some major mistakes, but my life has changed. I have the financial stability I didn't have nine years ago."

"Beck is ten." *And it takes more than financial stability to be a mother.*

"Quit throwing my mistakes in my face."

"I'm not doing it to hurt you"—*or maybe I am*—"but to remind you of things you should already know. If you come in tomorrow saying, 'happy ninth birthday'—well, that's just one step up from forgetting." Noelle pulled a pencil from her ponytail and tapped it against an order pad. "Mind if I ask a question?"

"Can I stop you?"

"I'm curious why you didn't tell Mac you were pregnant before you had Beck?"

Cheryl straightened her back, determination front and center again. "Because I knew what he'd do. Love me or not, he would have made me stay, because that's the kind of man he is." She shook her head. "I wasn't ready to settle down and be a wife and mother."

But now you are.

"Can I ask you a question?"

Noelle nodded.

"Why won't Beck open up to me?"

"Because you don't listen." When Cheryl opened her mouth, Noelle held up a hand to stop her—*case in point*. "You ask a question, he answers, then you start talking about yourself. You don't listen to his answers and dig for more info. You're more interested in telling him your stories than hearing about his. Ask him what he likes…and then *listen*."

"I can do that."

We'll see. Noelle held up the order pad. "What can I get you?"

"What's good?"

"Everything."

Cheryl glanced up. "I should probably have a salad."

"The burgers are great. I recommend The Eden if you like Swiss cheese and mushrooms."

Cheryl set the menu down. "I can't remember the last time I ate a hamburger."

"If it was longer than a week ago, it's time to broaden your horizons."

Cheryl pursed her lips and then nodded. When Noelle turned away, Cheryl added. "With fries."

Noelle went to the kitchen with an inkling of a soft spot. Everyone makes mistakes. Some couldn't be recovered from. Cheryl leaving Beck might be one of those, but maybe there was a solution. If she moved into the master bedroom—the thought made her knees weak—Mac could offer the guest room to Simon and Cheryl for an occasional visit. That might solve everyone's problem, save a day in court, and relieve a lot of heartache.

She stopped at Cheryl's side several times while the woman ate most of her hamburger and did a nice number on her fries. Their conversation didn't touch the subject of custody again and Noelle didn't ask any more "why" questions.

When Cheryl asked where she could go to get her nails done. Noelle looked down at her own un-manicured hands. "I have no idea. You can try Dahlia's Salon just across the square."

She leaned toward Cheryl, because she just had to know. "Are your eyelashes real?"

Cheryl batted them for show. "Nope. You can have a set just like them for about twenty dollars, though mine cost much more."

Of course. Why did Cheryl feel the need to add that last part? Again, Noelle wondered about her past.

When it was time for a ticket, Noelle waved Cheryl's money away. "It's on the house."

"I can't let you—"

"Let it go, Cheryl. We'll see you tomorrow."

*W*hen she walked through the back door, she was greeted by a black, brown, and white bundle of fur that wiggled so hard she was afraid its tail would fall off his body. "Hi, you."

"Isn't he cute," Beck said, sliding into the kitchen in stocking feet.

Noelle squatted down and picked up the frolicking puppy. "He is adorable. Welcome home, Quincy."

"Do you like him?"

"I love him." She laughed when the puppy licked her chin. "My shoes are off-limits, buddy. No chewing."

"He likes playing with the chew toys we bought."

She ran her fingers through Beck's hair. "Good."

"Oh, guess what?"

She tried to match Beck's enthusiasm with wide eyes. "What?"

"I get to ride on Patsy's Pastries float in the Christmas parade tomorrow night."

"That's fantastic, Beck. Did Patsy ask you?"

"Yep. She talked to Dad today."

"I can't wait to wave when you go by." She straightened when Mac walked into the kitchen.

"I see you've met our newest family member."

"I have." She tipped her face up for his kiss, which was more than the gentle peck they usually shared when Beck was watching. "Hello."

He grinned. "Hi, yourself."

"Ewww," Beck said on cue.

She turned the squiggling puppy for inspection. "So what breed of dog is Quincy?"

"Believe it or not, he's a Bernedoodle."

"A what?" she asked laughing.

"A Bernese mountain dog-poodle mix," Mac said, rubbing the puppy's head.

Noelle lifted a brow, "How big is Quincy supposed to get?"

"Anywhere from sixty to one-hundred-twenty pounds. And yes, I knew that before I agreed to take Quincy in," Mac said with a laugh.

*A*fter dinner, when Beck was tucked into bed and Quincy had settled down for the night, Noelle found Mac at the kitchen table, a warm smile on his face, his gaze as intimate as a kiss. She started to pull out a chair to join him, but he took her by the arm and settled her on his lap. "Did your insurance agent come by the café today?"

"Yes. She assessed the damage and will get back with me

before the end of next week. Has JT said anything about the suspects?"

He wrapped his arms around her and she settled back, thinking how nice it was to be held. Her parents weren't big on showing affection. "JT is probably going to up our hours until we can catch whoever's doing this."

She smoothed the pad of her thumb over an errant eyebrow hair. "The fire marshal came in and questioned me before lunch. I couldn't tell him much."

"Like JT said, whoever is doing this will mess up eventually."

"I'm going to have a cup of tea. Would you like something?"

"No thanks." When she tried to scoot off his lap, he didn't let go for a half second, which made her smile. She could feel his eyes on her as she prepared her tea and a delicious tingle snuck up her spine.

"How was the rest of your day?"

"Interesting." She poured hot water into a mug, carried it and a tea bag to the table, and sat across from him. "Cheryl came in."

The smile that had lingered on his face since she'd come home fell away. "What did she want?"

"Nothing. Well, a hamburger."

"You're smiling."

"I might have come up with a solution to this whole custody mess. What if you offered to let Cheryl and Simon stay here a few times a year to visit with Beck?"

Mac's chuckle held no humor. "Are you crazy?"

Mac's comment hurt, but Noelle tried to joke it away by crossing her eyes. "I thought we'd already established that."

"My ex-wife and her husband are not staying here."

She held up a hand. "Hear me out. After talking to her, I don't think Cheryl's fight is about taking Beck to California, as much as it is about proving something to her husband. "

Mac frowned. "She talks to you for a few minutes and you side with her?"

"I'm not siding with her, I just thought if we offered a solution, she might drop the—"

"We? You have nothing at stake here, Noelle."

His comment hit her like a slap across the face. Nothing at stake? Did he really believe that?

"I hope you didn't agree to anything. You didn't tell her—"

"I didn't tell her anything." She stood up and slid her chair back into place. "I just thought if you let her stay with you and Beck a few times a year, it might save you both a lot of heartache. Maybe she would drop the case all together, which could possibly save you from having the judge rule against you."

"You believe the judge will rule against me?"

"No, but there is no guarantee. I thought if Cheryl—"

"You thought wrong."

She picked up her untouched tea and placed it in the sink. At the door to the hall she turned. "Cheryl isn't a bad person, Mac. She made a horrible mistake and she's been paying for it a long time. She just wants to see her son. If you stop long enough to think of someone besides yourself and what you want, you'll realize it might be in Beck's best interest to get to know his mom."

Mac stood and slammed his chair under the table. "Stay out of this, Noelle."

"I will." She walked into the guest room and shut the door.

⌐∿

*N*oelle had no right to discuss the situation with Cheryl! She had no right to make Cheryl think this could work in her favor!

Mac tossed and turned and fumed most of the night. When she came into his room at four to get ready for work, he was awake, facing away from the door, still furious that she'd turned on him.

After she left the house, he got up to let Quincy out, but could tell by the wet leash Noelle had already done so, which made him even more angry. She'd inserted herself into their lives and taken over things he or Beck should be doing. They'd been surviving just fine without a woman cooking dinner or washing their clothes. Sure, the caramel corn was great, but it couldn't be that hard to make.

Beck woke up excited to show Grams his puppy, so they jumped in the truck and went to his mom's for breakfast. After Beck left the house to walk Quincy, Lily turned to him. "What's got you in such a snit? Are you worried about seeing Cheryl today?"

Mac was happy to unload his conversation with Noelle on his mom.

She blinked a couple of times like she hadn't understood a thing he said. Then stood and picked up her plate. "You're wrong, Mac. You involved Noelle when you married her. I can't believe you told her she didn't have a stake in this. She gave up her single life for you. She's been by Beck's side since the day she said 'I do'." You should have been thanking her for coming up with a solution that might keep Beck with you and satisfy Cheryl at the same time."

"She might have made things worse, Mom."

His mom turned with a hand on her hip. "How? Did she talk this plan over with Cheryl?"

"I don't think so."

"Then how did she make anything worse? If anything, she made a friend. If Cheryl believes she has an ally, she might be willing to compromise."

Mac threw up his hands. "Great, my wife and my ex-wife are allies, and my mom is on their side. That's just what I need in my life."

Lily stalked over to the table shaking a spoon at him. "This isn't just about you, Macoy Johnson. Stop thinking only of yourself and start putting others first."

Mac stood so fast his chair flipped backward and hit the floor with a *crack*. "What are you talking about? I've been thinking of what's best for Beck his whole life."

"Yes, son, you have…until now. Now you are the one who's front and center in your thoughts and it's going to ruin your relationship with Noelle."

"I'm worried sick about my son ending up in California and you're concerned about my relationship with Noelle?"

"I'm saying that you need to stop being so closed-minded. I doubt Cheryl will get full or even partial custody, but she may get some holidays and summers. If you invite her to stay with you a few times a year, she might drop this whole custody mess and take you up on the offer. I'm also telling you to apologize to Noelle or you'll lose a wonderful woman who's trying to help you."

"I'm going to lose her anyway. Remember, we're only married until this custody mess is over."

"But you don't have to be."

Mac shook his head as he righted his chair. "Don't start, Mom. A matchmaker you are not."

"I don't have to be a matchmaker. You're already married to her. Beck loves her. Open your eyes, son. Quit looking at what you could lose and grab on to what you have. Noelle is right in front of you. This is the second time she's come up with a possible solution. The first was when she offered to marry you and become a stepmother to your son. This isn't just about you. She is involved."

Mac grabbed his coat when Beck bounded into the house followed by a wet puppy. "We have to go."

"Are we picking up Noelle?"

"Not this time. Get a towel out of Grams's laundry room and dry Quincy off before he makes a mess." He turned to his mom, another traitor. "Are you sure you don't mind watching Quincy for an hour?"

"I don't mind. I'll dry him off, Beck."

"Is Noelle going to be there? Why aren't we picking her up?" Beck asked, panic in his voice.

His mom sent Mac a glare as she walked over to Beck and zipped his coat higher. "Noelle will be there in spirit, sweetheart. Remember not all things are black and white."

"Great. That's going to make a lot of sense to a ten-year-old."

"I wasn't telling Beck. I was telling you." She kissed Beck's cheek. "There will be warm cookies when you get back."

Once they got in the truck, Beck turned to him. "Why isn't Noelle coming, Dad?"

"She has to work."

"But she said she'd be there."

"Enough. I'll be with you."

He pulled into the parking lot of Owen's office. Noelle's car was in front of the Victorian. Beck jumped out of the truck and ran for the door before Mac could get his seatbelt off. When he got inside, Beck was hugging Noelle. Cheryl and her attorney watched from across the room.

"Dad said you weren't coming."

Noelle smiled at Beck. "Well, I promised you I'd be here, so I am. Why don't you take off your coat and hang it by the door?"

Owen came into the reception area. "If everyone is here, come on back."

They all trooped into the same room they'd been using for every meeting. Beck hung onto Noelle's hand, which only angered Mac more. Owen had a fire burning. The room was a warm and cozy contrast to the cold day outside which matched Noelle's chilly reception.

His mom was wrong about the situation, but maybe it wasn't as bad as he made it out to be. He knew Noelle thought she was helping, but he had no intention of offering Cheryl and her husband a place to sleep every month. They could afford to stay in a hotel.

Cheryl sat on the sofa opposite them, looking contrite. "I'm sorry I forgot your birthday, Beck. Noelle reminded me."

Beck looked down at the hem of his shirt as he always did when his mom spoke to him and mumbled something unintelligible.

"Beck, why don't you tell your mom what you did for your birthday party," Noelle said.

Beck glanced at her and then at his mom.

Cheryl leaned forward. "I'd love to hear about it."

"We went bowling."

Cheryl's eyes lit. "I used to love to bowl. I remember—" She stopped when Noelle cleared her throat. "Did you have a lot of friends at your party?"

Mac looked from one woman to the other, wondering what had just happened.

Beck started talking about his party.

"Why don't you tell your mom about Quincy?" Noelle said when the party conversation dwindled.

"I got a dog yesterday. His name is Quincy."

Cheryl clapped her hands. "I love dogs. Remember, I told you we have—"

Noelle coughed, and Cheryl shifted on the sofa. "What kind of dog is Quincy?"

Beck looked at him. *Finally. My son remembers he has a dad.* "He's a Bernese-poodle mix."

"What color is he?"

Mac was surprised Cheryl asked two questions in a row. Noelle nodded at her. *What is she doing?*

"He's black and brown and white. And he likes to chew on the toys we bought, huh, Noelle?"

"Yes." Noelle touched Beck's arm. "Beck is getting ready for a Christmas program at school."

Cheryl glanced at Noelle as if asking permission or seeking approval. "What are you doing in the program?"

"We're singing songs."

"Do you have to wear a costume?"

Beck wrinkled his nose. "Reindeer antlers."

"That sounds like fun." Cheryl looked at Noelle again and Noelle smiled at her.

"We get to jingle bells that Jacob's mom is sewing on leather straps."

Cheryl laughed. "I'd like to see that."

Beck glanced at Noelle and then Mac. *I'm second fiddle to my own kid.*

"I guess you could come."

Noelle turned to him. Every muscle in his body tightened when he realized what was coming. "If you're going to be in town on the Wednesday before Christmas, you'd be welcome to come to the school for Beck's performance."

Cheryl's eyes flooded with tears. What could he do but nod. Noelle had taken his freedom of choice away. She'd stripped him of his parenthood in front of his ex-wife. She'd invited Cheryl without discussing it with him first. And she had no right. Soon Cheryl would think she could come in and take Beck whenever she wanted.

He stood and looked at Owen for help as the visit ground on. Owen offered a smile. He wanted to shout, *What are you smiling about? This whole visit is a disaster. Noelle is ruining everything!*

When Cheryl finally stood to leave, she asked Beck if she could hug him. He looked at Noelle. Again. She nodded and moved aside. Cheryl didn't make a big deal of it, just gave him a simple squeeze, and thanked Noelle rather than him.

After Cheryl and her attorney left, Owen rubbed his hands together. "That went well. Really well. You catch more bees with—"

"Don't you ever speak for me again," Mac said, turning on Noelle. "You had no right to invite Cheryl to Beck's—"

"Mac," Owen said reaching for his arm and glancing at Beck. "Not here. Not now."

Beck stepped in front of Noelle. "It's okay, Dad. If Noelle is there, I don't care if my mom comes."

Mac felt as if his blood would boil right out of his pores. "Beck, go in the kitchen."

"Dad—"

"Go In The Kitchen."

Owen took Beck by the shoulders and led him toward the door. "I think I have some lemonade in the fridge."

Mac never took his eyes off Noelle's. She defiantly stared him down. Once the door was shut he said, "You had no right to invite—"

"I didn't invite her, Mac. Beck did."

"But you made it worse."

"Cheryl made some terrible mistakes, but she's trying to correct them." She touched his arm and he shook her hand off. "I understand—"

"No, you don't. You can't understand because you're not a parent. You're a pretend wife and mother. That's all."

Tears sprang to her eyes. He turned away.

"I know you don't want to lose Beck, but it's not right to keep him from his mother, either. Let him try and salvage a bit of a relationship with her."

"Because you have such a good relationship with yours?" He cringed as soon as the words escaped his mouth, but he couldn't seem to stop them.

Hurt contorted her mouth for a moment. She swallowed. "Mac—"

"You should leave."

He stalked over to the window overlooking the garden, but heard her close the door softly behind her when she left the room.

CHAPTER 17

Mac paced back and forth, furious with the way the day had turned out, furious Noelle had stepped in when she should have kept quiet, and furious he'd lost his temper in front of Beck.

Noelle's tears had affected him more than he liked to admit. He'd hit below the belt twice, which she didn't deserve after all she'd done to help him. Still, she shouldn't have interfered.

Owen opened the door. "I saw Noelle leave. Have you cooled down a little?"

"Yeah." Mac combed the fingers of both hands through his hair. "I'm sorry. This whole custody thing's made me crazy."

"It might not seem like it, but Noelle did a good thing today. She extended an olive branch that might make Cheryl back down a bit."

"Or not. You said yourself, you never know how these things will turn out." Mac turned back to the window. "The waiting, not knowing—I just want it to be over."

"We have a court date a week from Monday. I was going

to tell you earlier, but your ex-wife and her attorney arrived first. You and Noelle should have Beck at the courthouse a bit early that day. I think the judge will want to talk to him first. Call and make an appointment with Jolie, I'll walk Beck through some of the questions the judge might ask."

"I don't want Beck answering questions. He shouldn't be put into the middle of this."

"I would feel the same if it were either one of my sons, but Beck's opinion will make a difference with the judge. He'll want to know how Beck feels about going to California, and about his mother."

I know that! I still don't want Beck to have to go through this.

He was furious with Cheryl for putting them in this situation and at himself for not making sure there was some addition in their divorce decree that would have prevented this. "After this is over, I want to make sure something similar won't happen again."

"Sadly, there is no guarantee, Mac. We can put an inclusion in the documentation, but there's just no sure guarantee."

Beck appeared at the door. "Where's Noelle?"

"She had to go back to work."

"You yelled at her."

Can this day get any worse? Mac held out his hand to his son, who ignored it. "I shouldn't have yelled. I was upset. Sorry for getting angry in front of you, buddy."

"You need to say you're sorry."

Mac exhaled, depleted of all energy. "Yes, I do. I will."

～

*N*oelle left Owen's office and drove to the café. She let herself in the back door as Gertie was entering the kitchen.

"What are you doing here? You're supposed to have the rest of the day off."

"I'll work the evening shift. We won't have any customers once the parade gets under way, so I'll close early. You and Albert go enjoy the festivities."

She went into her office and called her mother-in-law. "Hi, Lily, it's Noelle."

"Hi, honey. How'd the meeting go?"

"Owen thinks it went very well. Listen," she said before Lily had time to ask any more questions. "Something has come up and I have to close the café. Can you watch Beck until I get off? I'm closing once the parade starts, so I won't be late."

"Of course. Are you okay?"

She felt the sting of tears, Mac's hurtful words still ricocheting around the walls of her heart. "I'm fine. I'll see you later." She hung up the phone, giving Lily no time to respond.

She'd planned to watch the parade with Mac, and the tree lighting with both men. Now she'd watch alone. Yes, she was cutting off her nose to spite her face, but Mac's comments about her relationship with her mother cut deep, leaving a huge chasm in her chest. He took aim, fired, and hit her right where it would hurt the worst.

He wanted her to stay out of it, said she didn't have a stake in the matter. *Well, Macoy Johnson, you can deal with this mess yourself.*

She tied an apron around her middle and went out to handle the dinner rush.

The crowd was in a hurry to finish before the parade started. She just hoped the place cleared enough that she could step outside and wave to Beck. She wondered how Mac had explained her absence to his son and Owen. Then shook her head. It really didn't matter. An event she'd been looking forward to was ruined because Mac was angry and pigheaded.

His comments hurt, but he was also correct to question her. What right did she have to stick her nose into Beck and Cheryl's business when she couldn't hold a civil conversation with her own mother? None. She should have stayed out of the situation. Naively, she believed she'd come up with the perfect solution for everyone.

When she heard the high school band coming around the square playing "Jingle Bells", the café was empty of customers. Grabbing her coat and twisting the open sign to closed, she hurried outside and locked the door. She found a space at the curb and stood with hands jammed in her pockets against the cold night air, careful not to look around for Mac. She didn't want to see him or speak to him. As the band passed, Lily appeared next to her.

"I saw you from the library steps and decided you have a better view. Rance stayed over there with our impossible son." At Noelle's glance, she nodded. "Yes, he told me what was going on, and, for what it's worth, I think he's wrong. Your idea could solve this custody battle in minutes. I told him so."

Noelle wished Lily's statement made her feel better. Instead, she started questioning herself again. As much as she loved Beck, she didn't have nearly as much at stake as Mac did. She wasn't a parent. As Mac said, she was a pretend wife and a pretend mother. She could sympathize with Mac's pain, but never really know the agony of losing a child. He was wrong to say she had nothing to lose, though, because she did. He and Beck had become a huge part of her world and she couldn't imagine being without them. "I'm sure that didn't go over well."

Lily grinned. "Nope, it didn't. I know he's worried about losing Beck, but he's also holding onto a grudge he needs to let go of. At first I was scared to death we'd lose Beck, but now…" She shook her head. "No judge in his right mind would give Cheryl custody. Still, it would be better if Mac worked with her rather than taking this to court, where Beck will have to talk to a judge. If he's forced to say he doesn't want to live with Cheryl, that will hurt her unnecessarily."

Noelle agreed with Lily, but to say anything against Mac —her husband—felt wrong, so she remained quiet.

Before Mac and Beck arrived today, Owen told her a court date was set. He said the judge would want to talk to Beck. He would ask Beck questions that would cut Cheryl's heart to ribbons. And there was no need.

Now that she and Mac had consummated their marriage, what would happen? She'd hoped they'd go on as a family, but after today… Did she really want to stay married after the things Mac said to her? Would he want to?

Her thoughts turned ugly. Had he told her he loved her just to get her into his bed? He'd never seemed like that kind of man, but what did she really know about Mac?

Lily pointed a gloved finger. "Look! Here comes Beck."

She and Lily waved wildly when Beck passed by on a float advertising sweets from Patsy's Pastries.

"I love to see that smile."

Noelle nodded as a cloak of sadness settled over her. She put her arm around Lily's shoulder and gave her a quick hug. "I have to get back inside."

"Surely you aren't keeping the café open tonight."

"No, we closed right after dinner, but I have to finish cleanup. Since Mac is on duty, I'll be by to pick up Beck as soon as I'm finished."

The front of the café was clean by the time the parade was over, so she bundled up again to join the crowd around the huge decorated pine in the square.

The new tree wasn't as tall as the original, but was as

much a part of Eden Falls as any transplant. She felt a kinship with the tree and looked out at it every time she got a chance.

Alex, in her role as mayor, gave a short have-a-great-holiday-season, love-thy-neighbor speech, then flipped the switch on the lights. The tree stood proud in its coat of many colors. She heard Beck calling her name before she spotted him sitting on his dad's shoulders. She waved. Her and Mac's gazes caught and held for a long, movie-drama moment before she turned and went back inside the café.

⁓

*M*ac watched Noelle go into the café alone. He'd tried unsuccessfully to keep his eyes on the tree lighting, but they strayed toward her repeatedly. Her facial expressions had remained neutral while talking with his mom. Just now, her smile was subdued, which was so unlike her.

His anger shrank, leaving him feeling petty. He might not agree with inviting Cheryl to Beck's Christmas performance, but Noelle was right. Beck had extended the initial invitation, yet he'd yelled at Noelle. He didn't like the idea of Cheryl visiting, but since being told of the court date, he'd begun to feel jittery. Maybe an invitation to Cheryl would soften her resolve.

He didn't agree with Noelle on every point, but she had his heart. She made his son happy. She'd turned their house into a home. He owed her more than he could ever repay.

Love had crept up on him, like the soft snow that piled up one inch at a time. He'd been unsuspecting, but now that it was here, it fit well and felt right. He'd never expected to come out of this loving Noelle, and he knew deep down she wouldn't have let him make love to her if she didn't feel the same way.

He spent a long, lonely night patrolling their small town with thoughts of Noelle crowding his mind. His shame over the things he said to her grew by the hour. He drove past the house, hoping to see a light. He wanted to go in and apologize, beg her to forgive him for the awful things he'd spouted in anger. He wasn't too proud to admit he was wrong. He wanted to tell her he loved her. Then show her.

～

*M*ac must have been held up at work, because he still wasn't home when Noelle and Beck left for church. Beck had to be there early to practice for a program the children were performing on Christmas Eve. When they pulled into the driveway after the service, Mac's truck was in the garage.

"Let's be real quiet so your dad can sleep."

"What can we do that's quiet?"

Noelle had planned to pull out Christmas decorations, but didn't know where Mac kept them, and searching might make too much noise. "I know. Let's make gingerbread men."

"Cool. I've never done that before."

"Ha," she said tweaking his nose. "We finally found something fun I've done that you haven't."

She loved his laughter that followed.

After a joyful greeting from Quincy, she sent Beck to change out of his church clothes while she tied an apron around her waist.

Luckily, she'd planned ahead. Thinking Beck might like to make gingerbread men, she bought the ingredients the last time she was at the grocery store. She got everything out and set it on the counter.

Over the short course of her and Mac's marriage, Beck had shown a real interest in the kitchen. She loved the excitement in his eyes as she taught him to measure ingredients and mix things together.

They did have to stop frequently to show Quincy love. He didn't like being left out.

While the first batch of gingerbread men baked, she fixed grilled cheese sandwiches and tomato soup, a perfect lunch for a chilly winter afternoon.

"Are you mad at Dad?"

Noelle looked at Beck as he took a second bite from his sandwich without quite meeting her eyes. He'd been subdued during church and she felt guilty for adding to his apprehension. Of course, he'd be curious about what happened in Owen's office after he'd been escorted to the kitchen. "No, I'm not mad." *Just hurt by the wounding remarks hurled in a tense moment.*

"Is he mad at you?"

An inner voice told her to tread carefully. "He's angry at the situation."

He glanced at her, then back at his sandwich. "Because I said my mom could come to the school program?"

"He's angry because he's scared. I know it doesn't make much sense." She stood, walked around the table, and squatted next to his chair. His brown eyes so much like his father's looked at her in question. "He loves you so much and—"

"He's afraid my mom will take me away."

How to answer? She didn't want to scare him or add more anxiety. "He wants what's best for you."

"I told him to say he's sorry to you for yelling."

Sweet boy. "Don't worry about us. Everything will work out the way it's supposed to."

She wasn't sure she believed that. She thought she'd found her purpose. Now, she wasn't so sure. She ran a hand over Beck's back. "Everything will be okay."

The timer buzzed and she straightened. "When we're finished decorating these cookies, we'll wrap some up to take to Gram and Gramps' house."

Beck smiled. "I'm going to frost one with a bald head to look like Gramps."

"We can put a blue apron on one to match your Grams's."

"Yeah!"

After lunch, she showed Beck how to mix food coloring into frosting. With no pastry bags to pipe frosting, she improvised by cutting the corner out of plastic sandwich bags.

They had a great time frosting the cookies with different personalities. Beck laughed more than she'd seen since she moved in with them.

Noelle lost all track of time while they baked and decorated and laughed, until Mac walked in, freshly showered, dressed in jeans and a blue oxford shirt. His handsomeness took her breath away.

Beck hopped off the stool to greet his dad. "Look what we've been making."

"I see. The fabulous smells coming down the hall woke me up." Mac pulled Beck in for their usual man hug.

Noelle loved watching them together, so in sync with each other. If Cheryl could see the way Beck's eyes lit up when Mac walked into the room, she might not be so adamant about separating them. Again, her idea struck as a good solution, but the decision was Mac's. She was determined to stay out of it as Mac had requested.

Mac looked over their gingerbread men. "Wow, you two have been busy."

"We had to finish before going to Grams and Gramps's for dinner. See this one? Who do you think it looks like?"

Mac laughed. "With glasses and a fringe of white hair, I'd say it looks like Gramps. Good job."

"Noelle helped me."

Mac finally looked directly at her. "That's great."

"Noelle said we could decorate our house on Tuesday after I get out of school. Can you get the Christmas decorations out?"

"I'll pull the boxes down from the attic tomorrow. After we decorate, we can celebrate with dinner out," he added without taking his gaze from hers.

"Can we go to Pablo's? We haven't been there in a long time."

Mac wrapped his hand around the back of Beck's neck. "That sounds good. We'll go to Pablo's."

Beck picked Quincy up. The puppy had been dancing around their feet for attention. "I'm going to take Quincy for a walk."

After the back door closed, Noelle said, "I hope we weren't making too much noise."

"I didn't hear a thing. It was the tantalizing smells." He picked up one of the gingerbread men. "Are these up for grabs?"

"They are." She gathered dirty mixing bowls and carried them to the sink. "Beck and I had grilled cheese and soup for lunch. There is some soup left. Would you like a sandwich to go with it?"

"No. I'll just warm up the soup."

Noelle pulled the leftover container from the fridge and popped it into the microwave. "Did you have a long night?"

"A long morning. An eighteen-wheeler ran off the road and highway patrol was busy with another accident, so I stuck around to help."

He turned her toward him with hands on her waist. Several emotions crossed his face before he settled her against him. "I'm sorry about yesterday. I'm sorry I yelled and I'm sorry for the terrible things I said. You've done more for Beck than I can ever repay. You didn't deserve my anger. Cheryl and this custody mess are driving me crazy."

Could she let go of the hurtful things he'd thrown at her yesterday?

"Please, forgive me."

His remorseful expression was genuine. She nodded. "I'm sorry, too. I can only try to imagine what you're going through. You were right, I'm not a mom."

"I shouldn't have said that." He rested his forehead against hers. "You've been more of a mother than Beck's biological one."

The comment made her heart glad. She's just spent three hours making cookies with Beck and had the time of her life. Her own mother hadn't done things like this with her. They'd never created lasting memories like she hoped this would be for Beck. "Owen told me about the court date."

"Can you be there?"

She raised her brows. "Are you sure you want me there?"

"Owen thinks you should be."

She pulled back slightly. "That's not what I asked."

"Yes. I'd like for you to be there."

As long as I don't say anything.

"And so would Beck." He tugged her close again. "Can we kiss and make up?"

His mouth tasted of gingerbread and frosting. The kiss quickly changed from soft and sweet to intense. Breathlessly, she pulled back a second time when the microwave buzzer sounded.

He nodded toward the hall leading to the bedroom. She glanced at the clock on the stove and shook her head. "Beck is just outside and we have to be at your parents' house in thirty minutes."

"I'll call and tell them we can't make it."

"Absolutely not. You know your mom has already started

cooking, and Beck wants to take a few gingerbread men over to show them."

He huffed out an exaggerated sigh. "Later, then."

His hungry looks muddled her insides and left them buzzing with anticipation. How had she gotten here, to this lovely place? Just six weeks earlier she was living with her cousin. Now she had a family, complete with dog. She was experiencing sensations she'd never imagined.

The court date scared her. What would happen to them after next week? And the week after that?

She removed the soup from the microwave and set it on the table. "Sit and eat."

❧

*T*o Mac's disappointment, they returned home too early to put Beck to bed. Adding to his frustration, Beck, with a wiggling Quincy, plopped down between them on the sofa while they watched an hour-long Christmas special.

He hadn't felt this tense since he was sixteen, at the public pool watching Marianne Summers slip off her shorts and T-shirt to reveal a very tiny bikini. The memory made him even more irritated, an emotion that was becoming too familiar in one way or another.

Noelle went to the kitchen to fill Beck's request for popcorn. Mac followed like a puppy looking for affection. "If you make popcorn, he'll stay up later."

She looked over her shoulder and smiled indulgently, the way people did when placating a kid. "He knows it's a school night. He'll go to bed as soon as the show is over."

He came up behind her and bit her neck gently. She shivered in his arms. "Stop."

"I haven't told you that I love you today."

She turned and her expression softened into a sweet smile. "I love you, too, Mac."

His chest tightened. "Say it again."

"I. Love. You."

The rest of their hour moved as slow as a hundred-year-old turtle crossing a two lane road. He couldn't get Beck tucked into bed fast enough, and then had to take extra minutes to settle Quincy down. Would this day never end?

~

*N*oelle lay in her husband's arms, listening while his heartbeat settled to normal under her ear. He ran his fingers over her hip as he pulled the sheet and blanket over them, the touch triggering goose bumps all over her heated skin.

I'm happy. Happier than I ever imagined possible. She never thought of herself as unhappy, but what she felt now was so huge, it was indefinable. Jubilant, exuberant, blissful —no word was big enough to describe the emotions flowing through her.

She turned her face up to look at Mac. "Tell me about when you were young. What were you like?"

He chuckled, the sound rumbling though his chest. "I was awful, in trouble all the time."

"I don't believe that. Your dad wouldn't have allowed it."

He snuggled her closer. "I grew up running through the woods and fishing in the river. My friends and I had Eden Falls as our backyard. On summer days, we left early on some adventure and usually didn't return until after dark. That was back in the days when parents didn't have to worry too much about their kids."

"Sounds wonderful." *To run wild and play for hours— what would that have been like?*

"I only hope Beck has the same chance."

She ran her hand over his chest. "He will."

"I need a little of your optimism."

"Think positive thoughts, Mac. You have to believe things will work out the way they're supposed to."

"I want to believe things will work out in my favor."

"I don't think a judge will give custody to a mother who abandoned her son at birth. The situation would be different if she'd tried to stay in touch or had visited him. A judge won't send a boy who doesn't know his mother off to live with her in California. Worst case scenario, Beck has to go to California for a holiday or two a year."

"That still sounds pretty bad, considering Beck doesn't want to go at all." Mac lifted her chin and kissed her. "I'm sorry, again, about yesterday."

"Me, too. It's in the past. Let's forget it happened."

He raised above her on an elbow, a smile curving his mouth at the corners. "I know how we can do that."

~

*N*oelle got to the café even earlier than usual. She gave herself an hour to get Christmas decorations up. Normally she would have done it yesterday, but making cookies with Beck was more important.

She pulled the big box from the storage room, stifling a yawn. Mac kept her up most of the night, not that she minded a bit. Their relationship cemented itself last night and she was still floating on the river of Deliriously Happy.

She dragged the box to the front of the café, opened the lid, and pulled out a large, red, distressed wooden ornament. She'd invested in the shabby chic decorations her first Christmas in Eden Falls and fell in love with them more every year. They lent a warm and cozy feel to the otherwise retro interior of her place.

After feeding a few quarters into the jukebox, she strung lights in all the windows and around the door. She topped the windowsills with greenery and her distressed ornaments. Boughs of green with red berries capped the jukebox as music poured from the speakers. She placed a sleigh filled with Christmas candy near the register.

She smiled as she worked, remembering jokes Beck had told her yesterday while they made their gingerbread men. She loved his smile and his easygoing nature and hoped it didn't disappear after their court date.

Just two months earlier that sweet boy and his dad were passing through her life regularly like so many others in this town. She saw them during the week on occasion, and always on Friday nights when they came in for burgers and shakes. Now they were an important part of her every day. They were in her thoughts when she woke up and planned her day out to be sure someone was with Beck. She thought about them when she went to bed, running over the events they'd shared, hoping to build lots of lasting memories.

By the time Albert came in the back door to start cooking for the breakfast crowd, the place was festively decorated, and she was still floating down Deliriously Happy.

CHAPTER 18

Mac dropped Beck off at school and drove to the station with a glance toward the café. Noelle's side of the bed was cold by the time he woke, so he knew she'd left way before dawn. He knew why when he saw Christmas lights glowing from her front windows.

After parking, he walked through the back door of the station, stopping at his mailbox, where he found new pictures of the arson suspects. Even though he'd seen them well enough to recognize them without a picture, he still examined each one carefully.

He turned into the break room and grabbed a blueberry muffin when he spotted a box from Patsy's Pastries on the table.

"Whistling." JT snagged a cheese Danish from the box. "You're in a good mood."

Mac was surprised to learn he'd been whistling, but he was in a great mood. "Who brought the pastries in?"

"Carolyn sent them over." JT studied him with a grin. "Things are going well between you and Noelle."

"They are."

JT nodded toward the papers in Mac's hand. "I see you got the updated pictures from your mailbox."

"Any more news?"

"No, but I want everyone on alert. The café didn't burn like it was supposed to, so they'll be back."

The words chilled Mac. "You think they'll try to torch the café, again?"

"I don't know, but I think we need to keep an eye out. Starting tonight, I want the night patrol to check behind businesses as well as the fronts. The town council is sending a letter out to business owners suggesting security cameras."

"Noelle already ordered some."

"Rowdy did, too."

Mac headed for the door. "I better get patrolling." He held up the photos. "I'll keep an eye out."

~

While chili simmered on the stove and cornbread browned in the oven, Noelle and Beck unloaded the boxes of Christmas decorations Mac brought down from the attic. They didn't have much, most were things a father would buy when a woman wasn't around. She decided she'd have to do a little shopping to make the house more Christmas-ready.

Beck unwrapped a piece from a nativity set and placed it on a table near the fireplace. "Grams gave me this when we moved here."

"I know you were very small, but do you remember living in California?"

"I remember I had a friend that lived next door. Her name was Ellie. I went to her house sometimes when Dad was at work." Beck unwrapped another piece of the nativity. "She was my age and her mom used to drive us to preschool. I remember I had a friend named Logan at school. I went to his birthday party, and I remember going to the beach with my dad and getting all sandy. That was fun."

Noelle grabbed Quincy by the collar and pulled a slip of paper from his mouth. He'd done a fantastic job of shredding the larger piece all over the floor.

"What do you remember from when you were little?"

She tugged a musical snowman out of another box and wound the key to hear the Christmas tune. "I also had a friend who lived next door. His name was Ian. He had red hair and freckles. When I was allowed, we'd go to a park nearby and play. The girls teased me because my best friend was a boy."

"Did the boys tease Ian for playing with a girl?"

Noelle set the snowman aside and rummaged until she found a Moose, his antlers decorated with lights. "If they did, he never said."

They heard the back door open and Beck jumped to his feet. "Dad!"

Noelle also pushed up from the floor. Time to greet her husband and take the cornbread out of the oven. Mac met her at the kitchen door, Beck on his heels. Mac pulled her into his arms and kissed her hard, setting her heart thudding against her ribs. "You started decorating without me."

"Not really, just unwrapping things."

"Every time I walk through that back door, my mouth waters." He leaned close, his breath tickling her ear. "And not just for food."

She couldn't help the silly giggle that bubbled up. She loved this side of him.

He ruffled Beck's hair. "I thought we were going out for dinner."

"Beck and I got a late start decorating, so we decided we could go out another night. Hope chili sounds good."

"If it tastes as good as it smells, I'm perfectly happy staying home."

She patted her husband's chest. "You have just enough time to change before dinner. Mike is joining us tonight." She turned Beck by the shoulders. "Let's set the table."

"Okay. Hurry, Dad, I'm hungry."

Noelle spent another wonderful night with her men, this time including her cousin. They all raved about the chili and polished off the plate of cornbread. Mike helped them finish with the decorations, all but the tree, which Mac and Beck always cut down themselves.

As she watched father and son wrestling on the living room floor, a yapping puppy in her arms, and Mike sitting near, laughing at Mac and Beck's antics, she doubted her life could get any happier.

$\sim$

*M*ac pulled into his side of the garage just as Noelle lowered the trunk of her car. He opened the door and slid from behind the wheel. "Where are you going?"

"Sleepover, Dad," Beck said, bounding out of the house in time to answer.

"I haven't had a chance to start dinner," Noelle said.

He rounded the car to kiss her, not having to be prompted by Beck anymore. "Let's go out."

She smiled. "Sounds good to me. I'll be back in about fifteen minutes."

Mac showered and changed quickly, thrilled to have an evening alone with Noelle. He knew the perfect place to take her. She told him about her day while he drove to a small town northwest of Eden Falls. He pulled into a parking space beside a small Italian restaurant, and couldn't help smiling when Noelle stepped inside and groaned. The restaurant was warm against the cold of the night, the air was filled with delicious scents. A string quartet was playing romantic love songs in a lighted corner.

They were shown to a table covered by a red and white checkered tablecloth. The centerpiece was a wine bottle with colorful wax drippings covering the sides.

"This place is as charming as Glenwood is quaint."

Mac pulled out Noelle's chair. "I thought you would like it. The food is great."

"How did you ever find this place?"

"After school dances, we'd bring our dates here, away from the prying eyes of town gossips. Afterward, we'd take them to Angel's Point."

"Angel's Point?"

"The high school make-out place. It's just up the road a little farther, a turnoff that overlooks the river. I could show you after dinner."

She raised her eyebrows. "Going to your high school make-out place might make things weird between us."

"I dated Phoebe Adams in high school. We made out plenty of times and I don't feel weird around her."

She set her menu on the table with a grin. "I didn't know you and Phoebe dated. What happened?"

He shrugged. "We were young and it didn't last. We only dated for a summer. Then someone else caught her eye or mine. I don't remember. Either way, we didn't break each other's hearts."

"Do you look at her and remember those days?"

He shook his head. "Not anymore."

After the waiter delivered their salads, he pointed his fork to her. "Now it's your turn."

"My turn?"

"Tell a high school story." He was mesmerized by the candlelight flickering in her blue eyes.

"Why don't you believe me? I didn't date in high school because that was considered fun and fun wasn't allowed."

"You can't tell me you never went out on a date."

"I went out a few times, but nothing worth mentioning."

"Make-out sessions?"

She laughed. A sound he enjoyed. "Once or twice."

Over a perfectly relaxing dinner, their conversation never lagged. Noelle revealed new tidbits about herself every time they talked. They'd done marriage backwards, wedding first, getting to know each other afterward, but the more she revealed, the more he fell in love.

He tried to focus on their conversation rather than her lips. After their high school dating discussion, he had two things on his mind—kissing her and how long it would take him to get her home to their empty house. She was saying something about her ravioli, but his mind was traveling down another road.

She smiled, and he imagined her doing that in the darkness of his truck as they searched each other's eyes breathlessly. He'd run a finger down her throat while he nibbled on that tender spot under her ear, the spot that had caused a shiver after his gentle bite just the night before.

"Are you okay?"

Mac blinked. "Yeah, I'm fine." He picked up his water glass, only to find it empty. He turned to signal their waiter and noticed a couple kissing in the dark corner of the restaurant. A hand touching his arm startled him.

"Mac, you can have my water."

Suddenly, all he wanted was to get her home.

"Are you sure you're okay?"

He took a deep, settling breath and focused on slowing his

pounding heart. "I'm fine. Sorry. What were you saying about the ravioli?"

~

*N*oelle floated into the café on a cloud of bliss. Things between her and Mac were dialed to wonderful. The café was doing fantastic. Beck seemed happy with their situation. She hadn't heard from her parents since Thanksgiving. Life was just about perfect.

She breathed in the scent of apple pie baking in one of the café's ovens.

Christmas was three weeks away. Mac had mentioned needing a new chainsaw and Beck had complained his base-ball mitt was too small, both great gift ideas.

How was Christmas celebrated at the Johnsons' house? A glimmer of expectancy shimmered through her at the thought of celebrating the holiday as a family. Her parents were never home Christmas morning, sometimes not even for Christmas dinner. Maybe it was petty on her part because her parents weren't running around irresponsibly. They were helping others. Still, the only happy Christmas memories she had were the times her family spent the day at Mike's parents' house. She wondered if Mac and Beck had traditions. Maybe, as a family, they could establish new ones.

Her soaring spirits settled back to earth when her thoughts turned to Cheryl. What if she wanted some time with Beck this Christmas? Would Mac be willing to share?

Stay out of it, Noelle.

She dropped her purse on her desk and shed her coat and scarf. "Good morning, Albert." She walked to his side while she tied an apron around her waist.

"Morning."

"The pies smell heavenly."

He glanced at the timer by the ovens. "They'll be out in about twenty minutes."

"Need any help?"

"Nope." He pointed a beefy thumb over his shoulder. "Gertie came in a few minutes ago. Said there's a woman out front askin' for you."

She knew who it was without looking. Gertie and Albert knew everyone else in town. How could she stay out of it if Cheryl kept dragging her in?

Noelle walked out front. Sure enough, Cheryl was sitting in a booth by the window. She scooted onto the bench seat across the table. "What brings you in so—" She stopped when she saw the tear tracks on Cheryl's cheeks. Her cloud of bliss evaporated. Cheryl's coffee cup was empty, so she motioned to Gertie for a refill. "Can I get you something to eat?"

Cheryl swiped under her eyes.

Noelle looked up when Gertie approached with a coffee pot. "Can we get an order of French toast and a side of bacon?"

Cheryl released a damp laugh as fresh tears appeared. "I haven't eaten bacon or French toast in—it's been so long, I can't even remember."

"Albert's French toast is the best in the state of Washington and bacon is yummy any time."

Cheryl glanced out the window toward the police station. "Is Mac at work this morning?"

No, I left him warm and cozy in our bed. "He works tonight."

She started to ask why Cheryl was in town two days before they went to court, but decided the woman didn't usually need any prompting. She waited.

"I'm not mother material."

Noelle wondered if her reaction showed on her face,

grateful that Cheryl was still gazing out the window.

"I want to be. I hoped I could change once I saw Beck."
She looked down at the table. "I've tried to change, tried to
picture my life with Beck at the house, but…" She
swallowed.

Suddenly, the compassion Noelle had been searching for
overwhelmed her, almost to tears.

"I told my attorney to drop the case. He's going to talk to
the judge on Monday."

Noelle had no idea how to respond, so she didn't. She
pulled Cheryl's coffee cup back when Gertie appeared with a
plate of French toast, another of bacon, and a small pitcher of
syrup. She set them in front of Cheryl, who was wiping away
tears again.

"Thanks, Gertie."

Cheryl nodded her thanks as she put a hand on her stomach. "I'm not sure I can eat."

Noelle poured syrup on a corner of the French toast. "One
bite and you'll be hooked for life."

Cheryl took a tiny bite. "Oh, my gosh," she moaned.
"This is the best syrup I've ever tasted."

Noelle smiled in satisfaction. She had that buttery cane
syrup shipped from Louisiana. "The French toast ain't bad
either."

"Delicious."

Noelle picked up a slice of bacon and ate it while Cheryl
downed a piece of French toast in record time.

"Mac hates me," she said without looking up.

"No. He's angry you messed up his and Beck's routine.
He's worried Beck will be miserable if forced to go to California, but he doesn't hate you."

Cheryl picked up a slice of bacon and took a bite. "Simon
was right all along. Some people are meant to be mothers,
others aren't. That doesn't mean I don't love Beck. It doesn't

mean I don't want to see him. I would like to visit. I plan to come back for his Christmas program."

"I think Beck would like that." Noelle didn't dare add that she thought it would be good for Beck to get to know his mom. "Most kids love knowing family members are watching and cheering them on."

Cheryl's gaze held expectancy and hope. "Do you think Mac would let me visit Beck once in a while?"

Noelle stood and held up an index finger. "I'll be right back."

❧

*M*ac met Cheryl in Owen's office thirty minutes later. He couldn't believe it when Noelle called with the news. Cheryl wanted to give up the custody fight if he'd allow her to see Beck a few times during the year. Noelle was right all along.

Owen mediated their agreement and said he'd get the paperwork to Cheryl's attorney first thing Monday morning. If both he and Cheryl agreed to what Owen recorded of their meeting, the two attorneys would go before the judge. Beck wouldn't have to be there.

Mac hugged Cheryl, told her thank-you repeatedly, and walked away from Owen's office feeling thirty pounds lighter. And he owed it all to Noelle.

Visions of their love-making last night flitted through his mind. His feelings for her were stronger than he ever could have imagined he'd feel for a woman. He'd never been in love before, but what he felt for Noelle was bigger than the four-letter word could possibly encompass. She'd been a part of their life for such a short time, but already it was hard to remember what it had been like without her.

He walked into the café, and Gertie pointed toward the

kitchen. He pushed through the swinging door. Noelle looked up eagerly. He had her off her feet and in his arms in two strides. "She agreed to drop the case if she can visit Beck a couple of times a year. If I'd only listened, this would have been resolved a week ago."

"I'm glad everything worked out."

He set her on her feet. "Owen is getting all the paperwork ready. I'll go over there before work Monday, read over the document, sign it, and he'll have it delivered to Cheryl's attorney. We don't have to go to court. Beck doesn't have to talk to a judge."

"Well, that's great news," Gertie said from the doorway. "Congratulations."

"You have to go tell your mom and dad." Noelle got up on tiptoe and kissed the corner of his mouth. "They'll be so relieved."

He nodded. "We'll celebrate tomorrow."

She grinned, her eyes sparkling. "I can't wait."

※

*M*aking Christmas cookies for the fire and police departments was something Noelle had done every year since moving to Eden Falls. This year she was doubly thankful for all they did to keep this town safe. The fire department had extinguished the arsonists attempt to burn down her café and the police department had given her Mac.

The fire department's cookies already delivered, she found a parking space in front of Town Hall and climbed out of her car with a basket of goodies. She, Mac, and Beck were still celebrating Cheryl's sudden decision to drop her custody case. They all met with Cheryl on Saturday, as previously arranged. She told Beck she planned to return to watch his

Christmas program, which Mac seemed okay with now that she'd dropped her plan to take him to court.

She'd promised Cheryl she'd take care of Mac and Beck forever, and she intended to do just that.

She entered Town Hall and turned right, stopping at the front desk. Gianna smiled. "Hi, Noelle. Are you here to see Mac?"

"Actually, I came by to drop off some holiday cheer." She held out the basket.

Gianna peeked under the napkins Noelle had draped over the treats. "I don't imagine they're fat-free," she said.

"No. These cookies are jam-packed with sugar and calories."

Gianna patted a hip. "I've already started on my winter padding. What's one more cookie going to hurt?"

Noelle waited while Gianna made her selection. "Is it okay if I drop these off in the break room?"

Gianna pointed down the hall when the phone rang, so Noelle headed that way. She'd catered lunches and dinners at the police station before and knew where she was going. She turned left, but stopped short when she heard Mac's voice.

"Yeah, it's a load off my shoulders, knowing Cheryl won't be trying that again. Beck was happy to know he wouldn't be spending Christmas away from home."

"Where does this leave you and Noelle?"

Noelle recognized JT's voice and waited with bated breath. *I've fallen in love with her. We're a family now. She is part of Beck's and my world. I can't wait to spend the rest of forever with her.* Any of these answers would have sent her heart pounding in the right direction.

The pause was long. Eternally long.

"Our marriage was a farce, just like you said when I first told you about it. We got married to convince Cheryl and her attorney, to convince a judge, if we had to, that Beck was living under a stable roof. Mission accomplished. Noelle—"

Noelle turned and hurried in the direction of the door. At the front desk, she set the basket of cookies down in front of Gianna. "Will you put these things in the break room for me? I forgot I'm supposed to be somewhere."

"Sure."

She got in her car and drove around the square, away from town, chastising herself for being so stupid, angry at Mac for telling her he loved her, furious she'd been naïve enough to believe him.

She drove past Harrisville, and past the next town, and the next, before finally pulling to the side of the road. Swiping at tears, she blew her nose, and settled her sobs to soft hiccups.

"Enough, Noelle. This was the plan from the beginning. You offered to marry Mac to help him keep Beck in Eden Falls." Mac's "mission accomplished" rang in her ears. "Time to get ahold of yourself and stop blubbering before someone drives by and notices." Mac accused her of being crazy, but not everyone had to know just how crazy she was.

What to do? What to do?

You'll move out before he asks you to.

Noelle drove back to Eden Falls and pulled into the parking lot behind Rowdy's Bar and Grill, glad to see Mike's car. She hadn't been inside Rowdy's since the Halloween party, since the night Mac nibbled her neck in front of the whole town.

Mike waved from behind the bar. "Hey, Noelle. I hear congratulations are in order."

Noelle slid onto the last stool at the bar. "Congratulations?"

"Mac's ex gave up the fight."

"Oh, right. Yes. Wow, word travels fast."

"Small town." Mike planted his hands on the bar in front of her. "What's up?"

She glanced around and didn't recognize anyone close by. Still, she lowered her voice. "Now the custody hearing is over, there's no reason to stay married. I just want to make sure I still have a bedroom."

Mike's expression clouded. "It's your apartment, Noelle. I'm the imposer." He came around the bar and sat next to her. "You told me this was temporary, but after seeing you and Mac together, I thought maybe…"

"No. We put on a good show though, don't you think?" She flashed what she hoped passed as a realistic smile, the one she'd used often when she and Mac were first married. "We went for believability."

"Well, you had me fooled." He studied her for a long moment. "You okay?"

"Me? Sure. I'm good."

"I guess your mom and dad will be happy."

She nearly choked on a pretend laugh. "Ecstatic."

"Can I get you something?"

"No thanks. I have to pick Beck up from school." Noelle slid off the stool. "Have a good shift."

"When can I expect you?"

"Soon."

❧

*N*oelle tucked the few boxes she'd packed into the guest room closet. Other than clothes and a few cooking supplies, she hadn't brought a lot with her when she moved into Mac's house. Before packing, she'd thought long and hard about staying through Christmas, but saw no reason to prolong the inevitable.

While cooking Beck's ham and cheese omelet for breakfast, she looked out over the backyard. The morning had dawned crystal clear and below freezing. Frost-covered branches sparkled in the sunlight. She'd miss the view from this window.

Beck talked about his part in the church Christmas program while devouring his omelet. She startled when the back door opened and Mac walked in. She'd been dreading this moment since last night.

He hugged Beck who'd jumped up to greet him. "Sorry I'm late. Layne had trouble starting his car in the cold."

She stood to put her and Beck's plates in the dishwasher. "There is an omelet in the oven. I have to get Beck to church early. They're holding another practice."

He came to her side. "You look nice."

She had to look down to remember what she was wearing. Right, a knit dress and boots. "Thanks. Beck, honey, get your coat."

As Beck ran for the back door, Mac smiled. "What? No good morning kiss?"

She stopped what she was doing to look into his eyes. "We don't have to pretend anymore. Mission accomplished."

Noelle felt his eyes on her as she skirted him and slipped into her coat. She tied scarves around Beck's neck and then her own.

Beck bent and gave Quincy a scratch behind the ears, then headed for the door. "'Bye, Dad!"

"I'll take a quick shower and see you in half an hour," Mac called back.

Minutes later, Noelle walked into the church, which she'd come to think of as a peaceful sanctuary. Odd that she'd never really thought of religion or the beliefs of others until living with Mac and Beck. She liked to leave the world behind for the short time she was inside the old building. Though she'd miss sitting with the Johnson family, she decided she'd continue to attend after the divorce.

She sat in the back watching the kids gather in age groups. Each one had a special part in the program. She'd been working with Beck on his few lines. He had it down, but was afraid he'd forget once he stood in front of the crowd. She told him to ignore the congregation and just look at her. If he forgot, she'd mouth a word that would trigger his memory.

Alex slid into the pew next to her. "Morning."

"Hi, Alex."

"Congratulations."

Yep. Yay, me! "Thanks. Mac and Beck are very happy about Cheryl's decision."

"Said with a little too much cheer," Alex said with raised eyebrows. "Are you okay?"

"Sure, I'm fine."

Alex leaned forward and scrutinized her. "You don't seem fine."

Noelle dropped her chin and closed her eyes. She was tired—tired of the emotions that had plagued her all night while she packed. Tired of the façade.

Alex looped her arm through Noelle's. "Want to talk?"

Do I? It might be nice to unload her troubled mind on someone, as long as it didn't get back to Mac. "Between us?"

"If you like."

Noelle inhaled a shaky breath. "I fell in love with Mac and Beck. I fell in love with the fake life we built. I fell in love with being a wife and mother. I thought Mac felt the same way." *He told me he felt the same way.* She glanced at Alex. "I was wrong."

"What happened to make you think differently?"

"I overheard Mac talking to JT yesterday. He said our marriage was a farce, we'd accomplished our mission."

Noelle shook her head. "I knew this was temporary. Heck, I'm the one who offered. I just got my hopes up and I shouldn't have."

Alex rubbed Noelle's arm. "Why don't you talk to Mac?"

"I don't want to put any pressure on him." She turned and smiled at Alex. "He's so happy about his ex-wife's decision. I'm not going to ruin it for him."

"Want me to talk to Mac? Feel him out?"

"No. Please, just let it go. He's had a rough couple of months, worrying about this whole custody situation. I don't want any bad feelings. I want to remain friends."

Alex wrinkled her nose. "Men can be so dense."

Noelle lifted a shoulder in a half shrug. "They probably say the same about us."

CHAPTER 19

Mac hesitated when he saw Alex and Noelle talking in the back pew. His thoughts were in turmoil. After his shower, he'd gone to the closet and discovered Noelle's side empty. And boxes stacked on the closet floor in the guest room.

She was leaving. The custody case was over. She'd fulfilled her agreement. Her promises of love had been empty.

He glanced up front and Beck waved from a choir chair. Pride filled his chest. How had he gotten so lucky? And how would he explain Noelle's leaving to Beck? His son, who thought the world of her, was excited about spending Christmas as a family.

Colton stopped next to him and shed his coat. "Our wives have their heads together. That can't be good."

"No, it probably isn't."

"If I know Alex, she's plotting to dress me in tights again and have me act as Santa's elf at her parents' Christmas Eve party."

Mac chuckled. "I'd pay to see that."

"Don't look so amused. You might be right there with me."

I doubt I'll still have a wife by Christmas Eve. How long does a divorce take? His and Cheryl's had taken six months, but the laws in Washington were probably different. He'd have to ask Owen.

Alex suddenly appeared next to them, sliding her hand into the crook of Colton's arm. "What are you two talking about?"

"Discussing how scary it is to see our wives with their heads together. What were you and Noelle plotting?"

Alex flashed a smile that lit her face. "You murder-mystery authors are overly paranoid. We weren't plotting anything. Just chatting."

"About?"

"About life. Come on." She pulled on her husband's arm. "Let's get a seat. Have a nice day, Mac."

"You, too." He walked over to where Noelle sat. She glanced up when he sat next to her. "Hey. How's Beck doing?"

"Wonderful. He delivered his lines perfectly."

"Good." Mac slid his arm along the back of the bench without thinking. Noelle tensed, but he kept his arm where it was. He wanted to ask about the boxes. He wanted to know what had happened, but now wasn't the time. Church wasn't the place.

He turned forward. Beck was paying rapt attention to what the program director was saying. "You've been great with Beck. Thanks for helping him with his lines."

"You have a fabulous son, Mac. Beck is amazing."

"He thinks you're amazing."

She glanced at him. They were close enough he could see himself reflected in her pupils. She opened her mouth as if to say something, but Beck plopped down next to him. Noelle leaned around Mac. "You did a fabulous job with your lines, Beck."

"I did what you said, and I wasn't even nervous."

She smiled.

Lily and Rance slipped into the pew and the prelude music started. There would be no time to talk until after the service.

～

*D*inner at Lily and Rance's filled Noelle with regret. They were more comfortable to be around than her own family. She'd come to love these people and their Sunday dinners together.

There was much laughter and gaiety now the court date didn't loom in the distance anymore. She took her time studying each person's face while they enjoyed the feast Lily had prepared. Tonight would be emblazed in her memory for many years to come.

She hoped she could remain on friendly terms with Lily and Rance after the divorce, but knew their conversations would be restricted to less personal subjects. Then they would grow fewer and farther between. They wouldn't have Beck and Mac in common anymore, only friendship. She'd thought about trying to stay close to Beck, but decided that might confuse him, especially if Mac met someone.

Once back home, she told Beck good night in the hall, then went into the kitchen to wrap Christmas presents. He'd be surprised to wake and find boxes and gift bags to put under the tree once he and his dad cut one down. She'd like to see his face, but would be gone by morning.

～

*A*fter Mac tucked Beck in, the sounds of Noelle in the kitchen drew him to her. He stood in the doorway and watched her wrap a scarf and gloves in red tissue, then place them in a box.

"You're spoiling him."

She jumped slightly at the sound of his voice and then smiled without looking up. "Yeah, just what every ten-year-old wants for Christmas, a scarf and gloves."

He waited for her to say more, to tell him she was moving out. Instead, she rolled festive paper out onto the table and set the box in the middle. She cut and taped the paper in place. Then she took a spool of green plaid ribbon and unfurled a long strand. She wrapped it around the package and tied a bow on top. She fiddled with the ribbon, getting it just right.

"I noticed you've packed up your clothes. Are you going to leave without a goodbye?"

"This is new territory for me." She stopped what she was doing, her hands still on a new baseball glove. "I wasn't sure how to say goodbye."

"Why are you leaving before Christmas?"

"I thought it would be easier."

"On who?"

She met his gaze. "On Beck. Now the hearing isn't going to happen, there's no need to prolong this fake marriage."

Her words stung his heart. "What if we don't want you to leave?"

She laughed. Laughed!

"Mac, I need to finish these last two presents and get to bed. I have to be at the café early."

He nodded. What else could he say? If they didn't live in such a small town, he might open his heart, tell her he loved her and thought she loved him. He'd kiss her and tell her he didn't want her to leave, but he was afraid to show that much vulnerability. Especially if she didn't feel the same. "Can I ask you a question?"

She glanced up from the box she'd taped closed.

"Was it all just a farce, because some of it seemed real. The last few weeks seemed real."

Noelle smiled, eyes wide. "Then we did what we set out to do." When she looked down, he noticed her hands shaking.

"I want you and Beck to be happy. The longer I stay, the harder it will be on Beck."

She finished wrapping the last present and wrote out a tag for Beck. "Owen should be able to file divorce papers quickly." She stood from her chair and faced him. "I'll always be around if you need help with Beck."

She picked up a couple of the presents and carried them into the living room. He stacked the rest and followed. After he'd set them on the floor near where the tree would stand, he turned around, but she was gone. He heard the guest room door close with a hollow click.

*B*efore dawn, Mac heard Noelle moving through the house. She was quiet, but his ears were attuned, listening. He'd been prepared to get up and help, but something kept him behind his closed door.

He waited until he heard her car drive away before venturing down the hall to the empty guest room. The bed was made with clean sheets. Everything was neat and tidy, except the air. The beautiful essence of Noelle lingered...or maybe he was just as conscious of her scent as he was to her soft footfalls.

A couple hours later he woke Beck for school. Beck got dressed and came into the kitchen. "Did Noelle have to go to work?"

Mac cleared his throat. "Yes, buddy, she did." He set a

plate with bacon and eggs in front of his son and sat in a chair facing him.

"Thanks, Dad."

"You're welcome." He sipped his coffee and waited until Beck had finished most of his breakfast before he said, "Noelle moved out this morning, Beck."

Beck looked up, confusion clouding his features. "Why?"

Mac tipped his head back and forth trying to seem nonchalant about what he had to say—not sure what he should say. "Things…just didn't work out."

"Is that why she slept in the other bedroom last night?"

Mac shook his head at his son's astuteness. Of course Beck knew. "That's part of it." He leaned forward. "Beck, I want to tell you the truth, but I'm afraid you won't understand."

Beck stood. "You married her so my mom wouldn't take me away."

Very astute.

"You need to tell her to come back. She makes ginger-bread men and laughs at my jokes."

"It's more complicated than that, Beck."

His son picked up his plate and set it in the sink. "Don't ruin this, Dad."

~

*N*oelle was at her desk when Albert knocked on her open door. "Beck is out front. He doesn't look happy."

She pushed away from her desk. It had been four days since she moved out and she hadn't seen Mac or Beck, which was both good and bad. She missed them even more than she thought she would, but felt not seeing them would cut her strings of dependency faster.

Beck sat in his usual spot, head down. Noelle went around the counter and slid onto the stool next to him. "Hi there, handsome."

"Hi."

"Want a chocolate shake?"

"I didn't bring any money."

"My family eats free."

"You moved out, so we're not family anymore."

Noelle's heart cracked. She put her arm around his shoulder. "You'll always feel like part of my family, Beck. Always. No matter what happens."

"What's going to happen?"

She and Mac had been so stupid not to take Beck's feelings into account before they married. She thought she'd be helping him. Instead she'd accomplished the opposite. "How about that chocolate shake, then we'll talk?"

Beck nodded.

Noelle went behind the counter and made a thick, creamy, shake. She added whipped cream and set a cherry on top.

When she turned around Mac was standing in the doorway, the look of concern on his face probably mirroring her own. She tipped her head toward Beck. He nodded and left.

She went back around the counter. "Beck, let's go sit in a booth."

Once settled, he spooned whipped cream and the cherry into his mouth.

Noelle waited.

"Will you still come to the Christmas program at school?"

"I wouldn't miss it."

"What about my program on Christmas eve?"

"I'll be there early so I can get a good seat."

"After the program, we always go to the Garretts' Christmas Eve party, then we come home and open one present."

"I won't be at the Christmas party."

He looked down when tears flooded his eyes. "What about Christmas morning?"

"I can't be there, either, sweetie."

Beck wiped one eye with the back of his hand. "But I made you a present."

"You can bring it to me here anytime, Beck. You'll always be welcome at the café."

"But I want you *there*."

This was not going well. Beck was going to leave hurt. When she offered marriage, she never imagined she'd grow to love this boy so much. Never imagined his feelings for her would grow so strong.

"I know why you married my dad and I don't care. You can sleep in the other bedroom and still live with us. I won't tell anyone."

"Oh, Beck…"

"I won't, I promise."

"Honey, it's not about that. It's about feelings. Your dad and I don't share the same feelings married people do."

Beck dunked his spoon into the shake a few times and then he looked across the table at her with solemn eyes. "Do you love my dad?"

Oh, boy. Tell the truth or lie? Keep my heart locked up or turn the key? "Yes, Beck, I love you, and I love your dad, but marriage is more complicated than that."

"Why?"

She released a small breath. "I wish I knew."

Beck slumped down on the booth bench. "Me, too."

Noelle laughed and Beck smiled through his tears.

≈

*M*ac pulled up outside the café when Noelle texted him that Beck had just left. "Whatcha doing, buddy?" he asked when Beck climbed into the front seat.

Beck shrugged, his young face looking more solemn than Mac had ever seen. In his mind, he tried to blame Cheryl, but in the end it was on him. His selfishness had caused this.

"Want to get a Christmas tree?"

Beck shrugged again. "Sure."

Thirty minutes later, they trudged through the snow in search of the perfect pine for their living room.

"I wish Noelle was here."

"I heard you the first three times, Beck." He pointed at a pine. "What about that one? It's got a nice shape to it."

Beck walked around the Fraser fir. "There's a big hole in the back."

"We can put that side in the corner, where it won't show."

Beck shrugged. "I guess, but I like the other one better."

"The other one was too tall." Mac pulled off his glove and wrapped an arm around his son's neck. "We'd have to cut a hole in the roof of the house to stand it upright."

"This one's okay, I guess."

"Quit moping." Mac pulled out a piece of chalk and marked the trunk. "This is where you aim."

Beck took the sheath off his ax and swung. Mac knew he'd be doing most of the work, but Beck always put forth a great first effort. Noelle would be cheering him on if she were here. "Great job, buddy."

Two hours later, Mac finished stringing lights on their tree and left Beck to decorate while he made hot chocolate, under orders to *do it the way Noelle does*, whatever that was. Would she think he was crazy if he called her for directions? *Beck won't drink my hot chocolate. What's your secret?*

From there, maybe he could… Could what? Tell her he loved her? He'd told her many times, had never done anything to make her question that. Or had he, without realizing?

He glanced around the kitchen. In her short time here, Noelle made their home festive and cohesive. She'd decorated the kitchen with snowflakes, from placemats to kitchen towels. There was a snowman cookie jar on the counter that still held the Christmas cookies Noelle left behind. Beck refused to eat them, like keeping them would preserve a piece of Noelle.

He pulled a cookie out with the intention of putting a couple on a plate along with a mug of cocoa. The cookie was a snowflake, blue frosting with white piped in a snowflake pattern. He'd eaten the same cookie at work.

He pulled out his cell phone, scrolled to Gianna's name, and punched the phone icon.

"Hi, Mac."

"Gianna, you brought a basket of cookies into the break room a couple of days ago. Where'd they come from?"

"Your wife." She pronounced the words slowly, as if explaining something complicated. "She started down the hall toward the break room, but turned and rushed out. She said she had to be somewhere."

"Thanks." Disconnecting the call, he thought about that day. He'd been in the break room with JT when Gianna brought the cookies back. Why hadn't Noelle come in to say hello? Something niggled at his brain, something important, something he should remember, but couldn't.

~

*M*ac sat in his truck, watching his son and his wife through the window of the café. They were laughing, which lightened his heart. He wanted to be inside with them, enjoying the same joke.

He missed Noelle more than he ever imagined possible. She had his heart and he wished he knew what had changed between them. Why had she moved out so suddenly when things seemed to be going so well? He'd come to know her over the past two months, was sure, even though they were married, she wouldn't have slept with him if she didn't love him. What had changed? It couldn't be just because Cheryl had dropped the custody case.

He had a work party tomorrow night at JT's and had offered to switch shifts with Phoebe Adams. He had no desire to go alone. He'd work so Phoebe could take the new guy she was dating.

He jumped at the knock on his passenger window. Patsy Douglas motioned for him to unlock the door from the other side of the glass. He pushed the button, and, much to his irritation, the town's platinum bombshell climbed inside.

"What are you doing sitting here in the cold?"

He glanced at the café. "Watching Beck. He's spending time with Noelle."

She rubbed her hands together. "Mind turning on the engine? It's as cold in here as it is outside."

He started the truck and flipped the heat to high.

"Thanks." Patsy nodded toward the window framing Beck and Noelle. "What are you doing out here? Stalking?"

He glared at her. "No. Just giving them some private time."

"Can't you do that at home? Oh wait, you guys aren't together anymore."

Mac shook his head, wondering how he'd gotten so lucky

as to attract Patsy's matchmaking attention. Sure, she'd meddled enough to help a few couples get together in their small town, but he didn't need her help. "Don't you have somewhere you need to be?"

"Nope. Here is as good as anywhere." She stared at him a long moment. "You and Noelle were a good match. You'd make pretty babies."

He choked on a sip of coffee. "Geez, Patsy."

"You're an idiot to let her get away."

He slumped in his seat. Why did it hurt to hear Patsy tell the truth? "My ex was trying to get custody of Beck. Noelle was helping me out. Our marriage was just for looks."

She made a clucking sound with her tongue. "Everyone in town knows that."

"My ex dropped the case, so there's no need to pretend anymore."

She laughed. "You might have been pretending in the beginning, but not in the end. You're in love with that girl and she's in love with you. Life is short. Get out of this truck and tell her how you feel."

He pointed at the café. "She's the one who left."

"And you're the one who's letting her go." She opened the door and slid out of his truck. "Do something about it before it's too late." She slammed the door.

∼

*N*oelle took special care dressing for Beck's school Christmas program. She tried to squelch her excitement over seeing Mac, but it zinged through her every couple of minutes. She wanted to wow him. She wanted him to be sorry he'd let her slip away. *This red dress is just the ticket,* she thought, running her hands over her hips.

Of course the insecurities her mother hammered into her

all her life made her question whether Mac's words of love had been as fake as their marriage.

She'd managed to avoid him for the past two Sundays by arriving at church late, sitting in the back pew, and leaving a little before the service was over. Chicken? Maybe, but it saved her heart the pain she felt every time she saw him walking around Town Square or driving past the café in a patrol car. He promised her they'd remain friends after they separated, but he and Beck hadn't been in on their regular Friday night.

She'd seen him several times in the last two weeks, but tonight he'd *see* her.

In the auditorium, she heard her name and spotted Lily waving her forward. As she started down the aisle, Mac stood and turned to watch. Suddenly she felt like she might throw up.

She hugged Lily and Rance gave her a kiss on the cheek. She had hoped to sit on the aisle, away from Mac, but his parents stepped back so she could pass to the seat they'd been saving next to her husband.

"Hello."

Mac's eyes traveled down the length of her body, making her breath catch. "You look beautiful in red."

She put a hand to her stomach. "I decided to wear something a little festive for the occasion. For Beck."

He leaned close and she thought he was going to kiss her. Instead he whispered close to her ear. "Cheryl and Simon are on the other side of me. They don't know you've moved out. Can we keep it that way until the paperwork for custody goes through?"

She got up on tiptoe and kissed his mouth, then leaned around him. "Cheryl, what a gorgeous dress. Simon, it's nice to see you again."

Once they all sat, she reached for Mac's hand and linked

their fingers where Cheryl could see. That's how they sat through the performance, which turned out to be more entertaining than she expected. Beck looked darling in his reindeer antlers. She knew the moment he spotted her in the audience. She smiled and waved.

She felt Mac's eyes on her and looked at him.

"He misses you," he said close to her ear.

"I miss him back. Thanks for letting him come to the café for a visit."

He nodded.

When the performance was over, they all filed into the foyer where cookies were being served. Mac kept his arm around her waist for observation purposes. Beck ran straight into her arms.

"You were the best reindeer up there," she said, hugging him tight. She turned him to Cheryl. "Look who came all the way from California to see you sing."

Simon shook Beck's hand. "Well done, young man."

"You did such a good job." Cheryl gave her son a light hug.

"Thank you for coming," Beck said, making Noelle so proud.

"I brought you a Christmas present. It's in our rental car."

Rance clapped Beck on the shoulder. "Grams and I will walk you out there."

When they were alone, Mac turned to her. "Thanks for coming. It meant a lot to Beck."

"You don't have to thank me for that, Mac. I've been looking forward to this performance as much as you," she said, cringing at the defensiveness in her voice. She pulled her coat on before he could help.

When she turned to leave, he caught her arm. "What put a bee in your bonnet, anyway? I thought things were going great between us. Then you suddenly moved out. Were you just using me for my body?"

She laughed. "Yeah, that's what I was doing." She leaned close. "I thought it would be fun to lose my virginity to someone who said he loved me when he really didn't." At his look of incredulity, she added, "I overheard you and JT talking."

He pulled her aside. "Overheard us talking about what?"

"You said our marriage was a farce to convince Cheryl and her attorney. 'Mission accomplished.'"

He frowned. "Which was true."

True.

"Obviously you didn't stay to hear the part where I told JT I'd fallen in love with you, and that Beck was thrilled you'd come into our lives."

Her heart thudded hard once. Twice.

JT appeared next to her. "He also said, and I quote, 'We're staying married, so the joke is on us.' Alex told me you overheard our conversation. I was just coming to clear things up, but I see Mac already has."

She glanced at Mac, tears filling her eyes. "You really said that?"

"Every word." Mac lifted her chin with his index finger and kissed her tenderly. "I love you, Noelle."

CHAPTER 20

Mac stood on the far side of the Garretts' living room watching Noelle laughing with Alex. Denny and Alice's house was full of family and friends for their annual Christmas Eve party. He'd been coming since he was a boy, since he and JT were old enough to run through the woods together. There were familiar faces and some he was still getting to know, like Noelle's cousin Mike. He'd looked lost in this sea of people until Tatum—looking as Christmassy as possible for a girl wearing Goth—snagged him by the arm and pulled him into some sort of block-stacking, tower-building game she and Rowdy had set up for the kids.

"Glad to see you came to your senses."

Mac recognized Patsy's voice before he turned toward her. "It wasn't me who had to come to my senses."

"But it was you who took the bull by the horns. You didn't let a stupid misunderstanding ruin a beautiful thing."

He smiled down at the town's pastry entrepreneur.

"Beck looks happy."

"Beck is in heaven since Noelle came home."

Patsy ran a hand through the crook of his folded arms. "And what about you? Are you happy?"

He patted her hand. "Yes." *Beyond happy.*

Mason Douglas, appeared, and she transferred her hold on him to her husband. "Now we just need a new baby to spoil," she said over her shoulder as they walked away.

Mac choked on his punch.

Colton laughed as he handed Mac a napkin. "Patsy did the same thing to me about twenty minutes ago."

Mac wiped his chin and the front of his sweater. "You got away without dressing like an elf."

"Only because I promised I'd play the guitar when the entertainment begins. Which looks like about now," he said when Alex waved him over.

"Hey, Dad, do you think Quincy is lonely?"

Mac ruffled Beck's dark hair. "I think Quincy is happily chewing my other brown dress shoe so I'll have a matching pair."

Beck's laugh filled Mac with joy.

Beck had talked to his mother on the phone twice since she left town, and both seemed content with that. Cheryl was planning a week-long visit to Seattle during Beck's spring break and Mac had agreed to drive him over. He and Noelle could use that time to tour the San Juan Islands for the honeymoon they never had while Cheryl spoiled Beck silly. He told Cheryl they'd come to California for another week during the summer. Beck seemed okay with that as long as Noelle was along, too.

Noelle's birthday was tomorrow. He'd picked up a beautiful antique angel ornament for their tree—a gift to celebrate the angel she was to him and his son. Eden Falls was lucky to have her.

≈

*N*oelle stood with her back against Mac's chest, his arms wrapped around her while they watched the kids at the party perform a play Alex had written and was directing. Beck was playing the part of Scrooge and loving every minute in front of his audience. Alex's son, Charlie, delivered a line, and everyone laughed. And then laughed again when Charlie's tiny cousin Sophia wouldn't cooperate.

"Patsy suggested it might be time for a baby."

Noelle froze. A baby? She'd barely gotten her feet wet as a wife and stepmom. She looked over her shoulder. "What did you say?"

"I choked on my drink and then thought…maybe she's right. What do you think?"

Noelle turned in his arms. "I don't know. I haven't even thought about a baby. What if I'm not good at—"

Mac pressed a finger against her mouth. "You are good at everything you do."

"I'm not sure I'd know how—"

His finger stopped her words again. "You thought the same thing about Beck and he idolizes you. It's time to put past fears behind you? You're not your mother, Noelle."

No, I'm not my mother.

He lifted her chin. "A little girl or boy with your blue eyes."

"What if that girl or boy gets your brown eyes instead?"

He grinned. "We'll have to try again."

The happiness that bubbled over was too much. She rose on tiptoe and gave him a noisy, happy, smacking kiss.

"Eww, get a room," Beck shouted.

The party crowd erupted in laughter.

～

If you enjoyed *The Angel of Eden Falls*, I hope you'll continue reading! The next book in the Eden Falls Series is *Touches of Eden.*

To keep up to date on new releases join my newsletter at TinaNewcomb.com.

Following is an excerpt from *Touches Eden*.

EXCERPT FROM: TOUCHES OF EDEN

CHAPTER 1

Jillian Saunders jumped when the phone on her desk rang. Since most people called her cell number or texted, she'd forgotten how annoying the sound was. She grabbed the receiver before it could ring again. "Hello."

"I need a personal training session today."

The voice on the other end of the line wasn't much more welcoming than the shrilling ring. She and the demanding woman were friends through mutual acquaintances. When their group from high school met for the occasional girls' night out or to celebrate a birthday, she and Misty Garrett were there along with four other women.

Jillian switched screens on her computer, looked over her completely booked schedule, and sighed to herself. This conversation wouldn't end well. At least not for her.

"Can you come in at five?"

"I can come in now."

Jillian was tempted to laugh, but to do so would only anger Misty. "I have classes and clients until five. If you can come in then for a consultation—"

"I don't want a consultation! I want a complete workout."

"It's smart to start with a consultation so I can see what level—"

"Are you forgetting that your employers are my in-laws?"

Jillian put an index finger to her left temple. "No, Misty. I'll forget the consultation, but I can't just drop my other clients and classes to meet with you. Five o'clock is the best I can do today. I'll be off work by then, so I can help you personally." *Not that you care whether I get paid for my time.* As soon as the thought flashed through her mind, she pushed it aside.

Misty was asking for help, which wasn't her' style. Demanding an appointment *right this minute* was. Mother-hood had smoothed many of Misty's rough edges, but obvi-ously not the I-want-it-now ones.

Jillian was a little surprised Misty had waited almost a year after giving birth to ask for help with getting back into shape.

"I have a baby, Jillian."

"I understand you have to work around your schedule and Sophia's, but I can't just drop my other clients to fit you in. If you can't come at five, I have a couple of openings next week."

"Next week!"

"You're always welcome to come in and work out on your own before that."

She closed her eyes as Misty continued to argue.

"Misty, there is nothing else I can do today. Come in at five, and I'll show you a few exercises you can do until we set up a permanent schedule. I'll send home a few diet plan options as well."

"You're welcome," she said after Misty disconnected without saying goodbye.

Misty, with her outrageous self-confidence, natural gorgeousness, and venomous tongue, intimidated Jillian to her toes. She always looked like she'd stepped off the pages of a fashion magazine, airbrushed perfection in real life. Beautiful enough to capture any man's attention, Misty could turn around and cut him in two with a single comment.

Jillian replaced the receiver and pushed up from the chair she'd been planted in for the last two hours. Reaching high over her head, she bent, vertebra by vertebra, until her hands rested flat on the floor. The stretch relieved the stiffness in her back and shoulders. Her hamstrings begged for more than thirty seconds, but that was all she could spare. Straightening, she did a minute of deep breathing to clear her mind of Misty's domineering demands and juggernaut approach. Then she plastered on a smile before going into the gym to deal with another uncooperative client.

She walked through the free-weight area. Get Fit was packed with New Year's resolution-makers trying to rid themselves of the ten unwanted pounds they gained over the holidays.

She turned her attention to the main floor and nearly missed a step.

Fireman Brandt Smith was running on one of the treadmills. His brawny arm muscles glistened with sweat while they pumped to the rhythm of his feet. A few locks of his honey-colored hair bounced every time his foot hit the running deck. She stood, mesmerized by the beauty of his shoulders, the power in his leg muscles. She imagined him on a beach, the waves slowly sliding over the sand, his feet leaving tracks as he ran toward a brilliant sunset.

She also noticed the puckering evidence of a burn mark on his shoulder and neck peeking from under his sleeveless T-shirt. She took a step to the left and could see the mark ran from shoulder to elbow on the inside of his right arm. She'd never heard—

"Like what you see?"

Brandt glanced her way.

Embarrassed that she'd been caught staring, she turned toward her next client while sucking air into deprived lungs. She didn't realize she'd been holding her breath until Marty Graw—yes, his real name—spoke. Loudly. He usually looked like he'd just sucked on a lemon, but today his sour expression was replaced with a self-satisfied smirk.

"Appreciating," she said, quietly enough that Brandt couldn't hear. "Just think, Marty. You could have a body like that."

Marty's belly, which hung over the waistband of his sweatpants, jiggled when he snorted. If Brandt didn't know they were talking about him before, he knew when Marty pointed at him. "Only in my wife's wildest dreams would I ever look like that."

Doc Newell told Marty the week after Thanksgiving that he was a dozen chicken wings and a banana cream pie away from a heart attack. For Christmas, his wife gave him the gym's Get Fit and Healthy package, and Doc Newell followed up with strict orders for him to follow Jillian's plan.

Marty was in his midforties, had never worked out a day in his life, and didn't want to start now. Gentle with Marty in the beginning, Jillian was tired of him taking advantage of her easy nature. They'd been working together three days a week since the first of the year. If progress was going to be made, it was time for her to step up his program.

"Not in your wife's dreams. Pure reality. Have you warmed up?"

He glared at her out of the corner of his eye in response.

"We've talked about this. You have to warm up before we

start. Spend a couple of minutes on an elliptical to get your heart rate up."

"I hate the elliptical."

"Maybe you'll remember that on Tuesday and warm up on one of the bikes before our pleasure-filled hour together. I'll be back in two minutes."

She replenished a stack of towels and polished the drinking fountain, giving her procrastinator time to build up his anger. He'd work a little harder that way. When she returned to get Marty started, her gaze collided with Brandt's in one of the wall mirrors.

He smiled.

This wasn't the first time she'd noticed his disarming smile or the tempting dimple in his left cheek. This was, however, the first time that smile had ever been directed at her. Or was it? She glanced around, expecting to see a gorgeous woman behind her. When she looked back at him, his smile grew.

She turned away for the second time, then mentally smacked herself. *Why did you do that? The least you could have done is smile back. He'll think you're a,...* She couldn't think of anything stupid enough to call herself. She also couldn't bring herself to glance his way again. To smile now would be as idiotic as not smiling in the first place.

Marty spent forty-five minutes sweating and sputtering rude remarks. As a fast-food franchise owner, he enjoyed what he sold way more than he should. Jillian gave him a simple, healthy diet to follow their first week together, but knew darn well he wasn't adhering to her suggestions. She coaxed and encouraged while Marty huffed, groaned, and hurled more insults. His strength and endurance were slowly increasing, which inspired her. Him? Not so much. She wondered if he even noticed the changes resulting from their three weeks of work.

Even though her attention was focused on her client, she noticed Brandt moving closer to them as his own workout continued.

"You made it through another hour of torture. Good work, Marty." She held up a finger. "No rewarding yourself with junk food. Eat an apple or an orange instead."

He scowled.

"One more rep, then walk two laps around the track to cool down."

"I used to like you," Marty wheezed.

"Sadly that's one of the drawbacks of my job." She fluttered her eyelashes dramatically. "By June you'll be sending me flowers."

"Don't count on it." He finished his rep, climbed off the rowing machine, and trudged toward the indoor track.

"I like Gerbera daisies," she called after him. "They're cheerful, and will definitely remind me of your smile. See you Tuesday."

"You have a thankless job."

She whipped around. Brandt was standing behind her. Heat washed up her neck and across her cheeks. "No. Well…. Maybe in the beginning." She turned toward her office, but stopped. *The guy just opened the door for you. Talk to him.* She sucked in some courage and turned back. "I thought the fire station had enviable exercise equipment."

"We do, but a Boy Scout troop invaded our weight room this morning to work on their fire safety badges."

"I worked with a troop last week on their personal fitness badges." *A tiny something we have in common. Sorta.*

He was close enough that she could reach out and touch the cute cleft in his chin covered in whiskers. Of course, she didn't, but she could have.

"You were great with Marty."

She huffed on her nails and polished them on her shoulder. "All part of the job."

He took a step closer and her heart thumped too hard, stealing her breath away. "Do you have many clients that cranky?"

She thoughts floated to Misty. "A couple."

They stared at each other for a long moment. She'd waited for him to notice her for two years. Amazingly the day was here, and she couldn't think of anything to say that might keep him talking. She wished she were witty enough to make him laugh or courageous enough to ask him out. Alas, she wasn't that person.

After a year of therapy, she tried not to hold herself responsible for what happened in college. Deep down, she still felt she could have stopped things.

"I have a class to teach." She thumbed over her shoulder. "Have a nice day."

～

"You too."

Brandt watched Jillian enter a glassed-off room and greet several people before he headed for the showers. He knew of Jillian, knew her friends, but they'd never really talked before and he wondered why. Other than her job as a personal trainer, he didn't know much about her. After observing her unfaltering good cheer during the hour she worked with Marty, he knew she had infinite patience. The fast-food king wasn't the most pleasant person to be around on the best of days.

He might not have noticed her before, but he made up for it today. Her toned body as she worked side by side with Marty, her beautiful brown eyes sparkling despite her client's constant grumbling. Though he might not have noticed, her smile and encouraging words had pushed Marty to work harder.

Despite all that, what really caught his attention was the blush that touched her cheeks the couple of times their gazes met. When was the last time he'd noticed a female's blush?

He showered, towel-dried his chair, and dressed in his jeans and a sweater. On his way out, he glanced through the glass windows. Jillian was still in the classroom teaching what looked like beginner yoga. As she walked around the room, she lifted a client's sagging elbow, touched another's back. Maybe it was time to look into yoga. He'd never taken a class. The thought surprised him in a way that made him smile.

Outside, the air was so cold his breath appeared as white clouds. Approaching his truck, he noticed Misty Garrett getting out of her car. When she spotted him, she frowned. Not unusual.

His first night in Eden Falls, after accepting the opening with the fire department, he'd gone to Rowdy's Bar and Grill at the invitation of his new crew. They hadn't been there fifteen minutes when Misty sauntered over to their table and propositioned him in front of the guys. She'd been single then, and a beauty, with a cascade of black hair and electric blue eyes. He'd met women like Misty, and her brazenness didn't appeal to him.

Manners, branded into him as a boy, wouldn't allow him to embarrass her in front of four other men. He tried to laugh off her proposition as a joke, but Misty wasn't one to back down. She turned an uncomfortable situation into tacky.

He finally lifted her off his lap and told her straight-out he wasn't interested. Misty threw out several insults about him batting for the other team. "Firemen are all brawn and no brains," and "If you'd gotten four more questions right, maybe you could have been a cop." She finished off with,

"You guys have the only job where you wake up when it's time to go home," before storming out of Rowdy's.

"One day her house will be on fire and she'll have to eat those words," one of the guys muttered.

Another had clapped Brandt's shoulder. "Congratulations. You just survived your first Misty encounter."

A couple of days later, he'd further insulted her when he asked her friend, Alex, out. She'd despised him ever since.

Misty closed her car door and walked toward him. She stopped a few feet away and, for the first time since he'd known her, she actually looked embarrassed. "I owe you an apology."

He glanced around, then pointed to his chest. "Are you talking to me?"

Misty looked skyward when the first snowflakes of the predicted storm started to fall. She held out her gloved hand and caught one. "I was pretty awful to you when you first moved to town. I shouldn't have…come on so strong. And I shouldn't have insulted you when you turned me down." She lifted her shoulders, and the bottom half of her face disappeared behind her raised collar.

Misty was apologizing? Brandt wasn't sure how to respond, but did close his mouth when he realized it was hanging open.

"I just want to say I'm sorry."

"Apology accepted. Thanks, Misty."

She looked down. "Apologizing is like step three of the twelve-step program we *mean girls*"—she made quotation marks with her fingers—"have to go through before we can earn our tiaras."

Not sure how to respond, Brandt nodded. He wasn't quite sure what had just happened, but relief at not having to sidestep Misty settled over him.

She started for the door of the gym, but turned back to him. "Why did you ask Alex out?"

Because she is the complete opposite of Kacie. "She was kind."

Misty's gaze floated past him as if she had to process his answer. "She is kind and considerate…and icky sweet." Her eyes met his, her smile genuine and un-Misty-like. "And I'm pretty lucky to have her as a friend."

"Me too." He and Alex had only gone out a few times, but it was enough to know they weren't a match. She was easy to be around, though, and had become his safety net in a new town. She'd introduced him around, helped him find his bearings.

She was married now and, like Misty, he felt pretty lucky to count Mayor Alexis McCreed as one of his friends.

Misty's mouth went behind her raised collar again. "See you around, Brandt" came out muffled.

"Yeah, Misty. I'll see you around."

The memory of Brandt's smile made her hour with Misty a little more pleasant. Though Misty was trying to change her mean-girl persona, the old Misty crept out while Jillian worked her muscles.

"Are you trying to kill me?"

Jillian raised her brows. "I suggested a consult. You're the one who insisted on a full workout."

Misty's blue eyes blazed. "Yeah, a workout, not a torture session."

"This won't kill you, Misty."

"You're working me like you're holding a grudge." Misty narrowed her eyes. "Is that it? I said something awful years ago, and you're getting back at me?"

Jillian laughed, but not enough to annoy Misty further. "No. You apologized, and I accepted. The past is the past."

"That's what you say, but—"

"Misty, I don't hold grudges. You're working muscles that aren't used to exercise. In a month, you'll consider this a cakewalk. Keep your arms straight."

"Have you ever done this? Do you have any idea how bad it hurts?"

"Yes. I do this exercise several times a week."

Misty set the weight down and rubbed her stomach muscles. "You're odd, and I'm not saying that to be mean, but anyone who enjoys exercise is just…odd. You know who you should date?"

This should be good. "Who?"

"Brandt Smith. He was leaving when I came in. I bet he loves to exercise. You two fitness junkies could work out together."

Jillian's cheeks heated for the second time that afternoon. *Nice idea, except he barely knows I exist.* Today was the first time they'd said more than hi to each other.

"You're blushing," Misty said with a cat-like grin. "You like him."

Jillian shook her head. She wouldn't reveal her feelings—not to Misty. She did forgive her for any infractions from the past, but that didn't mean she trusted her with long-guarded emotions. "You did really well today. Walk a lap around the track to cool off, then come into my office. We'll set up a workout schedule, and I'll get you those diet plans we talked about."

Jillian walked through the door of her basement apartment and headed straight for the kitchen—four feet away. She dropped her keys in a small bowl on the counter and plugged her cell phone into the charger nearby.

Henry appeared.

"Hey, handsome. Did you miss me?"

"Meeeowww."

She slid her hand under Henry's belly and tucked him against her chest. His deep purr vibrated along her collarbone.

Henry was a rescue her brother gave her for her twenty-fifth birthday. They got along fine as roommates, as long as she remembered her place in his kingdom. "How was your day?"

He blinked deep gray eyes and meowed mournfully.

"Really? It was that terrible, huh? You'd rather be out in the cold and snow than in this warm apartment? Tomorrow I'll trade places with you."

Jillian wandered from the kitchen to the living room and back again. The confines of her cozy little she-cave were a tight, slightly claustrophobic fit tonight. Her nerves were still jumpy after talking to Brandt. And working with Misty hadn't helped.

She'd been against renting a basement apartment. She was all about sunshine streaming through open windows, which didn't happen underground, but when she graduated college and decided to move into Eden Falls from her parents' farm, apartments were scarce and money was tight.

The outside door opened directly into her living area. The kitchen—a few cabinets hung on a wall, a single sink, a small refrigerator, and a two-burner stove—was to the right. To the left of the door was a short hall that led to her bedroom and bathroom. Seven hundred square feet turned out to be large enough for her and Henry.

Mrs. O'Malley had converted her basement into an apartment and started renting it out when her husband passed away ten years earlier. She didn't need the money, so the rent was low. With her children living in faraway states, Jillian suspected she just wanted someone she trusted close by.

Jillian ran occasional errands for her, shoveled the walks in winter, and mowed the lawn during the summer.

In exchange Mrs. O'Malley let her paint the dark wood-paneled walls as long as she supplied the paint and the labor. A beautiful cream had warmed the space instantly. Then Jillian's mom made colorful drapes for the small basement windows and a coordinated slipcover for the sofa Jillian scored at a garage sale. She splurged on the two comfy armchairs that filled the tiny space. The down comforter on her bed was well worth the cost, since the temperature in the basement was run by the thermostat upstairs, and Mrs. O'Malley kept things on the cool side of cozy. She added a few throw pillows, some bright prints for the walls, and was now quite content with her space.

She circled back to the living room and sat in one of the chairs. "Do you want to hear about my day? It was quite thrilling."

Henry pushed out of her arms and jumped to the back of the chair. "Meeowww."

"Guess who came in today?" She waved her hand. "Oh, I'll just tell you, 'cause you'll never guess. Brandt Smith!"

Henry lay down near her head, his purr rumbling close to her ear.

She turned to look over her shoulder. "I know. I was excited too. He worked out at Get Fit because a Boy Scout troop was using the exercise room at the fire station. We talked. Well, he talked, but still…."

Henry closed his eyes.

"You don't have to be so unenthusiastic about it. Especially since you know how long I've liked him." She sighed. "I know nothing will come of it, but it was a small bit of thrill in my not-so-very-exciting life. You could pretend to be happy for me."

When she got no response, she pushed up from the chair. "You're just acting like that because you want your dinner."

Of course, the word "*dinner*" got an immediate reaction. Henry jumped off the back of the chair, landing elegantly, and sauntered into the kitchen. He meowed his agreement when she chose his favorite cat food from the cupboard and opened the can.

"Oh, guess who else came in today? Misty. She said she gained fifty pounds over the holiday, when in reality it was only about eight. She wants to get toned for summer." Jillian spooned the food into her cat's bowl and set it on the floor. "She was a little demanding, but only half as bad as she used to be." She leaned a hip against the counter and crossed her arms. "Of course, she expects results without putting in much work, but that's not unusual. Most people want instant results. We both know that isn't how it works. I think these sessions might be good for me and Misty. Maybe we can get to know each other better."

Jillian released her ponytail band and ran fingers through her hair, separating a few tangles. "She actually suggested Brandt and I might make a good match." She touched the tip of Henry's tail with her toe.

He scooted out of her reach.

"I guess I'll shower before I cat. I still have the Sunday dinner leftovers Mom sent home."

Henry was too busy scarfing his delicacy to pay her any mind.

"Maybe you should take a breath. You act like you haven't eaten in days."

Still nothing.

Jillian glanced around her quiet apartment. She was having a full-fledged, though one-sided, conversation with a cat. A thought made her giggle. "At least I'm not talking to myself. Right, Henry?"

At the sound of his name, Henry looked up and blinked. "Meeeowww."

~

The next day, Jillian heard a commotion and jumped up from her desk. She headed for a group of people collected around the men's locker room door.

"An ambulance is on the way, Marty."

At the sound of Dawson Garrett's voice and the mention of the client she just finished with, Jillian pushed through the crowd. "What happened?"

Marty lay on the floor, head elevated on a couple of towels. When he spotted her, he pointed a chubby finger. "This is your fault. I'm having a heart attack because you're a sadist."

She knelt next to them. *You're having a heart attack because you eat too much fast food.*

"Now, Marty, there's no use in blaming Jillian," her employer said, patting her shoulder.

Suddenly Brandt was beside her, and she was afraid *she* was having the heart attack.

As the only paramedic in town, he usually arrived just ahead of the ambulance. He set his medical kit next to Marty. "What have we got?"

"Marty says he's having a heart attack. Glenda saw him come out of the locker room holding his chest," Dawson said.

"Then he just laid down on the floor," Glenda added.

"This is her fault!" Marty pointed at Jillian.

"I…." She had no words, but felt her cheeks flame when Brandt glanced at her.

Brandt tugged a stethoscope from his kit and listened to Marty's chest, took his pulse, asked him about the pain. He was in calm control, going through a mental checklist. And Jillian was mesmerized.

While checking Marty, he asked Jillian questions about the workout. He asked Marty about his diet and if there was any history of heart problems in his family. A stretcher was brought in, and Brandt helped load Marty into the back of the ambulance, then climbed in beside him. Right before the door shut, he glanced at her and flashed his beautiful dimple.

She melted into a puddle.

ACKNOWLEDGMENTS

I loved writing this book, loved sharing Mac, Beck, and Noelle's story. I've wanted to write about a marriage of convenience for a while, but it took some time for the story to develop.

As always, I'd like to thank my Beta Babes Chris Almodovar, Holly Hertzke, Jeanine Hopping, and Louise Weeks. Thank you for your time and thoughtful feedback. I love you all.

I'm grateful to Eliza, Ma'ata, Cristina, Belinda, and Ocee. The title, *The Angel of Eden Falls* was a unanimous decision.

Thank you to my editor Faith Freewoman of Demon for Details for your kind words of encouragement, for believing in me, and working so hard on my behalf. Your suggestions strengthen my work while allowing my voice to shine through.

To my proofreader Jennifer Bray-Weber/The Killion Group, Inc., I appreciate your time, talent, and patience.

I'm grateful to Dar Albert of Wicked Smart Designs. You see my vision for book covers so clearly. Once again your talent and insight amazes me.

Thank you to the members of my critique group. Dawn Annis, Mary Hagen, C.K. Alber, and Lori Corsentino.

I'm so grateful to my husband, Rick (the formatting king). Without you, my readers wouldn't have this book in their hands. And to our kids – be kind and never give up on your dreams.

Finally, thank you readers. I'm honored that you set time aside to read The Angel of Eden Falls. I hope you enjoy it as much as I loved writing it.

ALSO BY TINA NEWCOMB

The Eden Falls Series

Finding Eden

Beyond Eden

A Taste of Eden

The Angel of Eden Falls

Touches of Eden

Stars Over Eden Falls

Fortunes for Eden

Snow and Mistletoe in Eden Falls

Rumors in Eden Falls

Second Chance Romance Collection

When You Love Someone

Endless Love

Rhythm of Love

Second Chance Romance Collection

\

ABOUT THE AUTHOR

Tina Newcomb writes clean, contemporary romance. Her heartwarming stories take place in quaint small towns, with quirky townsfolk, and friendships that last a lifetime.

She acquired her love of reading from her librarian mother, who always had a stack of books close at hand, and her father who visited a local bookstore every weekend.

Tina Newcomb lives in colorful Colorado. When not lost in her writing, she can be found in the garden, traveling with her (amateur) chef husband, or spending time with family and friends.

Follow Tina on:

facebook.com/TinaNewcombAuthor

instagram.com/tinanewcombauthor

bookbub.com/authors/tina-newcomb

goodreads.com/tinanewcomb

pinterest.com/tinanewcomb

Printed in Great Britain
by Amazon

80177689R00196